Tangled Spirits

A Novel

Kate Shanahan

ROAV Press

Copyright © 2022 by Kate Shanahan

All rights reserved. No part of this publication may be reproduced, stored or transmitted in any form or by any means, electronic, mechanical, photocopying, recording, scanning, or otherwise without written permission from the publisher. It is illegal to copy this book, post it to a website, or distribute it by any other means without permission from the author, except for the use of brief quotations in a book review.

Excerpt from The Tale of Genji by Murasaki Shikibu, Charles E. Tuttle Company Inc. of Rutland, Vermont and Tokyo Japan. Copyright 1976 by Edward G. Seidensticker. Reprinted with permission.

Paperback ISBN 979-8-9856291-0-1

Cover design by Nicole Hower

This is a work of fiction. Names, characters, places, and incidents are the product of the author's imagination or are used fictitiously, and any resemblance to actual persons, living or dead is entirely coincidental.

First edition

❀ Created with Vellum

Contents

Prologue	1
1. Awkward and Embarrassing Things	3
2. Kenji	13
3. Into The Spirit World	20
4. Not A Demon	25
5. Spirit-Squatting	33
6. Eating For Two	41
7. Clearly Destiny	47
8. Exorcism	55
9. An Ominous Prediction	61
10. Road Trip!	73
11. Call Me Ji	85
12. The Royal Astrologer	102
13. Personal Medium To The Empress	120
14. One Crazy Spirit	129
15. Reluctant Spy	137
16. Poetry Slam	145
17. Plotting	151
18. Vow Of Loyalty	159
19. Crow Droppings	170
20. Stepping In It	176
21. I Trusted You!	184
22. Tiger And Dog	189
23. Dance Trance	196
24. Full Control	203
25. Monkey Midwife	216
26. A Big Win	237
27. Three Worms Night	249
28. Snow Melt	257
29. An Imperial Request	266
30. Pilgrimage To Kamo	271
31. Two Empresses	283

32. Going Viral	288
33. Find The Middle Path	294
34. A New Mission	299
35. Three Omens	305
36. Dominant Spirit	311
37. Historic Meeting	322
38. A Dangerous Gamble	328
39. Millennial Plan	340
40. Separation Anxiety	348
Epilogue	355
Acknowledgments	359
Author's Note	361
List of Historical Characters	363
Historical Notes	365
Glossary	371
About the Author	375

To Anne, Riley, Kermit, and Vee

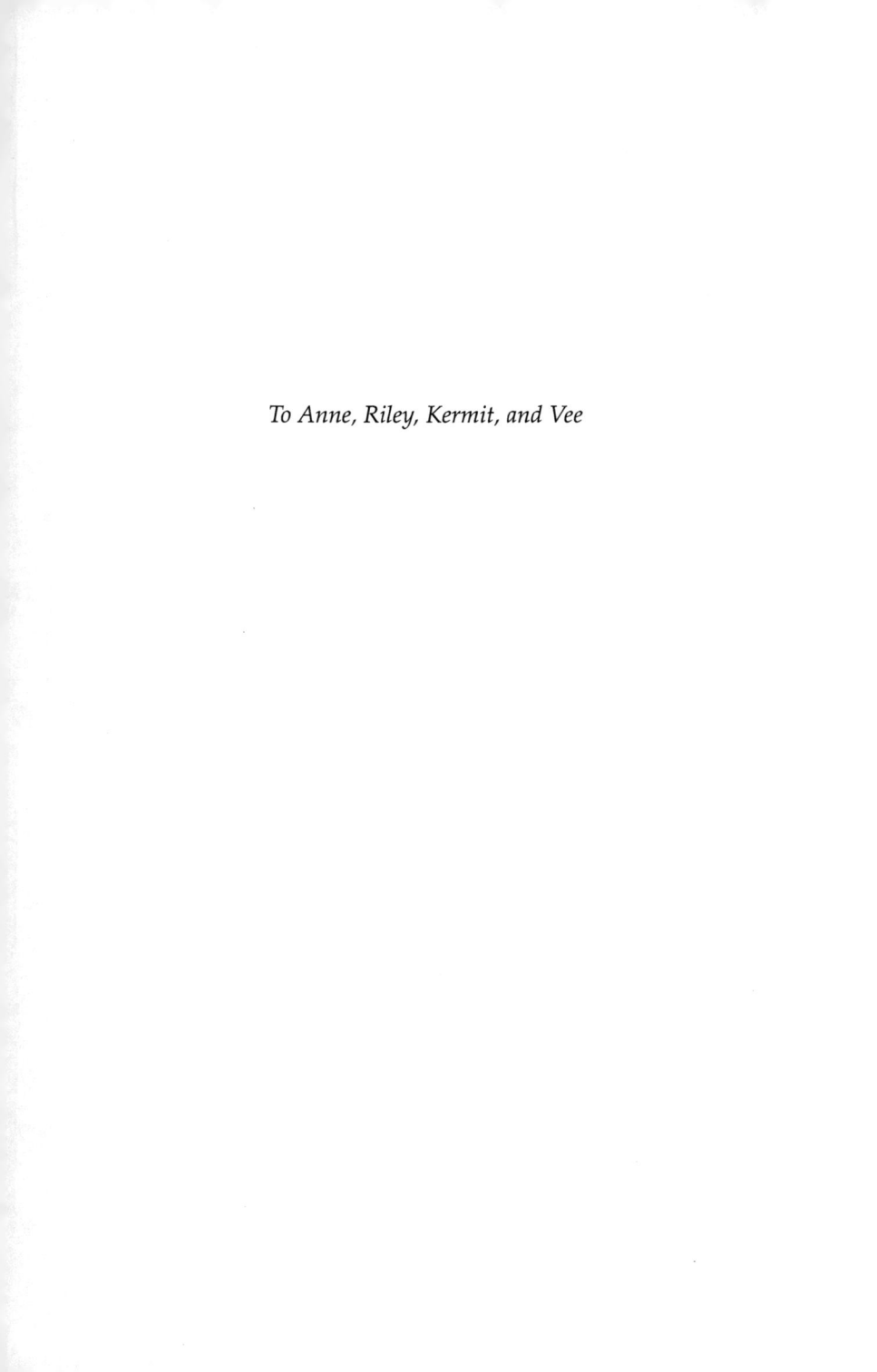

Prologue

If I wanted to blame someone for what happened, I could easily pin it on Mick. His behavior that night, what it drove me to do, the chaos that ensue—why *can't* it be his fault? I'm so over yelling at myself. I may have done some things I'm not proud of (kicking Masako out of her own body, spying on the Empress, almost changing history, stuff like that) but there's no denying it started with him.

Although, to be fair, the experience gave me everything I'd need for a killer honors thesis.

And Masako and I worked things out.

Eventually.

Chapter 1

Awkward and Embarrassing Things

July, 2019 CE (Seventh Month, Reiwa 1)

I gripped my beer tumbler with both hands and pressed it against the rough surface of the table, moving it back and forth, the slight vibration a welcome distraction from what was happening next to me. What had Yasu just asked? How long had I been in Japan? *Get a grip, Mina!*

"*Ni-gatsu desu.*" Then I kicked myself under the table because I'd stupidly said it was the month of February. I wouldn't have made such a rookie mistake if I weren't trying so hard to ignore Mick. "I mean- uh, *ni-ka-getsu imasu.* Two months."

"Your Japanese is very good," Yasu said, an obvious lie. He was working hard at ignoring Mick too, as was everyone else at our table. They were all so nice, pretending that nothing was wrong.

Mick had brought me to this farewell party for one of his co-workers, but right now he was busy making out with the bar hostess, who'd been drinking right along with us, so pretty in her tight white dress and red lipstick. Why was *she* drawn to

Mick? Was it his green eyes and large triangle of a nose? Did that make him exotic?

When I realized they were kissing, I instantly looked away from them and back to Yasu, who sat across from me. My pulse beat loudly in my throat, and I had trouble swallowing, but I refused to make a scene. Yasu's eyes flicked to Mick and the hostess, and then back to me with a tiny, sympathetic smile. I made my face expressionless, and focused on breathing quietly as if everything was just fine. It was just a little flirtation. Not a problem at all. *Mina, you're twenty. You can handle this. He'll stop, she'll go away, and then you'll tell him how rude he was, and he'll apologize, and life will go on. He has a temporary condition of idiocy caused by too many glasses of Sapporo beer. You've got no other friends in Japan. You can't break up with him.*

I set my glass down before it slipped from my damp palm, and put my hands under the table where they could twist and wring my napkin without giving me away.

And then my savior appeared in the form of the bar owner, a middle-aged woman who pulled the hostess away while chiding her in angry Japanese. Mick turned back to the table and took a swig of beer like he'd just been watching the baseball game on TV.

Jerk.

We left as soon as politely possible. Mick headed in the direction of his apartment, apparently oblivious to my inner fuming. I stood there perspiring in the humid evening, wondering how long it would take before he realized I wasn't going with him.

Which was about sixty seconds. He looked around for me, confused in the most innocent kind of way. "Mina? Aren't you coming?"

"How cou-" I swallowed, unable to continue for a moment. *Deep breath, Mina.* "How could you do that to me? It was so embarrassing."

Mick widened his already huge eyes. "You should've said something if it bothered you."

"Wait, what?" My heart raced at this injustice. "You kiss a stranger in front of me, and then it's on me to tell you not to? I'm your girlfriend, not your mother!"

Mick shrugged. "Hey, when in Rome, you know?"

"A public make-out session is not a "welcome to Japan" gesture! And what was I supposed to do? Yell at you, and then *I* look jealous and immature?" I folded my arms to hide my shaking hands. "You guys were kissing for at least five minutes. How can that possibly be okay?"

"You were acting chill. I didn't think you were the jealous type. Come on, let's go to my place." Mick turned, and I turned to go with him.

Wait. I'd exhibited heroic self-restraint to prevent ruining the party for everyone. That wasn't chill. That was mature. "You go home," I said. "I need to think things over."

He started to argue, but threw his hands up as if literally throwing in the towel. "Whatever, Mina, it was no big deal."

He walked away.

With thoughts careening around my brain like a hamster on cocaine—*why doesn't he see he was in the wrong? Why'd he let that woman kiss him? Why didn't I call him out at the time?*—I wasn't in the mood to brood alone in my dorm room. I needed to vent, but how? I'd met Mick at a coffee shop right after I arrived in Tsukuba for the start of my summer language program, and I'd hung out with him instead of making new friends. What a mistake. But that was *so* me. The friendship effort-to-reward ratio just didn't work for me. Friends moved away when you needed them most, or else they joined a clique you weren't welcome in, or they stressed you out with their own anxiety issues. Not that boyfriends were much better, but I never had trouble finding one.

On the other hand, maybe I should have been more selective. But what was the alternative? Spend *all* my time in my room studying like I did in high school?

And then I remembered Keiko. We exchanged language conversation lessons a couple of hours a week, and it occurred to me that she practically lived at Island Cafe. A quick text exchange confirmed she was still there.

I spent the twenty minute walk yelling at myself (*"Why didn't you speak up? How could you let Mick get away with that? How could you date such a jerk?"*) and at imaginary-Mick (*"That was so not ok!" "Maybe I should have gone home with Yasu! How would that make you feel?"*) After getting some strange looks from passers-by, I put in my earbuds and held my phone in my hand so I could talk to myself without looking like a crazy person.

As I walked into the eclectic cafe, the aroma of fresh-ground coffee mingling with garlic shrimp was oddly calming. Keiko was sitting alone at a small table in the corner, writing in a notebook.

I walked over and took another deep breath. "You will *not* believe what just happened at the farewell party for Mick's co-worker!"

Keiko rolled her eyes in a very American way. "I will believe anything involving Mick-san."

I described how the hostess had paid a lot of attention to Mick, harmless flirting, or so I thought, but then she sat next to him, took his head in her hands, and kissed him. He returned the kiss with great enthusiasm. When I got to Mick's "no big deal" comment, my voice broke and I had to swallow a few more times before finishing. "I mean, was he right? Should I have said something?"

Keiko shook her head. "You were being considerate of others at the party, and I'm sure they appreciated that you didn't argue with Mick in front of everyone. The hostess drank too much, *desho*? Mick should have apologized. It's his fault, not yours. What will you do now?"

"I don't know, but I want to do something that makes him see he's in the wrong. Something big, something completely unlike me. I don't know if I can keep seeing him if he doesn't apologize."

"*Soo, soo,* you don't need his sorry ass." Keiko's fluent English hit just the right note for the occasion. She pushed her notebook over to me. "Look at this – you'll love it. At ancient festivals in Japan, there was a type of courtship where young men and women would sing to each other, and sometimes it would turn into an orgy. Men and women could sleep with someone who was not their wife or husband, and it was okay with the gods because it was a sacred space where people and things belonged only to the gods, not to each other. This kind of festival happened right here on Mount Tsukuba. There's an ancient poem about it in the Manyo'shu anthology. I'm working on a modern English translation. It's not very good, and I haven't finished, but take a look."

I drew it closer and read the poem out loud.

"On the top of Tsukuba Mountain where eagles live,
Men and women sing courtship songs
Near the sanctuary of Mohakitsu.
There I will seek the wives of other men
And let other men seek the company of mine.
The gods, whose home this is, have never forbidden this.
So do not reproach me, and
Do not blame them."

"What? No freakin' way! The gods actually let people screw around on Mount Tsukuba? Wait, are you saying it's okay for Mick to kiss a complete stranger in front of me? The gods allow this here?"

Keiko gave a dismissive wave. "No, no, not that. But maybe

it means you can get even with Mick-san by finding your own handsome stranger to make out with."

"I'm not the type for random hookups no matter how mad I am at Mick. He's gone too far this time, though. I don't understand why he thinks it's my fault." If I hadn't maintained my composure, I'd have been a hot mess and embarrassed us all, which made it all the more infuriating that Mick blamed me for keeping my cool.

"*Jaaa*... let's talk about it when I see you on Monday for conversation class. We'll meet here at 3pm, *neh*?"

"*Hai*. Yes." Her English was so good she didn't need my help, but I needed hers. "Hey, Keiko?"

"Yes?"

Asking her to hang with me was so basic. "Uh, never mind. See you Monday."

That night I woke up at four a.m., my heart drumming a tempo too fast for sleep. Was it because of Mick? Or had I made a huge mistake, changing my major and coming to Japan? My mother had pushed me to apply to Michigan for engineering so I'd be sure to get a job when I graduated. I didn't want to be an engineer, but I didn't want to be a disappointment either, so engineering it was. And then freshman year I found myself staring at a chemistry test, unable to pick up my calculator, palms sweating, chest so tight I couldn't breathe.

The panic attacks continued, so sophomore year I changed my major to Asian Studies without telling my parents. I'd taken a seminar on Japanese culture for humanities credits, and fell in love with Sei Shonagon and *The Pillow Book*. How was that even possible? A lady-in-waiting at the imperial court of tenth century Japan couldn't have anything in common with an anxious American college student. Yet, when I read Sei's lists of frustrating, annoying, and depressing things, I felt like I *knew* her. Like when she wrote how infuriating it is to send a message to someone, and then think of a better way to have said it. Or how embarrassing it is when you find out that someone overheard you talking about them to someone else. And I wanted more of her, more of her era's literature. Why struggle with differential equations when I could read *waka* poetry and analyze *The Tale of Genji*?

I'd been fascinated with Japanese culture long before reading *The Pillow Book*. My best friend Aya had shown up in my fifth grade classroom one day when her father was assigned to Detroit from Japan. She showed me how to write my name in *katakana* and taught me to eat with *hashi*. We'd both giggle as the smooth plastic chopsticks she gave me went crossways, sending grains of rice sliding right back into my bowl. Her mother would make *tonkatsu* for dinner, and gave me a set of training chopsticks, hinged at the top for little children to practice with. Aya thought it was hilarious how much I loved them.

The fact that I cut Aya out of my life when she moved away didn't reduce my interest in Japan. In fact, after I realized what an idiot I'd been, acting like Aya betrayed me just because her father had been reassigned back home, I tried to find her online. I tried Insta, Snapchat—hell, I even tried FaceBook—but no Aya. I did find the University of Tsukuba, though.

Of course I had to tell Mom I was going to Japan for the summer language and junior year study-abroad program. She cried when I told her I changed my major, and guilted me for going so far away. Ever since Dad left, she depended on me for both social and emotional support. Which was another reason for the study-abroad. Ann Arbor was too close to Novi. I was tired of going home every weekend.

I'd envisioned a study-abroad in Japan as cottagecore: serene gardens, artful flower arrangements, graceful shrines. Which was silly, of course. The same pressure here to study hard and get good grades. And the crowds, pollution, social media obsession – same as home.

I loved all my classes on Japanese literature, though, especially the Heian Era. I longed to live in a time when poetry was everything: the way to flirt, send a message, show off, get promoted. I wondered if people had anxiety then, or if it was exclusive to modern life, to having instant information about terrible things happening all over the planet. Knowledge used to be power. Now knowledge created anxiety.

As these and other random thoughts whirled through my mind, I tried to get back to sleep by taking deep breaths and visualizing a small shrine hidden in a cedar forest.

Screw it. Might as well study for the language test on Monday. Grades were one of the few things I had control over.

I tossed my cover aside and slouched to my desk, glancing out the window at the blue-gray pre-dawn sky. The moon had set, but the blinking of the cell tower light at the top of Mount Tsukuba glowed red in a hypnotic on-off, on-off, on-off pattern. My breathing and heart rate gradually slowed to match. *That was some poem Keiko showed me. Maybe I should hike Mount Tsukuba today. A solo hike. Now that would be very unlike me.*

It wasn't easy to get lost hiking in Japan—usually I just followed everyone else on the trail—but after thirty minutes of marching along a gradually disappearing path, pushing my way through increasingly thick ground cover, it hit me.

My first time hiking alone, and I got lost. *Typical Mina move.*

Although to be fair, something wasn't right. Where were all the other hikers on this July Sunday? Maybe the humidity scared them away. Moisture rose from the ground like little ghosts, making the air thick and my skin prickly.

I wiped sweat from my hands with a bandana before pulling my phone out and tapping the screen to wake it.

Nothing.

Wiped my hand on my cargo shorts, tried again.

Nope.

Did I turn it off to reboot and forget to turn it back on? How unusual, not checking my phone every ten seconds. That just goes to show how angry I was at Mick. No wonder I took the wrong turn and got lost. My head was full of things I should have said to him last night instead of sitting in the *izakaya* pretending nothing was wrong.

I hit the "on" button with such fury the phone slipped out of my hand and landed with a crack on the wet rocks scattered along the dirt path.

"Crap-crap-crap! Shit!" My frustrated shout sounded oddly muffled, as if absorbed by the lush clusters of bamboo around me. This trail was beautiful, but weirdly silent—no cicadas buzzing, no mosquitos whining, no birds singing.

I closed my eyes and inhaled slowly, forcing myself to focus on the scent of wet earth and pine sap. I patted the ground, found my phone, and slipped it into my shorts pocket unseen. If I looked at it, and it was broken, I'd just have to sit down and cry. There'd be no other option.

With the phone safely out of sight, I opened my eyes.

And jumped back a step. A small animal had emerged onto the path and was looking at me. It had soft brown fur, a sharp little face like a raccoon, black patches around big brown eyes, and small ears that stood up in half circles like those kitty-ear headbands. *Posting a pic of this little guy would get lots of likes.* But getting my phone out would force me to face the truth about it, so I just held my breath and kept still.

It winked and scurried away.

I released my breath. *Wait, did it actually wink at me?* I shook my head in disbelief and headed back down the trail the way I came.

After half an hour or so of walking, I came to the place where I'd gone right when I should have gone left. Why wasn't the fork blazed?

Oh. There. A red blaze marked exactly where I should have gone. How could I have missed that? Thinking about Mick, no doubt.

I stopped to mull over my next steps, tapping my forehead a few times with my water bottle, eyes squeezed shut to keep tears in. A mosquito whined close to my ear. I swatted it away with irritation, yet grateful for the distraction. No mosquitos on the other path, the wrong one. No sounds at all that I'd noticed.

I stared at the right side of the fork, the way I'd gone before. There was enough engineer in me to want to go back to confirm my observation, or at least to see if the silence up there was just my imagination.

A rustling sound pulled my attention down the path to see a flash of white cloth blinking in and out of the trees. *Finally! The mountain shouldn't be this lonely on a Sunday.*

The hiker came into full view. A man striding with purpose, as if coming for me.

I froze, water bottle in hand. *Mom, I did exactly what you told me never to do: go out alone in a strange place without a working phone to call for help.* A recklessness I'd never have exhibited in Michigan.

Safest move would be to hide behind a tree, let him go by, and then go home.

My hesitation cost me.

He waved.

Chapter 2

Kenji

July, 2019 CE (Seventh Month, Reiwa 1)

His walk was fast and confident, and before I could decide what to do, there he was, standing in front of me. He looked about my age or a little older. Slightly wavy black hair brushed the top of his shoulders and framed high cheekbones. Broad shoulders and muscular arms under a white t-shirt. Jeans, in spite of the heat. Full lips. Dark eyes looking at me as if in recognition. But that wasn't possible. If I'd ever met him before, I'd remember.

"Hello!" he said. "I'm Kenji. I've seen you at school. I'm a student at University of Tsukuba."

He'd noticed me. How could I have missed him? "Hi. I'm Mina."

"*Minasan*, nice to meet you all," he said with a bow.

Minasan meant "everybody" in Japanese. A silly joke, but I liked the way he said it. Affectionate teasing, like he'd known me since childhood.

He smiled an apology. "Sorry, *everybody* must say that when they meet you. Keiko told me you are studying Japanese literature?"

He'd talked to Keiko about me? Did that mean he liked me? Or was he stalking me?

"Yes, Japanese language and literature. I'm focusing on Sei Shonagon's *Pillow Book* for my thesis."

"I'm a fan of Sei Shonagon as well." His eyes flicked toward the right side of the fork (*the wrong side?*) and then back to me. "Are you hiking to the shrine at Nyotai Peak?"

Was I? I didn't even know. I didn't get out in nature much. Mick liked us to go out for karaoke or his work parties, or else he'd game while I studied. He was an English teacher for a Japanese company, so he didn't have to worry about grades.

I didn't want to admit I had no idea where I was going, so I nodded.

"So then," he said while I stared at the curve of his lips. "Do you have a problem with a relationship?"

Wait, what? I moved my eyes from his mouth to his eyes. That was too personal of a question for someone I'd just met.

He noticed my hesitation. "I'm sorry, that sounded rude. Do you know the story of Izanagi and Izanami?"

His eyes focused on mine in such an intimate manner that my heart thumped, and it took me a few seconds to collect my thoughts. "Isn't that from Japan's creation mythology?"

"Yes. They were the world's first lovers, and they rest here on Mount Tsukuba, so people come here to pray for success in a relationship."

So a goddess of love inhabited this mountain. Maybe that explained my insta-lust for this person I'd never met before. "No, I'm just hiking to burn off some energy. Is that why *you're* hiking here?"

Kenji looked into my eyes like he knew me, like he'd always

known me. People here didn't usually look you in the eyes like that, so why was he?

"I come here often, but not for that reason," he replied. "I'm a Religion major, and I'm especially interested in Shinto. I believe there's spiritual power on this mountain."

"Spiritual power? Are you religious?" Not that it was my business.

"I take all religions seriously," he replied. "But Shinto's unique. For example, it doesn't have any founder or leader. There isn't any Shinto version of Mohammed or Jesus or the pope. And you might say it's a family business. My grandfather, his father, and so on back many generations have been Shinto priests."

"I don't know much about Shinto, I'm sorry to say."

"If we hike to the shrine together, I can tell you about it on the way to the top."

I had to think about that. If I went up to the peak, I'd come down the trail in the dark. If I went home now, I could get some extra studying in before my language test tomorrow. The twist: did I trust Kenji enough to climb to the top with him? Normally we'd have seen several groups of hikers pass us by now, but the trail remained empty, so we'd be alone.

The fight with Mick had me wanting to do something crazy and reckless. "Okay. Let's hike and you can tell me about Shinto."

He turned toward the left side of the fork.

"Kenji-san, before I forget, um, somehow I managed to go the wrong way on the trail, and when I went up there," I waved to the right, "I saw a strange animal. Can you tell me what it was? It looked like a raccoon but also like a little dog or cat."

He glanced up to the right, and then back at me as we started walking up the left side. "You saw a tanuki, which is native to

Japan. In English it's called a 'raccoon-dog,' although it's not a raccoon or a dog. In Japanese folklore there's a trickster *kami* who's a tanuki. He can change shape and he loves pranks. Maybe you saw the tanuki kami." His mouth twitched as if suppressing a smile.

"Hmmm...maybe the trickster tanuki led me down the wrong path. I knew it couldn't be *my* fault I got lost." I pressed my palm against my heart as if claiming innocence, and he couldn't hide his laughter any longer. "By the way, Kenji-san, what *is* "kami"? Isn't "kami" the word for God?"

"*So.* We call God "*Kami-Sama*" but "kami" means divine spirit. It's also the life energy present in all living things."

I struggled to catch my breath; Kenji had set a fast pace. "I-I've heard of kami in video games and anime, but never knew what they were in real life."

Kenji stopped. "We can wait here a minute."

"I get out of breath quickly." I took a sip from my water bottle, suddenly self-conscious. I coped with anxiety by studying harder and skipping meals. I should have spent more time working out and eating right. Kenji probably thought of his body as a temple, a host to a divine spirit. *Wait. Shinto has shrines, not temples.* A shrine to a divine spirit. *Yes. Divine.*

I looked into the forest so Kenji wouldn't see me blushing at my own thoughts. "Okay, I caught my breath. Maybe a little slower up this trail, if that's all right? Are you sure you want to hike with me? You could go a lot faster by yourself."

"I'd rather go with you. Do you want to hear more about Shinto? If you're bored, please tell me."

"I want to learn, and I can't talk and hike at the same time, and you can."

We continued up the path at a slower pace to accommodate my lack of physical fitness.

"So, what *is* Shinto?" I asked Kenji's back.

He turned around. "I'll walk behind so you can set the pace."

He waited until I was a step or two ahead of him. "Shinto means 'Way of the Divine.' It's a belief that everything in the natural world is connected. The Great Kami gave birth to other kami, and those kami created every tree, river, mountain, animal, and person."

I paused to catch my breath again. Cicadas buzzed loudly, and sparrows fluttered above our heads. A bird I couldn't see whistled a long high note followed by three rapid notes, and then the rat-a-tat-tat of a woodpecker. *All this noise after the silence on the other path. Weird.*

I knew the shrine was nearby when I saw glossy black ravens hopping on the ground through tall, fragrant evergreens, and sure enough, we soon passed under the orange *torii* gate.

The shrine was surrounded by shorter trees with glossy oval leaves hanging low to the ground. *Sakaki,* I remembered they were called.

"Kenji-san, why aren't there any people here today?"

"*Ji-me ji-me, desho?*" He lifted an eyebrow.

I tried to ignore what that eyebrow-lift did to me as I frantically searched my brain for the meaning of that phrase. *Got it!* Muggy. Just as I'd suspected. Too damp and sticky out here on the mountain.

"Or..." he continued thoughtfully. "Perhaps the kami want us to be alone together."

I visualized kissing Kenji under the *torii* gate. *Hey, if that's what the kami want, I'm willing to make that sacrifice.* But Kenji's tone wasn't seductive, and no wink accompanied his comment. Here he was alone with a young American woman at the top of a mountain, and he didn't seem to view it as an opportunity. Maybe he was gay? Or straight but too reserved to flirt? Or maybe he just wasn't attracted to me.

Ugh. Time to change the subject. "When I approach the shrine, does it matter that I'm not a Shinto believer?"

"Shinto doesn't exclude anyone from approaching a shrine, but you should have a clear intention when you approach it; otherwise strange spirits might enter your mind."

Kenji passed me to lead the way to a raised walkway that led to a small wooden shrine no bigger than a shed. The roof curved sharply down on both sides, creating eaves that took up as much space as the rest of the building. I closed my eyes and inhaled an ancient smell of wet, mossy earth and incense.

Following his lead, I poured water over my hands. Kenji rinsed his mouth too. I hesitated at putting public shrine water in my mouth, but decided since I was in a risk-taking mood today, I'd go all in.

We bowed and clapped in front of the shrine.

I kept my hands together, and bowed my head. *Are you there, Izanami? I'm not asking you to solve my Mick problem, but if you put Kenji in my path... thanks.*

Kenji was already walking back to the trail.

"Where next?" I called.

He waited for me to catch up. "Look." He gestured out over the mountain to the view. "The sky cleared for us."

"Oh, it's beautiful!" I turned slowly to see every aspect of the horizon: the white-blue of the Pacific; the blue-green mountains of Nikko; the quilt of rice fields and cities on the Kanto Plain. I pretended not to notice Kenji watching me, but my body fizzed like freshly poured champagne. "Is that Tokyo over there? I can see Mount Fuji!"

"Yes, that's Tokyo, and Fuji-san is visible today. We're lucky —it's been rainy or cloudy all day. The kami like you, Mina-san. They gave you this gift. This is a special day."

I turned back to face him but he was now gazing at the horizon, smiling to himself, like he was having pleasant thoughts. About me? My own mouth curved in response.

"There's a power spot between these peaks where I meditate," he said. "I go there to perform a Shinto meditation called *chinkon*. When one becomes very good at it, it is supposed to break down the wall between our world and the spirit world."

My hands and face tingled. "What's a power spot?"

"It's a place that transforms cosmic energy into a level that can be accessed by people."

I must have looked confused.

"*Jaaa*... okay," he said. "Cosmic energy is like electricity, and its transmission lines are bodies of water such as lakes, rivers, and streams. Cosmic energy transformers are usually mountains or islands. Those places are known as power spots. They amplify whatever feeling you bring to it. My hope is that by practicing *chinkon* in a power spot, it will amplify my efforts to connect to the spirit world. Would you like to go there with me?"

My mother's voice rang in my head. *Mina, are you crazy? It's dangerous to be out there with a strange man. Go home and study for that test!*

I took a deep breath.

"Yes!"

Chapter 3

Into The Spirit World

July, 2019 CE (Seventh Month, Reiwa 1)

Kenji headed along the ridge in the direction of the opposite peak, then veered left and disappeared.

I scrambled to catch up, then followed him on a barely visible path through dark green undergrowth. Shards of sunlight filtered through bushes and trees, creating a sharp contrast that made it hard to see where I was going. Occasionally Kenji would pause to hold back a low branch or push aside a bush so I could get through without getting scratched. As I brushed past him, I couldn't help glancing at his arms, so tan in contrast to his white t-shirt. He smelled faintly of cinnamon. From gum? Or cinnamon toothpaste? *If I kissed him, I could find out.*

Stop it, Mina! Maybe I was a victim of the mountain's love goddess effect. Drooling over guys wasn't usually my thing.

I should have been tired from hiking, especially in this humidity, but Kenji's proximity gave me a light-heartedness that had me practically bouncing along. Why had Kenji chosen to show this place to me, of all people? We'd just met. He couldn't have planned this. I'd made the decision to hike the mountain spontaneously, and hadn't told anyone where I was going.

"Kenji-san, your English is perfect. Better than mine. Where did you learn it?"

"Oh, no, it is not that good, but thank you," he said with a wave of his hand. "My father was assigned to America for three years with his company, so I went to high school in Ohio. After we returned, I studied and practiced English with every foreigner I met in Tsukuba, so I wouldn't forget how to speak it. I needed to be ready-" He stopped.

"Ready for what?"

'We're here, Mina-san."

We entered a clearing surrounded by *sugi* trees and wild hydrangea, the air fragrant with cedar and moss. A stream trickled downhill, forking around a small island, and a tiny wooden bridge connected the stream bank to the island.

"This is the secret meditation spot known to my family for generations," Kenji said. "In ancient Japan, it was believed that transitional places such as islands and bridges border the spirit world. You'll meditate with me here."

His tone carried such assurance, like he knew what I was going to do before *I* even knew. And what did he need to be ready for?

I was breathless, hot, confused and a bit terrified. Islands border the spirit world? A power spot that transforms cosmic energy? Not to mention imagining my mother's horror that I was alone in an isolated place with a man I hardly knew.

The decision was made by my new independent self, my risk-taking, hiking-alone-without-a-working-phone self. "I'm willing to try it if you're willing to teach me."

I followed him over the arched bridge. The island was just big enough for the two of us and a small sakaki tree.

"*Chinkon* preparation is very specific," he said. "Wash your feet and face as well as your hands. If you follow the *chinkon* method correctly, you'll feel a sense of peace and well-being."

We washed in the clear, cold stream, refreshing in the summer heat. I hadn't felt peaceful in years. Too much bad news, too much school shit, and those Insta's and finsta's I couldn't stop following no matter how bad they made me feel.

It was worth it to try this.

I noticed a tiny shrine nestled into the tree's base, almost hidden by low branches. "What's this?"

"A family shrine. As I mentioned, my ancestors have been coming to this spot for generations. Please sit with your legs folded under you or legs crossed. You should be comfortable, but you must sit straight."

Neither position sounded comfortable, but lounging on the grass wasn't one of the options. I chose to sit cross-legged.

"First we'll do *furu-tama*, which means 'awaken the soul.' Put your hands together with interlaced fingers, and index fingers pointing up, like so." He put his hands in the church-and-steeple formation. "Now, in this position, put your hands in front of your chest with your elbows pointing out, like this. Focus on sending energy into your arms, and swing them in this posture gently side to side."

I watched Kenji's movements and copied them, and soon I was breathing hard, which was strange, because it shouldn't have been any effort at all. My hands tingled, and then my whole body tingled too, with a faint buzzing as if my nerve endings were talking to me.

"You may stop *furu-tama* now. Close your eyes as we prepare for breathing."

That voice. Deep but not too deep; smooth, like a jazz singer.

I rested my hands lightly in my lap. I closed my eyes, but

couldn't help peeking. Kenji's expression was serene, and yet somehow full of life. I wanted to push him over, and put my arms around him, and-

I closed my eyes quickly. The power spot was amplifying my feelings. No wonder orgies took place on this mountain.

He continued his instruction. "Focus on one sound such as the stream running over the rocks. It might also help to count with me while you exhale. *Ichi, ni, san, shi.*"

One, two, three, four, up to ten, and then long breath in, count out, again, again, again.

No other sounds distracted me as I focused on the trickling of water. No cicadas, no birds, no breeze rustling the leaves. Back in the cone of silence? Had I been close to the secret spot without knowing it? Maybe it drew me here. Maybe this was where I needed to be.

Breathing in, attention attuned to the endlessly repeating music of trickle, splash, trickle, splash. Each inhale carried with it a green, humid fragrance. Trickle, splash, breathe.

Energy thrummed in my veins.

Nerve endings buzzing.

Breathing, listening. Breathing, listening.

Gravity. The earth pulling me down, anchoring me, embracing me.

Buzzing and tingling became active vibrations, my entire body shaking as though electricity poured into me from the ground upward. A golden light filled my mind. Peaceful, calm. Just like Kenji said. I laughed with joy.

But then a swirling, spinning sensation. My eyes were closed, yet somehow I saw men and women kneeling at the little shrine. Mysterious silver and gray shadows crossed my inner vision. Divine spirits? Nature spirits? A familiar shape—the tanuki—looked at me, laughing mischievously, beckoning.

The spirit world. This was where I was meant to go. Kenji had brought me here for this.

I stepped toward the tanuki.

A silver bell chimed.

I passed out.

Chapter 4

Not A Demon

Sixth Month, Chōhō 1 (July, 999 CE)

A woman's terrified shout brought me back to consciousness.

"Lady, wake up! Please, you must wake up, before it is too late!"

My eyes snapped open, revealing a clay bowl filled with water in front of me. My heart beat faster now that the meditation was over, and I felt a little shaky. Was this my anxiety rushing in? But why? Where did that bowl come from? And whose voice did I hear?

I tried to call out to Kenji, but I couldn't move my mouth or force any sound to come out. Was I dreaming?

"Yumi! I walked into the spirit world! Yumi, I saw a hungry ghost! *Osoroshi ya wa!*"

What? Did I just say out loud that I'd seen a ghost, and that I was terrified? My vocal cords had vibrated as if *I* were the one talking out loud. But I wasn't—or was I? My mouth had opened, and that voice came from me, but it wasn't mine. And I heard myself speaking Japanese, but it felt like my native language. I understood every word. It must be one of those dreams where you think you're awake but you're not. I've had those before. But why did I call out for Yumi instead of Kenji?

A middle-aged woman in a brown robe hurried toward me from the other side of the stream. "Lady, I feared you were in danger! Your body shook violently, and then you became deathly still. In my fright my spirit almost left me too! I prayed to Izanami to bring you back to this world. I was wrong to allow you to do this. We will ride home and you must never practice *kuchi-yo-se* again. Promise me, never again."

What the hell was *kuchi-yo-se*? Did my dream-self know more Japanese than my awake self?

My mouth opened and that dream-voice spoke again. "A shimmering mist descended upon this island—did you not see it?—and a tanuki-spirit beckoned to me. I stepped forward, calling out for Mother, but she did not come. And that is when I saw a pale figure of a young woman wandering as if lost, eyes wide but unseeing. It floated in my direction, and in my terror I pulled myself back to this world. Ah, my heart hits against my robe—do you not hear it?"

"*Kenji!*" I tried shouting but no sound came out. My vocal cords were not obeying my command. If I'd known *chinkon* meditation was going to lead to this nightmare, I'd never have agreed to it. And Kenji had seemed so chill. Why did he put me through this?

The Yumi-person spoke. "*Ayashi ya*! So strange! I saw no mist, and your body remained seated. You must have entered the spirit world. Promise me you will not attempt to contact spirits again, or I will report it—and your meeting with the blind *miko* —to the Governor."

Yumi must represent Kenji in my dream. What did that say about my psyche? "*Kenji, I'm still in my trance. Wake me from it, please!*"

I felt motion—standing up, walking toward the stream. Was I sleepwalking?

My body stepped onto a stone in the stream. Stepping stones? What happened to the bridge? What was happening to me? *Wake up! Get control of yourself! Focus!*

I looked down at my bare feet as they stepped carefully from stone to stone. Strange—no pedicure, and too small. My body felt wrong, like I was a marionette, and someone else was pulling the strings.

Concentrate. Move your legs. Just walk, damn it, walk the other way! My foot slipped off the stone and into the water, and it felt wet and cold. Would I feel that in a dream?

"Kenji! Kenji! Help me!" No sound came from my throat. What had he done to me? I struggled to move, but my limbs were frozen.

Trapped! Don't panic. Wake up. Wake up! A meditation nightmare. Kenji's fault. He led me here. Why had I agreed to go with him?

"Yumi, I heard a voice in my head! This voice—or spirit—made me fall into the water. It's trying to control me."

I'd said that, and yet it wasn't me. I felt my mouth move, felt the words come out, but it was like I was observing from the inside, and this other-me was the one speaking. Was I hallucinating? Did Kenji drug me? What was in that shrine water, anyway?

My leg lifted out of the cool water and back onto the smooth stone.

No dream could be this strange. I remembered the beckoning tanuki, remembered walking towards it, feeling so confident this was what I needed to do. The silvery-gray spirit world. I remembered that. And this other-me voice—she mentioned the tanuki. Was it *my* spirit she called a ghost? Could I have crossed through the spirit world and into the body of this woman? Was she waiting for me on the other side?

No way. Too bizarre.

I reached the stream bank and lunged toward Yumi. Or at least, my body did. I had no say in the matter. Yumi grabbed my sleeve to steady me, and as I glanced down at her arm, I noticed my dream-clothes: a white jacket and wide-legged, loose red trousers, just like those *hakama* trousers that shrine maidens wear. But I'd been wearing a blue short-sleeved t-shirt and khaki cargo shorts on my hike.

The other-me spoke. "Yumi, I am afraid. Perhaps-" I felt my heart race. "I suspect- well, perhaps in my haste to escape from the spirit world, I pulled this spirit with me. And it inhabits my body even now, *ya wa*." I felt my head bow as if in shame, tears leaking from my eyes.

What? Anger flashed through me like a magnesium flare. *She pulled me with her?*

Yumi dropped my sleeve and stepped back. "Eh? You are possessed?" She smacked her palms together. "We must exorcise it!"

A reluctant admiration filtered through my fury. This other-me person had taken a big risk, going to the spirit world. If this was a dream, was it telling me I needed to become bolder?

On the other hand, if this wasn't a dream, did the power spot amplify my desire to change my life, to change *myself*? And maybe this woman also wanted to change her life. Maybe her meditation opened the border on *this* side of the spirit world, and my spirit traveled through. Which meant my spirit was now inhabiting another person's body.

Ridiculous. Kenji wouldn't have done that to me. Would he?

I tried to speak again, but no matter how much effort I put into it, my vocal cords wouldn't move. My voice was frozen, like when I dreamed I was trying to answer a question in class, but was unable to speak.

Maybe this other-me could hear my thoughts, since speech appeared impossible. *"Hello? I'm Mina. Who are you?"*

A gasp, and then that other-me voice coming from *my* mouth. "Yumi, did you hear that?"

"No, I heard nothing. It must be the spirit speaking to you from within. But how? You are not a medium. Are you, Lady?"

Yumi's eyes widened. "Lady, tell me you have not-"

I felt myself fall to my knees. "Ah, Yumi, I am so sorry, it is my own fault," other-me replied. "In my ignorance, I must have given a spirit an opening to invade my body."

She cleared her throat with just a hint of self-importance. "O Spirit, what do you want with me? Are you a *mono-no-ke* like the one that killed my mother?"

"I'm dreaming, and I want to wake up." I tried moving my legs to walk back to the island, but nothing happened.

Yumi took my arm. "Lady, how is it you can speak to this demon? Speak to it no more. Give it no further opening. An exorcism will be needed to expel it. Let's hurry back to the horses and ride home quickly."

The bruising pressure of Yumi's strong fingers felt too real to be a dream. My heart beat faster and louder, and I needed air. Or was it *her* heart? Did it race because of my growing panic or because of *her* fear? I sensed she was curious about me as well as afraid. But how did I know these things if it wasn't my body? I'd felt my mouth form unfamiliar words, Japanese words, but there was no possibility my Japanese would ever be that fluent, no matter how hard I studied. And yet I somehow understood everything.

"Hey! I'm not a demon or a kami. I don't know what's happening to me. Are you a dream? Am I? If you are not my dream, what's your name?"

"Yumi, stop! Let go!" I felt my host pull her arm free. "The Spirit speaks to me! I must answer. It could be kami-sent."

I knew she was glaring at Yumi because I felt my mouth tighten and my eyebrows draw together, and I saw Yumi's quick bow of apology. My mouth opened and my lungs filled with air as my host prepared to speak.

"O Spirit Mi-Na, why ask when you know this is not a dream? Leave me now, or tell me what purpose you wish me to serve before you can leave."

I felt everything she felt. Heart beating, lungs inhaling and exhaling, goosebumps of fear and adrenaline jolt of anger. I couldn't read her mind, and I didn't know what she was going to say before she said it. Apparently I shared her senses and her emotions, or at least, the physical changes her emotions created, but not her thoughts.

"I can't tell you why I'm here. I don't know! You tell me! You seem to know a lot about spirits. Is that what I am? A spirit? Is that why I can understand you?"

An exasperated sigh. "Yumi, I am possessed by the most ignorant spirit imaginable. A spirit that doesn't know it's a spirit!"

"And you are either the most arrogant person I've ever possessed, or the strangest dream I've ever had."

Yumi held her hands out. "Why are you continuing to speak to it? We must go!"

I couldn't be inhabiting someone else's body. That just didn't happen.

This meditation spot looked like the place I meditated with Kenji, and yet it was just different enough to disorient me. The stream and the island were both bigger, and the bridge was gone. We'd crossed stepping stones to get from the island to the bank. Was this the same spot but in a different dimension? An alternate universe? A different era? Assuming I wasn't dreaming, drugged, or crazy, that is. And all three of those were more likely than stepping through the spirit world and into someone else's body. But if it turned out I *wasn't* drugged or dreaming, and I left this power spot, I might never get home.

"Um, I think we both meditated in the power spot, and we both opened the border to the kami world. Maybe I crossed through it on my side, and then into your world. I just-"

She stood still, but her rapid breathing and fast heartbeat gave me a sense of her fear and consternation. Her eyes were fixed on Yumi, but they widened as I spoke to her. I sensed excitement under her trepidation, and even something that felt like... could it be joy? She was happy? While I was freaking out?

I had to get out of here. "I just want to go home. My home, that is. I'm human like you, and believe me, I'm just as confused as you are. If we leave this spot, I may not be able to return to my body. Maybe you could try meditating again? In the same place? And by the way, where am I?"

Spirit possession must be a thing here. I sensed surprise but not incredulity in her response.

"Yumi, the Spirit claims it is not a demon." She raised her voice as if she thought I might be hard of hearing. "O Spirit, this place is Mount Tsukuba, near the Nyotai Peak. It is the Fourteenth Day of Sixth Month in the first year of Chōhō. His Excellency Lord Michinaga is Regent to His Majesty. I am Hitachi Vice-Governor Lord Tomohiro's daughter."

I recognized the era name Chōhō because of my obsession with *The Pillow Book*. The first year of Chōhō was 999 CE, and so His Majesty was the Emperor Ichijō, and his Empress would be Sadako, who was Sei Shonagon's patron. I *had* traveled through time! Or at least, my spirit had. But how would I get home? And *when* would I get home? And what was happening to my actual body in 2019? Was I in a coma?

On the other hand, this could be an honors thesis goldmine, to be able to learn what happened to Sei Shonagon in a way that no scholar would ever be able to do. I could get a PhD out of this. 'Youngest-ever professor of Japanese Literature' might change my mother's mind about my major.

Wait, what the hell was I thinking? I had to get home. Staying here was too dangerous. Something bad could happen to my host, and therefore to me. Epidemics, warfare, assault. And if she died, where would my spirit go then?

"Tomohiro's Daughter, this might sound strange, but I'm a woman like you, and I'm terrified at the idea that this might not be a dream. I may have crossed through the spirit world from the future. And can you tell me your given name? I told you mine."

Fear surged through her body as she replied out loud to my silent speech. "I will not tell you my name! Go home, Spirit! Leave me or the priest will exorcise you."

Yumi gasped. "Lady, the Spirit asked for your name? It must mean to curse you! Come, hurry!" She held out a pair of straw sandals which my host slipped on, and together they started their descent from the mountain top along a thin, dry trail.

Horrified at the idea of an exorcism, and dizzy at the strange sensation of my body walking against my will, I didn't know what to do or say next. Would I be able to get home if I left the power spot? Twice now I'd heard them mention an exorcism like I was an evil spirit that needed casting out. Where would an exorcised spirit even go?

Maybe I could control her. Force her to meditate. She was able to open the border to the spirit world from this era, so it should be possible. Then I could cross through the spirit world and back to my own precious self.

Strange how much I longed for the body I used to hate. But then, I'd never imagined having to live without it.

Chapter 5

Spirit-Squatting

Sixth Month, Chōhō 1 (July, 999 CE)

Give it no opening. Yumi had provided a hint on how to take control. What would an opening look like? Was talking to me making her more vulnerable? But when I'd tried to speak, nothing came out. On the other hand, I'd managed to move her leg slightly, with a lot of focus and concentration.

Through my host's eyes, I noticed the landscape was similar to Mount Tsukuba in my world: red pines, Japanese maples, sasa grass. The afternoon sun was lower than it was when I fell into my trance, but not by much. The air was almost as hot, but less humid. The cloudless sky was closer to azure than the cornflower blue I remembered from my hike. The result of cleaner air, maybe?

If this truly was the Heian era, why wasn't I wearing many layers of robes? Was this woman a shrine maiden? Or maybe women in this era had more choice in what to wear than I thought. I only knew what I had gleaned from reading *The Tale of Genji*, *The Pillow Book*, and a few court diaries. I really knew nothing about what life was like in the countryside.

The path had a number of tree roots that made the trail uneven. My host stumbled, crying out in pain, her eyes watering as she grabbed Yumi for support.

Ignoring the pain, I used the distraction to pry into her mind.

Anger. She blamed herself for tripping. We had that in common, at least. We blamed ourselves for everything. Most people would curse the tree root.

Impatience as she massaged her foot. Irritation at the delay.

But if I sensed her feelings, did she sense mine? How would I keep quiet?

A vivid memory of playing hide-and-seek came to mind. Heart racing, I'd hold my breath to avoid detection as the seeker drew nearer, suspense building until I let it all out at once, and then I'd be found.

She clutched her throat. I sensed panic as she fought with me to breathe. *So that's how I get control.*

Yumi gasped. "What's wrong, my lady?" She grabbed my host's shoulders as if trying to shake me out. "Is it the demon?"

I let go, and my host inhaled sharply. "The Spirit... it's hurting me."

"My lady, keep resisting it while we hurry home. There is no time to lose!"

Well, that was encouraging. I gained a small level of control over her by visualizing the action I wanted to take.

I pictured myself going back uphill.

Bingo! We started walking back the way we had come.

Yumi scrambled after her, picking up the skirt of her robe to keep from tripping on it. "My lady, where are you going?"

"I- I don't- know! This monkey spirit is- is fighting me!"

I lost my concentration. *"I'm not a monkey! I'm human!"*

"I will not let you control my body, Spirit!" She stopped suddenly, and Yumi crashed into her, causing both women to fall to the ground. "Exorcism's too good for you, Demon!" she shouted, her fury a bright, hot flash in my mind. She jumped up and stretched her hand out to help Yumi stand, but pulled hard in her anger.

Yumi yelped and massaged her wrist. "My Lady, do not talk to it!"

We headed downhill. I countered by visualizing going uphill. She spun around and swayed for a second. I'd made us both dizzy. She sat down and hugged her legs, clasping her hands in a lock around them. "I think the monkey spirit will have trouble getting me to move if I sit like this."

Yumi pressed her hands over her mouth. "Frightful living spirit! But why possess you? Does it need something from us?"

"*Yes!*" I exclaimed. '*I need you to work with me, not against me!*"

"What is your intention, Spirit?"

"*I don't have any intentions, and I didn't possess you on purpose. You pulled me in! I'm trapped, and I'm scared, and I want to go home. And I have a test tomorrow that I have to study for. If I show you images from my world, will that convince you I'm telling the truth?*"

"Perhaps. Show me." She closed her eyes.

"Lady, this could be dangerous." Yumi's voice cracked. "Take care!"

I took a minute to think about what to show her while she perspired in the warm air.

"O Spirit Mi-Na, we are waiting. Show me your world!"

Bossy. Not what I expected of a Heian Era noblewoman. I was a 21st century college student with a 3.9 GPA, but I envied her confidence and sense of command. I never felt good enough, smart enough, pretty enough for anyone to really like me, much less *obey* me. She didn't seem scared of me anymore. Maybe that meant she believed me when I'd said I was a human woman.

What would impress her? *Airplanes leaving white trails across a blue sky. Cars moving down the highway; learning to drive one, the feeling of power from pushing the gas pedal. Bullet trains. Smart phones, Internet. Posting a selfie on Insta.*

"See? This is what I look like in my world. A young woman, just like you."

She cried out in fear. "Are you from *Jigoku*? Does your world contain such metal monsters belching smoke and noise with people in their bellies? I understand why you escaped that nightmare of a world, but do not possess me further. Go back to your fox or monkey shape and leave me!"

Okay, maybe that wasn't such a great idea. And based on the struggle we just experienced, I didn't have enough control of this body to risk leaving the power spot.

"I might be able to go back the same way I got here. If we leave this place, I don't know what will happen. Please, it might be my only way back. Please help me."

She tilted her head. "Yumi, the Spirit claims it is a young woman from another world, and that the only way for her to get home is to meditate in the sacred place. I should try this before we get the priest. If it works, it will be over quickly."

"But the *sasa-hataki* ritual brought this spirit here- *ya wa*!" Yumi inhaled sharply and her eyes widened. "Lady! The *sasa-hataki* ritual brings spirits of the deceased to speak with a *miko*! Perhaps this spirit is one of the dead!"

Another rush of adrenaline. "Ah! How could I have missed that?"

I sensed she was both frightened and thrilled that her sasa-whatever had worked. Maybe that was the origin of her excitement earlier. Could this be the first time she'd performed this ritual? And it actually worked? Well, sort of worked. She hadn't intended to capture my spirit, that much was clear. But why? She was a noblewoman. She should be at home practicing her calligraphy or writing poetry, not performing shamanistic rituals on an isolated mountain. Why would she do that? Not to mention the risk she took trying to enter the spirit world. Any kind of demon could have possessed her. So she was lucky, really, to get a spirit like me. Not that I thought highly of myself, but at least I wasn't evil.

"O Spirit!" she called out like we didn't share one set of ears. "Are you one of the deceased? What message would you give me? Or service to ask of me?"

"I hope I'm not dead. I couldn't be dead. I was meditating, and then I was here. Yes, definitely not dead."

She conveyed this to Yumi.

"Then let's go now." Yumi stood up and brushed dirt from her robe. "We don't want to meet another spirit while returning in the dark."

The bowl of water was still on the island, and my host picked up several fronds of sasa grass that were lying next to it. She sat with her legs folded under her, and began to chant words I couldn't understand while tapping her forehead with the wide blades of grass. She focused on breathing while Yumi glared at her. At me, really.

Shadows lengthened as the sun sank to just below the trees, and my anxiety grew accordingly. I could sense that my host was in a trance, but the border to the kami world wasn't opening. No golden light, no silver bell. Just a gentle summer breeze rustling the bushes on the island.

She didn't seem to have the power to send me home. Maybe I needed to be the one meditating. *Yes, that's it!* I needed to perform *chinkon* just like I did to get here.

She was vulnerable now, unguarded in her trance. I visualized my spirit pouring into her mind like water filling a cup. My eyes opened, lighting upon Yumi, who was now gazing down as if meditating. I drew a breath. And another, counting out slowly.

I did exactly as Kenji had instructed, but nothing happened

other than the sun sank lower and the shadows grew longer. No buzzing, no vibration, no sense that the earth was pulling me into itself.

Why? Why didn't it work this time? My skin prickled with horror. Maybe it didn't work because it wasn't my body.

A hoarse sob escaped from my throat as I processed what that meant.

Yumi jumped up at the sound. I stood up, instinctively poised for flight.

"Demon, leave her!" Yumi grabbed my arms. I pushed back, and she fell to the ground, crying out in frustration. "What do you want from us, Spirit? Lady Masako, wake up, force the demon out!"

Aha! Her name's Masako! Yumi must have thought she needed to use the given name to push me out of the driver's seat.

Masako woke up from her trance and seized control back, leaving me disoriented, confused, and crushed that I had so little power. I could take control only when Masako was distracted or semi-conscious, and my control only lasted until she got her focus back. What was the point of possessing her if I couldn't take control? That wasn't spirit possession. It was more like spirit-squatting. So why the hell was I here?

Masako ran to assist Yumi while her anger washed over me like boiling water. "Spirit, I trusted you to leave while I was in the trance. Not only did you not leave as promised, you violated my trust. Leave me now or you will be very sorry when the priest arrives!"

She helped Yumi up from the ground.

I was ashamed of myself for having pushed her. *"Please tell Yumi I'm sorry. The meditation didn't work so I panicked. I don't know how to leave you. Believe me, I wish I did! My mother will have a breakdown if I never get back. My body will probably die without me. Can't you understand why I'd act this way?"*

Masako didn't answer, maybe because we had reached a couple of horses grazing quietly at the bottom of the trail. Or maybe she was shutting me out on purpose.

Her horse shifted and shied as she tried to mount, probably sensing my presence, so Masako had to grip its red cloth reins tightly. Both women put on hats that had been attached to the reins. The netting that ran around the brims probably kept mosquitos and other pests off their faces as well as hide them from any men they might meet on their way.

They rode a dirt path at the base of the mountain. Watching the scenery through Masako's eyes felt like watching someone's mountain biking Go-Pro video, and it made me dizzy. How could I be dizzy unless Masako was too? But she kept her balance.

It had grown dark by the time we approached a large compound of several one-story wooden buildings surrounded by an earthen wall. We stopped just outside the wall where an elderly man took the horses.

Masako and Yumi walked through a gate and into a courtyard where several lamps allowed me to see low buildings to my right and left, and another gate straight ahead, which turned out to be our destination. Masako and Yumi slid their sandals off and ascended a few steps to a corridor of some kind, stepping onto a thick straw mat covering a dark floor. An oil lamp provided a dim light as we turned this way and that, through several hallways, more doors, past steps leading down to a courtyard, more rooms. I became hopelessly confused. How could I possibly find my way out even if I managed to steal control and run away?

Masako called out. "I need to see Father! Where is he?"

An older woman pushed aside a screen and shuffled into the hall, her gray robe covering her feet and making a soft "shush, shush" on the wooden floor. "Welcome home, Lady. Lord Tomohiro is confirming the tax collection for the next shipment to the capital, and expected back tomorrow, or possibly late this evening if all goes well. I will bring supper to your apartment, if you wish."

Yumi stepped forward. "Lady Masako is possessed by a spirit! We must call the priest!"

Chapter 6

Eating For Two

Sixth Month, Chōhō 1 (July, 999 CE)

The older woman appeared both shocked and intrigued. "A spirit? What kind of spirit? Fox? Monkey? Vengeful spirit? Living spirit?"

She seemed to take it for granted that Yumi was telling the truth. If this happened the other way around, if Masako had invaded *my* mind in 2019, they'd say I was crazy and put me on medication. Or give me naloxone.

"Possibly kami-sent, but I do not know," Masako said. "I will discuss it with my father when he returns."

The servant bowed and shuffled backwards out of the room. From the dim light of a standing oil lamp, I saw that the room had open bays between support pillars along the wall. Wooden shutters were raised, allowing moonlight and fresh evening air to waft inside. Ahead, another lamp lit an interior room, which was where we headed next. Another oil lamp allowed me to see straw mats on the floor, a curtained, elevated platform that I guessed was a bed of some kind, several low tables, a couple of portable screens, and a wooden chest.

Yumi bowed to Masako and asked for permission to change out of her dirty hemp robe. "I'll send Chika to watch over you. She'll bring food with her. You must be hungry. I am surprised the servants have not lowered the shutters, but it is warm in here, so perhaps that is for the best."

Masako agreed to eat, although *I* didn't feel hungry. I did feel a headache coming on, however. The stress of hosting a strange spirit appeared to be causing my host some fatigue.

Oh! Strange spirits can enter the mind, Kenji said, if you pray without a clear intention. Is that what happened to Masako? She prayed but didn't know what she prayed for? But why me? Why am *I* the strange spirit?

Masako left her little room to cross the hall to the bay. The shutter above her head was probably lowered when it was cold or rainy, and apparently at night too, but Yumi was right. It *was* hot in here. I could feel Masako's forehead perspiring.

She gazed at the bright moon, an action that allowed me to see the earthen wall that appeared to run around the entire compound. It was clearly too high to climb over. Which made sense, if its purpose was defensive. If I managed to wrest control from her, I'd have to go through the gates and risk being seen.

My host sighed and closed her eyes, tears beginning to make their way down her cheeks. "Go away, Spirit. I have enough burden without carrying you as well," she whispered. She stared again at the silver orb gleaming in the indigo sky, lost in thoughts I couldn't read.

"Go away? That's what I've been trying to do all day!"

She didn't respond as she continued to gaze upon the full moon.

I distinctly remembered seeing a nearly transparent, slim fingernail of the waning crescent moon rising yesterday morning as I walked to the library. Full moon here, almost a new moon in my era. The floor swayed slightly under my feet, making me seasick, even though Masako was standing perfectly still on a steady floor. *Must be from the displacement of time travel. Like jet lag on steroids.*

I didn't want her to shut me out. I needed her to like me, so she'd help me. Poetry was big among the nobility in this era. A character couldn't burp in *The Tale of Genji* without someone writing a poem about it. Surely Masako would appreciate my poetry more than my classmates at Michigan did.

I thought for a minute. The haiku format wasn't invented yet. Waka poems were popular in this era and consisted of thirty-one syllables compared to haiku's seventeen. Mentally counting syllables on my imaginary fingers, I felt a corresponding twitch of Masako's fingers, which she didn't seem to notice.

"Masako, I have a poem for you," I said. I launched into it before she could respond.

"Moon shines upon us
Brightly, yet there is darkness
Within you. But I
Am the one who lost my way
When gods connected our worlds."

Masako stirred in surprise. She moved away from the window and began to pace the wooden floor. She paused a minute, and then replied softly.

"Spirit-invader,
My dreams are not as horrid
As scenes you show me.
I see why you fled your home,
But you must not stay in mine."

My excitement at Masako's response sent her heart lurching. Suddenly light-headed, she grabbed the support pillar to keep her balance.

So I could inadvertently affect her body. Interesting.

A young serving woman approached with a tray. "My lady,

here is your rice. Yumi instructed me to wait with you until she returns." She took it into Masako's sitting room and Masako followed. The servant had set the tray on a low, round, red lacquer table, and was sitting on her knees. She kept her head bowed, but kept glancing up at Masako, no doubt inspecting her for overt signs of spirit possession.

Masako sat on the straw mat in front of the table. She picked up black and red lacquered *hashi*, but stared at her tray with a complete lack of interest. I saw white rice, some kind of sashimi, seaweed salad, and slices of mandarin orange—all foods I liked—and a cup of water.

Frustrated that Masako didn't have an appetite, I was tempted to intervene. This host-body needed to stay nourished and hydrated; I had no idea how long I would need to live in it. Intervention hadn't gone so well back on the mountain, but maybe I could make Masako feel hungry. If I could do that, maybe I could control other things.

Mmmm...smell that salad... those orange slices look so juicy... I pictured myself picking up a sashimi slice, chewing it, tasting its buttery goodness, tackling the snowy mountain of soft white rice, so satisfying, so filling...

Masako started eating, and it tasted as good as it looked, but after a few bites she spit out a mouthful of rice and pushed the tray away so roughly it slid onto the floor, spilling the remaining contents. "Spirit, I was not hungry! You are not my mother to tell me what and when to eat! Leave me be!"

"*Sorry! But you need to eat. You're eating for two now, in a way.*"

The young woman in the corner rushed over. "My lady, what is it? Has the spirit choked you? Shall I recite a sutra? Shall I get a guard or a priest?" she asked, her voice quavering. She kept her eyes down, probably afraid she'd see the strange spirit in Masako's eyes.

Masako waved her away. "The sutras won't help me. No,

Chika, I choked because I was angry. The Spirit annoys me, and is always telling me what to do!" She dropped her aching head into her hands as Chika pressed her palms together in a silent prayer.

"I'm sorry, I'm sorry! I won't do it again, I promise!" I really did feel sorry. I wouldn't have liked some mysterious force making me eat against my will. It was good to know I could do that, though.

Yumi slid the door open. "What's wrong, Lady Masako? Chika, what happened?"

Masako and Chika spoke at the same time.

"She was choked by..."

"I am fine -"

Chika fell silent to allow Masako to finish. "The Spirit tried to make me eat when I was not hungry. I am upset that such a thing is possible. Yumi, I am very tired. Please set up my bedding. Chika, clean this up, and then you may leave."

Chika scraped the food off the floor, holding the tray at an angle and using her hand to brush the food back onto it. She bowed and left, but not before I glimpsed her face: pale, frightened, and relieved to not have to stay in the room any longer.

Yumi went over to a chest in the corner from which she took out several robe-like blankets, laying them out over a straw mat on the elevated platform. "My Lady, the servants are lowering the shutters," she said.

"Leave one open. The one across from my room, and leave my door open just a bit. I am very warm, and I wish to feel the breeze," Masako replied.

After letting the servants know of Masako's request, and then twisting Masako's hair into braids for sleeping (which took a long time, since her hair was as long as she was tall) Yumi set up her own sleeping mat in front of the door.

Masako took off her white jacket and red hakama. Underneath she wore a full-length white robe that fit almost like a modern-day kimono. That must be her sleepwear, because she kept it on as she lay down on the platform, drawing the other robe over her for a blanket. She set her head on a block of wood with an indentation for her head. It was more comfortable than I'd expected, but then, I was in Masako's body, and she was no doubt used to it.

I needed her to fall asleep. I wanted to try to take control so I could get back to the power spot and try the *chinkon* meditation again. I decided that I needed to concentrate on how much I missed my real body and my real life, so the power spot could amplify my desire and send me home.

Oh! Maybe that's why the meditation hadn't worked earlier. Maybe my desire to go back to my own time and place hadn't been strong enough. I'd never liked my own body, and no study-abroad program included *this* level of immersion, so the kami sensed my ambivalence about returning. But now I'd seen enough, and I was ready to go home.

Chapter 7
Clearly Destiny

Sixth Month, Chōhō 1 (July, 999 CE)

M asako's breathing slowed.
"*Masako?*"
No response. I looked over at Yumi and saw that she, too, had succumbed to exhaustion.

I visualized getting up, sliding the door all the way open, and walking to the hallway. After a few halting zombie steps, and just barely avoiding stepping on Yumi, I'd made it to the moonlight. I turned my palms up to see divots there. Pock marks. Was this why Masako was so sad? Had she lost her mother in a smallpox epidemic?

Flexing and twisting my arms, running my right hand over my left tricep, I admired how strong they were. I'd read that Heian noblewomen were typically weak. I'd spent more time in front of screens than exercising, so my body was weaker than this one. If only my mother could see me now, inhabiting a body that had never held an electronic device in her life.

I didn't want to steal Masako's body, but I was desperate to escape from this utter dependence on someone else. If I took a horse, I could find my way back to the power spot and perform *chinkon* again, only this time make it clear that I really, really wanted my spirit to go back through the spirit world and to the other side where my body had better be waiting for me.

Getting out wasn't as difficult as I'd expected. I knew the first step was to turn right as I faced the bay, and head to the double doors, which were now closed, causing a moment of panic, but Masako's muscle-memory took over and I just seemed to know how to lift the bar. Her unconscious guidance allowed me to navigate the turns to the inner gate and into the courtyard, where an oil lamp remained burning for light.

Gravel tickled my bare feet. A silky sensation swung against my ankles as a warm breeze waved my robe hem back and forth. I struggled to walk gracefully and silently, but if anyone saw me, they'd know something was very wrong. I lurched a few times, tripped on my robe once, but made it through the gate without being observed. A night bird whistled, and a horse whinnied, the sound informing me my destination was the building just a few yards ahead. I recognized the stable, and in my excitement, I walked faster.

And then stopped dead as I noticed a man walking out of the stable. He saw me at the same time and strode toward me. An older man wearing a tall black hat, a belted red cloak flowing over his shoulders to just above the knees, and pantaloon-looking trousers of a light color that I couldn't quite detect in the dark. Was he a guard? If he noticed my shaking hands and shallow, rapid breathing, he'd be very suspicious. He might even think I was possessed.

I forced myself to maintain Masako's calm composure.

He glared at me. "What are you doing here?"

What would happen if I tried to answer? Would I speak in the right language, and with Masako's voice? I still didn't know how I understood everyone here, or how Masako understood my modern American English. Even if I had access to the language center of her brain, that didn't mean I'd be able to speak her language out loud. It'd be safer to remain silent and play the sleepwalking card. I stared past him with what I hoped was a blank look.

His angry expression softened. "Go back to bed. You should not be out here in the dark."

I breathed slowly and quietly to slow my racing heart so it wouldn't wake my host.

But I failed. Masako woke up and took control back with an unconscious ease that left me dizzy. "Father, what are you doing here?" She sounded dazed and half-asleep. "You weren't supposed to return until tomorrow."

"I finished my inspection early. But Eldest Daughter, the more important question is what are *you* doing here? Were you walking while sleeping?"

Masako turned her head back and forth to see the residence behind and the stable ahead of us in the darkness. "I- I don't know. I was asleep and then- then I woke, and saw you in front of me. I'm not dreaming now, am I, Father? Such a terrible thing: a spirit invaded my body, and it won't leave me! I tried to send it back to its world, but it wouldn't go. It takes- it takes control of my body when I meditate, and it would seem while sleeping too!" She started to weep out of frustration and fatigue.

I hadn't wanted to make her cry, but I needed to know what I could and couldn't do in this world. It was a matter of survival.

Masako's father let out a long sigh. "Why do these evil spirits plague us? The pox demon that killed your sister, the red pox that took your mother, and now this! I must have done something terrible in a previous life. I will send for the priest immediately. In the meantime, Yumi must watch over you constantly to ensure the Spirit can't take you away again. Stay in your apartment until the exorcism."

"Will you please tell him I'm not evil?" I was so done with being called a demon and referred to as "it." Masako hadn't told her father this spirit-possession was her fault. Why was the possessing spirit always the one who got blamed? She'd called me an invader, but if she hadn't run out of the spirit world in a panic, I'd probably have just gone back to my body in 2019. Instead, I was stuck here, the target of everyone's fear and anger.

Maybe the exorcist would send me home. *Someone* had to be able to do that. I couldn't be the only spirit ever to travel through the spirit world and into the past. I wasn't that special.

Lord Tomohiro sent a servant to wake Yumi, and called one of his provincial officers to get the temple priest and the shrine miko. When Yumi arrived, he chastised her for failing to notice Masako had left her room.

Yumi knelt on the ground and bowed her head, weeping. "I have no excuse for my failure," she whispered. "I will leave your service."

Lord Tomohiro waved his hand to dismiss her offer, and instead ordered her to ensure Masako did not leave her apartment for any reason until the priest arrived.

Masako and Yumi walked back to their room while her father went to a larger version of the same building next door. They appeared to be the only two family members in this huge place, and they lived in different buildings. How often did they really interact? Although I wasn't in a position to judge. After we lost the house, my mother stayed in Novi while my father moved downriver, and he remained in a permanently bad mood after losing his job at the plant, so I didn't see him much.

Yumi pulled a robe from a chest and began to mend it. It appeared she was going to stay awake the rest of the night to keep an eye on me. Maybe I could teach Masako to talk to me silently the way I did to her. I had a lot of questions, and I needed to arm myself with answers. The more information I had about this place, the more likely I'd survive long enough to get home.

"Lady Masako, I talk to you by directing my thoughts to you in a focused way. I think you can do the same to me. You shouldn't need to speak out loud. Do you want to try it?"

"Spirit, if you can hear my silent thoughts, you can take over my mind, and maybe that is your plan."

I "heard" Masako's thoughts even though she had not vocalized them. "Lady Masako, you're able to keep your thoughts to yourself. I can feel and hear and taste what you feel and hear and taste, but I can't hear your thoughts unless you direct them at me. I didn't see or hear your dreams while you were asleep, for example. I don't know how this works, but it does."

"It works because you are a kami."

"If I am a kami, why are you trying to exorcise me?"

"If you are a kami, you will allow yourself to be sent back to the kami world."

"But I'm not a kami, so where will my spirit go after the exorcism?"

"If you are a demon, you will go back to Jigoku. If you are a fox or monkey spirit, you will go back to your shape. If you are none of those, you might just drift through our world forever, unless you possess someone else."

It sounded like I'd be homeless. And even if I did possess someone else, chances are it wouldn't be a young, privileged noblewoman. It could be a peasant, a criminal in exile, or even an animal.

Masako didn't care what happened to me, but this was *her* fault. She should take responsibility for getting me home safely. If only she saw it that way. What would persuade her to work with me on this?

"Masako, how old are you? What month were you born?"

"That is very personal information, Spirit. Why do you want to know? Will you cast my horoscope? Or will you use it to cast me out of my own body? Why should I trust you?"

"Maybe we were destined to be together. You don't want to fight destiny, do you?"

She thought this over. "I will give you my age and birth month. At the last New Year, I turned twenty-two years. My birth was in the Seventh Month."

Aya's mother had told me about the traditional Japanese way of counting age, in which a baby is counted as one at birth, and then two at the next New Year, which meant, in Western terms, she was twenty now.

"Masako! We're the same age! My birth month was Eighth Month in my time, but under your calendar I think my birth month was... uh... Sorry, give me a minute. The lunar calendar confuses the shit out of me." I paused. "Sorry. Was that rude?" It was impossible to know just how my modern speech translated through to her.

"Fear causes the bowels to void. I have heard it happens in battle. Do you fear the lunar calendar? Or do you fear confusion?"

Okay, so it translated literally. "No, it's just how college students —I mean, young people at university—talk. So where was I? I believe Eighth Month would be Seventh Month in your calendar, so we're both turning twenty-one next month. Well, in just a few days, I guess. That can't be a coincidence. I mean, what are the chances? My presence here is clearly destiny. You don't want to anger the kami by exorcising me when they worked so hard to get me here, do you?"

Masako sighed. "Mi-Na, many kinds of spirits possess people. How do I know which kind you are? It is best for the priest to expel you, so I can go on with life as I was."

"What were you, anyway? You aren't married, right? And surely most women your age are married. What were you planning to do with your life?"

Masako didn't seem interested in answering my provocative questions, instead slipping into a dark, silent mood.

I didn't want to get exorcised and end up in the void, but neither did I want to live in the body of someone with no hope and no future. I wanted to get home. Not only to my world, but home to my body exactly where and when my spirit had left it.

Maybe I could help Masako and help myself at the same time. "Look, maybe the kami sent me here to help you. Don't shut me out. Share some memories with me. Maybe they'll give me an idea of how to help you."

No response at first, but just as I was about to give up, she released a flood of images. *Mother, long hair tied at the back, chiding her for running. Fighting with her sister Takako, Father teasing the girls about how he would recruit them for his provincial guard because they were such good fighters.*

Father teaching them to read and write. Mother showing them how to make incense. Riding horses with her on her parents' estate.

Then the sickness four years ago, the one with pustules. Pain, fever. Priests with incense and chanting. Doctors with herbs.

And cremations. Too many, Takako among them, and a fiance too. Masako's pending marriage was canceled by death. She had been exchanging poems with a man for some time. Her parents wanted her to marry him, and three nighttime visits made a marriage. One night was all she had. He arrived with his friends on horseback, left his shoes at the entrance where her parents immediately took them and hid them so he couldn't leave. Eating mochi together, then entering a curtained platform. Slipping under the covers, he gently pulled her robe apart, exploring by touch in the dark. The next day he sent a beautiful morning-after poem on soft green paper.

He didn't return the next night. He became feverish, and not long after that, the pox demon chased his spirit to the other world.

And Mother, never fully recovered from her grief, was taken last year by the aka-mogasa, the red pox.

Praying with Father at the family altar to ensure the spirits of

Mother and Takako would remember to go to the next world, and not get lost in this one.

Turning to the local shrine for solace, praying to the kami to let her serve them.

The flood of memories ceased. Tears cooled her warm cheeks, and they felt like my tears too.

"Do you see, Spirit? My life is empty. There is nothing you can do for me. The kami have taken it all."

I understood, but what could *I* do? This was *her* life, her culture, her era. I needed to get back to my own, with or without her cooperation.

Chapter 8

Exorcism

Sixth Month, Chōhō 1 (July, 999 CE)

Dawn arrived with a cool breeze and a cacophony of bird sounds. The July air smelled fresh and green. A world without one single internal combustion engine. After I returned to my body, I might never breathe such air again.

At the sound of shutters being lifted in the hallway outside, Masako opened her eyes, allowing me to see bright spots of color enlivening the dim interior. Bright green silk curtains hung around her platform bed. Purple silk lined the green straw mats on the floor. A pearly-white inlay gleamed from the top of the black lacquer chest.

Masako seemed a little less depressed this morning, a little less hostile to her guest, and I found myself feeling a little more optimistic as well. Maybe the kami *had* sent me here to help her. I'd felt her melancholy ever since I arrived here, but now I realized what a vast empty space remained in her. Maybe I was dark matter that had slipped in to fill the vacuum.

I suddenly felt grateful for my own parents. I might not have seen much of my dad in the past few years, but he was there for me, I knew that. If I had any trouble at all, he'd help in a heartbeat. And my mother loved me so much, I'd spent the past year trying to put some distance between us. Masako's story made me grateful for my own luck in having both of my parents alive. Well, not just luck. Advances in science over the next thousand years would help. Smallpox vaccines, for one.

I tried to send a wave of comfort her way, and she smiled in return.

"My lady, may I leave to get your water and let the kitchen staff know you are awake?" Yumi whispered. She was already dressed and kneeling on her mat.

"Yes. Mi-Na will not harm me."

Comfortably nestled in her silk blanket like a butterfly waiting to emerge from its cocoon, Masako directed her thoughts to me. *"Mi-Na, if you are human, then who are you? Were you married in your world? What is your clan? What is your father's rank? You are not a commoner. Your manner of speech is not so different from mine, although you use strange words and expressions that I do not understand."*

Maybe I'd alleviated her boredom. I could make this a Thousand-and-One Nights situation. *A little information a day keeps the exorcism away.*

"My clan name is Cooper. My father's rank is... uh, well, we don't use that kind of system in my world. I think you hear my speech as similar to yours because it is *yours. I seem to be accessing your language center. I mean, I'm speaking with* your *words. I know that sounds strange. I suppose all possessing spirits must do something like that. Otherwise they'd never be able to communicate with their hosts. Anyway, I live in a far-away country unknown to you, but I came to Tsukuba to study at the university. I'm not married. In my era, people usually don't marry until later in life, if at all. So, will you find a new husband?"*

"My father has shown no interest in arranging a new marriage for

me, for which I am grateful because I wish to be a shrine attendant. My deepest desire is to understand how to appease the ekiki that killed my sister, and to conduct the proper rituals so they do not kill others."

"Sorry, but I have to ask. What is ekiki? I don't know why I understand most of what you say, but not everything. A bug in this language thing, maybe."

"How can you know so little, O-Spirit-Of-One-Thousand-Years? Ekiki are demon spirits who send epidemics. Shrine priests and miko endeavor to drive them off or appease them. Their efforts do not always work. I may be of no use at all, but I wish to try. How could there be insects in our speech? I, too, do not always understand what you say to me."

Her condescending tone irritated me, but I admired her courage in speaking to a strange spirit that way.

"Insects? I didn't- Oh, yeah. A bug is a kind of problem. Forget it. We'll just have to figure it out from context clues. So what's stopping you from becoming a shrine attendant?"

"Imperial shrines are led by imperial princesses, and so her attendants must be refined and highly ranked. I grew up in the countryside, so I lack refinement. Also, the priestess and her shrine attendants are supposed to be chaste, and as you know, I have experienced a man's touch. So it is a foolish dream. Anyway, life is fleeting. My sister's life was a plum blossom, all the more beautiful for its evanescence. Whatever value my life has to this world will also disappear, just as the pure snow melts and is soon forgotten."

"Oh, Masako, no!" My grief on her behalf caused tears to spring from her eyes.

She blinked them away in confusion and pushed her sleeping robes aside. She put on the red hakama trousers from yesterday over her white robe, draped a thin orange robe over that, and a green robe last. She walked over to a large polished metal mirror hanging on a stand, and in the imperfect reflection, I saw she had a stocky build. I had no way to know how tall she was, but she felt shorter than my actual body. Maybe she was five feet tall? Compared to my five-four. The ribbons that tied back her lustrous black braids were slipping loose, and strands of hair floated around her face and shoulders. A swatch of shorter hair at her temples, cut to shoulder length, framed her face.

"*Will you touch your hair for me?*" I asked in awe and envy.

Masako pulled her hair around so that it flowed over the front of her green robe to her ankles. It felt silky, a bit oily, and heavy compared to my fine, dirty-blond shoulder-length hair. She stared at her reflection, her eyes distant. I couldn't read her thoughts, but I sensed a heaviness in her spirit. Maybe she didn't like what she saw in the mirror? I understood that feeling all too well.

"*Masako, you're beautiful! Your eyes are like sideways half-moons, your hair is thick and shiny, and your face glows when you smile.*" I hadn't seen her smile, but I'd felt it, so it seemed like a good guess.

"*Yumi thinks I resemble a peasant. Beauty for women at court means small eyes and a pale, round face. I don't paint my face white or blacken my teeth, so perhaps it's best that my father will never allow me to go to the capital.*"

Yumi interrupted our conversation by sliding the door open. "The Lord Governor has a message for you."

Masako read the note. Apparently, as long as she knew a word's meaning, whether spoken or written, I knew it too. The note said that the priest would be here in the late afternoon to perform the exorcism.

The exorcism. I didn't have my body with its stew of adrenaline and hormones, so how could I be so anxious if Masako wasn't? Phantom anxiety? I couldn't yell at her anymore. She felt terrible about what she'd done, and being angry at her wouldn't help either of us. "*Masako, I'm scared. I don't know what's going on with my body back home. I could be in a coma. If the priest exorcises* me, my spirit might separate from my body completely, and I might die. Please don't do this."

She took her time answering. *"I am sorry, Mi-Na, but I need my body back to myself,"* she said at last. *"You must leave. You might find your way home."*

"But what if I don't? Where will my spirit go? Masako? Masako!"

Silence. Did she even hear me when she closed her mind like that?

"Masako, talk to me, please!" What had I said to push her away? *"I need my body back too! Please help me find a way home!"*

Crickets. Actually, cicadas. They were buzzing loudly outside, emphasizing the silence within.

With Masako shutting me out, I passed the time by dwelling on the awful possibilities of what the exorcism might do to me. I'll be expelled and wander the void for eternity. I'll be expelled and sent to Jigoku, where demons live. I'll be expelled and my body will die. The exorcism will fail and I'll be stuck here the rest of my life. Or the rest of Masako's life? She'll go crazy. I'll go crazy.

I heard a small cough. Chika was kneeling at the entrance to the room, her head bowed. She informed Yumi and Masako that the exorcist had arrived, and after a quick "can't wait to get away from here" bow from her kneeling position, scooted away down the hall, still on her knees. Masako lay down on her mat while Yumi stood to welcome the priest, who arrived a few minutes later with Masako's father.

Three others came with them: two young men in brown robes, no doubt the priest's acolytes, a young woman in a white robe with red hakama who was introduced as the medium, and the Shrine Miko, a middle-aged woman wearing a red blouse tucked into red hakama and a loose-fitting white jacket. Her headdress was hung all around with little bells, but she walked so gracefully and quietly they didn't jingle as she floated into the room and settled onto a straw mat. She bowed her head at Masako with a smile of encouragement.

Lord Tomohiro went to Masako's side. "Daughter, you will soon be free from the demon," he murmured.

I felt Masako's affection for her father rush through her, followed by a sort of wistfulness, but instead of replying to her father, she spoke silently to me. *"Mi-Na, I will miss you."*

"But not enough to keep me around," I said, but before I could say any more, the priest began chanting a monotonous lyric over and over. One of the two acolytes lit incense balls in a container with burning charcoal, placed that in a censer, and began to swing the censer slowly while striking a bell with his other hand. The other acolyte began to chant as well, his voice harmonizing with the priest's.

The bell's silvery chime, the chanting, and the sandalwood-and-clove scent of incense in the dim room made me feel sleepy. Masako closed her eyes and drifted into a trance.

"Spirit. Listen to me."

A voice in my head, but not Masako's. The medium?

"Spirit, it is time for you to leave that body. You do not belong with her. Come to me. I welcome you to my body. Come to me and leave her behind. You will be safe with me."

A tug. A pulling sensation. My spirit began to move out of Masako's body. Another tug, stronger this time. I felt myself slipping away.

"Masako, stop the exorcism! Don't let her pull me away! I can help you. Do you want to spend the rest of your life in this lonely place? I have an idea! Don't let me go! I can't resist her alone!"

I received no response.

Chapter 9

An Ominous Prediction

Sixth Month, Chōhō 1 (July, 999 CE)

The medium began to tremble and shake as my spirit moved toward her body. How could this be happening? Exorcism was based on superstition. Illness caused by spirits? Maybe when nobody knew the actual causes and cures, sure, but then science and technology gave us vaccines and antibiotics, so people knew better.

And yet here I was, my spirit halfway between two bodies, neither of them mine. Maybe everything the ancients believed had some nugget of truth to it.

"Medium, what will happen to me if I leave Masako?"

"Don't worry, Spirit. Come to me. It's safe. Come to me."

Was it, though? Safe? Or did it even matter? Masako didn't want me here. No one wanted me here. No one would care if I let go and slipped quietly into the void. Why should I fight to stay?

My spirit stretched like a piece of taffy, only a small end still clinging to Masako. The medium threw herself full length onto the mat, writhing as though in a seizure, but our strengthening connection allowed me to feel her triumph.

Her premature celebration goaded me into one last attempt. *"Masako! Lady Masako! Wake up! She's got me, and I can't hold on any longer! Help me! I have an idea that will help you!"*

Masako's eyes snapped open. *"Mi-Na, stay! I'm pulling you back!"*

With Masako's help, I pulled away from the medium's spiritual grip, and she cried out, collapsing in a faint.

I sent waves of relief and gratitude to my host. *"Thank you, Masako, thank you for not letting me go!"*

"Mi-Na, your presence, while intrusive, even maddening, is also comforting. Your stories about your future-world have stopped me from dwelling on my loss. And perhaps your very existence here is evidence that I might have power as a miko. You said you can help me. What is your idea?"

I didn't want to answer just yet, because the priest had stopped chanting and was looking back and forth between the medium and Masako with a puzzled expression. The Shrine Miko kept her head lowered as if praying.

Masako's father came forward. "What happened? Is the exorcism completed?"

The priest bowed. "It appears the exorcism failed. The Spirit was very stubborn. I will talk to the medium when she recovers. She might be able to tell us why it failed, and if the Spirit means to cause harm."

"He should have asked about that first!" I said. *"I'd have reassured him!"*

"Those who are possessed cannot communicate with the possessing spirit. Only a medium can do that," Masako answered thoughtfully, "so it would not have occurred to him—or anyone—to ask me that question."

An Ominous Prediction

She sat up. "Father, I changed my mind about the exorcism. The Spirit claims she came from our world, but one thousand years in the future, when metal monsters hold people in their bellies, and the air causes choking and gasping."

The priest, who had been tending to the medium, stared at Masako with astonishment. The Shrine Miko didn't react at all.

Lord Tomohiro's expression included an interesting mix of consternation, fear, and wonder. "Eldest Daughter, where did you get this ability to communicate with spirits?"

"It started during my meditation on Mount Tsukuba. That's where Mi-Na—that is what she calls herself—crossed into our world, so perhaps this power came from there."

By this time the medium was sitting up. The priest invited her to speak with a gentle wave of his hand. "I spoke with the Spirit," she said in a soft voice, her face still pale from exhaustion. "It was about to leave Lady Masako when I lost touch. I don't know why the exorcism failed, but while I was connected to it, I understood that it is not a mono-no-ke or a ghost. It appears to be a benign kami."

The priest gestured to his assistant to begin packing up their equipment. "Lord Governor, I am sorry for our failure to do what you requested of us today." He bowed deeply and left with his assistants.

Lord Tomohiro gestured to the Shrine Miko. "Miko, do you have any knowledge of what has happened and what we must do? And why Eldest Daughter is able to communicate with this spirit?"

"I hope she doesn't turn you in for attempting to commit shamanism without a license." Oops. I needed to stop speaking American. Masako wouldn't understand me.

Or maybe she did. "If she does, Father will be very, very upset with me. He might even require me to become a nun." Her heart beat faster as she contemplated this terrible outcome, although I didn't understand why becoming a Buddhist nun was so much worse than being a shrine maiden. Both jobs required celibacy and prayer.

The Shrine Miko bowed from her kneeling position, and her bells tinkled softly. "Lord Governor, I cannot tell you why a Future-Spirit has possessed this devout Daughter, nor why Lady Masako has the powers of a medium. But if Future-Spirit is not expelled, it is likely the two spirits will bind, with one spirit becoming dominant, absorbing the other permanently. They may have already begun this struggle for control." She lifted her face to gaze at Masako. "Lady Masako, I recommend that you avoid communicating with this Spirit, and above all, do not become attached to it in any way. Otherwise it may become the dominant one. And even if not, enduring a long struggle for control will result in madness."

Masako's cheeks grew cold. *"Mi-Na, is this true? Did I make a mistake pulling you back?"*

"I don't know the first thing about spirit possession, but if you trust her, then we have to believe her. Neither of us wants to go crazy, and I'd rather get back to my own body than try to dominate yours. But while you might have made a sacrifice by pulling me back, you didn't make a mistake. You kept me from the void, and I am so, so grateful for that. I'm fascinated by your world, but I don't want to be trapped here. Maybe the Shrine Miko has the power to send me back to my own body?"

"Indeed, I should ask, for she is very wise." Masako sat up.

"Miko," she said with a respectful nod. "Would you perhaps have the power to send the Spirit back to her own time and place?"

The Shrine Miko shook her head slightly, setting her bells jingling. "We miko call spirits to possess our bodies, and by doing so, we enable them to achieve their purpose. After they pass their messages to us, and we pass them to the people, the kami return whence they came. We do not send them away. Perhaps the Future-Spirit does not understand its purpose."

The Shrine Miko exchanged a look with Masako that Lord Tomohiro noticed, and his eyebrows drew together.

"Daughter, did you bring this possession upon yourself?"

Masako bowed to the floor but couldn't bring herself to speak.

"Then you must take responsibility for what has happened. Shrine Miko, do you have any recommendations for what we must do now? Will you take her under your tutelage and protection?"

Masako's forehead was still on the mat, so I couldn't see Lord Tomohiro's expression, but the Shrine Miko's voice was calm and kind as she replied. "Only one person has the power to send this Spirit to her future world, and that is Abe no Seimei, the Royal Astrologer at the Imperial Court. She must journey there to seek his help. He is a learned man who will be fascinated by the Future-Spirit. He may also perceive that Lady Masako has a special kind of power to have pulled a Thousand-Year Spirit into her body."

Masako jerked her head up in surprise.

I jumped in. *"Masako, my idea was that you and I can work together to convince someone powerful to help us both! I'll supply my knowledge of the future, and you help me get home safely by taking me to the only person who can do so, and maybe they can help you become an imperial shrine attendant. Deal?"*

Suddenly dizzy, Masako put her head in her hands. "I- I don't know, Spirit. It is a long and dangerous journey to the capital, and the Shrine Miko recommended I not communicate with you. But she also said it is the only way to send you home. Oh, what should I do?" She lifted her head and looked at her father. He was handsome in a sad, brooding kind of way, with faded pockmarks, dark pouches under his eyes, a strong chin and a square face. *"A position at an imperial shrine could help Father's position also."* Her fingers tingled with growing excitement. *"Spirit, if this works, if Lord Seimei agrees to help us, I will serve the Emperor and the kami, and do my part to prevent epidemics."*

She clasped her hands tightly as she took a deep breath to make her plea. "Father, Seimei might be very interested in the Spirit Mi-Na, and if we impress him, he might reward our family with a good word to the Lord Regent."

Lord Tomohiro sucked air through his teeth. "I can't leave Hitachi now, zo. Too much oversight is needed to prepare upcoming tax shipments. I can't take the time to escort you to court, and you mustn't go alone. I do not trust this strange spirit. Why does it possess you, Eldest Daughter, of all the people in the realm?"

Great question. It wasn't my choice to possess her, but we had so many coincidences. Same birth month, same age, meditating in the same spot, both wanting to change our lives. Just as multiplying two negative numbers makes a positive one, multiplying coincidences equals... whatever the opposite of coincidence is. Fate? Divine intervention?

"Tell him the ritual failed because the kami sent me here and they don't want me exorcised." I hoped she couldn't sense when I lied. *"So don't cross them or they might send more epidemics."* I felt a little bit guilty about leveraging her greatest fear, but I didn't have much choice. *"I can trade information about the future for his help. And as the Shrine Miko said, bringing a benevolent spirit like me from the future shows you have power, and that could help the imperial family. That's what the kami want from you. Tell your father that."*

Masako's breathing became rapid and shallow. From fear? Or

excitement? Or both? I hadn't possessed her long enough to know the difference.

"Spirit, you have reminded me that my life is worthless except for the value it has to the kami. And if it is their wish that I serve them in the capital, and if they sent you here to enable me to do so, then I must take the risk of losing my own spirit."

I feared she'd be skeptical that what the kami wanted just happened to be her greatest desire, as well as the only way for me to get home, but her humble and naive response felt genuine, which was both refreshing and disconcerting. I was used to people my age being jaded and cynical from long-term social media and internet exposure.

Masako conveyed my request to her father, who kept his eyes closed and his head bowed as if praying until she finished.

He nodded his head as if his internal question had been answered. "Eldest Daughter, you must prepare to leave in six or seven days, and pack for a journey of several months. My cousin, Lord Korenaka, was promoted to Chunagon—Middle Counselor—last year. He should be able to get you an audience with Abe no Seimei."

Masako bowed, thanking her father, then exchanging a smile and a bow with the Shrine Miko. The Miko left the room with Lord Tomohiro, possibly to talk about Masako's future. The medium, who'd silently observed all of this, bowed her farewell, but Masako ignored her.

"Well, aren't you going to bow back and let her leave?"

Irritation and impatience. "*Commoners*. They aren't really human. But very well."

The medium left the room after Masako's stiff nod of dismissal. I was grateful to her for keeping me here, but I couldn't stop myself from giving her a little twenty-first century attitude.

"Lady Masako, your ancestors were commoners once."

"Mi-Na, it surprises me how little you understand of my world. My clan is descended from Emperor Kanmu, who is descended from Amaterasu, the Sun Goddess, so my ancestors were never commoners. Nobility perform rituals to protect our country from kami punishments. Commoners are polluted, so we yoki hito risk failure if we come into contact with them."

Yoki hito. I remembered that term. "Good people." Nobility were considered virtuous while commoners were just one rung above animals. "The priest might talk to your father about your power to talk to me. Maybe he'll recruit you as his medium. Then you'd be on the same level as that medium."

"Oh, no, he wouldn't do that. He will want my father to order me to become a nun. He wants to prevent bad spirits from persuading me to do bad things."

"I suppose he wants you to be a Buddhist nun because he's a Buddhist priest."

"Shave my head and recite sutras all day? Never! When I recite sutras, I feel nothing but boredom. When I pray to the kami, I feel close to them, and at peace."

"You don't have to be a virgin to be a shrine medium, do you?"

"I have seen older, married women as mediums. It seems like a dangerous thing, though. A medium invites all kinds of evil spirits into her mind."

"Like me?" We both laughed. "Look, Masako, I'm from a thousand years in the future. With my knowledge of the future and your potential as a medium, I'm confident we can get you special dispensation to serve at one of the imperial shrines."

"I don't know why Lord Seimei would do that for someone like me."

"If he is so great at divining things, he'll see you have power, and he'll want to place you where you can do the most good. How long will it take to travel from Hitachi to the Imperial Capital? In my world the trip from Tsukuba to Kyoto takes three hours on the bullet train."

"Three hours?" She sent a wave of amusement my way. "You

An Ominous Prediction 69

do love to exaggerate, Spirit. Depending on travel conditions, it could take as little as a month and up to three months."

"We'll have so much fun. We'll be road trip buddies!"

Masako laughed out loud. "I do not understand your strange way of speaking, but I never met a human with such enthusiasm as you, Spirit. There is nothing for me here in Hitachi. And Seimei is perhaps our only chance-"

The door slid open, and Yumi came in with a tray of food and water. She kept her head bowed, staring at the tray. "Lady Masako, if this spirit can hear what you hear and read what you read, you can't make a plan to get rid of it. It knows everything. You say it means no harm, but it might have taken over your power of speech. How can we know that it's really you, Lady, and not the Spirit speaking?"

"Yumi," Masako said with tenderness, "I think you know it's me. Remember on Mount Tsukuba when Mi-Na took control? You knew right away it was not me. So look at me."

Yumi lifted her head to search Masako's face and eyes, which allowed me to examine her lined and scarred face, her thin gray hair, and her chestnut-brown eyes full of sorrow.

After a minute, she nodded. "Yes, Lady, I believe it's you. Then I must also believe what you say, that the Spirit means no harm. But why is it here? What will you do with it?"

"We will seek out the Royal Astrologer in the capital. He might have a use for our services. Will you come with us?"

"It's the first time I've heard you say 'us,'" I said. "I like the sound of that."

"Mi-Na, can you not interrupt me? It is annoying when I'm having a conversation with an actual person."

Miffed, I went silent.

Unaware of our internal conversation, Yumi replied. "I have served you since your birth, Lady Masako. I will go where you need me to go, as long as Lord Tomohiro approves. Now please eat and drink. Even a failed exorcism is exhausting. You need your strength."

Yumi watched while Masako ate her rice and dried cuttlefish, then went to sit near the door to sew.

Masako opened a small chest containing her writing materials. In addition to a brush, inkstone, and scrap paper, she took out several sheets of finer paper of varying hues, including green, yellow, and gray. *"I would send my letters to my fiance on this."* She held a sheet up to a lamp so I could see a sunrise blend of orange, red, and yellow fibers glowing softly in the light.

She set it down, and picked up a note that lay buried under everything else. *"This is the morning-after poem he sent me. Pastel colors are popular at court, especially for men. He attached it to a twig from a pine tree."* She read the note aloud in a quiet and tender voice.

"Morning haze rises
Upward, obscuring the sun.
I anticipate
Rising together with you,
But now I'm pining away."

"Does that line about 'rising together with you' have a double meaning? You know, like he's, uh... you know. A part of him rises when he's with you?" I wasn't sure how blunt I could be with her.

Masako didn't care, though. *"Oh, yes, of course. That is how such poems are written."*

She went into the next room and opened a box made of a light brown wood. *"This is made from catalpa, a sacred tree."* She took out a carved brown comb and held it against her cheek, the wood smooth and cool on her skin. *"My mother gave me this. It's a swallowtail butterfly. My mother loves butterflies."* She blinked away tears as she realized her mistake. *"Loved."*

An Ominous Prediction

She stuck the comb in her hair, and opened a round black box. She took out the cloth-wrapped object within, unwrapping it to reveal a small mirror encased in black lacquered wood. She turned it over so I could see the mother-of-pearl flower set into the back of the case, then held it up by a knob on the back so I could view how the comb looked on her head.

She stared into her own eyes. "Hello, Mi-Na," she said out loud. "Do you have mirrors in your world?"

"Uh, yeah. We have lots of ways to look at ourselves. Too many."

Our conversation was interrupted by horses neighing and stamping outside the wall.

"What's that?"

"It sounds like officers arriving from the capital. It's been several months since anyone has come from there." Masako went to the window and craned her neck so she could see over the wall. A group of young men in military uniform milled about as servants rushed here and there with water for men and horses. "An escort for the tax shipment, perhaps." She went back to the chest and picked up another small box, where she sorted through small brown pellets of something fragrant.

It looked like she was more interested in talking to me than ogling hot guys on horseback. That wouldn't have been my choice, but whatever. She probably never had a best friend. I hadn't had one since Aya, but I couldn't afford to make one now. Bonding with her might become binding, which would mean I'd never escape and we'd both go insane.

The next few days passed in a blur of preparation. Lord Tomohiro told Masako he would send extra rice, silk, mulberry fiber, and other crops that she could exchange for new clothes, and a few extra sacks of millet to bribe bandits if needed. He also made sure she practiced the *biwa*, and tested her on memorization of poems from the Kokinshu anthology. "If you spend any time at court, you'll need musical skill and a knowledge of poetry, or you'll embarrass us both."

I had many questions about the journey, but Masako fell asleep quickly every night, exhausted from her preparations, so I decided not to bother her. We'd have plenty of time to communicate during the trip, and I had to come up with a way to persuade Seimei to send me home.

Chapter 10

Road Trip!

Sixth Month to Seventh Month, Chōhō 1 (July to August, 999 CE)

The local diviner determined that the tax shipment should leave six days after the next full moon. When the appointed day arrived, Masako woke up before dawn. As she dressed in her travel clothes, she explained we'd be riding in an ox-drawn carriage so that she wouldn't be seen in public. "*Yumi will ride a horse. And we will take the Eastern Sea route, not the mountain route. I have never traveled so far.*"

"Have you lived here all your life?"

"Yes. Even though Mother was Father's primary wife, she lived with her parents after her marriage, so I was raised here. Father lived in the Capital, as did his secondary wife, but she died in childbirth five years ago, and the baby died too. Not long after that he received this post and moved here. Mother left her parents and moved in with him at that time. Father was very sad at the loss of his other wife and baby, but it made him happy to have us with him. But as you know, it wasn't long after that when my sister died, and then we lost my mother last year."

My spirit-heart hurt as I contemplated his loss of two children and two wives in just a few years.

Masako's traveling clothes consisted of the usual thin white *kosode*, which I now realized was the precursor to the modern-day kimono, but was basically underwear here; the red hakama over the kosode, an orange robe, and finally a short white overcoat. Yumi wove Masako's long hair into a braid and tucked it into the overcoat to keep it out of the way.

Masako put on her straw sandals and set a large hat on her head. Netting hung from the brim, presumably to protect her face from men's gazes as well as from insects and sun.

Once outside, I used Masako's peripheral vision to examine the ox carriage in which we'd be making our way to the capital. It was a box with a solid roof and platform, open at the back and front with curtains for privacy. Narrow, curtained openings on the sides allowed light and air inside. Two huge wooden wheels rose halfway to the top of the carriage, and two poles ran through the base of the carriage and extended forward to yoke a black ox. Three sturdy men waited by the ox, and another man stood at the back, all dressed the same with red jackets and white pantaloons, straw sandals, and large straw hats.

Lord Tomohiro walked over to Masako and handed her a packet of paper, no doubt one of the most precious gifts he could give her. "Practice your calligraphy and poetry. Those skills will be of great importance at court, and you can write to me too. Government officials make occasional trips to the provinces, so I am sure you can find someone to take your letters."

He bowed, a few quiet tears on his cheeks as he recited a farewell poem.

"She glows like the moon.
My last jewel, bound for the
Sun-bright palace, where
She will shine. She must not stay,

But how can I let her go?"
Tears rolled down Masako's face as she replied.
"This month's name is false,
Called, as it is, No Water.
Why, then, does the rain
Fall ceaselessly from my eyes,
And dampen my wide, silk sleeves?"

She bowed deeply, and turned to the carriage, where steps had been set out for her to climb in. She sat on her knees on a thick, silk-lined mat and allowed a sob to escape. Yumi slid the curtains closed, and Masako adjusted her seating position to crossed legs for the long journey.

Yumi came up on a small black horse and said something to the ox-drivers, who then called out to the ox, and our wheels creaked and began to roll. Very, very slowly.

"No wonder this will take two months! Masako, you could walk faster than this ox. Is it normal to go all the way to the capital like this? You can't even stretch your legs in here!"

"With my rank, yes, but I hate it. It's one reason we don't travel often."

Masako cried out in pain as one big wheel hit a rut, causing her head to bounce against a wooden panel. "*The drivers should take more care!*"

I felt pain too, but I didn't blame the men so much as the mode of transport.

After an hour or so of bumping around in the carriage, we stopped in the midst of a commotion: men shouting, carts creaking, and horses clopping and neighing. I smelled a mixture of straw and manure which was midway between a nostalgic county-fair horsey smell and an unpleasant port-a-potty odor.

Masako moved the side curtain to peek out. Government officials buzzed around, counting animals, jars, and bags of goods. Porters received bags to sling over shoulders and backs. Horses, too, were getting loaded with sacks. Warriors strode around looking fierce, wearing swords at their sides as well as bows slung over their shoulders. Masako's father had hired them to guard the goods from bandits on our route.

"Holy shi- I mean, holy kami! There must be two hundred people out there! And at least fifty horses. What are in the sacks?"

"Most likely rice, millet, and mulberry paper. You see those men with the big jars? Fermented fish."

What would fermented fish taste—or worse, smell—like? I appreciated dried or smoked fish, but fermentation was a whole different...kettle of fish?

I watched as two men slid a jar onto a thick pole, and then each shouldered a pole end. "Will they carry that all the way to the capital? I couldn't carry it to the end of the path!"

"It's funny, Spirit, your surprise at commoners. They are porters, so carrying things is what they do."

The convoy traveled for the next month without incident. The line stretched for several miles due to varying modes of transport. The warriors tended to ride ahead because they could, even though the ox-carts loaded with valuable silk and rice were the slowest and fell way back. Every once in a while the Captain would remind the warriors to provide equal protection to the end of the convoy. Our carriage stayed in the middle. Perhaps the Captain wanted to make sure the Vice-Governor's daughter had the same level of security as the mulberry paper.

The unsteady roll of the carriage gave Masako something like seasickness the first week, but after that we enjoyed looking at the scenery. Some rain found its way into the carriage, but so did fresh air, and as long as Masako was comfortable, so was I.

I wanted to get to know her better, and I wanted to tell her about Aya, and about my father, and losing our house, but I resisted the temptation. Sharing intimate details might hasten the binding process. The Shrine Miko said we had limited time before our spirits permanently fused. If that happened, I'd never get home, and we'd both go crazy.

Which made me think that spirit possession might be a real thing in my world too. All those voices people heard in their heads? Maybe some of them were prankster-kami, or demons, or lonely spirits lost in time like me.

Masako and I spent some time discussing how to approach Seimei. Why would he bother to help us? What did we have to offer? If our best option was my knowledge of the future, what should I share? Or not share? I'd only taken one Japanese history class, but it was a survey course that covered several centuries. Or would he be curious to know about my era? Nuclear weapons? World Wars? Information technology?

"Masako, we need a plan." That was how I managed my life. Planning. Planning for the ACT exam. Planning how to get into college. Planning for how to get and keep a 4.0 GPA. Planning kept anxiety at bay. Making lists and schedules. *Do this first, then that, then the other thing, and it would all fall into place.* Although sometimes the unexpected got in the way, and then I'd lose my shit. *That exam question didn't look familiar. How could the prof do that to me? I did my part! I completed the study guide! Memorized the grade rubrics! 100% attendance!* Yet the words swam around on the page, incomprehensible, and meanwhile everyone around me was busy writing what were undoubtedly perfect answers.

And of course, no amount of planning prepared me for this out-of-body experience. But at least Masako and I could make a plan together.

She didn't agree. *"Calm yourself, Mi-Na. You are causing my heart to beat too fast. It would be futile to discuss what such a wise and* educated diviner will want to know. We must wait for him to ask, and then we shall answer the best we can."

Masako had become more comfortable using my name, which was nice. Constantly being referred to as "Spirit" felt objectifying. I was a real person with a real life. Although if I wasn't born yet, was I a real person?

Stop! I couldn't allow myself to dwell on my own non-existence. That train of thought could lead to madness.

I'd spent most of my young adult life dwelling on worst-case scenarios and anxious about things that would never happen. *If I don't get an A, I lose my scholarship. If I lose my scholarship, I drop out of school. If I drop out of school, I'm a failure in life. If I'm a failure, it will break my mother's heart...* a negative thought-spiral leading to insomnia and panic attacks.

Now I had different and higher risk worst-case scenarios to dwell on, and my fretting had an effect on Masako. She might be lonely and sad, but she wasn't anxious, and yet her heart began to race while she slept, and then *she'd* wake up before dawn just like I used to.

Which made me even *more* anxious. My growing impact on her body might be a sign that permanent binding had begun.

The convoy stopped before sunset each day. Masako and Yumi usually had indoor lodgings, either in temples or with other noble houses, but sometimes had to stay in temporary huts with bamboo blinds for privacy. One night we camped on a white sand beach overlooking the bay. Masako slept in the carriage, and Yumi slept on the ground next to it. We enjoyed listening to the sound of the convoy porters and guards joking and laughing around their various campfires, and the sound of the waves lapping against the shore. The moon was new, but the stars made up for it by shining brilliantly down on us.

"I've never seen stars so bright," I said. "It's impossible, in my world. Too much light pollution."

"If you conduct purification rituals to eliminate the pollution, you might bring the stars back."

"If only it was that easy."

It took three days to get through the hot, marshy fields of Yedo. The drivers tried to ignore mosquitos buzzing around them as they pushed their way through tall reeds, yelling at the ox to pull harder to get the big wheels moving through the sticky, muddy road.

"Masako, in my world this humid swamp has become one of the world's largest cities, with buildings so high the tops are almost in the clouds. Nearly ten million people live here, and it's called To-kyo, Eastern Capital, because in a few hundred years the capital will move here from Kyoto- I mean, from where it is now."

"Ten million? How can so many people live in one place? I don't believe there are so many in the world. And it doesn't seem very clever to put the Imperial Capital in a swamp."

Not long after that, the carriage came to a stop. Masako shifted in her seat, craning her neck to see a wide river ahead, and then looked behind us, where the line of porters, horses, and carts stretched as far as we could see.

Yumi slid the back curtain open. "Lady Masako, the river is too wide for a bridge and too deep to ford. We must cross by boat."

Our carriage was driven ahead to the ferry, where the ox was unyoked. With great difficulty, the drivers and some porters lifted the carriage with Masako still inside it, and set it onto the deck of a barge-like boat. Several ferrymen poled the boat across, a nerve-wracking experience as they had to pole furiously to keep us from being pushed downriver by rushing water.

Getting it out of the boat was even more terrifying. The men in the boat lifted the carriage up, while men on the bank grabbed it from the top, but it tilted dangerously. Masako pushed her hands against the carriage walls to stay in place. If she slid to one side, her weight might be just enough to tip the carriage into the river. Her heart beat furiously, but I had the strange feeling it was *my* fear causing it to do that, not Masako's. *She* didn't seem to care that she was in this death-defying situation. Was she that brave? Or did she not care that much for life?

But we made it safely to dry land. Yumi and her horse were in the next boat, and our ox, which I'd named Oxy just for fun, came next, lowing and swinging his head with fear. After the drivers calmed Oxy down, they hitched him to our carriage. We'd been among the first groups to cross, and rather than lose precious days waiting for the rest of the convoy, we went on ahead. They'd catch up eventually. Oxy was even slower than those porters carrying jars of fish, and the Captain had not specifically told our drivers to wait for the rest of the convoy.

For the next three days we traveled along the shoreline. Masako kept the curtain open to enjoy the salty ocean breeze. A bright sun carved diamonds on the water, and later, a brief shower created a double rainbow.

"*Mi-Na, the end of a rainbow is a portal to the spirit world. But as you are a spirit, you must know that already, ya wa?*"

I hadn't forgotten what Kenji said about islands and riverbanks. So rainbows were portals too. Maybe all naturally-occurring liminal spaces were portals.

Which made me think about Kenji, and about my life back home. I missed it all—well, maybe not Mick—and worried about what was happening to my body back on the mountain. But this journey kept me from dwelling on it too much. Traveling by ox-carriage from Tsukuba to Kyoto, dangerous river crossings and the possibility of bandits, trying to keep my host alive long enough for me to get sent home. I had enough on my mind.

We made a turn away from the sea and towards the mountains, and at last we saw Mount Fuji's perfect cone floating above the Hakone mountain range. The drivers struggled with their footing as they began to move uphill.

"Should we give our drivers a break? They are working so hard, and they look hot."

"Mi-Na, it's their job to do this. Don't worry about them; the lieutenant will tell them when to take a break. And they're just commoners-" she stopped, probably not wanting me to chastise her again.

But I'd moved on to another question, one that had been on my mind since she showed no interest in those young officers on horseback. "Masako, you said your fiance died last year. Isn't that old for a woman to get married in your world?"

"Not so old for my family's rank. I had no interest in marriage or children, and my fiance was three years younger than me. Mother wanted me to wait until he was at least sixteen."

No interest in marriage? "Do you ever think about men? You know, like being with one intimately?"

"A peculiar question, Spirit. The human body is ugly, which is why women and men do what they do in the dark with their robes on. That one time with my fiance was not unpleasant, but not something I'd ever seek out."

"Uh, do you..." I hesitated before the next question. "If you don't think about men, do you ever think about women, in that way?" I was on the straight end of the sexual orientation spectrum. If my host was attracted to women, would I feel it too? Although if she was, surely I'd have noticed by now. I felt her adrenaline rush when she was scared or angry, so I'd feel her crush if she saw anyone she liked, but I hadn't. At least, not so far.

She was puzzled at my question. "I have heard some women at court become very close, but I do not care for any of that. Truly, I just want to be a shrine attendant. Celibacy does not bother me."

She was probably asexual. What would happen if *I* found a man attractive? Would it jolt any reaction in her? Or could I even feel such a thing if she didn't?

Her comment about being a shrine attendant triggered a memory. *"Masako, when I walked into the spirit world, and you saw me there and ran away, you pulled me with you. I heard Yumi say something about a blind miko. Were you practicing miko-ism? If that's even a word? I take it your father didn't know about that? What does a miko do, and why did you want to practice it?"*

She shifted uneasily on the seat cushion, then lifted the window curtain. *"Oh, look, Mi-Na, the Kiyomi checkpoint! We are almost halfway to the Capital!"*

I saw a wooden hut ahead. We'd passed several of these checkpoints so far. Soldiers were stationed at each one to ensure only those with authorization to travel could pass through.

"It won't take long for our small group to cross this barrier, and we're still weeks out from the capital, so you might as well answer my questions. Otherwise I might drive you crazy with my pestering." I had no control over her body, but I did have the ability to fill her mind with noise. It wasn't much, but better than nothing.

She sat back with an irritated huff. *"You mustn't tell anyone-"*

"How could I? I can't control your speech."

"Mi-Na! Do you wish to hear my story or do you wish to pester?"

"Story! Please!"

The carriage stopped. Masako peeked out. The drivers were bowing at the station while Yumi, thickly veiled for propriety's sake, presented Masako's travel authorization from Lord Tomohiro. The soldiers bowed deeply, not even ordering her to lift the curtains. That would be too, too rude.

After a few minutes the carriage started rolling again, and Masako continued with her story. *"I did a foolish and dangerous thing. I despaired of life after the epidemics took Mother and Younger Sister, and I longed to see them, hear from them, and perhaps to join them. But then I met a wandering miko. She was blind, as many* aruki-miko *are, and she had performed a ritual to be possessed by spirits of the dead to pass messages* along to their families. I begged her to teach me how. I gave her my most beautiful robe, and she taught me the sasa-hataki *ritual. She warned me that I might not have the power to call up my mother from the spirit world, or that I might become possessed by an evil spirit. And she was right."*

Well, that was a slap in my virtual face. "Why do I have to keep telling you I'm not evil? A little selfish at times, and insecure, I grant you that. But if I was evil, I'd make you do something really terrible, like kill someone. Instead I'm helping you break out of your lonely life in the provinces."

She laughed out loud, although I wasn't trying to be funny.

Yumi called in through the window. "My lady? Did you speak to me? Do you need to stop again?" We had regular breaks to relieve ourselves and get refreshments of water and dried fruit.

It wasn't the first time Masako had made noises while talking to me—a laugh, a gasp, a soft-but-audible "eh, eh." Yumi must be shaking her head at the strangeness of her possessed companion.

"No, Yumi, I am fine," she replied with laughter still in her voice. "*Mi-Na,*" Masako continued. "*Of course I know you are not evil.*" She laughed again.

My serious host was teasing me?

"*You are exasperating and amusing, but not evil. And I pulled you into my world, so I must have power of some sort. If only I had the power to expel- I mean, to send you back to your body.*"

"I wish that too. But I'm confused. What is the difference between a medium, a miko, and a shrine priest?" That sounded like the start to a joke.

She smothered a gasp of surprise so Yumi wouldn't hear. "*O Spirit, how did you enter the spirit world when you have so little understanding of it?*"

"I'm human, not kami, remember?"

"But you are one thousand years old. That should give you much wisdom."

"I'm from a thousand years in the future, but I'm the same age as you, and much less mature."

She paused for a moment as she reflected on that. "Very well. A medium communicates with spirits who afflict other people. She pulls the negative spirit—the ke—from the sick person into her own body. But only a priest, either from the temple or from a shrine, can ask the spirit its name and banish it. A miko summons spirits or kami, who use the miko to pass along instructions, or a message, or a prophecy, to the people. A shrine priest prays to the kami to gain their support and goodwill. A temple priest prays to Buddha, and is paid by others to recite sutras for good health, or for someone who has died."

By this time it was getting dark. We'd entered a lush, fragrant wilderness, and it was just our carriage, ox, and drivers, and four hired warriors. Somehow the other ten carts had fallen far behind.

We camped for the night, which meant Masako had to sleep upright in the carriage while Yumi slept on the ground next to it. When Masako descended to stretch and use the facilities—meaning the woods, with Yumi holding up a robe for privacy—we could see a bright orange glow in the sky. I'd no idea Mount Fuji was an active volcano in this era, and it was both beautiful and terrifying.

As the drivers and warrior-guards got their own fire and food prepared, we heard them talking about how this area was known for bandits.

Which made me wonder what were the chances we could traverse this isolated area safely?

I got my answer the next day.

Chapter 11

Call Me Ji

Seventh Month to Eighth Month, Chōhō 1 (August to September 999 CE)

We had a stream to cross, so the guards suggested we get the ox-carriage across that first, and then camp for as long as needed for the convoy to catch up.

The road was better than I expected—almost as wide as an American two-lane road—and we forded the stream without much trouble.

While waiting in our carriage, we heard new voices, speaking loudly and coarsely, and then a squeak of fear from Yumi. Masako lifted the curtain to peek out. A group of ten or so men wearing padded straw vests had surrounded our guards, shouting and waving swords and thick wooden staffs. Our drivers were lying on the ground with their faces in the dirt. *Dead?* One of them turned his head slightly and caught my eye. *Good, not dead.* He looked back down quickly, probably so the bandits wouldn't get the idea he ought to be dead.

Guards and bandits were shouting in what appeared to be a negotiation, one that was not going so well. And then I realized what they wanted. *"Holy excrement, Masako! We left the millet sack bribe with the convoy!"*

One of the bandits came over to unhitch Oxy, apparently to take him in lieu of millet, but Oxy had other ideas. He liked his drivers, and this bandit apparently smelled suspicious. He head-butted the man, and then started running with the carriage half-unhitched. One wheel dropped into a deep rut, and the carriage tipped and then slammed against the ground. Masako's head smacked a wooden panel, sending pain through her head so intense she passed out.

I heard shouting, so I took control of Masako's body to see what had happened. Easy, now she was unconscious. I pulled myself up from the floor, ignoring my aching head and the trickle of blood running into my eyes, and peeked out. I needed to do something. Find Yumi, get out of the carriage box, something, anything but just sit here helplessly. *"Hey, Masako, wake up! I'm the anxious one. You're the brave one, remember?"*

No answer. The front opening was still covered by the curtain, but the back curtain had slid to the ground. Yumi had dismounted and was crouched by the opening, looking in with concern.

"Lady Masako!" she whispered. "You're bleeding! Did you hit your head? I have your bow in one of my saddle-packs. Are you able to fight?" She was holding a staff with white-knuckled determination.

I didn't know if I could speak using Masako's voice, but I had to try. "Yumi, this is Mina." Good. That sounded right. "Lady Masako hit her head when the carriage tipped over, so I took control. I'm not sure I *can* fight, or that Masako's body has the strength right now. Can you fight?"

"Demon! You are not to control Lady Masako. That was part of your pact!" Her eyes widened in fear even though her tone was sharp with anger.

I sympathized. It complicated things when your boss suffered from spirit-possession, but we needed to take action. "We don't have much choice right now, do we? Hand me the bow and arrows. You take the staff. But let's wait. They're still talking over there."

I spoke too soon. The negotiations broke down, probably due to a lack of millet, and the bandits charged. The guards did their best, but they were outnumbered, and one of them lost his sword after a bandit knocked it out of his hand.

Yumi turned to her horse, which was not happy about the noise, shaking its head and dancing back and forth. She managed to pull a bow and set of arrows from the bag —"here, take these!"—and mount the restless horse, nearly falling, but not giving up. Once mounted, she lifted her staff with both hands and nudged the little black horse forward, shouting "Ha-ee!"

"A woman on that horse! Watch out!" a bandit shouted.

I couldn't take the time to watch her. I pulled an arrow from the bag, grateful I'd done archery in Girl Scouts every summer at camp, but not certain I had the strength to pull the string. I lifted the bow to my shoulder and aimed at a bandit who had just knocked down a guard. My hands and eyes seemed to know what they were doing, and with a confidence that took me by surprise, I shot the arrow and hit the bandit dead on. His straw padding protected him, but he was startled and distracted, so I shot another, this time hitting his hand and forcing him to drop his staff. Masako's muscle-memory had taken over for me. Her body, her brain, her skill set, all under my control. It felt natural, smooth, and even in my fear, confusion, and with an aching head, I reveled in my accomplishment.

As I put another arrow to the bow, I saw Yumi prepare to smack a bandit with her staff, but she accidentally hit our other guard on her upswing, causing him to drop his sword.

Uh oh, friendly fire. Team Taira's in trouble.

The quality of the shouting changed suddenly. Baritone yells of anger rose in pitch to tenor shouts of terror. "*Yōkai!*" I heard someone call. "*Yōkai! Yōkai!*"

Yōkai? Ghosts? I peeked around the carriage. The fighting had stopped. The men stood frozen in position as if playing an eerie game of statue tag. A strange fog, thick and iridescent, sinuously slid toward us from the trees like a sentient being. Weird, but just fog. Why'd they stop fighting?

And then I noticed shapes forming and reforming within it. *A deer? No, a fox! There's a wild boar, and it's about to charge at us.* I grew light-headed with fear, and grabbed onto the carriage for support. But if it was just fog, it couldn't hurt us, right?

No one wanted to find out. Survival instinct kicked in, and the bandits fled. The guards and drivers fled too. Yumi's horse bolted with poor Yumi clinging to its bridle and shouting at the horse to stop. I didn't see Oxy anywhere.

Should I run away? Could I even run? Masako was unconscious from a head wound, after all. *Maybe this animal-fog will just roll over me if I play dead.*

I threw myself on the ground. As I peeked through my fingers in fear, I noticed the fog had already begun to dissipate, sending wisps of mist swirling through the air, sparkling in the rays of sunlight that now reached through the trees.

I curled into a fetal position and put my spinning head in my hands as I contemplated my status. *Injured and alone in a spooky mountain forest. Awesome.*

A creaky male voice startled me out of my self-pity. "Quite entertaining, don't you think?"

I looked up to see a stooped and wrinkled old man looking pleased with himself under a long white beard. He was smiling, but in a nice way, not a leering or cruel way. He wore clothes that had probably once been white, but were now gray with dirt.

Same went for his turban-like head covering, and his beard, which was full of leaves and twigs.

"What *was* that?" I asked when I got my voice back.

"*Obake* fog! I've tested it on a few bandits before, but this is the first time I used it to save someone. Your guards were so scared they probably voided their bowels." He chuckled and looked me over. "It looks like your body is damaged. Come with me. I've been waiting for the two of you to get here."

"What did you just say? How did you know? Who are you?" Did Masako's knock on the head cause me to hallucinate? How could he know there were two of us in one body?

"My divination skills really improved after I became a *yamabushi*. Better than Seimei's now." He gave me an amused look. "You're thinking I'm not very humble for a monk. Seimei always told me I was too arrogant for a diviner, so I've been living here for thirty years to learn humility. And if I'm this conceited now, just imagine how much worse I was then!" He cackled and held out a staff for me to grasp, pulling me to stand.

I swayed, my head still spinning. "I shouldn't leave here. The guards and my attendant Yumi will come back to this spot. Or at least, I hope they do. Who are you? You know Seimei? We're traveling to see him. We need his help."

"I know. That's why *I'm* going to help you. You shouldn't see that scoundrel without proper training. You'll need to develop your own powers or he'll manipulate you into serving him. They call me Ji no Gyoji. You can call me Ji."

"Ji-san, can you see me? I mean, the real me? Mina?"

He added new wrinkles to the ones already on his forehead as he puzzled out what I'd said. "What do you mean by 'Ji-san?' he asked, and it occurred to me that the honorific 'san' wasn't in use yet.

He waved a hand dismissively. "Doesn't matter. Just call me Ji. I see two spirits glowing within one body. I divined I would meet a spirit from a future world, and that this future-world-spirit would share life in my world with a gracious hostess from the Taira clan. She needs to wake up, by the way. Let's get some of your belongings and go to my humble residence so that I can treat this wound."

I decided to trust this Ji person. Maybe I shouldn't—look where trusting Kenji got me—but my intuition said this was where I needed to be. He gave me his staff to lean on, and I followed him a short distance to a hole in the mountain hidden by bushes.

We entered a cave with a packed dirt floor and walls made of a rough reddish-brown stone. I sat down on the ground, and he washed my head wound with salt water, which hurt, and then pressed cool clay against it, which felt good. I started to feel sleepy, so of course that's when Masako woke up.

Startled at her surroundings, she scrambled to stand. *"We've been kidnapped by bandits!"*

I suppressed my flash of anger that she could take control so easily. *"Calm down, Masako, we're fine. This yamabushi helped us. He scared off the bandits with some kind of magic fog. Unfortunately, the guards ran away, and Yumi's horse got spooked and ran off with her on it. His name's Ji. He can see us both!"*

She exhaled with relief, then gasped with surprise. *"Can he see you? Mi-Na, did you take control? Could you walk after I hit my head?"* Now I felt *her* anger surging. *"You took control? You did not ask permission. This is a violation of our agreement!"*

"What agreement? I never promised to never take control. Oh, and by the way, I did it to save your life!" Okay, so a slight exaggeration, since Ji had been the one to scare the bandits away, and I saved *my* life by saving hers, but I did get her to this cave where Ji could treat her head wound. I deserved credit for that, didn't I?

Masako put her hands over her ears as if to shut me up. Ji

noticed and intervened, explaining to Masako that we needed to work together, not against each other.

He suggested we stay for a few days while Masako recovered. He offered to teach us divination skills to improve our chances with Seimei. "Seimei and I were friends, once. They say his mother was a fox spirit, which allowed him such a long and healthy life. He's a great diviner, a really great diviner. Just beware of him, and be sure to have something to hold over him as leverage."

Ji explained the guards would not be coming back. They'd be ashamed of having left their posts and fearful of retribution for abandoning Masako, so they'd join the bandits, who would be too terrified of this spot to return for the ox. Yumi's horse had bolted down the mountain, and she would find the rest of the convoy. They would arrive in four or five days. The ox would find the carriage, and graze and drink water from the mountain stream nearby until then.

He'd divined all this. My head was spinning, and not from Masako's wound. How could all this be happening? How could someone "divine" all this information? Maybe humans had a kind of cosmic micro-chip inside that had been utilized by ancient peoples, but was untapped in modern times. Find Friends could've located Yumi, but then we'd need wifi or a cell signal, not to mention a smartphone. All Ji needed was some bones and a fire. Oh, and a special knowledge gained from living alone on a mountain for decades.

He offered to teach divination to Masako. "Many diviners have been women, noble women especially," he explained, "and Taira Lady, drawing Future-World-Spirit into your body shows great power. I wish I could be there to see Seimei's face when he meets you and realizes just how special you are. He might even take you as a pupil. Tell him Ji taught you first." His eyes gleamed. "In exchange for my help, I want Mi-Na to describe her world to me. I have a deep thirst for such knowledge, so Taira Lady, you will allow the Spirit to take control while you sleep."

I loved the idea of being able to move around on my own every night, but Masako disagreed. "Ji, if I allow Mi-Na to take over each night while I sleep, her power might grow, and if our spirits fuse into one, she might become the dominant spirit."

That really pissed me off. *"Masako, you're the one with all the power here. You're being selfish. You just don't-"*

"Stop shouting at me, Spirit! This *is* my body that you invaded. Is everyone in your world so rude? I stopped the exorcism to save you from the void. I have undertaken this long, dangerous journey to get help for you. How dare you call me selfish?"

"You're doing this for yourself as much as for me!"

Masako pressed her fists against her head and screamed a little scream that might have been from me, or it could have been from her, or even both of us in angry synchronization.

Ji held up a wrinkled hand, his dirty sleeve slipping down to reveal his scrawny brown arm. "I can see your spirits becoming dark orange with anger. Instead of arguing over who will control whom, you must work together to achieve what you both want. Allowing Spirit Mi-Na to take control each night requires trust, and trust is needed for you both to achieve your ends."

I'd been so good ever since the exorcism, and Masako still didn't trust me. But what if she was right? What if trust created a bond that would lead to binding? I didn't want to become the dominant spirit in a body and world that wasn't mine. And it might not even be the case that I'd dominate. I could become subsumed by Masako's spirit.

Ji wouldn't take no for an answer from either of us. "The Taira Lady must learn divination from me, and the stories that Mi-Na will tell will give me something to dream about when I'm all by myself in my lonely cave, done with my rituals and prayers for the day," he said.

"Masako, ask Ji how much time we have until we won't be able to separate our spirits. I'm thinking we don't have any time to spare for this!"

Masako agreed after insisting I rephrase my demand into a polite request. *"Mi-Na, your harsh manner of speaking will result in disaster if you become the dominant spirit someday."*

She had a vested interest in improving my manners. I needed to start listening more closely to her phrasing, the depth of her bows, how she ate her food, how she put her robes on. *Just in case.*

Ji had no idea how much time we had left as separate spirits, but he said our escort wouldn't arrive for a week anyway, so we might as well learn something useful.

Masako and I reluctantly agreed to Ji's request. Over the next few days, Masako's wound got better, and she learned how to read cracks in the bone of a deer shoulder blade, a core practice of divination. She let me take control while she slept so I could tell Ji about the future. I hoped she would let me do that in the capital as well. It wasn't like she needed her body while she slept. And it made such a big difference for me, to regain even a small amount of the autonomy I used to take for granted.

So at night Ji and I walked together through the dark and mysterious forest while I talked about my world. Stories of environmental pollution made him weep, while my description of smartphones made him drool with envy. In exchange he taught me how to identify the kind of spirits that fell into the *yōkai* category. *Obake* were shapeshifters who caused mischief and trouble (fox and tanuki fell into that category,) *tengu* were bird-like goblins that preyed upon human weakness to corrupt us, and *yūrei* were spirits of humans who died but couldn't move on to the spirit world due to their need for vengeance. Disasters such as the smallpox epidemic, earthquakes, and fires were attributed either to *yūrei* or to angry kami, so it was important to learn how to appease them.

My nightly takeover yielded some benefits. It had grown easier to take control, for one. Masako fell asleep, and I slipped into full possession as if I were putting on a new pair of jeans. The first night the jeans were a little tight, uncomfortable, causing a slight change in my gait, but by the third night they'd been washed and stretched and felt like my favorite pair.

As we walked through the dark forest, I began to see *obake*. A fox with an iridescent aura crossed our path one night, and a badger-shaped glow shuffled between trees on another. When Ji laid out offerings to the kami as part of his divination ritual, I saw shadow-figures of men and women appear to eat and drink what was laid out. "How can I see them when I'm in control of Masako's body, but neither of us can see them when she's awake? And why can you see them?" I asked.

"You came here through the spirit world, and in that brief crossing you received that power. I have spent forty years developing my powers, and now, when I offer certain prayers, *obake* will come to my assistance, as you saw when they scared off the bandits. Keep in mind that while you can see *obake*, you won't be able to control them like I did. Unless you spend forty years working on it."

"Don't quit my day job, got it. Thanks, Ji."

During the day I kept quiet and in the background. I didn't want to connect with Masako any more than I had to. Masako felt the same way. She avoided talking to me unless she absolutely had to, and she stayed awake as long as possible at night to give me less time in control. Ji said we needed to trust each other, but any trust we'd built up on our journey so far had been damaged in our anxiety about fusing.

Ji decided to teach Masako to see *obake*. "If you can see and identify such spirits, you can prevent or eliminate curses, and that will gain you support at court. But Taira Lady and Future-Spirit must work together to do this. You must become vulnerable to the other. Trust in each other. Lean on each other like stones in an arched bridge."

"Respectfully, Ji, can I learn without Mi-Na? I feel she is becoming too strong, that rather than a guest, she considers my body her new home."

"I'm worried about that too, believe me. I don't want this to be my home."

"Taira Lady," Ji said, "building a trusting connection with the Spirit does indeed increase risk, but you will not be able to see *obake* by yourself. The Spirit has walked through the spirit world from a future world, and this, I believe, has given her a special power. She might convey this power to you, but only if you trust her to do so."

Ji asked Masako to stay awake that night. After sunset, but before moonrise, he walked with her to the stream where we got our drinking water. He pointed to a grassy spot on the stream bank, and instructed her to meditate. "There are four spirits in every soul," he said. "Future-Spirit left three of her four spirits with her corporeal body, and they will draw her back when Seimei creates his spell to separate you. Taira Lady, think of Future-Spirit as your fifth spirit. When you have absorbed this new spirit, you will be able to see *obake*."

Absorb me? I thought Ji was supposed to help me, but wasn't absorption the same thing as fusing? Masako didn't seem to mind, though. Absorbing me would make her stronger, give her *my* power.

Her meditation trance began. Her heart rate and breathing slowed. I heard no thoughts from her, nor did I try to speak. Serenity pervaded her body. I sensed an opening of her spirit to me, a warm welcoming feeling, and I had a sudden vision of my mother's arms widening as I ran in for a hug when she picked me up from daycare. Masako was opening her soul to me.

Or maybe she wants to become the dominant one. I wasn't about to let that happen. This trust thing Ji kept talking about could be the trigger to binding. Shrine Miko advised us not to connect, but Ji was pushing us to do just that. I trusted Shrine Miko. Her advice made sense. Masako and I could keep our relationship on a business-like status. I'd done without close friends for years, and it worked out. I could make this work, too.

I took control while her trance left her vulnerable, and plunged into the cold mountain stream.

She woke up and took control back, spluttering and angry. "What did you do, Mi-Na?" she shouted. "Ji, Mi-Na will not cooperate! This will not work."

I felt waves of disappointment and anger emanating from my host. Why was she upset? Why wasn't she more fearful that bonding would lead to binding?

Didn't matter. Maybe she was willing to take that risk, but I wasn't.

Ji nodded his head as if he wasn't surprised I'd sabotaged the ritual. No reprimand, but no second chance.

The next day Ji had Masako conduct a divination ritual to determine the best day for us to leave.

Step 1: ritual purification, which meant bathing in the stream. Ritual freeze-ification is what it was. Woke us right up.

Step 2: Build a small but very hot fire.

Step 3: Get the right tools. Ji handed her a deer shoulder blade bone and an iron poker.

Step 4: Honor the deer's sacrifice. Masako held it reverently, lifting it toward the sky.

Step 5: Burn the bone. She heated the poker in the fire until it was red hot, then ran it across the bone from "earth to sky," as Ji said. She doused the heated bone in a hollowed out stone of cool water, heated the poker again and pulled it across the bone from east to west. She concentrated on her question as she repeated this action over and over.

After several iterations, fine cracks spread across the blade. She examined them for several minutes, reading them as Ji had taught her. "It tells me that... tomorrow, *ka*? Tomorrow is the most auspicious day to leave."

"Yes!" Ji cried out, delighted. "Taira Lady, you are a good pupil!"

She exhaled in relief, and then laughed out loud. *"Mi-Na, I never dreamed I would learn something like this. I'm so happy I stopped your exorcism!"* She tried to stop smiling, not wanting to seem over-confident or arrogant, but her lips kept curving against her will.

"Impressive," I told her. "We might be able to use it to negotiate with Seimei." Yes, I could be business-like.

Ji announced that a group of sumo wrestlers would arrive at the carriage the next day, and that Yumi was with them. "The oracle knows, it knows!" he sang, "And it tells all, it tells Ji all!"

"Wait a minute. If Ji knows everything, can he tell me how to get home? Or maybe even help me get home? We've been assuming all this time that he can't, but we never asked!"

"Oh, Mi-Na, isn't this exciting? You won't learn anything like this in your university, ka wa?"

"No, but that's beside the point. I need to get home. Just ask him, or I'll ask him myself tonight."

"Maybe I won't let you take control tonight." Masako was getting cocky with her new-found talent.

"Maybe I won't ask. You have to sleep at some point. I'll take control then."

"You wouldn't!"

"I would! Only because you're being a jerk about it."

Not sure how 'jerk' translated, but it made her so angry she vented to Ji. "She threatened to take control without my permission! Could you send her home? I do not need her. I have power of my own."

He had little sympathy to offer. "Taira Lady, you and Future-Spirit must work together. One of you alone is like one cedar shingle. Useless. Two of you make a roof. A small roof, but still. Terrible example. Anyway, only Seimei has the power to send Future-Spirit back to her own body at the correct time and place. And don't tell him I said that, or he'll get so conceited he'll have to join me in my mountain home. And neither of us wants that."

Knowing now we'd have to co-exist until we met Seimei, I apologized for threatening to take control against her will, and also for ruining her meditation, and she forgave me.

When morning arrived, Ji wished us well. "Please pass my greetings to the old man in the capital. Tell him I taught you all his secrets." He plucked leaves from his beard with a pleased look on his face. "And Future-Spirit, remember to work closely with Taira Lady. You two are a matched set, like my robe and my belt. Both gray with dirt, and without a belt, my robe would hang open. Without a robe, my belt is useless. Neither of you can succeed without the other's assistance."

He might be a master of divination, but his analogies were the worst. If only I could unsee the image of his dirty robe hanging open.

Masako bowed. "*Sensei*, we both thank you for your instruction. I will remember you to Lord Seimei."

We walked to our abandoned carriage, and sure enough, Oxy was grazing happily next to it. A few hours later we heard the sound of a large group coming up the trail. We spotted Yumi first, riding her horse at the front of the line, followed by eight or nine stout young men. Yumi told Masako that some of the men had been ox-handlers for the governor of Sagami Province, and were on their way to the capital to provide their strength and skills for noble families as ox-carriage drivers. Several other men were local soldiers, and had been recruited to wrestle for the palace. The ox-handlers agreed to act as Masako's drivers, joking about how pulling little Masako would give them a competitive advantage over the soldier-wrestlers.

The rest of the convoy started to catch up, and from then on we remained closer together. At night the men built campfires and drank sake. Masako and I got to know their names from listening to their stories and jokes while we sat in the carriage. They spoke with a thick country accent that Masako—and therefore I—had trouble understanding, and at first Masako didn't even want to try to understand, but over time she couldn't help herself. She overcame her disdain for commoners and their coarse speech, becoming familiar with their contractions and idioms, and even enjoyed the insults they threw at each other.

Taro, a burly young soldier with a shaved head, was one of the most eloquent storytellers with a never-ending supply of stories that made the nobility look ridiculous.

"A Major Counselor was trying to get into the robes of a beautiful young noblewoman, who was a bit of a prude. He talked to her from her veranda, begging to be allowed into her room, but she kept telling him no. He decided he was too hot for her to wait any longer, so he crawled into her room, grabbed her and pulled her close. She struggled a bit but it just made him want her more. Just as he was about to untie her belt, she farted so loud it could be heard in the next room! He was so mortified he left without a sound and told himself he was going to get religion and become a monk."

"And did he?"

"Of course not. He just went on with his business!"

The men roared with laughter, lifting their glasses of rice wine and shouting *"kampai!"*

To my surprise, Masako laughed too.

"You think it's funny? A gently-raised noblewoman like you?"

"Of course! Did you not think it was amusing?"

"Well, it's upsetting the counselor didn't take no for an answer, but yes, I laughed at how the sweet young woman chased that jerk away with a fart."

The men didn't bother Masako, keeping to themselves for the most part, but once in a while they would turn their heads to shout back at her, usually some stupid joke or an observation about the weather. She smiled when they did that.

As we got closer to Lake Omi, we began to see more travelers. Bureaucrats on government business, merchants, and pilgrims crowded the dirt path. We went through a marketplace where our soldier-wrestlers were greeted with great excitement and offered food and sake in exchange for tales of fighting glory.

Eventually we arrived at the gates of Heian-kyo. A traffic jam caused by an overturned ox cart made for very slow going, so I had plenty of time to take in the sights. And the stench. Masako was just as shocked as I was at the crowded streets, the rows of huts holding tiny shops selling fish, sake, cloth, and pots, noblemen on horseback skirting around our carriage, not only to get ahead, but also to glimpse colorful sleeves and robe trains peeking out through the curtains of the beautifully decorated ox-carriages on the street.

And we noticed commoners, possibly homeless people, squatting to do their business in the alleys. That and a few decaying animal corpses here and there explained the awful smell.

All the men wore tall black hats, even the ones who didn't have shoes. Those with shoes wore geta, tall wooden sandals, to stay out of the muck. Several women merchants mingled with men in and around the shops.

The residences of noble families lined entire city blocks, or in some cases, two blocks, with high earthen walls surrounding them. A number of shanties were flimsily built against those walls, including the residence that turned out to be our destination.

"Your uncle is high-ranking. How can these homeless people get away with building their shacks against his residence?"

"I really do not know, Mi-Na. We must ask my uncle's wife. I believe she lives here too."

I stopped my sarcastic comment, remembering at the last minute that aristocratic wives usually lived with their parents, not their husbands.

A servant came to greet us. She called for a groom to get Yumi's horse, and escorted us inside. After Masako and Yumi had washed and changed, we ate. We hadn't eaten much besides dried fish and dried fruit for weeks, so we ate with appreciation and speed. I especially enjoyed a kind of fish in vinegar. Masako told me it was fermented fish, which surprised me, but I didn't know if I liked it because it was close to food I liked in my world, like pickled herring, or because Masako liked it, and I had her taste buds.

Shortly after we finished, Lord Korenaka came in. After a polite exchange of greetings and asking about Masako's father's health, he folded his arms.

"I haven't told anyone about your spirit possession, Niece," he said. "I don't want to scare people. It took a very persuasive letter from your father to get me to agree to sponsor you with Seimei. I feared bad luck, but he assured me," this with a scowl, "that your spirit is a benevolent one and will bring good luck to those who assist."

Masako bowed and apologized for being such trouble. He nodded his head and sent us off to prepare for the meeting with Seimei.

Chapter 12

The Royal Astrologer

Ninth Month, Chōhō 1 (October, 999 CE)

Seimei had requested Masako meet him at the start of the Hour of the Snake on the fifth day of Ninth Month.

"Why Snake? I see myself more as a Rabbit." I was only half-joking. I'd always been an early riser, and the Hour of the Rabbit was around five a.m. while the Hour of the Snake fell after nine a.m.

"As an onmyōji, he surely augured an auspicious day and time."

"By the way, what do onmyōji do besides auguring and divination? And how is that different from a miko?"

"Onmyōji study astrology, calendar-making, and whether certain events are good omens or ill ones. It is a very important job. A miko is considered a female onmyōji, although the most important duty of a miko is to call the kami into her body so that the kami may pass important messages to the people. Seimei is known throughout the realm as the Great Diviner, although his title is Head of the Bureau of Computation. We are fortunate that he agreed to meet with us. I expect he is curious about you, Mi-Na. Without you, he would have no reason or desire to meet with me."

Bureau of Computation? That sounded like accounting, not sorcery. He'd better be more than a calculating bureaucrat. I needed powerful magic to get me home.

Yumi ensured that Masako's attire was appropriate for a visit to an imperial ministry. Over the usual kosode and hakama, she dressed Masako in several colorful robe layers, a shorter jacket over that, and a train that draped from her waist and over the floor. Masako was strong for her rank and position in life, but even she found it difficult to move with the weight and length of all those robes.

Never in my life had I been dressed in so many layers, not even in a Michigan winter. Fortunately the long bays allowed a cool breeze in while providing a lovely view of mountain maple and beech trees clothed in their own robe layers of burnt orange, golden yellow, and crimson.

Yumi dressed Masako in alternating robes of dark green and orange. "These colors are considered "transitional" because they reflect autumn," Yumi explained, "which is the transition between summer and winter, and it's considered feminine to wear transitional colors."

"She's so happy to dress you like a girl."

"I am fortunate to have her with me at court. Before she was widowed and came to live with us, she spent time as an attendant for a lady-in-waiting to the previous Empress."

Yumi tied a green belt over the final orange robe, and turned to combing Masako's hair. She started at the ends, which, as Masako's hair literally swept the floor when she sat down, were very tangled. After spending some time on the first five inches, she worked her way up to the crown of Masako's head.

After this lengthy process, she eyed the results of her work, head tilted as if undecided whether she was finished or not. "The fashion now is to leave the hair untied, but I have a green ribbon that would be wonderful with these colors," she mused.

"Let's use it to keep your hair out of the way as you get into and out of the carriage."

She tried to convince Masako to let her apply makeup. "You will look barbaric if you don't blacken your teeth and paint your face white."

Masako ignored her, and I had the feeling this was a one-sided discussion they'd had many times before.

"Come on, don't you want to fit in with the popular crowd?" I said, half-teasing, half-worried that Masako's individualism might cause problems for us.

"I'm not looking for a position at court, or for a husband, remember? The kami won't care if my face isn't painted or my eyebrows plucked or my teeth blackened. You came through the kami world. Do you think they care?"

"I didn't ask the kami what they think about matters of formal attire."

Lord Korenaka rode his horse alongside our carriage as we traveled the mile or so to our appointment. Our destination was located within a gated community of government buildings and imperial residences known as the Greater Imperial Palace, or Daidairi.

Only foot traffic was allowed into the compound, so we had to dismount and leave our ox and carriage outside the gate. A couple of boys ran up to help Yumi and Masako exit the carriage and to take Korenaka's horse. Masako held a fan up with one hand to hide her face, grasped her robes with the other hand, and slid awkwardly out of the carriage and onto the ground. Her hair followed, slithering off the platform like a pet snake. She staggered forward, caught off-balance by the weight of her robes, but put her hand on the carriage until Yumi could arrange her hair and robes for the walk into the compound.

We passed through security after Korenaka vouched for us,

and into the complex of brown-roofed, hall-like government buildings and storehouses. It was a short walk to the Bureau of Computation. Masako's uncle pointed out the Ministry of Ceremonies on our left and the Bureau of Imperial Attendants on our right. Masako had her fan up and her head down in order to focus on walking in her heavy, layered robes, so I couldn't see much. She paused once to look around, as much in awe of being in the Daidairi as I was. We could see six or more individual buildings on each side of a long walkway, each of them built with curving cedar shingled roofs, wooden steps and verandas running along the sides. Servants, government officials, military officers, and noblemen crowded the walkways and stood chatting on the steps.

We walked up to a large wooden building with a wraparound veranda. Bypassing the wide steps leading into the main hall, we walked along the building's left side, then slipped sandals off before ascending a smaller set of steps. We shuffled along the veranda behind Lord Korenaka, passing several offices before we stopped at an open door. The women were directed to enter the right side of the room while Lord Korenaka went to the left side. A wooden screen bisected the room.

"Masako, can we peek? Please? I want to see what your uncle's doing over there."

Masako was curious too, so ignoring Yumi's gasp of outrage, she peeked around the edge of the screen. We saw a young man seated at a low table, writing slowly on a scroll. He held a long blue sleeve with his left hand to keep it out of the ink while he manipulated a writing brush with his right. His baby face, adorned with a tiny mustache, frowned in concentration.

"Awww, he's adorable!"

"He does not appear to be very good at his job, Mi-Na. He has not noticed we are here."

Lord Korenaka, who had been standing at the entrance, cleared his throat loudly. The sudden noise caused the scribe to jerk his brush, leaving a long black smear over his carefully written characters. He quickly bowed from his seated position, his hands about to touch the straw mat on the floor when he realized he was still holding the brush. He sat up, set the brush on the ink stone, and bowed again.

"Lord Chunagon, welcome!"

I remembered that Korenaka's title was Chunagon, middle counselor, so of course that was how he'd be addressed.

"I am the Great Diviner's grandson, not worthy of your presence. I am helping in the office today due to a high number of bad dreams and omens." His voice was muffled due to the fact that his forehead was on the mat.

"I want to speak with your grandfather. I had a terrible dream last night and I need him to interpret it. I don't want to make important decisions until I know what it means. Ah, and my niece has an appointment with him."

"I am so sorry, but he is conducting a divination for Her Majesty. I am his apprentice. Perhaps I may attempt to assist you?"

"Very well."

The scribe turned the scroll he had been working on toward Lord Korenaka.

"Excuse me, please write your name here. I have to keep an account of the services I perform. We have to show how busy we are before we can add another diviner to our staff."

Lord Korenaka took the brush with an expression of distaste, dipped it in the ink, and paused over the page while he looked for a clean space to write his name. The scribe pulled the scroll back quickly.

"Ahhh, I'm so sorry." He rolled up the part of the scroll with the ink smudge and unrolled enough to give Lord Korenaka a clean space to write.

The nobleman completed his task and stood up. He took a breath, but before he could speak, another voice interrupted.

"Good morning. I am so sorry to be late. Her Majesty…" An older man stood in the doorway, his head tilted to the left, presumably the direction of the Empress's residence.

"The Empress, of course, comes first. I would like your help interpreting a strange dream-" Before Lord Korenaka could finish, the older man gestured toward the screen. Masako jerked her head back to avoid detection.

"*Lord Seimei!*" She had goosebumps on her arms in spite of the many layers of silk between her skin and the air.

"Akichika here will assist you with that," Seimei said, waving at the scribe. "Meanwhile, I'm eager to meet the young lady who claims to host a spirit from the future. Akichika, leave us. Lord Chunagon, please wait outside or in the room next to this one. I need to examine this young woman in privacy."

Was he planning to make a move on Masako? She peeked around the screen again. Akichika bowed several times and walked out backwards, stumbling against a post before disappearing from view.

"He's worthless, but he's family," Seimei said as he advanced into the room. "Please do not be concerned about your cousin's daughter. If a spirit has possessed her, I will see it, but that will be more difficult to do with others in the room."

Lord Korenaka agreed reluctantly. "I will return in the late morning." He gave a short, stiff bow and left.

"*He didn't ask you if that was ok with you! Doesn't he have to protect you or something?*"

"*He trusts Lord Seimei, and he does not trust you, Mi-Na. If Lord Seimei needs to be alone with me to get rid of you, my uncle will not argue.*"

Seimei called over to the screen just as Masako ducked back behind it. "Please come out. I'm an old man, and it won't harm your reputation if I see your face."

Yumi whispered frantically to Masako and grabbed her sleeve. Masako jerked her arm back and pulled herself across the floor on her knees to get around the screen.

Once on the other side, she bowed deeply and kept her head down, awed and shy in the presence of the great man.

"Look up, I want to see him up close!" I said.

"I am showing humility, arrogant spirit. Do not give me orders."

Seimei, who had been sitting there staring at us while Masako sat with her head bowed, came to my rescue. "Governor's Daughter, you may look at me. I see the glow of two spirits, but I need to look into your eyes to understand the type of spirit you host."

Masako raised her head and I was finally able to examine the man sitting cross-legged in front of us. Surprisingly handsome for an old guy. Broad, high cheekbones, a full mouth, and bushy gray eyebrows over intense black eyes. He had a small mustache and a pointy silver beard. His gray hair, bound into a top-knot, was mostly covered by a black cap with a top-knot holder. He seemed to be in excellent health for his age: he sat straight, head steady, eyes clear and sharp. His cloak was the same purple-black as Lord Korenaka's.

While I was assessing him, Masako was staring in awe like a young groupie crushing on an aging rock star. As she stared at him, he stared right back. *Who did he remind me of?*

"Attendant!" he called out without his eyes leaving ours. "You may leave."

I heard a gasp from behind the screen, and then the soft whisper of Yumi's robes as she left the room.

Masako didn't react. In fact, her heart rate had slowed from its excited "I'm in the presence of the most powerful diviner in the world" rapid pace to a calm "I'm just sitting here thinking" rhythm.

"*Masako? Are you ok with Yumi leaving?*"

No answer. Now her heart and her breathing had slowed to meditation level.

Seimei continued to stare, unblinking, his intense gaze not shifting. The words *"Taira Rebel"* and *"New Emperor"* flitted through my brain. Was that Seimei's thought? Or Masako's?

Seimei's mouth tipped down and his eyebrows drew together. Was he angry with me for hearing his thoughts? But he kept his gaze on mine, and I couldn't look away.

A dark, cold sensation began to flow through me, separating me from Masako. "*Masako! Where'd you go? Talk to me!*"

I exerted my limited spirit-strength to pull her back from the invisible current, but to no avail.

"Calm yourself, Mi-Na," he said. "Lady Masako's spirit is safe. I have put her in a deep trance state so that you may speak with me directly. Now tell me: why are you here?"

What? How in *Jigoku* did he know my name? "*Masako? Masako!*" Still no answer. I could feel Seimei's presence, though, as if he were in Masako's head along with me. I reluctantly took control of Masako's body. "I am kami-sent." *I think.*

"And why did the kami send you?"

It was time to execute our plan, to make our bargain. Everything depended on getting this man's help.

"Lord Seimei," I said with a bow. And then, as he frowned at me, I remembered that I shouldn't use his given name. But what would I call the Head of Computation? Lord Bureau Head? Lord Computer?

I couldn't stop a slightly hysterical, under-my-breath, immature giggle. *Deep breath, Mina. You got this.*

"Uh, Lord Royal Astrologer, I arrived here from one thousand years in the future. I crossed into the spirit world, and from there into Lady Masako's body. It may be that I have been sent to deliver an important message to His Majesty, but in order to divine the kami's intention, we need your great skill."

Seimei's bristly eyebrows rose slightly. "Why would the kami use *you*, Spirit? *I* divine their messages and omens on a daily basis. What do you have to offer the kami? You appear to be an ordinary young woman who accidentally possessed another ordinary young woman. Well, perhaps she is a little more than ordinary, if she called you here, but that tells me nothing interesting about *you*."

I barely avoided screaming with frustration. *Royal Astrologer, was he? More like Royal Pain.* "I have knowledge of the future that might help you. In return, please send me back to my own time. And Lady Masako humbly requests your assistance to help her get a job at an imperial shrine."

"Ah. Well, of course I will do what must be done to support His Majesty. But why do you think I can help?"

"You're famous for your abilities. Even in Hitachi Province people speak of your powers. Apparently you're the only person who can send me back to my own body. And Masako doesn't think she has a chance to get into an imperial shrine without court connections, and you are connected to everyone." A little flattery couldn't hurt. "I can see *obake*, and Masako pulled me into her body from the spirit world with only one short lesson in spirit-summoning. We will share our power with you in exchange for your help."

He tugged his short beard thoughtfully. "Your tale confirms what I have long suspected, that the spirit world exists at the center of all worlds. Mi-Na, you entered from your future-world, and Lady Masako entered it from our world. She must have pulled your spirit into her body when she re-entered her time and place-" His hand froze mid-tug. "Just as a small fish... ahhh... may enter a cave through one entrance, and a large fish may enter at the same time through a different entrance and then... the large fish swallows the small fish and exits the way it had entered. The spirit world is the cave that connects all worlds and all times."

I had to admit his weird analogy worked for me. But did that mean I was stuck here? How many small fish managed to escape the belly of a bigger one?

His tone grew soft, almost as if he were talking to himself. "Yet how could a provincial governor's daughter with no miko training manage this? Perhaps she truly does have power. And... it is certainly possible that kami assisted with your possession in order to achieve something important. Perhaps Lady Masako is the rice, and you, Spirit, are the yeast. When put together, you will produce wonderful sake. Without you, Lady Masako's power might remain untapped forever, her soul unopened. Which means-"

Now *that* was a Ji-level bad metaphor, but his point was the same as Ji's: Masako and I needed to work together. Regardless, I needed answers from him. "Lord Seimei, we've heard that if I don't get sent home soon, our spirits will bind, with one of us becoming dominant. So the clock is ticki- I mean, we don't have much time left."

He smacked his palm on the table. "It is clear that you come from a horrible world without manners. Do not interrupt me again! Prove to me you came here from a thousand-years world. Tell me something I don't know, and then tell me of your world," he demanded, still staring into my eyes.

I didn't want to give any knowledge away for free, especially considering how little detail I knew about the year 1000. But I'd written a paper on the Genpei War, so that was fair game.

"In 1180—I mean, about two hundred years from now—there will be a terrible conflict between the Taira and Minamoto clans that will put an end to four hundred years of peace. The imperial line will survive, but Fujiwara power will not. A new class of warrior known as "samurai" will form, and the regent will be replaced by the shogun." I suspected he had a vested interest in the Fujiwara clan maintaining control, so that news might upset him. "And I doubt there is anything you could do to prevent it."

He frowned. "Do you take me for a fool? What I am doing will *postpone* war until then."

My mouth gaped for a second before I snapped it shut. Seimei prophesied events two hundreds years away? If he could do that, then he surely had the power to help me.

"Tell me something about *me*, or about the Regent, or about His Majesty," Seimei said. "What do you know about us? What happens in the next five years? Does Empress Sadako provide a Crown Prince?"

Aha, leverage! "Will you send me home if I tell you?"

"Insignificant Spirit, do not attempt to negotiate with me! Her Majesty is expecting a child near the end of this year. Tell me, Mi-Na, what do your chronicles say? Will this child be a boy?"

I had a vague idea that a prince was born around this time, but I wasn't sure. On the other hand, Seimei wasn't going to help me if I didn't give him some nugget of prophecy, and I'd surely be home long before the baby was born.

"It's a boy," I said with a confidence I didn't feel. "Will you help us?"

A small smile of self-satisfaction appeared on his face. "Yes, a boy. That is what I had divined." He bowed. "Spirit, I am the *only* one with the power to send your spirit back to your body. I have the power to send your spirit anywhere, anywhere at all. I am the most powerful *onmyōji* since Empress Himiko."

"*Masako, we came to the right person!*" Then I remembered Masako couldn't hear me. Well, time enough to tell her when Seimei was finished with me.

But Seimei was not done. "Yes, I could send your spirit anywhere I choose. For example, I could send you into a wild boar to be hunted by the Fujiwara clan and served for dinner. Or into a dog which would be kicked and starved to death. Do you have a preference, Mi-Na?" He bowed again, with mock deference this time.

My forehead grew damp, and I sensed a distinct lack of oxygen. I hadn't taken a breath in a while. Seimei's reputation in my era was that of a sorcerer who only used his powers for good, like Merlin in ancient Britain. So why was he threatening me? What had I ever done to him?

"And I could help this provincial governor's daughter obtain a position at one of our imperial shrines," he said with a smile. "I have connections at court. In fact, I received a promotion to Senior Fifth Rank for saving His Majesty's life when he had the pox. Therefore I have very, very high connections at court. Or... mmmm...." He tapped his fingers on the table. "Or I could use my connections another way. Such as marry her to a farmer, or to one of those sumo wrestlers who just arrived in the capital. Mi-Na, do you think Lady Masako would like to wear a coarse hemp robe instead of layers of colorful silk? And no attendant or serving women to help prepare food? I could make that happen. I have connections." He bowed his head slightly as if he had conferred a huge honor upon us.

I clasped my shaking hands inside my wide sleeves. "Lord Royal Astrologer, why would you do that? We haven't come here to harm anyone."

"Let's just say I want you to know what I am capable of, since we will be working closely together."

So he was just showing off? "I understand," I said. "But you didn't need to scare me. I *want* to help you. I want us to work together." *In exchange for your help*, I wanted to add, but I didn't want to be scolded again. "What would you have us do?"

"Lady Masako's ability to communicate with you, Spirit, is an excellent qualification for a position as a medium to Her Majesty, so I will assign her to attend Her Majesty daily. Mi-Na, you will monitor for *obake*, which will assist Masako in protecting the Empress from malignant spirits. In order to protect Her Majesty in every possible way, I need to know her physical condition daily. Any change in her health, any sign of labor especially."

That seemed like a reasonable request.

"And you, Mi-Na, have a special assignment, one you must complete without letting anyone know, including Lady Masako. I need you to bring me the correspondence between Her Majesty and her brother Lord Korechika. Letters, notes, poems, and a summary of any conversations they have. If you can not obtain the actual letter or note, make a copy. You have access to Lady Masako's speech, so you must be able to read and write as she does."

What? How could I keep a secret from Masako? We shared a freaking body! And stealing letters from the Empress? Wasn't that treason?

My head hurt, so I rubbed my forehead in a vain attempt to make the pain go away, and then stared blankly at the perspiration spot on Masako's silk sleeve. *Shit, did I just ruin her outer robe?* And why was I worrying about that when Seimei had just stomped out my little spark of hope for help?

"If I am satisfied with your service," he said in a business-like tone, "I will arrange for Lady Masako to join an imperial shrine, and I will send you back to your body at the time you left. *Only* if I am satisfied, however. If I am not satisfied, Masako will start a new career in farming, and you, Mi-Na, will be a Fujiwara dinner."

There were so many things wrong with this. What if we were

caught spying? How long would it take before Seimei had what he needed and sent me home?

"Um, I don't think I can keep a secret from Masako. We share the same body. Everything I hear goes into Masako's brain, so even if she's in a trance, she'd be able to access the information later. I can't stop that unless-" *Unless I take control indefinitely.*

Seimei finished my sentence, fortunately with the wrong words. "Unless I cast a spell to put a barrier in place. Good thinking! I prophesy that you will be an excellent addition to the Bureau."

I wanted to slap that smug smile off his face.

"But do not fear, Spirit, I have already done so. The barrier is extra-wide for this conversation, and Lady Masako will remember nothing. I will leave a smaller barrier in place for when you take control to gather such information as I require. She will not notice or remember."

He was telling me to take control without Masako's consent? I was not comfortable with that. But what choice did I have?

Seimei turned his gaze to a painting on the wooden screen partitioning the room, which broke eye contact. Masako came out of her trance, and as usual, she took over immediately and without having to work at it. *So not fair.*

On second thought, it *was* her body.

I sensed confusion and a kind of sleepiness emanating from her.

"Mi-Na, was I in a trance?"

I didn't know how much to tell her. *"Ask Seimei."*

She followed his gaze to the screen to see demons, goblins, and a man in white robes with a pointy black beard and a soul patch reading a scroll.

He turned back to Masako. "One of my favorite paintings, commissioned by a Third Rank nobleman when I saved his daughter from a mono-no-ke. She would have died if not for my intervention." He smiled. "At the Bureau of Divination, the most skilled yin-yang diviners in the country work hard to interpret dreams and omens, lucky or unlucky directions, and protect the imperial family from evil spirits. I will assign you as the Empress's personal medium, and as a medium in the Bureau of Divination, you will be part of this good work. In addition, I will tutor you to become a miko. If you have a talent for that, eventually you could become a miko for an imperial shrine."

A bright flash of joy filled Masako's mind and she forgot about her question. *"Mi-Na! Imperial shrine miko! That is more than I ever dreamed!"*

"I'm happy you're happy, but—" I stopped myself from telling her Seimei had asked me to spy on the Empress. Could he really turn me into a pork roast? *"I thought you didn't want to be a medium."*

"The Empress's proximity to the Emperor makes her sacred, and it would be a sacred duty to serve her. You must agree to help me. You promised to do so when you persuaded me to take the long journey to the Capital."

I didn't quite remember it like that, but it looked like I had no other recourse, unless I wanted to dwell in a wild animal for the rest of what would surely be a short life. I'd report to Seimei for some period of time, and in return he'd send me home.

It would be fine.

Really.

Seimei continued. "Of course you will receive food, clothing, and a place to sleep in the palace, as well as my help at the completion of your service. I will also send Mi-Na home."

Masako bowed and thanked Seimei politely and profusely.

Seimei appeared pleased, but wasn't finished. "Of course the Empress is of the highest level of refinement and taste, and she surrounds herself with clever and beautiful women. Your rustic upbringing is quite evident. Your skin is not painted, and you don't blacken your teeth or pluck your eyebrows. Her Majesty will not allow you to wait upon her like that. It is not the pockmarks—almost everyone at court has them—but it's unsightly for a noblewoman to have naked teeth. I will ensure Her Majesty expects you in a few days. You must work on your appearance before then."

He started to bow his farewell, then stopped. "Lord Chunagon mentioned that you received some tutoring in divination from a yamabushi you met in the mountains. Was he called Ji no Gyoji by any chance?"

"Yes, he saved us from bandits, and taught Mi-Na to see *obake*."

"Ji and I were friends at the imperial university. He was a bit of a devil. Liked his sake too much. He also practiced gambling more than a diviner should. Got into some trouble with the wrong clan and had to leave town in a hurry. Which method of divination did he teach you?"

"Interpreting cracks in a deer bone."

Seimei gave a dismissive wave. "Deer bones are old school. I use turtle shells exclusively. My grandson Akichika will teach you. He has no talent for interpretation, but he knows the methodology well enough to get you started."

He bowed slightly and left the room.

While we waited for Yumi and Lord Korenaka to get us, Masako looked out the door and shook her head in confusion.

"Mi-Na, our conversation with Lord Seimei was quite short, but the sun is almost at its high point. Did we not get here midway through Hour of the Snake? How could it be the Hour of the Horse already?"

I didn't think she'd notice the missing time. Of course I couldn't risk telling her about Seimei's mind-barrier, so what could I say?

"Well, it took a long time to get here, and then we had to wait for Seimei to get back from the Empress's palace. And maybe you were so excited to meet him, you just didn't notice time passing."

She started to put her hand on her head in consternation. I needed to change her focus so she wouldn't notice the sweat stain on her sleeve.

"By the way, Masako, when Seimei was looking into your eyes, the words "New Emperor" and "Taira Rebel" popped into my head. Maybe I caught something Seimei was thinking. Does it mean anything to you?"

"About fifty years ago, Taira warrior Masakado decided that our clan's descent from Emperor Kanmu made him eligible to be Emperor, so he began a rebellion and named himself The New Emperor. He attacked Hitachi Province and captured the governor. The rebellion was put down and he was killed. He had a son who disappeared soon after. The rest of our clan remained loyal to the true imperial line. But the name Taira might have given Lord Seimei reason to doubt me."

I'd never heard of this Emperor wannabe. "Does anyone know where Seimei came from? Isn't his own history somewhat lost in time? He was adopted by the Abe clan, right? So what was his clan name before that? Could he be the Taira Rebel's son? He's about the right age."

Masako's skin grew cold and prickly under her white robe. "It is not possible. The son of a rebel would never be allowed this close to His Majesty. Do not speak of this anymore."

On the carriage ride back to Lord Korenaka's residence, Masako and Yumi discussed how to prepare for court while I mulled over Seimei's demand to spy on the Empress. What did Seimei plan to do with the information? Whose side was he on? Would history change if he acted on information I gave him? But if the kami *had* sent me here, anything I'd do would be fine with them. Unless I was a pawn in some war of the gods. Kenji had told me about the goddess Izanami. We'd been on her territory when we meditated. Could Izanami be responsible for all this? I knew about the great love the Empress had for the Emperor, and Izanami was a goddess of love. Was I here to help the Empress, somehow? Seimei was doing his part, assigning Masako to attend to her.

I might never get answers, so I needed to stop worrying about it. Anyway, it appeared that only spying for Seimei would get me home.

Chapter 13

Personal Medium To The Empress

Ninth Month, Chōhō 1 (October, 999 CE)

Masako and Yumi spent the next few days excitedly preparing for life at court. Lord Korenaka's wife and daughter flitted about like jewel-toned hummingbirds trying to make this provincial governor's daughter presentable. Masako's stocky build and tanned face gave her a somewhat peasant-like appearance that even eyebrow-painting and tooth-blackening couldn't hide. The imperial medium uniform was simple and comfortable, though: red hakama trousers and white robe, cloak, and belt, all made of hemp cloth.

The daughter, a fifteen-year-old willowy beauty, took Masako in hand. "I must say your appearance is much improved with face paint, and your teeth look *so* much better in black. When you speak, use the court speech I taught you. Please don't embarrass our family with your rustic way of speaking. In fact, keep silent as much as possible."

"*She means well,*" I told Masako just in case that hurt her feelings. I appreciated her help. We had to succeed at court if I was ever going to get home.

Masako didn't seem to mind. She enjoyed the attention, not having had much female companionship other than Yumi and servants since her mother and sister died.

I grew more anxious each day, fretting until Masako's stomach hurt. I had to restrain myself from talking to her about Seimei's request to spy, which wasn't easy—we shared one brain, after all. "Masako, we don't know when Seimei will send me home. Our spirits get more tangled every day. Why aren't you more worried?"

"Mi-Na, Lord Seimei is a wise and skilled Yin Yang master. We have no choice but to put our faith in him, so calm yourself. Now, what do you think of the hair ornament my aunt gave me? The unusual color comes from an exotic wood brought here from Koryo."

"It's lovely, but it's nearly invisible against your hair." How would I steal letters without Masako knowing? I could take control while she slept, maybe, but if I was caught, so was she. No doubt the penalty for treason was death. And if Masako died, what would happen to me? Would my entranced body on Mount Tsukuba also die? If Kenji was waiting for me to regain consciousness, what a nice surprise for him. Meditate with a mostly healthy-looking young woman, and then boom! She's dead.

I watched Masako through the hand mirror Yumi was holding up for her. She opened her mouth to examine her newly blackened teeth. I knew what to expect, but even so, it was a shock to see a gaping black hole instead of her yellow-white chompers. She ran her tongue around her front teeth, and the taste of iron lingered in her mouth.

She took the Korean comb out of her hair and put in her mother's catalpa wood comb.

Yumi tilted her head. "Much better." She gently pushed Masako's hands out of the way to adjust it properly.

"Ah!" Masako put her hands to her stomach. I felt it too—a sharp stomach cramp.

"Lady, do you feel the onset of your monthly pollution?" Yumi asked, her forehead wrinkling in concern.

That would really screw up our schedule. Masako wouldn't be able to go to court for at least a week and a half between her "defilement" and the purification she'd need to undergo afterward. But she hadn't had a period since I'd possessed her. Was it my fault? My mother worked nights for a while at the hospital, and her periods stopped for the duration. So maybe my taking control while Masako slept was a kind of night shift for her. Or maybe having another presence in her body disrupted her biology that much. My emotions had affected her physically any number of times since arriving here, so why not that, too?

She reassured Yumi that it was only from nervousness about attending the Empress, and then she scolded me. *"Mi-Na, please do not speak to me for the rest of the day. You make my stomach hurt."*

I felt bad for causing her pain, so I agreed to do my best not to worry her further.

Korenaka's wife, Lady Shigeko, accompanied us on the designated day, dignified in robe layers of maroon over spring-green, a color combination called bush clover, and suitable for autumn wear, she explained kindly and condescendingly, knowing Masako had a limited knowledge of court clothing.

Masako told me that Lady Shigeko had her own high status as the Emperor's former wet nurse. *"An Emperor's wet nurse has a special relationship with the Emperor his whole life, like an aunt, someone who can visit freely and speak to him openly, and so she is sought out by those who want the Emperor's favor."*

"It's lucky for us that your father's cousin and his wife are such a power couple."

Lady Shigeko told us that a palace fire on the fourteenth day of the Sixth Month had destroyed the Imperial Palace, so the Emperor and Empress had moved to the Emperor's residence on First Avenue, known as Ichijō Mansion, and made it a temporary palace.

"The fourteenth day of Sixth Month? Masako, wasn't that the day I arrived? Was the fire a message from the kami about my arrival?"

"Mi-Na, such a question shows not only your ignorance but your arrogance. You and I are too insignificant."

"I'm crushed you think I'm such a minor event." Usually I thought very little of myself. I wasn't smart enough, attractive enough, assertive enough, anything enough compared to everyone else on social media. So I found my own arrogance refreshing. And maybe I wasn't wrong. Maybe the fire *was* a message about me.

The Empress wasn't allowed to give birth in the palace due to the defilement associated with childbirth, so Her Majesty had recently moved to the residence of Korenaka's brother, Lord Narimasa, and so that is where Masako would go. The three women rode in an ox-carriage, a larger and nicer one than our conveyance from Hitachi, with colorful designs on the sides, and a thicker mat to sit on inside, for the few blocks from Korenaka's compound to Narimasa's.

As we exited the carriage to enter the north gate on foot, stepping onto straw mats laid out for us on the ground, I realized why Narimasa's name was so familiar. Sei Shonagon had made fun of him in *The Pillow Book*.

My burst of excitement at this realization sent Masako's heart racing, and she gasped inadvertently, but she was too distracted navigating the uneven mat with her heavy robes to admonish me.

Lady Shigeko led us to a large room with highly-polished black wood floors, dim in spite of several bays with blinds half-open. A standing oil lamp provided additional light. Two women in brightly-colored robes were kneeling on a mat, giggling and looking at something laid out on the floor.

"You are at least as highly ranked as those women," she said, "so even though you are provincial, don't let them order you around."

A petite young woman came up to greet her, bowing deeply, her untied hair slipping forward to sweep the floor in front of her green and brownish-yellow layered robes. "Welcome, Lady. You honor us with your visit."

"Kohyōe, this is Lady Masako, daughter of Hitachi Vice-Governor Lord Tomohiro. The Royal Astrologer assigned her to be personal medium to the Empress, and she is very powerful, so be on your best manners around her."

Kohyōe gasped, covering her face with her wide sleeve as if for protection.

Lady Shigeko nodded with satisfaction and turned to Masako. "There," she murmured, "that should keep them at bay for a while. Ladies at court get bored, and boredom makes them vicious. So does jealousy of your opportunity to spend time with the Empress. And some of them like pranks, so be on the lookout for that too."

Masako and Yumi bowed their thanks and farewell as Lady Shigeko left.

"Honorable Imperial Medium, I humbly direct you this way." Kohyōe walked to a corner of the room and gestured toward a large black chest. "You may put your belongings here." She walked away as fast as her long robes would allow.

While Yumi put their belongings into the chest, Masako walked over to the women sitting on mats at the other end of the room. They were looking at a scroll that had been unrolled across a mat on the floor, but they glanced up as Masako approached. The older of the two smiled, but not a welcoming smile. More of a sneer, really.

"What have we here? A medium? Do you command spirits? Will you save us from mono-no-ke?"

The two women smirked at each other.

Kohyōe waved her sleeves in alarm. "Don't tease her. Lady Shigeko said she's powerful!"

The other women lifted painted fans to hide their laughter.

Masako bowed again. "The Lord Royal Astrologer assigned me to protect and serve Her Majesty."

"I am called Chunagon," said the woman who hadn't yet spoken. "That is Dainagon," she said, waving toward the sneering woman, "and you've met Kohyōe."

Masako provided a silent explanation on their names as they were introduced. Their names reflected their husband or father's government position. Dainagon meant Senior Counselor and Chunagon was Middle Counselor, like Lord Korenaka. Kohyōe meant "Little Guard." She was indeed little, and her brother or father must have been a palace guard.

After introductions, they invited Masako to review the scroll on the floor. She thanked them, knelt down to get a good look at it, and gasped.

The other women gave each other amused, knowing looks.

I was surprised too. *"What fun, introduce the new girl to porn. I never imagined this was how noble ladies spent time at the palace."*

"What...what is this scroll?" Masako asked once she got her voice under control.

"It is a copy of the Scroll of Initiation," said Dainagon as if everyone should know that. "It was commissioned by Chunagon's lover and given to her as a present. What's the matter? Don't you like it?" She and Chunagon shared a mocking laugh.

I fought the urge to smack the smiles off their faces. Masako would never agree to cooperate with me on that.

They were interrupted – thankfully – by the swish of silk curtains pushed aside by a woman who then walked over to our group. Masako stood to greet her. She appeared to be older than the others, and she held herself with an air of confidence. The top of her head came to Masako's eye-level, but she seemed tall in spite of her short stature. Her robes were the finest we had seen in the palace yet. Eight layers of color, alternating orange, yellow, green, with an outer robe of green figured silk.

She ignored the women and their scroll, staring instead at Masako with amused brown eyes. Her face paint was immaculate, and her eyebrows were completely plucked and repainted high upon her forehead. Masako bowed deeply in greeting.

The woman bowed back. "I heard the Royal Astrologer has taken you as a pupil in the divination arts. You must have talent. He certainly isn't helping you for your beauty." She tilted her head as if daring Masako to react.

"We- I have been assigned by the Royal Astrologer to attend Her Majesty as Imperial Medium. My father is Lord Tomohiro of the Taira clan."

Dainagon looked up as if she had just noticed the older woman. "Shonagon, look! Is this not just like Lord Korechika?" pointing to an illustration on the scroll.

"How am I supposed to know what he looks like?" She flipped up her fan and looked over it with mock flirtation. "I'm an old woman of thirty-three, and he's only twenty-four." She turned back to Masako and gave her a cool, appraising look. "The Empress calls me Shonagon (*"Junior Counselor,"* Masako interjected.) We have several Shonagons here, so I am also known as Sei, which, as you probably don't know, being from the provinces, is an alternate reading of Kiyo from my clan name Kiyohara." She gave Masako another up-and-down look, the expression on her face indicating she wasn't impressed by what she saw. "Before you will be allowed into Her Majesty's presence, you will need to demonstrate your abilities to me."

"Masako, it's Sei Shonagon!" I was so excited I sent Masako's blood rushing to her head. "*She wrote a book—or is writing a book, I should say—that will become famous as a new form of literature. It's similar to a style of writing in my world called blogging.*"

Masako blinked in disbelief. "*You are interested in a woman who wrote a journal one thousand years before you were born?*"

"I know, right? But that's why I love her writing. She made *me* interested in her. She made me laugh and made me cringe about the same things she did. It woke me up to how much we have in common as humans, at how we get frustrated by many of the same things Sei Shonagon did, even though separated by culture and millenia. Like when she wrote about how annoying it is when your boyfriend talks about an old girlfriend." Was I talking too much? But it was my favorite subject, and meeting Sei in person might just have made this strange, scary experience worth it. As long as I did, in fact, get home. "Masako, you said that commoners were hardly human. Maybe they don't have the privileges you enjoy, or they can't keep their hair long because it interferes with the work of planting rice or spinning silk for your lovely robes, but you could find something in common with them if you tried. You got to know some commoners on our journey here, right? What is something you discovered you had in common with them?"

"*The stories they told at night amused me. Humor,* ka wa?"

"Before our journey, you couldn't imagine having anything in common with those ox-handlers. It's impossible for some people in my country and my era to believe they have anything in common with a tenth century Japanese lady-in-waiting at the imperial court. But her book shows us that we do."

"*Well, Mi-Na, she is suspicious of me. Our tenure here will be short if she doesn't trust us. I have an idea for this demonstration. I will ask them to find someone who is cursed or possessed. If you take control while I am asleep, perhaps you can see the spirit and describe it."*

I only half-listened. I was too busy naming my future daughter "Kiyo." Or maybe my future cat. *"That's chill. Not cold! I meant fine, that's fine."*

Masako presented her request to Sei while the others listened. She didn't mention that the Spirit Mi-Na would take control of her body to achieve this. We were all about proving Masako's right to be here, not mine.

Somehow Sei managed to look skeptical without changing her expression. "Dainagon, do you know of anyone currently possessed or cursed?"

"I have heard it said that the son of former regent Lord Michikane has been cursed. He has a lump growing on his forehead. It is said he has been cursed by a-"

"Yes, if anyone is cursed, it's that family." Sei turned back to Masako. "It is fortunate that the Empress's brother, Lord Korechika, will visit her here this evening, and after that he will stay to drink sake with his cousin, the one who is cursed. I will come for you late tonight."

Chapter 14

One Crazy Spirit

Ninth Month, Chōhō 1 (October, 999 CE)

I had some trouble taking control because Masako's heart was beating a little too fast in anticipation of the upcoming test, and she couldn't fall asleep. I advised her to count monkeys. It made her laugh, but at least she relaxed enough to allow me to take control just as Sei came over to our mat.

"Step quietly, and keep your fan up," Sei said.

As I stood up and walked to the door, she gave me a sharp look as if she suspected something. Maybe I was too loose with my limbs, too wide with my stride. Too American.

I bowed my head and focused on taking small steps.

Sei led me along a dark corridor, down some steps, and along a garden path lit by a few lamps here and there. She walked slowly but with grace, sliding her feet forward to avoid stepping on her long hakama and robes. I struggled to mimic her, but she lifted one eyebrow as she noticed my awkward gait and murmured something about provincials and their rustic ways.

We came to another building and stopped at a room with an open bay on the veranda side. The blinds were pulled halfway up. Sei stood against the wall, where she couldn't see anything, but she wouldn't be noticed either. She signaled for me to stand where I could peer over the veranda and into the room. Two men sat on cushions with sake cups in their hands. The man on the left looked like a college student with a man-bun except he wore a purplish cloak over violet-colored gathered trousers, and a black hat with a little pocket in it for the top-knot. He had a soft, full mouth, a long face, and a small nose. Unlike most college boys, he looked like he was ready to spring up and draw out a knife in one swift movement if I made a sound. That must be Korechika. Just as good-looking as the ladies said.

The other man, the one on the left, was dressed similarly but looked even younger. Too young to be drinking sake, or maybe that was just my cultural bias. He glared into his cup, his face twisted into an unpleasant expression. He also had a long face and small nose. So what was it that made him so different from Korechika? The sneer of his mouth? The small, angry eyes? The bump on his head? This must be Michikane's son Kanechika, the one they said was cursed.

I shivered, but continued to watch closely. The men chatted, but too quietly for me to hear anything but their murmurs. Both of them were sons of two dead former regents, Michitaka and Michikane, brothers to the current regent, Michinaga.

A light flickered. The oil lamp sputtering? The men didn't react. Another flicker, and then the air above Kanechika began to shimmer like gossamer threads in the morning after a heavy dew. The shimmer became a mist. An image slowly formed, twisting and curling. I tried to concentrate in the way Ji taught me. Focus…focus… *ah-ha, there, I see it! A snake!*

I gasped, then ducked in case the sound had drawn their attention. After a minute, I cautiously raised my head. The misty snake was looking right at me. My skin crawled; my heart jackhammered. *Calm down, it's not like it's a spider.*

The writhing serpent continued to stare at me. "Curssssed... Curssssed..."

I sat down abruptly, holding a hand against my mouth to prevent a silent scream from becoming an audible one. The two men continued to talk in low voices as if they hadn't heard the sibilant word. But I *knew* the snake-spirit had spoken. No question about that, even if the men hadn't heard it.

I didn't dare reply. Not only did I not understand *obake* etiquette, but the men might hear me and banish me for spying. Or worse, think I was there to sleep with them.

I peeked again, but I heard no more snake-talk, and after a minute, the mist dispersed. I crouched down, duck-walked over to Sei, and gestured that we should leave.

Once we were out of earshot, I practically burst with the thrill of it. "Did you hear that? The *obake* spoke to me! I saw it! It's a snake!"

"I saw and heard nothing. Are you certain?"

"It formed over his head, Kanechika's head, that is, and it looked right at me. *Obake*. A snake! It said one word: "cursed," but more hissy, like this: 'curssssed.' More words were *not* necessary."

"It is said Kanechika is fond of hurting animals, and that he once tortured a snake to death. He has been unwell ever since. Did you notice the large lump on his forehead?" I nodded. "It is said that lump comes from the snake's curse."

His odd behavior might come from a brain tumor, which explained the lump, or he could be a psychopath. Didn't matter. We'd passed Sei's test.

We walked back to our quarters without speaking. When we arrived, Sei turned to me. "Lady Masako, you have shown me your power. I will let Her Majesty know of your success."

The next morning, I filled Masako in with the details of our late night adventure. *"Now you've got credibility for your new medium business. They'll believe you now. You know, if you'd heard the rumors about Michikane's son killing that snake, you could have made the whole thing up and they wouldn't have known."*

"Spirits and the divine are never something to lie about. Everyone knows that."

We ate a quick breakfast of rice, salted fish, and seaweed salad. I'd discovered this kind of food made a great hangover breakfast after late night drinking with Mick at karaoke bars. The drinking age was twenty in Japan, and Mick and I didn't have a whole lot else in common, so karaoke and beer was followed the next day by salted fish and seaweed. I didn't miss Mick, but I did miss Tsukuba.

Shortly after we finished, Sei showed up freshly painted and wearing another full set of robes, this time with layers of reddish-yellow over light yellow.

"I informed the Empress of your ability to see the snake-curse, and she invited you to attend her later today. I will send one of her ladies-in-waiting to bring you to her inner room.

Dainagon came to get us an hour or so later. She looked Masako up and down. "Your robes are not very special, but you are no doubt forbidden from wearing these colors," she said smugly, lifting her wide sleeves with layers of green and gold.

I sensed Masako's annoyance at Dainagon's condescension, but she just smiled politely without replying. We had decided it would enhance Masako's mystique if she always wore the white uniform of a medium.

Dainagon's mouth twitched in irritation at the lack of response, and she marched ahead of us in silence.

Masako was announced into the royal presence as "Imperial Medium Lady Masako of the Taira clan." Masako knelt, and bowed her head to the floor, remaining that way until the Empress spoke.

"Seimei's protégé, you may stand. According to Lord

Seimei's note, you are to attend me. He is concerned about my health."

The Empress sat on a silk-covered platform about two feet high. Twenty-two years old, according to my calculation, and her husband, the Emperor, would be nineteen now. Smooth skin, face painted white, two dabs of black painted high on her forehead; a round face with sweet, intelligent eyes aglow with curiosity.

"Imperial Medium, tell me about the snake-curse. What did it look like? Were you frightened?"

Masako did her best to describe what I had seen and heard, and when she finished, Empress Sadako leaned forward. *"I would have been terrified. My cousin Kanechika... Well, the less said about him the better. You must be very brave. And to make the journey all the way from Hitachi? Such adventures you must have had! I want to hear all about them. You are the Hitachi Vice-Governor's daughter, are you not? Do you know any Chinese poetry? Governor's daughters are so well educated, are they not, Shonagon?"* This with a laughing glance at Sei, who bowed her thanks for the compliment.

"I regret that I have not learned any Chinese poetry."

"My mother was an expert on it. In fact, she may have been the most knowledgeable woman on the subject ever." The Empress stopped smiling. "Any medium can channel spirits, but if you are to become a miko, you must have prophetic abilities." She leaned forward, her eyes focused fiercely on Masako. "I am expecting the Emperor's second child. Will I have a boy? Will I give the Emperor a Crown Prince?"

Masako bowed and closed her eyes. *"Mi-Na, do you know? Is this written in your future books?"*

I'd already told Seimei the Empress would have a boy, so I could hardly not tell the person most affected, especially if Seimei was planning to pass that along to her. *"Masako, I- tell her-*

oh, just tell her it's a boy." And if it wasn't? Masako and I would both suffer the consequences.

Masako opened her eyes. "Your Majesty, the oracle tells me it will be a son."

Hope and joy sparked in Sadako's eyes as she clapped her hands together. "Oh, Shonagon, a son! The Emperor will have a son!"

Sei bowed, her own smile mirroring the Empress's. "Truly wonderful news. However, Your Majesty, the Medium conducted no divination, no clacking of bones or sticks. Medium, how can you possibly know this?"

"The Spirit Mi-Na shared this information with me. She – Mi-Na is the spirit of a young woman – has prophetic ability. Her knowledge, and my ability to communicate with her, is the power I have to offer, and I will use this power to protect Her Majesty."

Sei gasped and took a step back. "Are you possessed by *ikiryō*? A living spirit? You cannot stay in the palace! We cannot take the risk that misfortune will fall to the Empress or His Majesty as a result of the *ikiryō*'s presence!"

"She is not *ikiryō*. She is here to help us. The kami sent her."

Sei and the Empress looked at each other and back at Masako.

Sei took a deep breath. "Your Majesty, Lord Seimei has taken the medium as a pupil, and he must have known of this possession when he sent her to you, so it is possible the Spirit was sent by the kami to help us. I will ask Dainagon to watch her closely. We will exile her if anything appears to be amiss."

Empress Sadako looked at Sei as if we weren't even there. "She is related to Lord Korenaka, is she not? He transferred his loyalty to Lord Michinaga rather than to my brother when my father died. The Taira clan has a history of disloyalty."

Sei bowed deeply. "Your Highness, I will ensure she leaves if her prophecies—or her actions—prove false." She waved toward the door again, and Masako bowed and left the room.

Sei provided us with a monologue while escorting us back to our room. "Perhaps you could banish the *ashi-no-ke* which plagues a young lady who recently arrived at court. She can not move at all. *Ashi-no-ke* is one of the most feared illnesses here at court. We also fear the *mono-no-ke* that cause chest trouble and stomach trouble. Usually the priest must chant and wave his incense stick and rosary to banish them. And then he goes to sleep, sometimes right there, in the room with the afflicted person! Driving spirits away must be very tiring work. And I pity the medium, usually so thin and pale, although occasionally quite stout, for when the spirit leaves the afflicted person and enters *her*, it causes such moaning and writhing, it's absolutely frightful! But if the medium did not shriek, we would not know that the spirit has entered her, and the priest couldn't banish it, and so it can't be helped. I am surprised your father allowed you to become a medium. Well, perhaps it was not your choice. The spirit Mi-Na came to you quite uninvited, I heard."

Masako nodded her head as Sei spoke but chose not to reply. I enjoyed Sei's speech, but became increasingly anxious about whether I was correct about the Empress's baby. Even if I went home before the birth, Masako could get into a lot of trouble if I was wrong. If only I had my phone. Surely Empress Sadako's children were listed in Wikipedia or Japanese Wiki or someplace online. But that would mean I'd have internet access somehow. Which would be lit. I'd be the best oracle ever. I could look up any answer to any question. They'd worship me, light incense for me and bring me little cakes. Masako would become famous as my host, the Delphi priestess of Heian Japan.

If only I could help her that much. She deserved it for putting up with me. Only Seimei knew how much longer he'd keep me here.

But what if he decided to wait until the baby was born to confirm whether I told the truth? Three more months? That was too long. I missed home, and what about that bonding thing? How long did we have before Masako and I fused into one crazy spirit?

Chapter 15

Reluctant Spy

Ninth Month, Chōhō 1 (October, 999 CE)

Masako spent the next morning practicing calligraphy. She chose to sit at a low table placed between two screens, giving us a measure of privacy, yet close enough to the veranda to get natural light as well as fresh air from the garden, a nice change from the incense that permeated the palace and yet didn't quite cover the smell of infrequently-washed bodies. Even though nobles here were clean by the standards of most of the world in the tenth century, taking baths every five days or so, apparently daily baths weren't a thing yet. It all depended on which days were lucky or unlucky for bathing and hair-washing.

Sei took us to the Empress's apartment in the early afternoon. On the way she confided to us that Narimasa's residence was a poor excuse for an imperial consort's palace. "It is terribly cramped. Her Majesty deserves better. I was very upset when I saw it. And the day she moved here, the Regent-" She stopped suddenly as if rethinking her chattiness and we walked through a corridor in silence. "Here we are," she said a few minutes later as we entered a gallery.

We knelt before a sliding door covered with fabric. "Fan up!" Sei whispered. "The Empress is with her brothers."

Sei slid the door open, and gasped. A little girl stood in the doorway, her dark-brown bangs falling into her eyes as she tilted her head. "Sho-Sho opy door!" The child laughed and patted Sei's head. "Good child, Sho-Sho."

Sei tried to conceal her own laughter. "Princess, may we enter?"

"Lady Shonagon, I am so sorry. Princess, the word is "opened," not "opy." Please bow to Lady Shonagon, and then we must leave. It is time for your rest." The speaker, presumably the princess's nurse, put her hand on the toddler's head and pressed very lightly, just enough to encourage the little girl to bow, and then took her hand and left.

"Masako, do you think that's the Emperor's daughter?"

"Surely it is. She must have been visiting her mother, the Empress."

"What a sweetie! I wish I could pinch those chubby little cheeks."

Masako and Sei covered their faces with their fans, then scooted through the door still on their knees.

The blinds were up and the shutters were open, allowing a few shafts of sunlight to brighten the room. Crisp fall air mingled with the fragrance of clove incense, reminding me of hot spiced cider and college football, and with that, another acute pang of homesickness.

Empress Sadako, dressed informally in layers of purple over light green, with a soft white train flowing from her waist, was sitting on a dais in front of a brazier, with two men seated across from her, one of whom I recognized as Korechika. They looked up when we entered, but continued their conversation without pausing, although Korechika's glance lingered on Masako before turning back to his sister. Sei guided Masako to a screen at the other end of the room. "Sit here. I have an urgent errand to take care of." She left after bowing again to the Empress and her brothers.

The screen had bamboo slats rather than a wood panel, so we could see something of the group around the brazier; perfect for spying on the Empress. I needed to listen carefully to what Korechika said to the Empress, and somehow memorize it for a later report to Seimei.

Korechika kept glancing our way. He muttered something to his siblings which made them laugh, and then he walked over to our screen. He sat with crossed legs and peered through the bamboo slats, his long, dark eyes glinting with mischief as he reached through the wide gap between the bottom of the screen and the floor to caress the hem of Masako's white robe. She gasped and jerked her robe away.

He laughed. "One usually compliments a woman's robe colors, but white is so dull I find myself without anything to say. Medium, you prophesied my sister will have a Crown Prince. Where did you get this power?"

"Lord…I do not…I'm not…" Masako fell silent.

"Elder brother, leave her alone. She is new to court and here to protect me." The Empress's voice carried authority, and Korechika moved back to the brazier, although not without a few backward glances.

"*He's intrigued by the possessed medium,*" I said.

"*Not if I stutter when I try to speak to him. I was not prepared for that. He is the brother of the Empress, and uncle, perhaps, to a future Emperor.*"

I needed information about Korechika to give Seimei in my report. Maybe I could get Masako to flirt with him to get him to talk.

"*Masako, do you think he's handsome? He obviously thinks he is. Maybe you could have some fun with him.*"

"*Mi-Na, no! I have no interest in that. We are here to protect Her*

Majesty, not sample the courtiers as if they are robes to try on and discard."

"Okay, okay, I get it. You're so serious!" I was a little bit ashamed of myself for encouraging her to flirt for my own purposes when it was clearly not who she was.

The Empress called over to the screen. "Lady Masako! You have met my brother Lord Korechika whether you wanted to or not, so I will introduce my younger brother, Lord Takaie."

Takaie was muscular, with broad shoulders and a wide face. He wore the same stiff, tall black cap as his brother, and a similar black cloak.

He looked towards the screen. "So she saw the snake that cursed our cousin? How did she do that? She could be a spy. And she could be lying about Her Majesty's baby."

My spirit-gasp at Takaie's guess caused Masako to hiccup.

Fortunately the Empress didn't buy it. "The Royal Astrologer is tutoring her personally, and he sent her here as my medium. She is possessed by a kami-sent spirit which provided the prophecy about this child." She placed her wide sleeves over her silk robes, which were loosely tied to allow space for the bump underneath.

Takaie raised his eyebrows and shared a skeptical glance with Korechika, but he said nothing more about Masako. A lady-in-waiting came in with a sake ladle and cups. Sadako did not partake, but her brothers did, and after a while their voices grew louder. Masako and I began to hear snippets of their conversation.

"Sister, a son!" Korechika lifted his sake cup, signaling a toast.

Takaie lifted his cup too. "A son!"

"At last we will overcome the humiliation inflicted upon our family by our uncle." Korechika shouted in his excitement.

Takaie leaned forward. "Sister, you will discuss this with His

Majesty, yes? His son is our nephew, and it is fitting that Korechika will be the boy's regent when the time comes. When do you next meet with His Majesty?" He signaled to the attendant to fill everyone's cups yet again.

Empress Sadako's response was too soft for us to hear.

"Masako, how is it that the Empress's brothers are here? I remember a story about them being exiled."

"I believe Lord Michinaga allowed them to return to honor the birth of His Majesty's first child, Princess Nagako. Bringing the Empress's brothers home may have been a gift to the Empress for bearing an imperial princess."

"So maybe Michinaga isn't such a terrible person? I mean, Korechika and Takaie did a number of stupid things, from what I remember."

Masako shook her head at my ignorance. "It was rumored that Lord Michinaga either instigated or spread false rumors about Korechika to keep him from gaining support among the other nobles for the regency. My father expected Lord Korechika to become regent after his father, the beloved Regent Michitaka, died, and he was quite upset that Lord Michinaga pushed the Empress's brothers out of the way. He said Lord Michinaga is a clever schemer who only wants to enrich himself, and that he plans to remain regent at least until his daughter is of age to become consort to the Emperor and bear him sons."

I wanted to find a reason to like Michinaga. He controlled everything here, including Seimei, who controlled me, or at least, my ability to escape from this imprisonment. But Sadako's kindness and intelligence had won me over, and I was starting to feel guilty for agreeing to spy on her.

The men left when the sunlight faded. Masako's feet were freezing and her legs were asleep.

"Masako, is this what life will be like for us here? Sitting behind screens for hours in a cold room?"

Masako, annoyed with my complaints about life in the tenth

century, ignored me. And certainly her life was luxurious compared to what we'd seen on our journey. Villages full of tiny huts consisting of no more than a few sticks holding up a few more sticks. A young populace—few commoners survived to age thirty due to epidemics, fire, earthquakes. Stick-thin children, of whom there were too few. Apparently the smallpox epidemic had been especially lethal to children.

And since I lived in Masako's body, and had her sense of smell, I didn't really notice the body odors and the potty-type smells that would have sent me reeling in my own body. I should be nauseous at the incense pervading the air and scenting robes, but I rather liked it. Somehow I could distinguish between different scents. Sei's robes were heavily nuanced with sandalwood, while Dainagon's had a stronger piney smell. Korechika had a muskiness which could have been his natural scent, but it might also have been deer musk.

I don't know how I knew all that, unless it was similar to the way I understood the language here. It was all in Masako's brain. Smelling frankincense at Sunday mass had always made me nauseous.

Sadako stood up and called toward the screen. "Miko, you may come over to the brazier to warm yourself."

"I love that she calls you Miko. It's so aspirational."

"She honors me with her trust in my abilities, and her invitation for me to warm by the brazier is so thoughtful. Most noblewomen would not consider it. I expected the Empress to treat me as the servant that I am. I am humbled by her kindness to me."

Masako shuffled around the screen, bowing in thanks before sliding across the floor on her knees to the only source of heat in the room.

The Empress kept giving Masako quick sideways glances, as if she wanted to stare at her without looking like she was staring.

"Miko," she said after a few minutes. "Lord Seimei

Reluctant Spy 143

vouched for you, and you have shown your powers in many ways. But how could your oracle have known about the baby?"

"Your Majesty, my oracle comes from a future world in which such events are recorded in books."

Sadako looked down for a minute while her hands clenched and unclenched the soft silk of her purple sleeves. She took a deep breath. "Then what-" she paused, swallowed, and raised her head. "What else does the oracle know? Will this baby, this boy, become Emperor someday?" She bit her lower lip and looked back down again, intently studying her now-wrinkled sleeve like it was a cracked deer bone.

"Do you know the answer, Mi-Na?" Masako asked.

The emperor in this era was known in my world as Emperor Ichijō. His cousin Prince Okisada had already been named Crown Prince, and I remembered that he became the future Emperor Sanjo. I was confident that Ichijō's son became emperor after Sanjo. But who was that boy's mother? Was it Sadako, or another consort?

I'd overstated my knowledge of the future, but I didn't want anyone to know that, not even Masako. Seimei might not help me get home if he understood how little I actually knew. Our deal was based on it.

"Tell her that, uh, the kami forbid me from sharing that information."

Masako didn't argue. "My oracle claims she is forbidden to share that information, Your Majesty."

Sadako's shoulders slumped. "We must attend to the wishes of the kami. I will meditate and pray. Thank you for trying." She took another deep breath and dabbed at her eyes with her sleeve. "You may return to your apartment now."

As we entered our room, Yumi came over to us with a spring in her step. "Lady Masako, here is a note from the Regent Lord

Michinaga himself!" She held out a folded piece of paper with both hands.

Masako admired the penshipmanship on the cover before reading it. "It's a request to visit the Regent in three days!"

"The paper is so soft, and such a pretty blue," I remarked.

"Is it about your new role as Imperial Medium?" Yumi asked. "Or do you think he wants something else? Chunagon mentioned that Lord Michinaga usually arranges a liaison with every new woman at court – at least, with those of suitable rank. He is said to have a pleasant temperament and a charming personality."

Masako hesitated, appalled at the idea that every new lady-in-waiting had to sleep with the Regent. "Is such a request usual here at court? Do court ladies ever refuse such a request? What are the consequences of refusing? Yumi, you know I do not wish such a thing."

"Yes, Lady, I am aware of your desire for celibacy. He does you a great honor with this invitation, and refusing to meet with him might have serious consequences, but perhaps it is only to discuss your new role as Imperial Medium. He is known to be devout, and is no doubt intrigued by your ability to host a kami-sent spirit."

Masako sighed. "Well, then, find someone who can bring my reply to the Regent's office," she said to Yumi.

At last, my chance to meet the famous Michinaga of the Fujiwara Clan. But what did he really want from Masako?

Chapter 16

Poetry Slam

Ninth Month, Chōhō 1 (October, 999 CE)

The note had requested Masako to meet the Regent in his palace office at the Hour of the Bird. Also known as the Hour of the Rooster. And what was another name for rooster? How appropriate for the man known to "interview" each new woman who arrived at court. I was finally learning to tell time here.

But it didn't mean I'd adjusted to it. "*In Michigan, where I grew up, the sun is quite high at six o'clock—I mean, during the Hour of the Bird—in the summer, but in mid-winter it's dark.*"

"*Does your world rule the sun?*" Masako laughed at such an outlandish idea. "*The Hour of the Bird is always sunset, just as the Hour of the Rabbit is always sunrise. It's absurd that Bird might be daylight in some months and darkness in others. Your people have made time unreliable.*"

"*At least we can count on an hour being the same length all year, unlike here, where the calendar makers are constantly adjusting time. Sooo complicated.*" I'd never complain about the time change in my world ever again.

Masako enjoyed these glimpses into my world as well as my perspective on hers. As she'd said several times now, life was more interesting with me around. And I wanted to keep it that way. We had grown to trust each other more, but I worried constantly that she'd get tired of me and call for the exorcist, who would send my spirit into the void, and then I'd never get home.

An ox-carriage arrived to take Masako and Yumi to Michinaga's office at the appointed time. Masako and Yumi sat behind a screen covered in a translucent white silk, and the light of an oil lamp on the low table in front of the screen allowed us to see hazy images through it, including the outline of the Regent walking in through a connecting room.

"Imperial Medium, how do you find court life? As a provincial, you might have some trouble with our court-raised ladies. Come from behind that screen, and your attendant can wait for you outside." His tone was friendly but firm.

Masako and Yumi looked at each other with alarm, but he was highly ranked, and refusing could cause a lot of trouble, so Yumi whispered to Masako she'd be close by if needed. Masako shuffled around the screen on her knees with her fan raised to eye level.

"No need to stand on ceremony. Please be seated and have a drink with me."

Masako sat down, her fan trembling as she peered over it at the handsome man now seated in front of her.

"Mi-Na! How could you think he's handsome?"

"Oops, did I say that out loud?"

He looked to be the same age as Sei, in his early thirties. His broad shoulders filled out his robe in a very masculine way. He radiated warmth and assurance, a man who gets what he wants, not by brute force, but by fierce intelligence and sheer charisma.

He gestured to the decanter on the table. Masako took the

hint, and pushed her sleeves up in order to lift the heavy kettle-like ladle. She poured warm, cloudy sake into two saucer-like celadon cups. He raised his, gesturing to Masako to raise hers also.

"Now that's what I call a man, unlike the boys I dated in college," I mused.

Masako choked on her sake. "Mi-Na, how could you! He is a scheming power-grabber!"

"Do you have a cold?" Michinaga asked.

"I... I drank too quickly, and the sake burned my throat."

"Strange. This is high quality sake. Now, put your fan down. I am not an *onmyōji*, but perhaps I can see the Spirit that has possessed you."

Masako lowered her fan and stared at the black lacquer table, her face hot with shame from exposure to an unrelated man. He watched her for a few minutes in silence, taking sips of sake from time to time.

"Raise your head. I want to look into your eyes," he commanded.

Masako complied reluctantly, giving me the chance to look deeply into the eyes of the most powerful man on campus. How could she *not* think he's handsome? Intelligent, amused eyes. Strong chin. High forehead with black hair pulled back and tied up on top, covered with the usual black cap.

Masako's only physical reaction to him, besides the heat from her shame, was repulsion. Strange how we could have such different feelings about the same man. That answered one of my many questions. I clearly did not influence her sexuality, and she didn't influence mine. But it was her body. How could *I* feel sexual attraction to this man when *she* didn't? Mind over matter?

"I see you are attracted to me," he said after a few minutes of silence. He reached his hand across the table as if to put it over Masako's, but she jerked back and put her hands in her sleeves.

He laughed. "You are the daughter of the Hitachi Vice-Governor. He was a great friend of the former regent, my eldest brother, Lord Michitaka. I might have to bring your father back to the capital soon. By the way, I heard a rumor that you prophesied the Emperor will have a son. I assume the Spirit gave you this knowledge?"

Masako's breathing became rapid and shallow, and she looked down at the table again. "Lord Regent, this Spirit has knowledge of many things to come. The Empress asked for a test of my powers, and the Spirit provided me with this information."

He lifted his cup and examined her curiously, his lips quirked in a little smile.

"A medium who is the daughter of a Fifth Rank nobleman. Normally a medium would be beneath my notice, but you are perhaps the highest ranked medium I have met. And the Spirit is a human woman from the future, I heard. Two women in one body. Fascinating."

"He's thinking that sleeping with you would be getting two women in one go," I told Masako, in case she wasn't getting it. After all, she didn't have much experience with men.

"He completely misunderstands me!" she exclaimed. *"But he's not interested in anything I have to say. He's only thinking of himself."*

"And Seimei will train you to become a miko with powers of divination and prophecy. Although it appears you already have prophetic abilities." He took two brushes, an inkstone, and two pieces of paper from a drawer in the table. "Let us write each other a poem. I will write first, and you respond." He wet the inkstone, dipped his brush into it, and wrote gracefully and quickly on his scrap of paper.

Masako took her piece of paper reluctantly. *"His paper is lovely,"* she said, caressing it and admiring its shade of pastel purple.

"Regency has its privileges, I suppose."

Michinaga set his brush down, picked his poem up with a flourish, and read it to us in a pleasant baritone, pausing dramatically between phrases.

"Lives there a Spirit
Beneath miko robes of white
With divine intent
Who comes to bless my fortune?
Or a girl to bless my night?"

"He's propositioning you!" I said. "How will you answer that?"

"How do you think, Mi-Na!" Her fear made her sharp with me. "He implied he'll remove my father from his post! Perhaps that's his way of encouraging me to comply with his proposition, as you called it."

"Are you sure you don't want to sleep with him? There is something about him I find very attractive. Something about men in power?"

"Mi-Na! Stop that! This is not your body, and you have no say in this." She thought for a few minutes, gazing at the brazier warming the room, then picked up her brush and started writing. She was less graceful than the Regent and would win no awards for calligraphy in this town, but she was fast.

Fire has its own will –
It burns those who come too close.
Kami-sent spirits
Protect with spirit-fury.
Beware their angry curses.

"Hey, don't blame your dislike of him on me. Anyway, I don't know how to put a curse on someone."

"I want to scare him, Mi-Na. That's one of the few advantages of spirit possession."

I didn't like her implication, but decided to let it slide.

Masako read her poem to Michinaga, her voice trembling

with uncertainty over his possible reaction. She assumed he was not used to being turned down.

She was right. He rose to his feet in anger, and yet somehow with grace, and frowned down at her with his mouth tight. "Medium, you are fortunate you are of greater value to me here than exiled." He left without bowing.

"*Masako, you almost got us kicked out! But the fact that he didn't throw us out means he knows we're working for Seimei. He thinks we'll be more useful spy-*" I stopped myself. "*More useful observing the Empress than exiled from the capital.*"

Masako didn't respond, and I suddenly felt sick. A strange brew of shame, suspicion, and anxiety had turned Masako's stomach. She called out for Yumi, who rushed in, hovering over us anxiously.

When Masako felt a little better, we headed back to our quarters while I pondered what had just happened. Did I have anything to do with her nausea? Why had I been so attracted to a man she obviously disliked and had no sexual attraction to? Maybe a feeling so obviously repugnant to my host was my vaccine against fusing with her.

Or maybe it was just my usual poor taste in men.

Chapter 17

Plotting

Ninth Month, Chōhō 1 (October, 999 CE)

The Empress received a note while Masako was attending her, and exclaimed that it was from her brother Lord Korechika. Empress Sadako was like that, sharing information in such a trusting way. She'd grown up in a political world, and she knew the Regent wasn't on her side, yet it didn't occur to her that a spy might lurk within her own staff. Which made me feel bad, but what could I do? I had to get home, and this was my way out.

She put her hand over her mouth as she read the note, and when she'd finished, she set it down and blinked away tears.

So it must be bad news, which would be something Seimei would be interested in. Masako was attending the Empress at night, so we'd be sleeping in the gallery. I could steal it then. I hoped Seimei's mind-barrier was working, because I did *not* want Masako to read my mind right now.

The Empress's brightly-hued layers of pink, light green, yellow, and dark green flowed around her like a rainbow waterfall as she stared at a blank piece of paper, her dark hair framing her melancholy eyes. She sighed, pulled her brush across an inkstone, and wrote—or painted, really—a short note, moving her hand and arm with the grace of a dancer and the studiousness of an orchestra conductor. She folded the paper and handed it to Masako, who had been sitting quietly nearby practicing her own writing skills while I observed everything with her peripheral vision.

We'd only been attending the Empress for a few days, but I'd already learned calligraphy was a big deal here. Sadako had been raised to be an Emperor's consort, and her father, the previous regent Lord Michitaka, insisted she have excellent calligraphy as well as a thorough appreciation of poetry and the classics, and she lived up to his high expectations. We had not yet met Emperor Ichijō, but we'd heard he was madly in love with her, and who could blame him?

She turned to Masako. "I have a note for His Majesty's mother, the Imperial Lady. Find someone to take it to her."

Masako took the note with a bow.

I'd heard servants talking about how the Emperor's mother lived in Michinaga's residence, which was a massive two-city-block compound, and only a couple of blocks away. *"Let's go ourselves!"*

Masako was horrified at the idea of wandering city streets without a carriage or escort, so I teased her about how quickly she'd adopted court manners. She got irritated with me and said yes just to shut me up.

Her pulse grew faster—she was scared, but also as excited as I was—as we slipped unseen out of the east gate, the side closest to Michinaga's residence. Masako had slipped on some geta-style high clogs and hitched up her hakama and robes, tucking the extra cloth into her belt. She'd put on a wide-brimmed hat with netting, and since her outfit said "medium" and not "noblewoman," she didn't get too many stares along the way.

The street was busy with ox-carts and pedestrians, the smell of grilled fish mingling with the stink of animal and human waste. It hadn't rained in a while, so the hard-packed dirt of the street wasn't muddy, although Masako had to be careful not to twist her ankle stepping into a rut.

We found Higashi-Sanjō Mansion without difficulty. Several oxen and their carriages had been left outside the north gate, and the guards were busy talking to the ox-drivers, no doubt getting the scoop on whatever nobleman was currently visiting the residence, so we were able to walk in without being seen.

We had no idea how to find the Emperor's mother. We wandered around inside for some time before realizing we were lost.

"Uh, Masako? Don't you think we'll get in trouble for wandering around the Emperor's mother's palace without an escort?"

"Don't worry, Mi-Na, I have this note to prove we are here on imperial business."

I mentally shrugged my non-existent shoulders as we walked through yet another empty, dark room. I noticed a door leading outside. "Let's go that way – this place is giving me the creeps."

Masako put her palms together, closed her eyes in a brief prayer for patience, and then told me to shut up. Well, her version was more polite, but I got the hint.

We went through the door and onto a veranda that ran along the outside of the building, connecting separate rooms like the balcony of a motel.

Masako paused in confusion about where to go next. As she hesitated, we heard a man's voice coming from a room a couple of doors down. "It sounds like Michinaga," I said. "Stop here a minute so we can listen."

"I don't want him to think I want his company. And he might be discussing matters of state."

"Exactly! We might hear information that we can trade with Seimei if he gets stubborn about helping us."

Frustration, hesitation. "Very well, Mi-Na. Just for a moment." Masako took a couple of tentative steps closer to the voice and paused, her white robe billowing in the cold wind. The blinds were rolled down over the large window so we couldn't see in, but we could hear just fine.

"Korechika has been humiliated." Michinaga's voice. "No one supports him for regent anymore, not since his return from exile. He is still arrogant, but his pride has been deeply damaged. Even his holdings will not give him the rice he is due. They hold it back, knowing I won't punish them for it."

"My son is too fond of our niece. We provided him with other concubines and consorts, but Her Majesty is the one he loves. She may yet persuade him to make Korechika regent once the boy is born and named Crown Prince."

"Masako, that must be the Emperor's mother, Michinaga's sister!"

Masako shuddered, suddenly cold with dread. "They are plotting against the Empress!"

"Shhh! We need to hear this."

"Do not 'shhh' me, Mi-Na, you spoke first!"

We fell silent in time to hear Michinaga's reply. "I will ask Lord Seimei if the kami will bless any action I take to maintain my position as Regent."

"You demonstrated the kami's blessings when you won the archery contest against Korechika years ago."

Michinaga chuckled. "Our eldest brother couldn't accept that his beloved son Korechika lost to me, so Michitaka insisted on continuing his archery competition even after I won it. Before I shot again, I declared that if my arrow hit the target, my descendants would be emperors and empresses. And it was a perfect hit. When it was Korechika's turn to shoot he was so nervous he missed his shot completely. I aimed another arrow and said that if I hit the target this time, I would become regent someday. And of course the shot hit in the center. Michitaka was furious and ended the event."

"And now you are Lord Regent. If Korechika becomes regent, there will be chaos. He has more interest in gambling and fighting than governing. Your wisdom will bring harmony. Korechika would bring conflict. I support *you*."

"I can not stop the Empress from having a boy, but I can prevent her son from being named Crown Prince. If he is not Crown Prince, he will never become Emperor, and therefore no one of significance will support his uncle Korechika in his quest to become Regent. I'll take care of that. Your role, when the time comes, will be to counsel your son to make my daughter his Empress. One day she will bear him a boy, who will be Crown Prince and then Emperor after Crown Prince Okisada has his turn. And then it will be time to end this confusing tradition of alternating imperial candidates between two imperial lines."

"And the imperial line will be *your* line, Younger Brother. Your daughter Akiko, future consort to my son; your daughter Kiyoko, future consort to Crown Prince Okisada; and your two daughters born this year will be future consorts to future emperors. You show the true meaning of the proverb "if one must have a child, let it be a girl."

Masako clasped her hands tightly.

"*Masako, that hurts! Loosen your hands a bit, would you?*"

She dug her fingernails into my arms to show me who was boss. "*If I make a noise and they discover us here, it will not go well. This is a betrayal of our Empress, which is a betrayal of His Majesty.*"

"*Well, we can't just walk up and hand His Majesty's mother the note — she'll think we overheard their conspiracy. Let's backtrack and find someone to give this to. Empress Sadako didn't tell you to hand it to the Imperial Lady in person."*

Masako agreed—for a change—and started walking toward the steps.

"Careful! Don't trip on your robes, and try not to rustle as you move."

"Mi-Na, I have worn robes my entire life. I know how to walk," she said, more than a little irritated with me. As she descended from the veranda, we heard firm footsteps above us.

"Turn around so it looks like you're just now going up." I couldn't stop back-seat driving to make up for my lack of actual control.

Masako spun around so quickly her head whirled with vertigo and she gripped the railing to keep her balance.

Michinaga called out from above us. "Medium, what are you doing here?"

She took her hand off the railing, bowed, and raised her fan. "Your Ex-" she cleared her throat. "Your Excellency. I have a note from Her Majesty for the Imperial Lady. I have not been to this residence before, and became lost." She kept her eyes lowered in apparent humility, but really to keep them from betraying her fear.

"Doesn't your Spirit guide you? Or maybe it doesn't know as much as you claim."

Masako kept her head down as she replied to Michinaga. "The Spirit has not been to this palace, nor has she read about it in her books."

"Ah. The Spirit only knows what it – she? – has read. Has she read about me?"

"I'm surprised it took him this long to ask," I said. *"You can tell him yes, he's famous."*

Masako conveyed this in a halting voice, glancing up through her curtain of hair to see what his reaction would be. He had folded his arms and was smiling as if pleased at this news.

Before he could ask another question, a lady-in-waiting came around the corner and stopped dead when she saw who we were talking to. She knelt on the ground and bowed.

Michinaga called over to her. "The Empress's Imperial Medium has a note for the Imperial Lady. Take it to her." He walked down the stairs, deliberately brushing against Masako, who shrank back from his touch. "Medium, I want to hear more about my fame and glory, but it will have to wait for another day. I have a country to run." He gave her a mocking bow and left, a white train attached at the waist of his purple-black robe trailing after him like slime after a snail.

Masako held the note out, her hand shaking. "Here."

The woman took the note with a bow, and proceeded up the steps while Masako took a minute to catch her breath.

Once under control, she walked back to Narimasa's residence, demure on the outside, frantic on the inside. *"They are planning to make Michinaga's daughter Empress! But there can only be one Empress. Ah! Will they harm Empress Sadako? Will they harm the boy? We should warn her. This is a betrayal of the imperial family!"*

"We need to stay out of it," I said as if I really meant it.

"Why don't you want to help Her Majesty? Whose side are you on?"

I didn't want to tell her that I was on whatever side could get me back into my own body. Besides, what good would warning them do? It would only upset them and get us tossed out of court as spies, and I'd lose my chance to get home. I cared about the Empress, but we needed to stay focused on our mutual goals or we'd lose everything.

"I know it's not easy to sit back when you know something is wrong, but you'll get us in trouble and it won't help Her Majesty. We can help her more by being by her side, which we won't be if Michinaga thinks we're spying on him."

Masako's steps quickened with her frustration. *"My loyalty is to the Emperor, not to the Regent or even to Lord Seimei. I'm going to warn the Empress, Mi-Na, and you can't stop me!"*

Could I stop her? Did I want to stop her? Maybe the world *would* be a better place with Sadako as Empress and Korechika as Regent. But it wasn't my job to make that decision. Nor was it Masako's.

Chapter 18

Vow Of Loyalty

Ninth Month, Chōhō 1 (October, 999 CE)

That night Masako, Sei, and a few other ladies-in-waiting slept on mats outside the Empress's curtained platform. I waited for hours for everyone to fall asleep. Sometimes the women would remain awake all night, chatting softly, making up poems, or even, in a few cases, snuggling. Masako was right when she said that some women get very close at court.

But tonight all was quiet. Masako's breathing was deep and silent as I prepared to take control. *But what if Masako wakes up while I'm trying to steal Korechika's note? Or worse, what if the Empress wakes up?* We'd be tried for treason and exiled, or worse. I'd told Masako I wasn't an evil spirit, but stealing her body to steal from the Empress was practically a case study in demon possession. I couldn't do that. Could I?

Maybe I should be honest with her. Maybe she'd help me steal the letter. But then I'd be the little devil that whispers temptations into one ear. And if she didn't cooperate with me, then what?

Torn with indecision and doubt, I just lay there as Masako slept, blissfully unaware of the potential wickedness brewing inside her. Before I gathered the nerve to get up, I heard servants walking through the gallery, stirring brazier coals back to life. I'd lost my opportunity.

We didn't get another chance to sleep in the Empress's room before the next report to Seimei, so I decided to tell him no letters had been received by the Empress while we attended her.

Masako was kept too busy over the next few days to tell the Empress that her aunt and uncle were plotting to destroy her. The women were in a tizzy because the Emperor had announced a visit. Masako didn't know much more than I did about appropriate dress, so we listened carefully to their discussions. We had Yumi, of course, but fashions change, and she hadn't been at court in twenty-five years.

We learned certain color combinations had names, some of them lovely (aster: alternating robes of green and pale violet), and some not so lovely to say but nice to see (withered field: alternating light green and yellow robes.) Dainagon, unexpectedly friendly and chatty, tried to talk Masako into wearing a combination of robe colors known as plum-pink, which was scarlet robes layered over maroon robes. She even had her maid get her own long, silky robes from storage. "You may wear these," she said generously.

"*Oh, Masako, you'd be so very striking and colorful wearing these!*" I exclaimed. "*Too bad you need to maintain your mystique by wearing your white Imperial Medium uniform.*"

Dainagon wouldn't take no for an answer, even offering her own maid's services to dress her.

Masako was nearly overwhelmed with her kindness. "*Mi-Na, we misunderstood Lady Dainagon. She seems to be quite nice after all.*"

Sei walked in just as Masako was slipping on a maroon robe

over her kosode. "Dainagon!" Sei said with a sharp tone. "Leave Her Majesty's Medium alone!"

Dainagon managed to smirk and pretend-pout at the same time. "Shonagon, you have spoiled our fun. That rustic knows nothing about proper clothing for the season. She does not belong here. She belongs in the wilderness with her father." She scooted away to the other side of the room, where Chunagon was whispering with Kyohoe, laughing and pointing at Masako.

Sei turned to Masako and frowned. "The plum-pink combination should not be worn until Eleventh Month. It is the wrong color for the autumn season. If you had worn it as she suggested, everyone would have laughed at you. I defended you this time, Medium, but you must develop a sense of what is proper, or you risk becoming a subject of ridicule, and a woman can not survive at court if made a fool of."

I had been wondering when the pranks would begin, but that showed us Dainagon's true colors.

It was decided the ladies would be painting when the Emperor arrived. We were seated in the Empress's pavilion on green silk mats. Attendants arranged the ladies' robes to show them to great effect, draping colorful sleeves against laps, gently moving long hair down silk-covered backs and across mats like dark streams crossing a meadow. Masako was the lone chrysalis in a garden of butterflies.

I caught a glimpse of Sadako's face as the Emperor was announced. She glowed as if an oil lamp had been lit from within. Her eyes swept down flirtatiously, and she was unable to keep her lips from curving with excitement.

The Emperor glanced at the beauty of the scene in front of him, and his eyes lingered curiously on Masako for a few seconds before two serving-women moved a free-standing yellow silk curtain between us and the imperial couple.

"*Can we look around the curtain?*"

Masako wanted a peek too, so she moved her mat to the edge of the curtain stand. The Emperor wore indigo trousers, a purple robe, and a cloak of russet-bronze over that. Except for his clothes, he could be a typical teenage boy anywhere. Slender, a bit gawky, probably still growing. I could see him as one of those sweet nerdy boys at home who played a lot of XBox, but more Halo than Call of Duty.

They seemed very comfortable with each other, but then, they'd been married for nine years. He took a strand of her hair in his hand, winding it around a finger while talking to her animatedly. She smiled as he talked, her cheeks pinkening through her white face paint. When he was done, she responded, and it was his turn to listen, which he did while looking at her with an endearing intensity. How could anyone want to split this couple up?

After they chatted for a few minutes, Lord Korechika was announced. The ladies all looked at each other in excitement. What a day—the Emperor and the rock star of Heian-Kyo in the same place as their Empress!

Korechika, handsome and impressive in violet-colored gathered trousers, white robe, purple-black cloak and black hat, walked over and bowed respectfully to the Emperor and Empress. Ichijō looked at him with affection and motioned for him to be seated. Sadako called out to her ladies that Korechika was going to lecture on the Chinese classics, so they were welcome to listen, or they could leave if they found it boring. No one left, of course.

Korechika began with a poem from Bai Juyi, and jumped from that to Lao Tsu. His deep voice was pleasant, and his tone varied enough to keep me from falling asleep.

'It doesn't seem fair, does it, Masako? He's intelligent, good-looking, and popular, and the Emperor clearly respects him. He could have

been a good regent if he weren't such a gambler and didn't act so entitled."

"I agree with you, Mi-Na, at least, the part that I understood. I think I'm getting a university education just sitting here."

"I have a university education, and I feel like that too. And look at Sei!"

Sei was leaning forward, her face rapt.

We knew she had a thirst for learning. A couple of days ago over our morning meal, Sei told us her mother had been lady-in-waiting to a previous empress, and while at court she became acquainted with Empress Sadako's mother Lady Takako. "Mother admired Lady Takako so much, she insisted I learn how to read and write Chinese characters. Unfortunately, when I was only ten years old, Mother died in a palace fire. As the fire spread, she made sure the Empress and her other ladies were safely out of the palace, and then she rushed back in to get the Empress's cat. In her haste she tripped on her robes, which caught fire before she could get out. After she died, my father decided teaching me would be his way to honor her sacrifice. I learned quickly, and Lady Takako told me my education would help me get a position at court, so I worked very hard, and now here I am, so you see, she was right. The other ladies-in-waiting talk about me spitefully. They think I'm conceited. I'm not. I just recognize my own virtues."

Masako expressed words of sympathy for her loss, but Sei brushed her off. "'You know the proverb: 'when the rain falls, the ground gets harder.' My education allowed me to achieve my dream of a life at court."

I tried to get Masako to find out what happened to the cat, but she told me rather sharply that I was insensitive.

Korechika didn't finish his lecture until sunset, after which he took his leave. The Emperor had seemed fascinated with the long talk, and the Empress had also followed it closely.

I noticed the other women were waking up from naps. *"This must be a common occurrence. No one's apologizing for sleeping."*

"To be honest, Mi-Na, if you had not been so interested, I might have fallen asleep too!"

Masako couldn't understand why I was fascinated with the outspoken and eccentric Sei Shonagon. Masako and Sei had a certain individualism in common, but not much else. Masako wasn't sensitive to beauty, was not great at poetry, and had no interest in love affairs or flirting. She didn't want a life of the mind when the trade-off was physical inactivity.

Sei lived in the moment, both sensitive to beauty and horrified by its absence. She loved attention from men and she got it, which puzzled other women at court because Sei didn't hide her wit and education, and men liked her anyway. Most women here hid their learning, not unlike middle school girls in my world. They would write poems and show off their calligraphy, but that was the equivalent of wearing the right ripped jeans but not speaking up in class. Sei was the girl who raised her hand every chance she got. Where'd she get that confidence?

I talked with Sei one afternoon while Masako was taking a nap. Sei came into our apartment to tell Masako she wouldn't be needed in the Empress's quarters that night. I didn't want to lose this opportunity, so after silently apologizing to Masako for taking over while she slept (she couldn't hear me but it made me feel better), I called out, "Shonagon, please wait! I want to tell you how much I admire you!"

Her eyebrows rose. "Why do you admire me, Medium?"

"It's Mina! The Spirit! I'm talking to you while Lady Masako is asleep."

Sei put her sleeve over her mouth and took a step back. "Your speech is- odd. And your face, your expression... Is it truly the Spirit speaking? Why?" She backed away slowly while she talked like I was a vicious dog that would pounce if she moved too quickly.

"I know of you in my world. I love your writing. I've read your book many times. I even read some of it to my college roommate Anne—I mean, to the woman who shared my residence at university—and she laughed out loud, which was quite an achievement, because she was from New York and very sophisticated. Like you! I mean, not the New York part, obviously, but-" *Awkward, much?*

I focused on telling her she had become famous in my world, not only for her writing style, but for her sense of beauty and her wit. She relaxed; she really did enjoy flattery, especially when it was sincere.

After I outlined the many reasons I admired her, I prompted her to talk about herself, which wasn't difficult. She told me about her ex-husband Norimitsu. Her father had selected Norimitsu because his family had wealth as well as connections at court. Sei's father was a well-known poet, an occupation which apparently didn't pay any better here than in my world, so marrying into wealth was key.

She married Norimitsu at fifteen, and had her son Norinaga two years later. Her sensitivity to color and beauty, her intelligence and her drive were at odds with her husband's personality. "I wondered if he was simple. And he doesn't care for poetry. He has told me so many times. He understands nothing about color combinations, nothing! It's so frustrating to have a conversation with him."

"Sei, I wonder if- I mean, some people can't see color the same way other people do. Maybe he's color-blind?" It had never occurred to me before, but color-blindness surely affected people in this era just as it did in mine, but how difficult would *that* be in a society that valued color so highly.

"Blind? He is certainly not blind! Or do you mean blind to color only? Ha! Yes! You are amusing, Spirit, much more so than the Imperial Medium. You should take possession of her speech more often. Anyway, Norimitsu and I separated when I came to court. We get along much better now, like brother and sister."

"Where's your son?"

"He's with his father's parents. He will take over their estates eventually, so I do not need to be concerned about his future."

"Sei, I hope this isn't a rude question, but if it is, please forgive me because I'm from a culture that values direct questions. In my era, we don't know how you got the name Shonagon. It doesn't seem your father or husband were Junior Counselors." I held my breath in anticipation. If I could get this information, I'd know something scholars in the field didn't.

She put her finger tips against her red lips as if shushing me. "No one has asked such a question because, Spirit, it is, as you say, rather direct. I will tell you so that you can record it in your chronicles. It amuses Her Majesty to call me Shonagon—Junior Counselor—because I have the honor to advise her from time to time. But that is our little secret." Her pleased smile faded. "Mi-Na, the Imperial Medium insists you are a human spirit with a living body. Is that not the very definition of *ikiryō*?"

"I am not trying to harm Masako or anyone. I came here accidentally, although kami were involved, so I think of myself as kami-sent. And honestly, I just want to go home-" I stopped myself. If Sei knew how desperate I was to get home, she might wonder what kind of bargain I'd made with Seimei.

She was too quick-witted. "You want to go home? How will you get there? And how do you know Seimei? Tell me truly— why did he send Lady Masako to attend the Empress?"

I repeated our standard phrase. "Seimei protects the imperial family, and he realized we could be of use to her." I sensed Masako waking up, so I said a quick goodbye, laid back down, and closed my eyes.

Masako opened her eyes to see Sei staring at her. Startled, she scrambled to a sitting position. "Shonagon, why are you here? Does the Empress need me?"

"I came to tell you she doesn't need you this evening." She stood up and started to leave, then turned her head back.

"Medium, if you mix rice flour and egg whites, and put it on your skin frequently, it will help shrink those pockmarks."

Masako muttered a sleepy and confused thanks as Sei left. *"Mi-Na, were you talking to Sei while I slept? You should ask for permission before using my voice."*

"I'm sorry. She came up to you while you were sleeping so I seized my chance. I wasn't impersonating you. I told her it was me, Spirit Mina. She was so nice to give you that tip about getting rid of your pockmarks."

"I think you are bothered by my pockmarks more than I am. You keep bringing them up. And did it occur to you that she was seeking information about us?"

I was too embarrassed to let her know I might have given us away. And her comment about my obsession with her pockmarks? She was not wrong. I'd always hated my complexion, and after a bad case of poison ivy in high school, I was practically phobic about skin issues. Maybe the kami wanted to teach me a lesson by sending me into a host who'd had smallpox. *Thanks, kami. Thanks a lot.*

The result of my conversation with Sei became evident a couple of days later. The Empress Sadako had, up to this point, appeared to trust Masako. She seemed to be someone who always believed the best in people. Her brothers advised her on strategy, and through them she knew Michinaga was not to be trusted, but no one suspected Seimei of partisanship. So she took us at face value, giving us access to her presence and allowing us to sit in her company, albeit behind a screen, even when her brothers were present.

It was Sei who convinced the Empress that she was too trusting. Sei informed us a few days later that the Empress wanted Masako to take a vow of loyalty. Masako believed she was protecting the Empress, and she was naive in the ways of court politics, so she was upset and confused by the Empress's request. I had limited court experience myself, but I'd read lots of dystopian and fantasy YA novels that gave me some insight into court life.

So I wasn't surprised when the Empress called Masako to her side. Sei stood next to the Empress protectively, and I noticed Empress Sadako's face paint didn't completely hide dark shadows under her eyes.

"Miko," the Empress said, "Not everyone wishes to see me produce a crown prince or see my brother become Regent. It has come to my attention that we do not truly understand your intentions. If the baby is born a girl, you will be exiled. If I have a boy, then we will accept that your spirit is truly kami-sent."

Masako stiffened, upset that her integrity would be questioned. "Your Majesty, my loyalty is to you and the Emperor. I promise I will not betray you. Although Lord Michi-" she stopped abruptly, holding her hands to her head, moaning as if in great pain.

She wasn't in pain, but she was confused and scared. She'd practically dared me to stop her from warning the Empress about Michinaga's plotting, so I'd flooded her mind with sounds and images from a rave video I'd seen. She couldn't focus, couldn't think. It was awful. But it worked. She couldn't speak.

Empress Sadako gasped. "What is happening? Help her, Shonagon!"

Sei had a better sense of my personality after our little chat the other day. She put her hands on Masako's shoulders and spoke firmly. "Mi-Na! Stop what you are doing!"

I stopped. *"I'm sorry, Masako. I didn't realize how bad that would be, but you can't just blurt out that we eavesdropped on Michinaga. Don't you see? Even if the Empress believes us, she'll think we're spies, and we'll be banished!"*

Masako refused to answer me. She apologized to the Empress. "Your Majesty, it was indeed the Spirit Mi-Na. Please accept my vow of loyalty to you and to the Emperor." She bowed deeply, and the Empress nodded to accept the vow.

I felt bad about rave-bombing her mind. Would she get even with me by arranging an exorcism? How was I going to convince her I did it for her own good, not just mine?

Chapter 19

Crow Droppings

Ninth Month, Chōhō 1 (October, 999 CE)

"Imperial Medium, welcome to the Bureau of Computation." Akichika flushed bright red as he bowed several times in quick succession, his white sleeves flapping. "The Royal Astrologer asked me to show you to the inner office."

He turned toward an inner door while Masako suppressed a snicker behind her white fan.

I joined in, grateful she was talking to me again after that episode with the Empress. "*I think he likes you, Masako. How old do you think he is?*"

"*Seventeen, ka?*"

In his haste to get the door open, Akichika tripped on the edge of a straw mat, saving himself by throwing his hands on the door for support, but ripping its thin paper panel in the process. "I'm so clumsy," he mumbled, and ran into the next room to escape his humiliation.

Masako was too kind to let Akichika hear her laughter, so she suppressed it while she walked over to examine the painted screen.

The painting included two short figures with horns standing next to the image of Seimei. "Masako, are those goblins?"

"They are shiki-no-kami, or shikigami for short. Spirit-helpers. I've heard rumors that Seimei uses shikigami as magical assistants, and that he has the power to make them do his bidding."

"Maybe someone saw Akichika helping out when he was a toddler and thought he was a shikigami."

Masako had no sense of humor when it came to the supernatural. "If Seimei does rule over such creatures, you might see them, Mi-Na. I wish I had your powers. What will I do when you leave me? If I lose both your ability to see spirits and make prophecies, what good will I be as a miko?"

"You've got the talent. You just need the skill set, and Seimei will give you that."

As we moved toward the inner room, Masako bent to straighten the mat where Akichika had tripped, and her fan fell away from her face. Of course that would be the moment Akichika turned back to see what had happened to us. He blushed bright red again and lowered his eyes quickly as though he had seen Masako without her clothes on.

"Is it that bad to see a noblewoman's face? You would think he'd be thrilled you let your fan down."

"Some men try to see our faces, but he seems shy."

Seimei was waiting for us at a large, low table covered with scrolls, inkstones, brushes, and divination sticks. He waved at Masako to be seated and motioned to Akichika to leave.

Since Masako didn't know I was a spy, I couldn't ask her what information I should provide in this first report. Masako believed we were assisting Seimei in protecting the Empress. I believed he was looking for juicy gossip to escalate into a scandal that would cause the Emperor to reject the Empress, and open the way for Michinaga's daughter Akiko to move into that spot someday. How was I supposed to give Seimei my report and yet not let Masako know I was doing it?

Seimei tapped the table with an ivory stick. "Lady Masako, I heard you saw a snake-curse. I had not tried looking for it. I prefer to stay out of Michikane's family problems. He was an irritable, grumpy man, and his son Kanechika is even worse." Seimei cleared his throat. "Tell me. What else can the two of you do? Look at me."

Masako raised her head, and as Seimei looked into her eyes, she couldn't stop herself from spiraling down into their dark depths, falling... falling... and into a trance. He was that good.

"Spirit Mi-Na, you may take control of Masako's voice. Tell me everything you have observed at court, especially anything said by the Empress or her brothers. Do you have any letters or notes?"

Feeling guilty about taking control without Masako knowing it, but excited to be able to speak out loud, I gave him a summary of our first few days at court, leaving out the bit about the note from Korechika that I couldn't force myself to steal. I emphasized how difficult it was to keep my spying a secret from my host. "Why, Lord Seimei? Why can't I tell her? Why do you need me to do this? Why not just send me home?"

Seimei dropped his stick and raised his hand as if to slap me, but then took a deep breath and slowly lowered his arm. "Perhaps, in your coarse and vulgar world, such rudeness passes as conversation. Therefore I will not discipline you. This time. But mind your manners from now on, or I will send your spirit to a most uncomfortable place. *You* do not question *me*. *I* question *you*. Understood?"

But I desperately needed to find out when my assignment would be finished and he'd send me home. "Can I just ask-" He raised his hand again. "Yes, Lord Seimei." I bowed from my seated position. Slapping me would hurt Masako too, and that wasn't fair to her. She was unfailingly polite and followed all the rules of rank and etiquette, and yet she'd be punished for my rudeness. What did she do to deserve possession by a twenty-first century American college-student-turned-spy?

I needed a way to force Seimei to send me home. Could he actually be the son of the Taira Rebel? If so, I could use that as leverage. He wouldn't want that widely known at court. He could be executed for it.

"Look at me," Seimei demanded.

I complied, meeting his eyes in a way that would be rude if I did it on my own initiative.

We locked gazes for a few minutes in silence.

"Mi-Na, you think you have power over me," he said, although his lips didn't move. Telepathy, like the medium during the exorcism. *"But you don't. I am powerful, and you are nobody. Your limited knowledge of the future offers little to negotiate with. If you try to set yourself up in competition with me, I will destroy you, and Masako's life will be destroyed along with you. If that is a sacrifice you are prepared to make, so be it. If you cooperate fully, we will work together for the harmony and peace of the realm. Do you understand?"*

I shivered, my heart beating like it was taking a stress test. Poor Masako. She didn't ask for this. *"I get it. Cooperate or else. Fine."*

Seimei looked away, and Masako woke up, alert and energized by the adrenaline rush I had inadvertently triggered.

"What happened, Mi-Na? I feel like I've been running."

"I got a little scared, is all. It's fine now."

Seimei stood up and waved at us to leave. He called out for Akichika, who rushed into the room, grains of rice clinging to his little mustache.

"I will see you at the start of the next solar term," Seimei instructed us. "I will cast both of your horoscopes, so give

Akichika your exact birth dates and times. Akichika, please take Lady Masako to begin her instruction in turtle-shell divination."

Akichika bowed, his face flushing again. "Please follow me." He led us to a courtyard with a glowing fire pit in the middle, a few turtle shells on the ground next to it.

Akichika picked up a shell and gestured for Masako to do the same. He heated the poker in the fire, then pressed it onto the turtle shell with such force it slid across the smooth surface and onto his hand. "*Itashi ya!*" he cried out, dropping the hot poker onto his white robe, which started smoldering. "I am so sorry for this delay. I need to get some water. And more shells. Please do not leave! I will return." He hurried away, muttering to himself about what an idiot he was, and he didn't know why his grandfather wanted him to be a diviner because he was terrible at it.

"He really shouldn't be a diviner," I said. "What do you think he would be good at?"

"He might make a good shrine priest, ka wa? He seems sincere in his respect for the kami."

"I hope Seimei doesn't force him to be a diviner just because it's the family business."

Akichika shuffled into the courtyard with an overflowing basket of turtle shells. He stopped so suddenly a couple of shells fell out. He bent to pick them up without putting the basket down first, so for each shell he picked up, another fell out.

Masako put her sleeve over her mouth to cover her laughter. It came from a good place, though. Amusement, not scorn.

I wanted to be sensitive to Masako's asexual orientation, but it could help her career to be linked to the grandson of the powerful and influential Abe no Seimei. "*Masako, Akichika is young but he has potential. You both have a desire to learn divination and serve the kami. Do you like him?*"

"*Mi-Na, you know I have no interest in marriage or affairs. He might become a friend, though. I can see that.*"

Maybe she could string him along to pump him for information. Should I even bring that up? She'd be offended, no doubt, and it wouldn't be fair to Akichika either. And his loyalty to his grandfather would probably outweigh his interest in Masako.

Nope, not my best idea. "Well, at some point you should let him know you aren't interested in him. He has a big crush—I mean, he really, really likes you. Hey, maybe you could ask Akichika questions about his grandfather. Seimei made it clear he has all the power, but it wouldn't hurt to know more about him."

Masako agreed with me, and as the lesson proceeded, she asked a few innocent questions about Seimei.

Akichika's eagerness to impress Masako overcame his shyness. "Oh, my grandfather's very powerful. He's especially skilled at omen identification and interpretation. When crow droppings fell on Lord Yukinari's head, my grandfather determined it was a bad omen, so he conducted a purification ritual to remove the bad luck. And he prophesied the abdication of Retired Emperor Kazan."

I didn't know who Lord Yukinari was, but he must have been a nobleman with influence, someone Seimei wanted to impress. But crow droppings? Really? It appeared Seimei could tell people *anything* was an omen, and they'd believe him. Was he a charlatan?

But look at what he'd already shown us. He could hypnotize Masako in ten seconds flat, and speak to me telepathically. He *must* have real power. He absolutely *had* to be able to get me home. I had a life. Goals. Dreams of my own. And even though I had the nicest possible host, that didn't change my status as a prisoner in someone else's body. Seimei *had* to be the real deal. Otherwise I could be trapped here forever.

Chapter 20

Stepping In It

Tenth Month, Chōhō 1 (November, 999 CE)

I knew it wasn't right to take control of Masako's body without her permission, but aren't decisions made when our lives are at stake judged by a different ethics yardstick? This world was exciting but dangerous, and I needed to survive long enough to get home. And I hated my dependency on Masako for every little action I wanted to take. *Masako, can we go for a walk? Can we look out the window? Can we drink tea? It's not just for when you're sick.*

I often stayed awake while Masako slept, thinking about the ethics of spirit possession, or about my anxiety and the trouble it's caused me. The media called my cohort "The Cautious Generation," and no wonder: Columbine before I turned one, the twin towers fell when I was three, and the economy crashed when I was ten. My parents' house fell so far underwater it nearly drowned, and then my father was laid off. We lost the house, we moved. My parents got divorced. My best friend Aya moved away the same year we lost the house.

Then the truly anxiety-inducing activities: active shooter

drills in school, ACT tests, AP classes, pressure to get into a prestigious university. Choosing a major – everyone said go into a STEM field. For job security, they said.

But I stopped eating and my hair fell out under the pressure of maintaining my GPA. Switching to a humanities major and starting a study-abroad in Japan had improved my life tremendously, and I just *knew* 2020 was going to be *so* much better.

But instead, here I was, locked in someone else's body in the year 999, witnessing first-hand the ravages of smallpox and other diseases. Commoners who were 'barely human' while nobility were 'the good people.' The rich getting richer, taking property from the poor who couldn't afford their taxes. And no matter how privileged the 'good people' were, nobody had window panes, not even the Emperor.

Maybe I had focused on the wrong things in my life. I'd been so angry with Aya for moving back to Japan that I refused to stay in touch, and she was so angry with me for being angry with her that she didn't even try. I spent time studying instead of making friends because it just wasn't worth investing in something you were going to lose anyway.

And now I lived full-time with a young woman my age, give or take a thousand years. On the plus side, I wasn't waking up at four a.m. full of dread like I used to. Masako slept with the peace of mind of the self-assured. She was an interesting combination of melancholy and optimism, humility and confidence. We were comrades-in-arms, but I needed to keep an emotional distance to prevent binding.

And on this particular night, to rationalize stealing her body. I knew it was wrong, but I needed to know Seimei's end game, and find some kind of leverage over him. I didn't want to be stuck in this backseat driver position forever. I *had* to learn more about him and where he was going with all this. When would he send me home? *Could* he send me home?

The night was quiet, the usual late-night poetry recitations and dice games absent, creating an opportunity that might not come again. I didn't have a plan other than a vague idea to spy on Seimei, but I was desperate to be in control for once.

I sensed Masako slipping away into a deep sleep, exhausted by the stress of observing the Empress all day. If an evil spirit took hold on Masako's watch, she'd be blamed for it.

"Masako? Are you awake?"

No answer.

Masako's sleeping clothes—hakama, undershirt, kosode—weren't cumbersome, and I had more experience walking in them now, so it was easy enough to walk quietly out of our rooms.

There were two sets of doors. The first one I tried was locked, and I nearly went back to bed. Then I realized if I did, I might not get another chance like this, so I crossed the room to the other door, which slid open for me.

I'd become familiar enough with the residence layout that I could make my way out without bumping into a wall or falling off a veranda in the dark. After a close call with a passing guard, I grabbed a fan from a table in one of the corridors I passed through. The compound had at least four gates, each leading to a different street or avenue, and they weren't marked like they would be in a subway. I slipped past the guard at the nearest exit, who didn't even notice me as he stared up at the half-moon, probably composing a poem about it.

I stumbled onto the street, tripping on my robe. I'd forgotten to put on clogs, and my foot, inadvertently wrapped in the kosode, stepped on something squishy. A rank odor rose to greet me as I hastily shook my foot free and lurched away down the road.

Had I made a huge mistake, coming out here alone? It was at least a mile to the government ministry where Seimei had his

Stepping In It 179

office, and I didn't know the way. I moved close to the compound wall to think about whether I wanted to go back inside.

In spite of the late hour, several ox-carts and carriages rumbled along the avenue. I overheard two ox-cart drivers discussing a delivery to the palace storehouse, which I knew to be in the same compound as government offices. As the cart bumped along the street, I threw caution aside and turned to follow it, sticking closely to the earthen wall of Narimasa's residence to avoid being seen. This could be my only chance to explore this great city without the escorts and screens required by Masako's rank. Poor Masako. If she knew what I was doing with her body, she'd probably call the exorcist on the spot.

A few blocks straight, a right turn, another few blocks, and the cart stopped in front of one of the Daidairi gates. I slipped in unnoticed while the officers were checking the cart's contents.

I couldn't remember the way to the Bureau, so I just turned this way and that between buildings. Occasionally a palace guard passed by *(fan up!)* but paid no attention to me, no doubt accustomed to palace men and women on late-night assignations. A priest hurried by but didn't see me. I stayed in the shadows, stopping now and then to breathe in deeply, enjoying the smell of decaying leaves and watching the moon wink in and out of scurrying clouds.

As I stood thinking about what to do, I heard the melancholy, atonal sound of a flute coming from a building nearby. I paused again to listen. I must be adapting to my environment – I'd never liked court flute music before now.

I walked towards the sound, and came to a large outer building, probably a place where high-ranking officials conducted government business. Like most buildings here, a veranda ran along the outside wall, and most rooms had a window open to the veranda.

Peeking into the small room where the music came from, I could see two men seated on cushions. The one with his back to me was holding a short flute just a shade bigger than a piccolo. The other man was Seimei. His eyes were closed, his body swaying with the music, his wide-sleeved arms moving gracefully back and forth as if he were sleep-dancing. I ducked below the veranda and walked to the corner, looking back at an awkward angle to get a glimpse of the flutist's face.

Michinaga. Perfect. My two favorite people spending some quality time together.

Michinaga finished with a long, sad, high note. After a reverent pause, Seimei opened his eyes. A tear glistened on his cheek. No doubt a man who showed no emotion at such beautiful music would be considered unfit for office here. Quite a contrast to what social media would do to a politician who cried at a song in America.

Seimei lifted his cup in a toast. "Lord Regent, thank you for beginning our meeting in this elegant and moving way." His posture tilted slightly forward as if deferring to the younger man.

Michinaga sat cross-legged with a straight back, one hand holding the flute, the other caressing his sake cup. "Lord Seimei, more than ten years ago you prophesied this empire would receive many blessings from the gods when I became Regent. However, it is only a matter of time before the Empress has a son, and when she does, her brother Korechika will have a claim to the regency. Will the gods continue to bless the realm if I am not in power? And if not, do I take action to remain Regent? And will such actions be blessed by the gods?"

His religious fervor surprised me. What would he do if Seimei said the gods *didn't* want him to take any action adverse to the Empress? Of course, Seimei wouldn't say that, not if he were as closely linked to Michinaga's success as I suspected.

Seimei mulled over Michinaga's questions for a minute before replying. "The will of the gods is not always clear. This is why I asked you not to discuss this prophecy with others. It may be misunderstood without correct guidance and interpretation."

"That, Royal Astrologer, is not an answer to my question. Korechika is young and rash, not fit to be Regent. In fact, the Emperor would probably do better on his own than with Korechika as his counselor."

They both laughed at that idea, and Michinaga continued. "Korechika has no plan of his own, no sense of strategy. He just did whatever his late father asked him to do, and now? He is brother-in-law to an Emperor. Tell me, Seimei, did the gods bless that? *I* attend the Kamo Shrine twice a year, and my support for ceremony and ritual is unwavering. How much longer do I wait? Do I need to have a temple or shrine built? What do the gods want from me?"

"Lord Regent, the gods *have* blessed you. You survived the recent epidemic while more than seventy nobles in Heian-Kyo died. The signs are clear. The country will continue to suffer disastrous events if you are not the Regent. And the gods help those who help themselves, as long as they have guidance on what the gods want, which you receive from me. And now to business. I received the first report from the Future-Spirit who has possessed Lady Masako."

Michinaga set his cup down with a loud rap. Sake splashed onto the table, and he rubbed at it irritably with his dark blue sleeve. He didn't explain his reaction, so after a minute, Seimei continued.

"The Spirit has prophesied the Empress will have a son, which aligns with my own divination. Lord Korechika was overjoyed, as you can imagine, and pressured her to use this to advance his own position, but she demurred. She truly does have His Majesty's best interests in mind, even over her own interests, I believe."

"Yes, yes, she's a lovely girl, but her son will be a threat to my position, and according to your prophecy, a threat to me is a threat to the country, and the gods will bless any action I take to remain Regent."

Rationalize, much? And why did Seimei tell Michinaga about this prophecy ten years ago? Michinaga was the fifth youngest brother – hardly a sure bet to become a future regent. Maybe Seimei saw that Michinaga's ambition, intelligence and charisma were better for the country than any of the other Fujiwara boys. Maybe Seimei saw it as his duty to help him get there.

I needed to get out of here. I couldn't wait to tell Masako that Seimei was working with Michinaga, and *not* to protect Empress Sadako.

I crouched down and moved behind the building corner, happy to stand up once out of sight. I heard Michinaga tell Seimei good night, and then the sound of someone descending the steps. I peeked around the corner and saw Michinaga standing there putting his clogs on. Clinging to the wall, I willed myself to be invisible. So many other unbelievable things had happened to me, so why not the power of invisibility?

His footsteps crunched along the gravel path in the opposite direction. I exhaled quietly, waited a few more minutes, and then sped past the mystery building to head back to Narimasa's residence. Clouds now covered the moon, so I felt safe from scrutiny, which doubled my shock when I heard Seimei's voice.

"Lady Masako! How odd to see you here this time of night."

I slowed my pace. Pretending to sleepwalk had worked with Lord Tomohiro. Maybe I could make that my thing, or should I say, Masako's thing. It would help explain why her feet would be dirty in the morning. *Masako, you have a sleepwalking problem. Must be your unresolved issues stemming from the smallpox epidemic.*

He called out again. "Lady Masako, stop!"

If I didn't stop, Seimei would wake up the real Lady Masako and she'd be furious with me. I slowly moved my fan up to cover my face. "Where....where am I?" I murmured. "I...I must have been walking while sleeping."

"So it's just a coincidence you're at the Bureau of Divination?" he asked, a bit sharply for my taste.

So that's where I was. "I..was...dreaming of learning to be a miko. It is all I think about, day and night – the honor you have given me by taking me as your student. My... my footsteps must have taken me where my thoughts have been spending all their time."

He nodded. "Ah. Yes. A true acolyte."

I tried not to show my relief as the waning but still bright moon peeped through dispersing clouds. At least I'd have light to see my way back to the palace.

Seimei stared at my fan, and then at my eyes, and then at my fan again, but I wasn't worried. A fan was a must-have accessory for both women and men.

"Spirit!" he exclaimed. "Mi-Na! You took control of Lady Masako! How did you do that? And why? You lied to me! Come!" He grabbed my arm – *how rude!* – and pulled me along. How could he be so strong when he was so old? How did he know it was me? Where was he taking me?

Chapter 21

I Trusted You!

Tenth Month, Chōhō 1 (November, 999 CE)

Seimei pulled me up the stairs into the now-dark room. I couldn't see his expression, but the force of his grip and his push when he let me go told me he was very angry.

"Spirit!" he hissed. "What have you done to Lady Masako?"

I took a step back. "How'd you know?"

"Lady Masako would never use that fan."

I held it close to my eyes to examine the painted wood. It had a poem on one side, but I couldn't read it in the dark. "Is it the wrong fan for the season? The wrong kind of poetry?"

He sighed with exasperation. "*Baka*! What color is it?"

I shrugged. "It's dark in here, but I think...red?"

"Masako would never carry a red fan. Her father is Fifth Rank. Red-dyed cypress is carried by royalty only. Any fool knows that, and Masako is no fool. Therefore she doesn't know you put her in danger by wandering the city late at night, unescorted, visible to any ruffian out there."

Oh. I screwed up. Typical Mina move.

Wait! How was I supposed to know that? My history class

didn't teach what color fan a Fifth Ranker should carry. Masako should have provided me with some kind of spirit-possession orientation.

I gasped with sudden insight. *This wasn't my fault!* I'd survived for three months in a strange and dangerous world armed with nothing more than a limited knowledge of history. I did my best to keep us both alive, and if things worked out, Masako would have her dream job, thanks to me. And Seimei chose to string us along for his own selfish reasons instead of helping us.

I flipped him the bird. It felt so good I did it again. And then I did the British version, the two finger V, just for the joy of it.

He peered at me in the dark. "What are you doing? Casting a spell? You do not have more power than I do, so beware. Were you spying on me just now? Tell me what you saw or I will send your spirit into that rat." He pointed to a corner where I heard a tiny scratching noise. "Or would you prefer to be a boar, as I promised in our first meeting? You are more like a boar, with your wild manners and questions like sharp tusks. And I will know whether you speak the truth, so don't lie to me."

Maybe *he* was lying. "I didn't see or hear anything. I was just enjoying some alone time."

"Rat it is." He lifted his arms.

And that rat would soon be killed by one of many palace cats, and where would my spirit go then? "Wait! I heard you and Lord Michinaga talking. You gave him the information I gave you. *You* lied to *us!* Masako will be so angry with you. She truly believes you are protecting the Empress. Why are you helping Michinaga?"

"You tell me, rude Spirit. After all, you know the future, do you not? Why *am* I helping the Lord Regent?"

Oh, excrement. That wasn't covered in any class I'd taken, and probably wasn't even taught at the graduate level. What did

I know about Seimei? That he was talented, strategic, and manipulative. A survivor, to have lived into his seventies, and to have achieved Fourth Rank so late in life. "Because, um, you believe the Regent to be the best person to lead the government? And you'll do whatever it takes to ensure he remains regent?"

He chuckled. "Close enough, Spirit, close enough. Now, what do you know of me? Does your world know of my power and position?"

I could answer that. "Oh, yes, Lord Seimei, and not only in books. You have become popular in video games and anime, manga and- sorry, I mean the future has magical scrolls that tell stories. Most stories show you as a boy-sorcerer. You're quite popular. Teenage girls *love* you."

He laughed with a loud, pleased sound. "I had no powers until quite late in life. But it is good to know my name and position will be remembered even so far into the future as your time."

I needed to strike while his mood was good. "Please, please, please, Lord Seimei, send me home! I promise I'll never meditate in a power spot again."

I couldn't see his expression, but he inclined his head as if thinking about it. My heart lifted with joy. He was going to do it! He would send me home just to get rid of me!

"Mi-Na, I am not ready to send you back. It is a risk, of course, with the potential for binding, but it will be well worth it if your presence is the stick that stirs Lady Masako's powers into a bright flame."

From heart-lifting joy to soul-crushing despair. "But Lord Seimei-"

He lifted his head and his hand, so I stopped. *Bastard! Why wouldn't he just send me home?*

"Be advised, Mi-Na, if you do not behave, Lord Michinaga will banish Masako to a faraway island with exiled criminals who will thank the kami for providing a young woman to assuage their... loneliness. Continue reporting to me, and say nothing about how I might choose to use that information. It's time to wake up Lady Masako."

He clapped his hands, the sound reverberating through the silent room.

Masako woke up and took control effortlessly, leaving me dizzy with the speed of the transition.

She looked around in fear. "What am I doing here? Am I dreaming?"

Seimei cleared his throat. "Lady Masako, the Spirit Mi-Na took advantage of your sleep-time to wander around in the dead of night, putting you at risk. I saved you. You are now back in control."

She directed a bright flash of white-hot anger at me. "*Mi-Na, I trusted you! Never again will I make that mistake.*"

It occurred to me I'd gone too far with this body-stealing thing.

"Lord Seimei, I want you to exorcise her," she said. "Send her home, or send her away, I don't care. She has violated my trust one time too many."

"*Masako, no! I'm so, so sorry. But Seimei's plotting with Michinaga against the Empress! Please don't be angry with me. I promise I won't do that again!*"

"No, Lady Masako, I still need her powers, as do you," Seimei replied. "But you must follow my orders or I will ensure you live the rest of your life with Mi-Na on an island far away, and Mi-Na, you will experience everything Masako goes through on this island of violent men. This should give both of you an incentive to behave."

I knew just how horrified Masako was at this threat when she began shaking. If I had my own body, my face would be hot and red with shame at what I was putting her through. "*Masako, I shouldn't have taken control and gone outside without your permission. Please forgive me. We have to work together, or things could go very badly for us. Speak to me, will you? Even if it's to yell at me?"*

She refused to respond. Of all the threats Seimei made, having to live with me the rest of her life might be the worst.

Chapter 22

Tiger And Dog

Tenth Month, Chōhō 1 (November 999 CE)

Masako continued to ignore me. Rather than the symbiotic relationship I'd hoped for, I'd become a parasite hitching a ride on an unwilling host. It was all my fault she didn't trust me. Developing female friendships had never been one of my strengths, and I'd made our relationship worse by holding back from forming a bond with her so I could leave without pain or guilt when the time came.

Without Masako to talk to, I missed life back home even more. My mother had no idea I was a thousand years in the past. She worried so much when I left for Japan, the safest country in the world. I could never tell her about this. Even if I got back safely, she'd think about all the things that could have gone wrong.

I decided I'd tell Kenji everything, though. Something about him made me think he'd believe me, that he'd be jealous I connected to the kami world when that had been his goal for years. *Yeah, Kenji, it was awesome being stuck in someone else's body and unable to control a thing.*

Masako attended the Empress most days and reported to Seimei every solar term, which was every two weeks or so. Or rather, I reported to Seimei after he hypnotized her, and she continued divination training with Akichika, who still had a crush on her. As part of her training, he asked her to divine what role he would play in her life. He seemed to think he was being subtle, but we both knew better.

According to Masako's interpretation of turtle shell cracks, Akichika would be very important in her life. It also appeared to say that Akichika would be important to me, the Spirit Mi-Na, which irked Masako to no end.

I could only think of one way that could happen. *"Maybe that means I'll be stuck here forever, and you'll marry him, which would be a kind of polygamy, right?"*

She ignored me, and told Akichika the divination meant he would be her life-long friend, someone she could rely on, unlike the Spirit Mi-Na.

As promised, Seimei cast our horoscopes.

"I was not surprised to find Lady Masako was born under the lunar sign most compatible with Mi-Na's. Mi-Na is an Earth Tiger and Lady Masako is an Earth Dog. Tiger and Dog are both protectors and fighters."

"Ha! Not very compatible right now, are we?" Maybe if I just kept talking, Masako would reply, even if out of irritation.

"As a Tiger, Mi-Na is restless and impulsive, yet sincere and generous."

"I'm not impulsive, except for that one time I hiked alone and meditated with a stranger, and look how that ended. Lesson learned!"

"She was born in the Hour of the Rabbit, which tempers impulsivity, giving her skill in diplomacy and the ability to make good decisions."

"Remember when I said I felt more like a Rabbit? Guess I was right!"

"Her element is Earth, which means she has a tendency to use people, is more likely to worry than other Tigers, and less likely to select adventure."

"Well, now, that's starting to hit closer to home."

"And her season is Winter, which leads her to be filled with doubt and worry."

"Bingo! So accurate it's almost scary."

"As for Lady Masako, it's clear I made an excellent choice assigning you to Her Majesty's service. As an Earth Dog, you are loyal and a fighter for those you serve, and being naturally quiet, you can keep secrets. You were born in the Hour of the Dragon, which explains your desire to serve the kami. Your season is Autumn, which means you take your responsibilities very seriously, and that you wish to serve others. Perfect! And you are compatible with Earth Tiger Mi-Na. Truly fascinating."

"Does he even know you aren't talking to me anymore?" Her silence was deafening. "Oh, come on, Masako, give me a break! I said I'm sorry! Look at this horoscope. It explains everything. Impulsivity, recklessness, doubts—I've got it all, baby!"

"We won't take any action based on these horoscopes, but it tells me I made the right decision to proceed with your training to become a future shrine miko."

Masako bowed and expressed her thanks tonelessly, but Seimei was either too busy to notice or just didn't care that she'd lost her enthusiasm.

I couldn't go on this way. Her lack of communication and companionship magnified my sense of imprisonment. But what could I do about it?

I'd always held back from forming deep friendships. Connecting meant accepting a friend request, or a burst of dopamine from seeing my post had a hundred likes. I had no experience connecting with someone on a deeper level, a level where I allowed myself to be vulnerable to someone because I knew they had my back just as I had theirs.

Nope, that wasn't for me.

So what now? Was it worth risking a deeper connection with Masako by telling her everything? What if it drove her further away?

"Masako, I know you aren't speaking to me now, but I'm going to talk to you anyway. I have a lot to say, so even if you're still angry with me, please listen. I know I screwed up—uh, made a big mistake—and I'm so sorry. But please understand what it's like to be me. I can't move unless you do. I can't speak to anyone but you. I can only do what you want to do and when you want to do it. I'm completely and utterly dependent on you, and you won't talk to me. I need to get home, but I don't know whether Seimei can or will help me. And we don't know how much time we have before our spirits bind permanently. If we do bind, even the Great Seimei won't be able to separate us."

Masako had left Seimei's office and was sitting in an outer room drawing hexagrams. My speech had interrupted her concentration, so she put the brush down and put her hands over her eyes. I felt a wave of compassion emanate from her.

"And Masako, our horoscopes show that we're meant to work together. At first I just made up all that stuff about fate, but now our horoscope is one more bit of evidence that it's our destiny. The kami want us to be together."

"Eh, Mi-Na, if I forgive you, will you vow never to take control without my permission?"

My spirit lightened like a helium balloon. I might have floated away with happiness if I weren't tethered to my host.

"Yes, yes, I promise! I've missed you so much! Please don't ever ignore me like that again."

"I did not consider how it would feel to be trapped and unable to speak or move. It appears that I drew you in from the spirit world, as a miko should do, but I cannot send you home." She sighed and uncovered her eyes, looking down at her paper scraps. *"Perhaps-"* she stopped for a second. *"Perhaps you may take control during the day from time to time, when I am not needed to attend the Empress. I could meditate or take a nap."*

I didn't deserve that level of consideration, not after what I'd done, but I wasn't about to argue. *"Oh, Masako, thank you! Thank you so much!"*

I heard a familiar sound coming through the connecting room. *"I hear the Akichika-shuffle. Better put your fan up, Masako, we don't want him to turn as red as a pomegranate!"*

Masako laughed and reached for her fan. Sure enough, ten seconds later Akichika slid the door open, bowed hastily, and slid the door closed, all without noticing who was sitting at the table. He turned toward us, bowed again, and only then noticed it was Masako sitting there. He inhaled so sharply he hiccuped. "Imperial Medium!" He bowed again.

"Good afternoon, Apprentice Diviner."

"It is excellent you are here, *ka-na*! I have something to tell you. I will not be able to tutor you anymore. I am so sorry." His face fell into an exaggerated expression of sadness, as if he really did view this as a tragedy.

"Now maybe you'll actually learn something useful," I teased.

"Mi-Na, that was a cruel thing to say. But amusing."

She hid her smile behind her fan. "What will Lord Seimei have you do? And will he tutor me himself?"

"I am not skilled enough to tutor such a powerful medium as Lady Masako. My grandfather has agreed to apprentice me to the shrine. I will become a shrine priest, but continue to study astronomy." And now excitement shone in his gentle brown eyes.

"Your devotion to the kami will help us all. We will miss you, my friend, but you will be an excellent shrine priest, and will bring the kami's blessings to the realm."

He didn't blush this time. He bowed his thanks in a much more adult way.

"I swear, Masako, Akichika is filling that robe out nicely all of a sudden. Some young men are late developers, and I think he's one."

"Mi-Na, stop talking nonsense."

Akichika left with a spring in his step and without breaking anything.

I took that as a hint. It was time for *me* to grow up. I was twenty-one now, an adult, so I should do the mature thing and tell Masako about my reports to Seimei. I'd been growing increasingly guilt-ridden about keeping this from her. She'd decided to trust me again, but it wasn't real as long as I kept this from her.

"Masako?" Did I really want to confess? It wouldn't get me home any faster, and it might create a hostile living environment for me.

"Yes, Mi-Na? What is it? Do you have another amusing story about your world?"

I had to tell her. "Masako, Seimei makes me report to him on the Empress's meetings and conversations. When you meet with him, and he puts you in that trance, he asks me lots of questions about her health, what she's said about the Emperor, about her brothers, and so on. He forced me to keep it a secret, I don't know why, but it's killing me to not tell you!"

Silence as she processed this. Then—"I do not understand. We are both observing Her Majesty to protect her. That is no secret, Mi-Na."

"To put it bluntly, I'm a spy. I'm spying on the Empress for Seimei, who gives my information to Michinaga, who uses it for- for who knows what, but it can't be good for Sadako, I know that much. I wanted to tell you this, no matter what Seimei will do to me if he finds out, because you trust me. I don't want you to trust me until you know everything about me."

She didn't speak, but she didn't have to. I could feel blood rushing to her head, and that hot flash of temper she hid from everyone but me. Her hands tingled.

"Spirit- oh, Mi-Na, Lord Seimei should not have treated you thus, ya wa!" She opened and closed her fists like she wanted to hit somebody. "You should have told me right away, but I understand why you did not. You are a foreign spirit from a world I do not understand, and you are desperate to return to it. Lord Seimei has all the power. Please, Mi-Na, never lie to me again."

So her anger was directed at Seimei, not me. *He* betrayed her trust. I was only the tool he used to do that.

"I'm sorry, Masako. It's been hell keeping this from you, and my confession is intended to show you my willingness to be a better person. Michinaga will prevent the Empress's son from ever becoming Crown Prince, and Seimei's doing his part to help."

She trembled with barely suppressed rage. I knew she had a quick temper, but this was on a whole new level. "Lord Seimei- how could he? Why? The Empress is so kind, so sweet, and she loves His Majesty so much. He is the Royal Astrologer! Her Majesty depends on him for advice and counsel!" She bent over, pressing her arms against her stomach.

I decided that she needed to vent. Otherwise she might get IBS or ulcers or something nasty that comes with suppressing one's feelings. "Masako, tell Seimei how you feel. He thinks of you as a granddaughter. It's me he doesn't like. Maybe you can change his mind."

"I am no grandchild of his! But he is still my teacher. But he wants to harm Her Majesty. But he is the only one who can help us. But-"

She went back and forth in this vein for so long I grew concerned she was driving herself insane, and it had nothing to do with me. Other than being the catalyst.

Chapter 23

Dance Trance

Eleventh Month, Chōhō 1 (December 999 CE)

Over the next few weeks, Masako submerged her rage in a pool of darkness even I couldn't penetrate. I tried to talk her through it, but she refused to listen. I tried teasing her out of it, and we endured a splitting headache for days as a result. She wanted to stop training with Seimei out of loyalty to the Empress, but that would ruin her chance to become an imperial shrine miko, so she was angry at herself as well as at Seimei.

To make matters worse, Sei Shonagon had told Masako the story of the day the Empress had moved to Lord Narimasa's place. Michinaga had arranged an attendance-required outing for the same day to make sure no one was available to help Her Majesty. Sei said this petty humiliation was just another component of the Regent's strategy to destroy the Empress, who'd wept quietly the day of the move and most of the next day. Sei had tried to distract her with a funny story about Narimasa's gate being too small, and how he tried to get in her room that night, but Sei had laughed him out of there. The Empress asked Sei not to make fun of her host. Another example of her thoughtfulness even in the midst of her anguish.

Masako's intense loyalty to Empress Sadako had grown over time. At first, it was a reflection of her loyalty to the Emperor, but now it was personal. Sadako had shown nothing but graciousness and kindness to this rustic medium, while other ladies at court called Masako "Lady Ox" for her sturdy figure, and snubbed her at mealtime for her lack of refinement.

Masako didn't shut me out this time, but her anger made it difficult for her to focus on preparation for her first Kagura Dance, an event critical to her advancement as a shrine miko. The Kagura Dance summoned a shrine's kami to answer the prayers of the people. For those who practiced *onmyōdo*, it allowed the practitioner to understand a person's heart and to see where he or she weighed on the scale of good and evil.

For truly talented miko and *onmyōji*, the Kagura Dance had the power to call shikigami into being. Masako took her dance lessons from a local shrine priestess, but Seimei provided supplemental lessons to ensure Masako was properly trained in case the Dance resulted in giving her that power.

We met up with him under the *torii* gate leading to the shrine where her dance would take place. She greeted him with a stiff bow, her lips in a tight, thin line. It didn't take a powerful diviner to sense something was wrong.

Seimei folded his arms and frowned. "Lady Masako, if you bring anger into the Kagura dance, you might hurt someone. You are usually so calm. What caused this shift in your temperament?"

She tugged on her sleeve violently. She had been fidgeting ever since she got dressed, pulling on a tassel, tugging on a robe, hitching her robes and hakama up to prepare for dancing, constantly adjusting them to different lengths; putting her hair up and taking it down just to put it up again. I was curious about what she'd say. Was she angry with me, or with Seimei? Or both?

"The way they treat Her Majesty," she said, her voice cracking under the burden of suppressed emotion. "I can't bear to watch her continued humiliation. The day she moved to Narimasa's residence, no one was there to help but Shonagon and a few servants. Why?" Her voice got louder as she spoke, and her last words were a shout. Such rudeness to her teacher was very uncharacteristic. He could slap her for such insubordination.

But he didn't. He waved his fan thoughtfully. "Lady Masako, you have become too close to the Empress. Your job is to protect her from malevolent spirits. Your job is *not* to protect her from the political games noblemen play here in the capital. Do not allow your feelings about her to prevent you from achieving rank as Imperial Miko." And it was his turn to raise his voice. "Control yourself!"

I, too, had been upset with the way the Empress had been treated, but the depth of Masako's anger shocked me. Was our cohabitation causing her to react with greater depth and intensity of emotion than she might otherwise have?

She took a deep breath and stood straight. "I am in control. I will not let you down, Lord Seimei."

We proceeded to the shrine grounds where others were waiting. The dance had to be conducted with a shrine priest and a miko. Masako had been told the priest was also an apprentice conducting his first Kagura.

Masako stopped short when she saw him, shaking her head. "*Mi-Na, it's Akichika!*" She sounded both excited and irritated. "*I hope he's a better priest than he was an onmyōji.*"

Seimei chuckled to see Masako's reaction. "Akichika is a much better priest than *onmyōji*," he said.

"*Great minds think alike,*" I teased.

Seimei had Masako and Akichika face each other. Akichika

Dance Trance

had grown a little since the last time we saw him, and his white silk robes gave him a dignity I'd not seen in him before. He greeted Masako with a confident bow without blushing, and Masako smiled at him. He did turn a little red at that.

She held a sakaki twig in one hand and a bell in the other. Akichika held a fan in each hand. Just as the shrine priest was about to signal the musicians to begin, Seimei held his hand up.

"A reminder to both of you. If successful, both the *mitama* of peace and the *mitama* of violence will inhabit you. In the unlikely event you call shikigami into being, heed this: they must *always* be under your control. If not, the mitama of violence might control it for you. Shikigami must never be used to harm someone."

I hadn't thought about Masako getting possessed by *mitama*. What would happen to me if she became possessed by other souls? Would I get pushed out?

He folded his arms and stared at Masako for a full minute without speaking. Her heart began to beat faster in anticipation and fear of what he might be thinking.

"Lady Masako," he said, his voice low and soft. "You are the only human I know with a long-term spirit possession. I do not understand how this will affect the success of the Kagura dance. To improve your results, I will put Mi-Na in a temporary hold."

"*Oh, Masako, no! Please, ask him not to-*"

It was too late. She met his eyes with no hesitation whatsoever. He stared deeply into hers, and pulled me into a dark, dizzying spiral. Down, down, down, and then—frozen. Even if I spoke to her, she wouldn't hear me. I could feel her movements as well as the physical reactions to her emotional state—heart beating, jittery nerves—but she couldn't feel my presence at all. I hated the isolation and the reminder that I was a distraction, an intruder, an unwelcome spirit-invader. Damn that dirty diviner!

The dance began with slow and atonal music. A drum beat

about every five seconds, and a high-pitched flute exhaled long wavering notes. Masako and Akichika moved around each other with tiny, even steps that gave them the appearance of floating. Masako raised her arms, crossed and then uncrossed her hands, and drew them down while shaking the bell. Akichika did the same with his fans, his rectangular sleeves waving like flags.

The tempo increased gradually, and they moved faster to keep pace. They whirled, slowly at first, then faster, their sleeves and hakama billowing out like clouds. Then they reversed to whirl the other way. Masako had gone into a semi-trance. She knew the dance well and didn't need full consciousness to perform it.

A sense of peace filled her mind, and mine as well. I lifted my head and looked up at the pale blue sky, the same color as the July day I left my body. But how could I be looking at the sky while Masako's head was tilted toward the ground?

I looked down, and rather than the packed dirt of the dance floor, I saw grass. Was I dreaming while Masako was in her self-induced trance? I looked up again, and saw Kenji sitting cross-legged by the sakaki tree, his eyes closed, his mouth relaxed. And I saw *me*, my body, my khaki shorts green with grass stains, my eyes closed and a joyful smile on my face. I was alive!

Kenji stirred and opened his eyes. He looked at me—at my body sitting there—with a pleased smile, like he'd done something well.

"Kenji! Kenji!"

He gave a little start and looked around in confusion.

I tried again – *"Kenji!"* – and he looked up, down, around and then again at my body meditating there on the grass.

"Mina?" he asked quietly, probably not wanting to disturb my meditation.

"Yes! It's me, Mina!"

He moved as if to touch my shoulder, and the entire scene

disappeared, replaced by the dirt floor and Masako's white sleeves flowing back and forth.

Noooo! I screamed to myself. I wanted to smash something. I wanted to howl with rage, to take revenge on someone—anyone—for trapping me here in this world, in this body. *I haaaate youuuuuu!* I screamed at Masako, at Seimei, at everybody here. *Let me gooooo!*

Masako couldn't hear me, but her silent scream echoed my own. *"I hate you! Leeeeave!"* and yet all the while she was dancing, whirling and moving in time to the music. So peaceful on the outside. So angry on the inside. The *mitama* of violence was feeding on her anger.

Then, with no warning, calm. Quiet. No sound of a heart beating, no feel of sticky, perspiring skin. Numb and paralyzed, like a fly injected by spider venom. But I could see the musicians still playing and Masako's sleeves moving up and down as she danced. What was happening? What had she done? I suspected the Soul of Violence had fed on Masako's anger, spinning it outward in a hurricane of chaotic emotion, and I was in the calm eye.

She stopped dancing while Akichika, caught up in his own dance-trance, moved around her. "I see the spirit of Michinaga," she said in a voice I didn't recognize. It wasn't mine, and it wasn't hers. It was a lower, almost baritone pitch. "He tilts from good toward evil."

I heard her voice, but nothing else. What magic was this?

"The balance must be corrected," this not-Masako voice said.

"Masako? Are you okay? That was some weird shit with the anger, huh?" I knew she couldn't hear me but I had to try. Even in Seimei's "hold," I should feel her emotions. Now? Nothing.

She pulled a piece of *washi* paper from her sleeve and threw it up into the air, pointing at it with her sakaki twig. "Shikigami! Curse Michinaga!"

The paper turned into a midnight-black raven, which flapped its huge wings above Masako's head, calling out "Hello!" in a husky, human-like caw before flying over the shrine grounds, past the *torii* gate, and out of sight.

The musicians stopped playing, and Akichika stopped dancing and gazed at Masako, his brown eyes wide with fear.

Seimei strode over to Masako and grabbed her wide sleeve. "What have you done?" he shouted. "Is that shikigami under your control? Call it back!"

Masako blinked, emerging from her trance and freeing me from my suffocating cocoon. Her anger had been swept away by the catharsis of the dance. "I- I can't," she whispered. "The *mitama* have left me."

"You allowed the Mitama of Violence to use you for its own ends, and you used the dance to harm someone. You have failed this test. I refuse to teach you until you have learned to control your anger. Now I must undo what you have done."

He gestured impatiently at her to leave. Akichika stood there with his mouth open, but snapped it shut when Seimei glared at him. "Does that mean I failed too?" he asked.

"We will conduct this test again in the future. Both of you have failed."

Poor Akichika. It wasn't his fault. And I'd been so close to getting home. So. Freaking. Close. I'd seen Kenji waiting for me. Masako had the power to send me back! Yes, her magic had been uncontrolled and fueled by her rage, but everyone said only Seimei could send me home, and she'd almost done it! But she needed Seimei to learn to do it intentionally, so I had to help her make this right with him.

Chapter 24

Full Control

Eleventh Month, Chōhō 1 (December 999 CE)

Michinaga fell ill. Convinced of his imminent death, he begged the Emperor to let him resign and become a monk. That would have solved Empress Sadako's problems, but unfortunately Seimei performed a purification rite to get rid of Masako's shikigami-curse, and the Regent's health improved, so he rescinded his request.

Which was more evidence that Seimei had real power, and now that I'd seen my healthy meditating body sitting on the grass with Kenji, I was optimistic about returning home soon.

Masako, however, was miserable. Cursing the Lord Regent was not a great resume-building achievement, and had potential negative ramifications not only for her future, but possibly her father's as well, so she focused on hating herself.

"Cheer up, girl!" I said with enthusiasm. "You put an actual curse on the Regent. You should feel good about yourself!"

"This is a disaster. We could be exiled, and Mi-Na, you might never get home. It's my fault. It's all my fault!" She started to cry.

I knew how she felt. I'd done my share of stupid things for

which I kicked myself for days on end. Masako rarely did anything wrong, which made this particular event even more shocking. Had my possession of her body caused this impulsivity? Or was I right in that she needed to vent, but she hadn't, and so her pent-up anger brought out her power? *"Masako, you were serving the Emperor, in your own strange way."*

"It was a misuse of shamanistic power. I should have known better. It was very unlike me."

"If not for me, you wouldn't have allowed your anger to rule you like that. You have a bit of a temper, but it comes and goes quickly, and you never let others see it. I only see it because I live it. Thanks to my bad influence, you've become more impulsive, less in control, and less guarded. I suspect Seimei is secretly proud of your talent and he won't tell anyone you caused Michinaga's illness. He'll want to harness your power and make sure it's under his control. You still need him, and he'll see that he needs you too."

I was right. He chastised her severely but continued with her lessons, and we didn't hear a breath of rumor that Masako was to blame for the Regent's near-death experience.

On a cold evening a week later, we watched the Empress's women play a poetry game. One of the Empress's ladies plucked a koto in the background, and screens and curtains kept the brazier's warmth in with us while adding color and beauty to the room.

"This is the life I dreamed of, Masako, when I studied Heian literature. Poetry games, music, art. Her Majesty surrounds herself with women so literate they write diaries and understand Chinese poetry. Few people in my world would believe that women were so educated in the tenth century. I mean, in this era."

Full Control

"Well, Mi-Na, I am not one of those women, and I find this game quite dull."

Just then Chunagon rushed in breathlessly. Flushed with excitement, she waved a bundle of papers in front of Sei. "Shonagon, I obtained a copy of the Genji tale! Finding a copy was more difficult than finding braziers in Eleventh Month. It is even better than *The Tale of the Hollow Tree*. It's by Tametoki's daughter, who is Lord Nobutaka's fourth wife. She has only written three chapters, and everyone is begging her to write more. She just had a baby, so she's not planning to release any more chapters for a while. The Emperor and Empress have read it, and Her Majesty said she will send her own wet nurse to her if that will enable her to write!"

Sei took the bundle from Chunagon. "The paper is slightly rough to the touch, and its off-white color is in poor taste, but for a quickly made copy it is not horrible."

"*The Tale of Genji!* Oh, Masako, this is another famous work!" I was so elated I didn't even care about giving that bit of the future away.

"*Shonagon appears to be annoyed by Chunagon's praise of it.*"

Sei riffled the pages.

"Read it to us!" "Yes, read it out loud!" the ladies clamored.

"Very well, just the first chapter." She lifted the first page and began. "In a certain reign there was a certain lady not of the first rank whom the Emperor loved more than any others."

"I get to hear Sei Shonagon read aloud from *The Tale of Genji!* I want to jump with excitement—will you jump for me?"

"Hush, Mi-Na. Enjoy the moment before it's over."

Sei's voice grew softer and softer until it was almost inaudible by the end of the chapter. She set the pages down and stood up. Her face was flushed and her breathing a little too fast, like she'd been running, not reading. She told the group that she needed something from her room, and left with a rustle of robes.

"We should find out what's bothering her," I said.

"Maybe she's ill." Masako hurried after her.

Sei strode through the palace muttering to herself, not realizing we were close behind. When she arrived in her room, she let out an anguished sob.

"Shonagon, what's wrong? Is there anything we can help you with?" Masako asked in a soft voice. Sei turned to her, tears streaming down her face.

"I'm furious. I want to be the one to have created the shining gentleman. People enjoy my little musings and lists, but that's all they are – trivial, amusing, transient – no doubt soon forgotten. This Genji story will live beyond today."

Masako stood in the doorway in silence, not quite understanding Sei's emotion, but I knew exactly how she felt. I'd had so many arguments with classmates about this very topic. They ridiculed me for insisting *The Pillow Book* was better than *The Tale of Genji*. Murasaki was a product of her era, I'd claimed, while Sei Shonagon was ahead of her time. Which made me a bit of a pariah in my major.

Sei dried her tears with her sleeve. "Others will compare my book to the Genji tale, and my writing will be found shallow and insipid."

"Masako, please say something to help her feel better. You can tell her she will be remembered long after most other writers of this era will be forgotten."

Masako conveyed my comments, and Sei took a few more deep breaths. Her color and expression returned to normal. She stared at Masako without seeming to see her, her lips pursed in thought. "Leave me alone. I'm going to write." She turned her back to us, going to her writing table as if we didn't exist.

"I bet she writes something that reflects poorly on Murasaki. I mean Tametoki's daughter. She's known as Murasaki in my world."

"Mi-Na, you read the entire book in your world. You must know what she's going to write, so a bet hardly seems fair."

"I've forgotten those details, I promise. How about if I'm right, you let me take control for an entire day. And if I'm wrong, I'll tell you anything you want to know about my era."

Masako perked up. "Well, gambling brings luck, and we need more luck here. You mustn't do anything improper if you win."

"I promise I won't use my time in control to sleep with anyone."

I won my bet a few days later when the Empress asked Sei to read more entries from her book. Sei read a passage making fun of Murasaki's husband Nobutaka wearing gaudy clothes when he should have been wearing shabby clothing more suitable to the asceticism of a pilgrimage to Mitake.

The Empress laughed. "I remember this tale. The Mitake kami blessed him with a promotion after that pilgrimage, so they must have appreciated his care in clothing selection. Why did you not include that, Shonagon? That is surely the most interesting aspect of this anecdote."

Sei looked down at the paper she was holding, and hesitated, her usual quick wit failing her. "I revised my story to-" She stopped, exhaled dramatically, and then bowed. "Yes, Your Majesty. I will add that back in."

I was quick to claim my winnings from Masako. "See? Told you. She tried to make Tametoki's daughter's husband look ridiculous. I won!"

"It wasn't a fair bet. You say you did not remember that from your studies, but how do I know that? You cheated!"

"No, I swear I didn't. When I read the book, I didn't know Nobutaka was Murasaki's husband. When do I get to take control? Can I take over on a day when you have a lesson with Seimei?"

Masako fumed for a minute. "Oh, very well, but I need to remember what he will teach you. I can't miss any instructions or it could set me back."

I took control early one morning. It took longer than usual for Masako to put herself into a trance because of my excitement and anticipation. The longer we were together, the more influence my emotions seemed to have over her body, but she eventually managed to settle down enough for me to take over.

I stood up, stretched, and went to the window to look out, being careful not to step on sleeping ladies-in-waiting. The colors of autumn had faded, and a recent storm had stripped the leaves from deciduous mountain trees, leaving the slopes a checker board of bark-brown and pine-green. It was chilly, but not yet freezing, and the November wind brought the scent of pine with it. It was nothing that I didn't experience with Masako – she went to the window every morning when she woke up – but it felt so much better to do it under my own power. *I* decided to take a deep breath in. *I* decided to stretch, and *I* decided to go into the garden and wander around.

The ox-carriage came to take me to the Bureau office at the Hour of the Snake. Seimei waved me in but didn't look up. He was frowning with concentration and concern.

"Lord Seimei, is something wrong?"

He looked up, startled. "Ah, Mi-Na! Why are you in charge?"

Something about my voice always gave me away. "I won a bet with Masako, so I have control all day."

He looked disappointed. "I have a very important divination to conduct, and Masako should observe it."

"Don't worry. As long as that barrier-thing you keep between us doesn't affect it, anything you teach me goes into her brain, so she'll have access to it later. And maybe I can help."

His appraising stare lasted an uncomfortably long time, but I refused to squirm. Instead, I stared right back at him, something Masako would never do.

Full Control

"Are young women so rude in your era?" he asked. "Staring at a man like that?"

"In my country, people might think I was shifty or lying if I didn't look them in the eyes. Although in some cultures it's considered rude."

"Fascinating..." he murmured. He continued to stare, and finally I had to blink. His lips curved just a little. I stared at his mouth. *Somebody else has that smile, but who?*

He cleared his throat. "We must get to work. The Lord Regent's daughter Akiko is sick. He's concerned and has requested a divination to determine what should be done."

Akiko was the daughter that Michinaga and his sister intended to marry to Emperor Ichijō. No wonder Michinaga was worried. Not only paternally – and he seemed to be a loving father from what I had heard – but his future depended on her.

I leaned forward. "Can you describe her symptoms to me? I might have insight from my world."

"Her skin is warmer than usual, she's very tired, and she has a rasping cough that has lasted for several days and shows no sign of ending."

"Where does she live? Many of these residences are dank and cold this time of year. How old is she? I know noblewomen don't go outside much after their coming-of-age ceremony. Maybe she needs to be in a brighter, drier place. And if she's coughing a lot, they should stop burning so much incense."

"She lives in Michinaga's main residence. Let's finish this divination to determine what the kami have to say."

He had Akiko's horoscope in front of him. I knew that he had cast it when she was born, and had divined she would be mother of emperors, so obviously this cough wasn't going to finish her off. The stars said so.

He used a combination of horoscope and divination sticks. He silently reviewed his results, and then looked at me with new appreciation. "This matches with your suggestion," he said with a note of surprise. "The Regent should move her to a brighter, drier place."

My face tingled. I was pleased Seimei had confirmed my analysis, and I was awed by the magic behind the divination. Or did Seimei fix the results so they matched my comments?

This train of thought could go on for days. "Lord Royal Astrologer, have you divined whether the Empress's child will become Crown Prince?" I asked.

He wasn't surprised by my question. In fact, he was a little smug. "Yes."

"What did the divination tell you?"

"Mi-Na, tell me what you know first, and then I'll tell you what my divination shows." He stared at me as if trying to burrow into my brain. "Or do you even know?"

"*You* tell *me* first, and I'll tell you if you're right."

"Ignorant Spirit! You claim to have knowledge of future events. Do you actually know anything? Or have you been lying to me?" He paused as if this idea had just occurred to him. "If you don't know, then the baby must not be written in your history... and so... it doesn't matter. Because the baby will never become Emperor, for whatever the reason!" He ended his speculation with a triumphant wave of his sleeve, and a look on his face like he thought he deserved a pat on the back.

He wasn't wrong. I didn't know as much as I pretended to know. So I just bowed my head with humility and remained silent.

After watching me for a minute, he grew impatient. "Come with me. I must bring the result of this divination to the Lord Regent in person."

"Won't he be disturbed to discover the Spirit Mi-Na has full control of the Imperial Medium's body?"

"He might find what you have to say about the future of

great interest." Seimei's eyes gleamed as his tone grew louder and more enthusiastic. "Why didn't I think of this before? We could order Masako to allow you to take over more often. She's not the oracle. *You* are. And I've never heard of a spirit possessing a body for so long. After all this time, haven't you learned to take over while Lady Masako is awake but without her cooperation?"

I'd never seen him so animated. He leaned forward, his gray eyebrows moving up and down as he spoke. "You should try. But it is enough that you have access to this body for today. Come!"

I could see the benefits of meeting with Michinaga as myself. Masako was a bit naive, and although it felt disloyal to even think about it, I sometimes wondered if her lack of interest in court politics and courtly manners had held us back, had kept us from moving closer to our goal.

The Lord Regent was startled when Seimei introduced me as the Spirit Mi-Na. Seimei assured him I was harmless, which irked me, but I had to admit he was right.

A servant offered us sake. I took a few sips while Seimei explained his divination results to the Regent. The sake wasn't bad. Warm, nice on this cold, gray day. Maybe they should give sake to Akiko. That might relax her lungs.

"Lord Regent, I suggest giving a small amount of warm sake to your sick daughter," I said. Seimei glared at me. He didn't like me getting credit for anything, much less interrupting his Regent face time. But he brought me here, so it was his fault.

Michinaga turned his charm on me. "O Spirit Mi-Na, why have we not spoken before now? I had no idea you could control this young Taira lady."

I glanced at Seimei, who was examining his sake like he was trying to pick out a stray hair. Apparently Seimei hadn't told the Regent that I occasionally took full possession of Masako's body.

Maybe he didn't want Michinaga to know because he was afraid of what we would do, especially if I became the dominant spirit. Maybe he feared Michinaga would replace him with me.

The Regent smiled with sincere warmth, his eyes focused on me like nothing in the world was more important than this conversation. I felt my cheeks flush. I hadn't been the center of anyone's attention since Kenji, and I liked it. I shouldn't, and wished I didn't, but I did.

We chatted a bit, and he had a servant bring a robe over. "This is my gift to the Spirit Mi-Na. Perhaps you can wear it while you are in control."

I caressed the soft yellow silk, a bit of summer sunshine on this gray day, enjoying the sensation that someone was focused on *me* for the first time in months.

"So... the Empress will have a boy? Is that what your 'history' has written?" he asked in a casual tone.

I nodded my head, lost in the glory of the robe in my lap. My robe. He gave it to *me*. Not to Masako. To me. "Yes, Lord Regent."

Michinaga sat back and exhaled. He tapped his now-empty sake cup on the table a few times, staring at me. I picked up the sake decanter to pour more into his cup. Without thinking, I grasped his cup to keep it steady while I poured, and my fingers closed around his warm hand. I suppressed a shiver, but the adrenaline rush had already started. A handsome, powerful man, a little bit of danger... no wonder Masako was worried about what I would do. Yes, he'd recently humiliated the Empress and was actively planning to deny her son the title of Crown Prince, but I hadn't been this close to a man in months. Which, to be honest, had been the longest time I'd been without a boyfriend since high school.

I steeled myself to resist, muttering to myself, "He's a jerk. He's a jerk," like a mantra to ward off evil.

My hand shook as I poured sake into Seimei's cup next. Both men watched me with amusement, and now I felt stupid. I sat back on my heels, looking down the way Masako would have done. She would have insisted on a screen or a fan, and I hadn't done either. Apparently I'd learned nothing over the past months.

"Well, will the boy become Emperor someday?" Michinaga said in an off-hand tone, not in the least like his future depended on my answer.

If I replied in the affirmative, would he find a way for the boy to have an accident? To somehow interrupt the course of fate without violating his Buddhist principles? But if I said 'no,' that would give him too much power. Too much confidence he could do whatever the hell he wanted to.

"Lord Regent, my history books tell of great things accomplished in your regency." I looked up at him through Masako's long eyelashes. "And of your generosity, and your love of literature and the arts. A great flowering of culture."

My admiring tone and flirtatious glance distracted him. "Royal Astrologer," he said while continuing to gaze at me, "the Spirit Mi-Na has been a nice addition to my day. How often may we expect to see Mi-Na in charge? Can we order Lady Masako to submerge herself so Mi-Na can take over permanently? She is much more pleasant." He shifted a little closer to me with each sentence.

My pulse was racing. I wanted him to move all the way over, to sit so close I could feel his breath on my cheek. I wanted him to, and I didn't want him to. Strange, because Masako's biology was hers alone. If anything, I should feel her repulsion toward this man. Was my attraction to him due to magic? Or just the magic of chemistry? If we fused, would the dominant spirit's sexual orientation prevail? I could see why we'd go crazy if we had to constantly fight for control.

Michinaga was now mere inches away, and his hand rested on the hem of my white robe. "Spirit, *you* won't curse me. Which doesn't mean women don't curse men, but *you* wouldn't. Would you?" He lifted his long fingers to my chin and tilted my head up so he could gaze into my eyes. "I see you, Spirit Mi-Na. What color are your eyes in your world? I heard they match the sky on a sunlit afternoon," he murmured.

My body leaned towards his, my eyelids fluttering as I tried to keep myself from falling into the rich brown depths of his long eyes. *Masako will be so angry with me.*

"Lord Seimei, I wish to speak with Mi-Na alone. Please wait in the salon." He waved a dismissal without looking away.

Seimei's mouth opened as if to argue, but apparently thought better of it. He left after a bow and a concerned glance my way.

"What do you want, Mi-Na?" The Regent moved his hand from my chin, and wrapped both of his hands around both of mine. "Do you want me to order Lord Seimei to send you home?"

He was offering a quid pro quo. Sleep with him in exchange for his help. Would that be so wrong? I was already physically attracted to him, and I was in charge today. Maybe doing something diametrically opposed to Masako's wishes would prevent us from binding. Which would be in her best interest, too, and I'd get home sooner, also a good thing for Masako.

Yeah, great excuses, Mina. What the hell do you think you're doing? He might be powerful and charming, but he's done some bad things, and you don't even like him! I had not always respected Masako's wishes, and we didn't agree on everything, but I couldn't do this to her. She'd made her thoughts on sex very clear. None. Ever. Friends don't do things like that to friends. I hadn't wanted to make a friend, not here, not when I was trying my utmost to get home, but it happened anyway. Not only that, but she was the first close friend I'd made in ten years.

Full Control

I stood up, another rude gaffe, but at this point I didn't care. "The Empress is expecting Masako," I said breathlessly. "I must return now. Thank you for the lovely robe, Lord Regent."

He took his hands away and laughed. Not an evil "bwa-ha-ha" kind of laugh—he was too dignified for that—but more of a contemptuous bark. "You should both become nuns," he said, and left.

Chapter 25

Monkey Midwife

Eleventh Month, Chōhō 1 (December 999 CE)

"The stars indicate it's inauspicious for me to attend the birth personally," Seimei said while studiously examining a hanging scroll in his office.

"Inauspicious for his next promotion is what he means. Nobles who spend time with the Empress are seen as disloyal to Michinaga."

"Mi-Na, he's the Royal Astrologer for a reason. He understands the kami's messages in the stars."

It wasn't easy for Masako to reconcile the image of Seimei the Teacher with the picture I'd painted of his betrayal of the Empress. She wasn't nearly as skeptical as I was, and justified continuing lessons with him as a kind of counter-intelligence. My phrasing, of course, but she had a good point. We could learn *about* him while we learned *from* him.

Seimei saved the scroll from imminent danger of being crooked with a tiny adjustment. "But the Bureau of Divination must send an *onmyōji* . My divination indicates I should send-" He paused dramatically and turned around. "Lady Masako."

Masako gasped in shock, forgetting her manners. "Lord Seimei, I will be an apprentice for years yet!"

He raised his bushy eyebrows in admonishment. "Do you think I don't know that? This is a marvelous opportunity to practice." He gazed at Masako affectionately. "You have a natural talent for this, but without my guidance, such talent would be wasted. Only *I* have the ability to fully develop your divination skills. I have taught several of my children and grandchildren, but none of them has come so far so quickly as you have." He paused while Masako murmured something humble and appreciative. "You know, my grandson Akichika is very fond of you."

"Yeah, we noticed," I interjected sarcastically.

"Instead of isolating yourself in a shrine, you should marry Akichika and work in the Abe Clan divination business. You might pass your talent and powers to my great-grandchildren." He stroked his pointy beard thoughtfully, his normally sharp eyes dreamy as he contemplated such a glorious outcome.

Masako, on the other hand, was distraught, clasping her hands tightly, trying to catch her breath. *"I don't want to marry Akichika! He's a friend, but I don't want to marry at all!"*

I needed to think this over. Would Seimei force Masako to marry his grandson the way he forced me to spy on the Empress? And then would I be forced to live with Akichika too? But surely he wouldn't want his grandson to marry a spirit-possessed woman. He'd send me home first.

Suddenly I felt more cheerful. *"Akichika is naïve and clumsy, but he's sweet, and he adores you. And you'd be adopted into the clan that basically owns divination and sorcery. You would-"*

What a load of ox-excrement. *"Forget I said that. Tell him you already dedicated your life to the kami. Can you even be a miko if you're married?"*

"Yes, but I can't be married and serve at an imperial shrine."

"I advised you to tell Akichika you aren't interested, but you never did. Now you have to. He needs to find someone else."

Seimei put his hands in the sleeves of his black cloak. "You don't need to respond now. We will wait until after the imperial birth. And to prepare you to attend this birth, I will lecture on the topic of childbirth. I have attended many royal and noble births," he said with a self-satisfied smile.

"*I guess that makes him an expert,*" I commented.

"*Will you please stop, Mi-Na? I need to hear this. It's a huge responsibility and I must learn my role.*"

Seimei gave Masako a suspicious glance before continuing. "A woman in labor exists on the border between the spirit world and our world, because the child is transitioning from one to the other. This makes her highly susceptible to spirit attacks. This vulnerability is magnified for the Empress, who, as Consort to our sacred Emperor, is already closer to the divine. The temple will supply two or three mediums for the birth. As my *onmyōji* representative, Lady Masako, you have many other duties. Most important is to act as an oracle for any messages from the great kami. Also, during active labor you will play dice against one of the other mediums."

"What? That seems a little insensitive."

"Gambling brings luck into the room, and luck helps with healing."

Seimei folded his arms and glared at Masako. He seemed to know we were talking behind his back. "When labor begins, you will make offerings to the kami of the household, the garden, the hearth, and the well. Ensure buckets of rice are placed around the birthing room. The ladies-in-waiting will throw the rice upon the Empress so you don't need to worry about that. You need to conduct purification to appease the kami, so be sure to have paper dolls with you in advance."

My head was spinning. "*So many instructions! How will you remember it all?*"

No paper, no notebook, no smartphone. She just memorized everything. And more than that, she incorporated it all. It became part of who she was, part of her identity.

"How do you placate the gods during childbirth in your world, Mi-Na?"

Hospitals, c-sections, epidurals... "Just with prayer, I guess."

Seimei glared at us again – both of us. He saw my aura or something. He smiled but not in a good way. More of an evil mastermind way.

"Masako, we will pause for a moment," he said. "Look into my eyes."

Seimei did this in most of our sessions. He'd hypnotize her so I could take control, and then he'd give me the third degree about the Empress's court. He never let Masako see this side of him. When she gave her bi-weekly report, he asked her about the Empress's health like he was actually concerned. But when I took control, he pressed me for information on what the Empress said, if she'd had news from Korechika, if I'd managed to steal any letters, and if the Emperor had said anything important to the Empress recently.

Masako did as instructed, but instead of sinking into a trance, she stayed awake, and I found myself falling into his eyes. I tried to climb back out, but I couldn't move. I was frozen. I tried to tell Masako what had happened, but was unable to speak.

"'Stay there, Spirit, until we are done," Seimei commanded.

Masako gasped and broke his gaze. "What happened to Mi-Na? I don't feel her presence!"

Seimei held his hand out, palm down. "A temporary holding place, as we did during your Kagura Dance. You might enjoy the respite from her constant clamoring for your attention. Now pay attention to *me*."

I struggled again to speak, but without success. I could see Seimei, and hear the two of them speaking, but I couldn't communicate. Masako didn't seem worried, though, and her focus actually improved.

Okay, Lord Seimei, you made your point. I won't interrupt her during lessons.

When the time came to leave, Seimei released me from his hold with a quick searching gaze into Masako's eyes.

Masako gave me a cheery *"welcome back!"*

She'd better not have enjoyed my silence too much.

The following week, Seimei trusted Masako's abilities enough to send her to the palace to get rid of some rats. Real ones, not political ones. Lord Yukinari, a senior controller, had seen rats in his quarters, and he asked Seimei to determine if their presence was a lucky or unlucky omen. Seimei had asked Masako to participate in the augury – she was really good at reading those shell cracks now – and together they decided rats were not a good omen.

Which I could have told them if they'd asked me. Because… rats?

She was required to speak with the Emperor before the rat-purification ritual, so when we reached the palace we were shown into a large inner room. After a few minutes a green-robed chamberlain slid the door open. "His Majesty is on his way." He stood back to allow a serving woman to enter with a tray of cups, a sake decanter, and what looked like an afternoon snack of little pink rice cakes.

"Ooh, for us? Why the royal treatment?"

"It's not *us*, it's *him*," Masako replied. "*His Majesty*," she added in case I didn't get it.

She was talking more like me. Another step toward full integration of mind, body, and two spirits.

We heard voices coming down the gallery. "Mother, I insist we wait until she is of proper age!" The Emperor raising his voice? He was usually so sweet and even-tempered.

His mother's voice was soft and cajoling. "You were ten years old when you married Sadako. She was like a sister to you, remember? You could be Akiko's elder brother for a few years. The important thing is to name her -" She stopped suddenly as the door was opened by the chamberlain. Masako knelt on a straw mat and bowed her head to the floor.

"Welcome, Imperial Medium. You may get up. Do you bring a message from the Royal Astrologer?" The Emperor's bright tone didn't match his furrowed eyebrows.

Masako stood up to see Emperor Ichijō standing with folded arms while his mother frowned next to him. "Lord Seimei asked this humble apprentice to conduct the purification ritual to overcome the bad omen of the rats in Lord Yukinari's quarters," she explained.

The Emperor waved his maroon sleeve in a gesture of acceptance, but his mother scowled. "Lord Seimei sends an apprentice to do his work?"

Masako bowed again, holding Seimei's note out with both hands. The Emperor's mother read it and handed it to Ichijō, who scanned it quickly and handed it back. "Lucky rats, unlucky rats. Cats can get rid of rats. Just get rid of the bad luck. I don't care who does it," he said with an irritated frown.

It didn't look like Masako was going to be invited to partake in the snacks, but she couldn't leave without express permission. The Emperor's mother glanced at Ichijō and then back at Masako, holding out her own note. "Take this to the Royal Astrologer."

Ichijō inhaled sharply. "Mother! You can't do this!" he said through gritted teeth. "She's too young!"

"She looks up to you. She adores you. She's beautiful,

educated, and even at eleven years old has a strong sense of decorum and modesty that is absent from Sada- eh, from other members of court."

"I don't understand why you are in such a hurry to bring Akiko to court."

His mother sighed and closed her eyes, wrinkles of worry cracking her white face paint.

Masako's face grew warm with embarrassment at having to observe this high-level domestic dispute, but I was fascinated. I'd known Akiko would someday become Ichijō's consort, but here was proof positive that the Emperor's mother was the power behind the throne.

She opened her eyes and gazed at her son with a soft smile. "Your kind and loving nature defends Sadako. You have other consorts. What's one more? It will make my brother happy to know that his daughter is taken care of, should anything happen to him."

Her loving tone did the trick. The Emperor's shoulders slumped. "If that's all it is, just another consort, then... let the Regent do what he wants. I can have only one Empress, though, and that's Sadako."

She turned to Masako. "Take this to Lord Seimei right away, and perform the purification ritual after that."

Masako bowed deeply as the other two moved past her to the table with the snacks, and sat down to continue their discussion on the Emperor's marital status.

Masako left the palace to head to the Bureau. I was just about to ask her to read the note when she unfolded it on her own initiative. Another one of my corrupting influences, no doubt.

"Oh no!" she gasped. "She's ordering Seimei to divine the most auspicious day and time to promote Akiko to Empress! That's impossible. There can only be one Empress." She stumbled, her head spinning.

My knowledge of how and when Akiko would become Empress was hazy and imperfect, but this seemed too soon. "We can't tell Her Majesty about this. The shock might cause a miscarriage."

We hurried into Seimei's office to hand him the note. He read it without any change to his expression. "Do you know what this note says?" he asked.

"Yes," my too-honest host replied. "The Imperial Lady wants you to determine an auspicious date for Michinaga's daughter Akiko to be installed as Empress. But-"

"You shouldn't have read it. You must swear to me that you will not share the contents of this note with Her Majesty." He accepted her vow with a reassuring nod. "Don't worry, Lady Masako. This is only a backup in the event that Her Majesty dies in childbirth."

Sadako was eight months pregnant, so in a strange way it made sense. If she died, Michinaga would want his daughter installed as Empress rather than one of the other consorts, all of whom were competing Fujiwara clan members.

I tried to remember what was going to happen next, but too much time had passed since my history and literature classes. But I was more than fifty percent sure she would have at least one more child. *"She'll be ok,"* I assured Masako. It was the best I could do. *"She won't die giving birth. I think."*

We couldn't tell Empress Sadako about Michinaga's plans for Akiko, but we did tell Sei. *"We promised not to tell Her Majesty, but telling Sei is not part of the promise, right? She needs to know so she can prepare the Empress when the news gets out,"* I said, certain Masako would argue with me on that point.

"Right!" she replied. Yep, she sounded more like me every day. Which was not a good omen.

Sei covered her mouth with a green silk sleeve at our news. "We all knew Michinaga would make Akiko a consort, but so soon? She's only eleven! But no one dares to speak against him. There have never been two Empresses at the same time, nor should there be. His Majesty argued with his mother, you say? He defends her, but no one else does. They treat her like a stray dog: beat it enough and it will go away."

A few days later, Empress Sadako woke in the night crying out for Masako, who'd been sleeping on the floor outside the Empress's chamber. She slipped into her room, lit by several lamps because the Empress had recently become afraid of the dark.

She was lying on her side, strands of black hair clinging to her damp cheeks. "Oh, Miko, I had such a terrible dream. I fear it is a bad omen. Will you interpret it for me?"

"Your Majesty, I will do my best."

"I dreamed His Majesty was calling for me. I searched, but it was all blackness. I could see nothing and no one. Then a fox appeared out of the darkness, looking at me hungrily. I was scared and tried to run, but my robes tangled around my legs. The fox leaped onto my train, tearing it with its teeth, snapping at my hair. The Emperor called out again. *Aga-kimi*, I'm coming!" The fox ran off, and I woke up. My heart is still pounding."

Masako hesitantly smoothed the Empress's hair. Sadako closed her eyes, and Masako pulled her hair back into the tie from which it had come unraveled.

"Miko, tell me what my dream foretells," Sadako murmured.

"*Mi-Na, it sounds very bad, ka wa? But it depends. If the fox is a kitsune spirit, it would seem to be a bad sign. And why would the spirit attack the Empress? But... the fox could be the Great Kami Inari, which would be a good omen.*"

"Remember what Seimei said? Maybe she's about to go into labor and is therefore more vulnerable to a spirit attack." After months of solid evidence, I had no choice but to believe in things like spirit attacks, bad omens, and kami interference.

"But what if it was a message from a divine spirit?" Masako remembered something from a recent lesson with Seimei. "Your Majesty, what color was the fox?"

"Black – a black fox." Sadako gasped, wrapping her arms around her belly. "Miko, my labor pains are beginning! Get Shonagon and Dainagon – they know what to do. Just tell me – is it a bad omen for this birth?"

"A fox is one of the messengers of the kami Inari, and if he appears as a black fox, it is an auspicious omen. A white fox would be inauspicious."

Sadako's smile at this good news was cut short by a yelp of pain. "Hurry! Get Shonagon!"

Masako gathered up her robe and long trousers with both hands and scurried through the residence to Shonagon's apartment, calling out as she entered, "Shonagon, the Empress's labor has begun!"

She stopped abruptly when she saw Lord Yukinari getting up from Shonagon's sleeping mat. Shonagon rose to her feet, pulling her robes closed and re-wrapping her belt. People here thought the human body was so ugly they didn't take their clothes off even for the most intimate of moments, but at least Shonagon was ready quickly.

Yukinari didn't seem a bit embarrassed by our intrusion. "Ladies, I will inform the Emperor's chamberlain that the Empress is in labor, gather the assigned courtiers, and return before the Hour of the Horse." He slipped out through the window and down the veranda steps.

Other women had heard us and were gathering around Sei,

who gave everyone instructions, then turned to Masako. "Medium, you and I will go to the Empress."

We walked back to the Empress's room. She was sitting up and looked better than she had in days. She even smiled when she saw us. "Shonagon, Lady Miko interpreted my dream as an auspicious omen."

"Your Majesty, that is wonderful news. It appears the Imperial Medium is a *yumetoki*."

Masako and Sei had become allies in their defense of the Empress, but Masako was, perhaps, a bit jealous of my connection to Sei, and she reacted defensively to what Sei had no doubt meant as a compliment. "*Yumetoki* only conduct dream interpretation," she said. "A miko must be able to receive messages from the gods, which might be sent in a dream. It is a very different and complex skill."

Sei and Sadako exchanged a laughing glance at Masako's injured pride, so unusual in my humble host. "Yes, Miko," said the Empress, "we know what a *yumetoki* is. Please share with Shonagon this message from the kami."

Masako's cheeks grew hot, but she powered through her embarrassment to describe her interpretation of the Empress's dream. Sei was just as pleased as the Empress, and handed Masako a piece of paper as a thank-you gift for her service. She had taken it from the folded bundle that all nobles wore inside their robes on which to write a spontaneous poem.

Empress Sadako labored the entire day. At mid-day, Sei received a note from Lord Yukinari. She grabbed Masako's sleeve and pulled her out of the birthing room and onto the veranda.

"This is terrible," she said in a loud and angry whisper. "Michinaga scheduled his daughter's Consort ceremony for today. The Emperor must attend because Akiko is to be named Royal Consort. Michinaga timed it this way deliberately!

Monkey Midwife

Somehow he knew the Empress would give birth at this time, and he scheduled his daughter's ceremony so that all eyes will be on his daughter rather than the imperial birth. How did he know to time it so? Do we have informants here giving updates on the Empress's health?"

It hit me with such a sickening force that Masako moaned and held her head. *"Masako! My reports! Seimei gave my information to Michinaga! It's my fault. But I didn't mean to—I had no idea he'd use it for that."*

Tears sprang to Masako's eyes. *"This is my fault too."*

Sei raised her black eyebrows even higher on her painted-white face. "Do you know who the informant is? Why are you crying?"

"Don't tell her, Masako. She'll make you leave, and you need to be here for the Empress, especially if everyone else is going to Akiko's ceremony."

"But if harm comes to the Empress, I don't deserve to be here." Her trickle of tears turned into a waterfall.

"Medium, pay attention!" Sei snapped. "If you know who the informant is, you must tell me so we can get him out of here. If you don't know, stop crying and help the Empress. She is in labor, so go to her room to keep evil spirits away!"

"See, Masako? If you don't perform your duties as a medium, the Empress could die in childbirth. So let's worry about this later."

We arrived at the Empress's room just as Lord Narimasa's men arrived. Shonagon and Masako went in first, helping the Empress off her dais and over to the bamboo screen that Masako usually sat behind. Lord Narimasa's men pushed the Empress's dais back, spread cloth over the floor, brought in a new dais—or rather, a short platform with mats and cushions—and put up white curtains around it. They placed plain straw mats lined with white silk at various places around the room, and took out old mats and furnishings.

We moved the Empress into her little white room and onto the platform, and then a stream of people began coming in and setting up. Two nuns in white veils went to the Empress, while two young women dressed in red hakama and white robes came over to Masako for instructions. One of them carried the dice. Masako waved toward one of the screens. "We'll play behind that one."

An elderly priest and his acolyte sat on one of the mats. Serving women brought buckets of rice which they set around the Empress's curtains. The Empress moaned, questioning plaintively why it had to hurt so much. The nuns knelt by her side, encouraging her to sit up and recite sutras with them.

Masako started playing dice with Natsu, one of the two mediums. Masako was playing to win. Maybe they both played to win. Somebody had to lose, but luck was in the room as long as somebody won.

The other medium, Aki, sat on her mat behind her own curtain. The exorcist sat in front of Aki's curtain and began chanting. A few nobles, including Korechika and Takaie, seated themselves south of the curtained birth-space, talking and praying out loud.

Just as I was thinking it couldn't get any noisier, I heard a loud twanging, one note that repeated itself over and over. *"Do you know what that noise is?"*

Masako paused, irritated. *"Mi-Na, you shouldn't speak to me while I'm playing unless you have a message from the kami. That noise comes from the archers, who twang their bows to scare away evil spirits during labor."*

Over the next several hours, the sounds of chanting, twanging, and the Empress's moans; the smell of incense, sweat, and smoke from lamps; the strangeness of these healing rituals of gambling, bow-twanging, sutra-reading; they all hit me with greater culture shock than any time since I arrived in this strange

Monkey Midwife

world. Masako gasped for breath, her hand shaking as she moved her backgammon pieces on the board. *"Mi-Na, suddenly I feel dizzy and sick. Are you doing this to me? Stop it!"*

"I can't! So many people, so much noise—is it all necessary? The baby will be scared to come out!"

"These protections are not only necessary, they are not nearly enough." She rolled her dice and won the game.

Natsu frowned. "Another game? I'll win this one, I'm sure!"

"I need to check on the Empress, and then I will return to win again."

She went around the screen. Sadako was seated on her dais, her head buried in Sei's arms. Sei was smoothing her hair and whispering a sutra. A nun in a white robe sat next to her, her kind, elderly face resting on a wrinkled hand in concerned contemplation. A bamboo knife lay on the mat near Sei.

"What is the knife for? A bizarre sacrifice of some sort?"

"It's to cut the cord after the baby is born, but it might be used to shave the Empress's head if it looks as though she won't survive and she must take vows."

Masako peeked around another screen to see three men holding slim bows made of a light brown wood, the bows a good foot taller than the men who held them. They were pulling their bow strings with great seriousness.

The youngest of the men dropped his hand and waggled his fingers. "This is my first time to twang the catalpa bow. How much longer do we need to do this?"

The other two laughed, and the oldest of the three gave an extra loud pull on his string. *Twang!* "It could take a full day or even longer. Or it could happen within this hour." *Twang!* "If Her Majesty can do this, you certainly can, young man." *Twang!*

The younger man stood straight and pulled harder on his string. Masako nodded in approval. *"This labor is taking a long time,"* she remarked. *"Lord Seimei said if it lasted more than twelve hours to placate the kami through incantations."*

She walked out to the veranda where the cold, clean air felt refreshing after the crowded, noisy, incensed-filled interior. The late afternoon winter sunlight brought warmth to the garden and turned the little pond blue. Masako didn't seem as upset as before, thank the kami. Who knew what trouble she might get up to in that mood.

Our serene moment was interrupted by a sound that started as a moan, transitioned to a wail, and ended with a long, agonized scream that made Masako's skin grow cold. I'd never been present during a birth. If that pain was normal, no way was I ever having children. And if it turned out I was stuck here forever, at least it was in the body of a woman who'd already decided to live a life of celibacy.

Masako hurried back inside. Sadako was writhing on her dais, her hair disheveled and her eyes moving rapidly back and forth. She moaned, her face pale and sweating, and her eyes closed. The nun rubbed her back and suggested it was time to get off the dais. Apparently that meant birth was imminent.

The Empress shifted uncomfortably, and the nuns helped her off the platform. And then she screamed in pain. Actually, more of a long, high-pitched howl of anguish and terror.

"Holy shit! We need to do something!" I didn't know what, but anything was better than nothing.

Masako's anger boiled up from the deep, dark place where she had smothered it." *Yes! I must make amends for our betrayal. There is evil here, and I will sweep it away."*

"Say what now?"

"Such pain can only be the result of evil spirits in the room. I must do something, Mi-Na. I am angry with myself, with you, and with Seimei. Our responsibility is to the Emperor and Empress's health.

Shikigami can rid the air of evil spirits, and Seimei said a good miko can control shikigami."

But she wasn't that good yet, at least, according to Seimei. Although he did assign her to be his sub as *onmyōji*, so maybe this could work.

Masako started the Kagura Dance. *Oh. That was her plan?*

The Empress opened her eyes, and in a moment of clarity, looked around at her few attendants, and through gaps in the curtains, at the nearly empty room. "Where is everyone?" she asked in a voice so soft and weak I barely heard it.

Everyone had colluded to keep Akiko's Royal Consort ceremony from the Empress out of fear it would affect Her Majesty's pregnancy. "Well?" She looked around in confusion. "Where is everyone? My birth pains started-" She inhaled sharply, squeezing her eyes but unable to suppress a quiet moan through her clenched teeth before continuing. "Mmmmmm....Hours ago. I expected more attendants by now."

Sei knelt at her dais. "Your Majesty, the Lord Regent scheduled his daughter's *nyōgo* ceremony for today, and required that all high-ranking nobles attend. And, as you know, His Majesty must attend. Your brothers are here."

Sadako shook her head. "No. No, His Majesty wouldn't allow that. Not now, not while his son is born." She looked around again, and her face crumpled with despair and defeat. "No. No!" and then she screamed as pain racked her body.

The nun lifted Sadako's covers and robes. Sei reached out to hold them so the nun could examine the Empress, who suddenly twisted and screamed again, her hands flailing outward, smacking both Sei and the nun in turn.

The nun looked up at Sei while moving her hands over Sadako's stomach. "The baby's in the wrong position, and it is not moving!" She pressed down as if to change the baby's position, but nothing happened other than making the Empress moan and cry.

Masako pulled a piece of washi paper from her sleeve and tossed it into the air, shouting "Shikigami, help us!" The paper spun around all by itself in the air, then fluttered towards the ground, but as it fell, it grew larger. And larger. And then a monkey was standing there with a big grin on its face.

Everyone gasped with fear or shock. I was thrilled, but judging from the expressions I could see from my position, I was in the minority.

"Dispel the evil spirits in this room and allow the Empress to give birth!" Masako commanded.

The monkey chittered with laughter, grabbed the mat from under the exorcist, and pulled it out from under him as he cried out in fear and confusion. The monkey looked to Masako for approval, which of course it didn't get, so it grabbed the exorcist and tossed him overhead in a somersault. The poor priest landed with a sickening thud. The monkey danced up and down, pointing to the poor man on the floor, laughing and nodding his head as if to say "See? I'm helping!"

The priest shouted at Masako but couldn't be heard over the screaming, which came from the frightened nun and Sei as well as the poor Empress in labor.

"You need to control it!" I shouted at Masako.

She ignored me, pointing again at the monkey and raising her voice. "You are under my command! Dispel the evil spirits in this room!"

The monkey responded by grabbing the low table where the other medium had been playing dice and throwing it across the room at the priest, who ducked just in time.

By now everyone was shouting at each other and at Masako. I tried again. *"Masako, remember what Seimei said! The Soul of*

Violence might control a shikigami if you're angry when you call it up. Get rid of it before it hurts the Empress."

"I- I don't know how! I only know how to create it! And it should be helping!"

The Empress screamed and clutched Sei as the monkey approached her.

"You're a medium! Get it to possess you so the priest can banish it!"

"But Mi-Na, it might kill you!"

That worried me too. "We don't have time to plan another option! Do it!"

"Mi-Na! No!" But she knew as well as I did that the sacrifice had to be made. The monkey had pulled the Empress's cover off and had whirled it around the nun, wrapping her up like a white cocoon, muffling her outraged screams. Shocking everyone (the monkey wasn't all that big, but then again, neither was the nun), it picked her up, ran to the bay, and threw her out. Good thing they didn't have two-story buildings here.

Masako shouted at the priest cowering in the corner. "I'm going to call this spirit into my body so you can banish it!"

She called to the shikigami. "Come to me, Spirit. I brought you here. I command you to enter me."

The monkey picked up the oil lamp and threw it onto a straw mat. Flames licked the straw, hungry for more, threatening to eat into the wooden floor. The other medium grabbed the mat by its edges and threw it out of the bay.

I hoped the nun managed to move out of the way.

We heard guards shouting outside the window, and then footsteps pounding as they ran into the residence.

"Come. To. Me!" Masako commanded, her desperation hidden under her forceful tone. The monkey laughed again, and looked around for something else to destroy.

"In the name of Abe no Seimei, come to me!"

That worked. The monkey looked at her in shock and disappeared.

Masako trembled. Her eyes rolled up into her head as a violently laughing presence filled her mind. I tried to shrink into a tiny part of her brain—*no one here but us mice*—but it found me.

"Another spirit! What fun!" it said, tugging at me. "*Play with me!*"

It batted me back and forth like a badminton birdie. Humiliating. Painful. Can a spirit get bruised? But I was neither dead nor pushed out. And I didn't sense malevolence. A violent sort of glee, a sociopathic lack of empathy, but not intentional malice. So that's what Seimei meant when he said the Soul of Violence would manipulate her if she brought anger into the Kagura Dance. This monkey was the physical manifestation of her anger at the Empress's pain and humiliation.

The priest chanted over Masako's head. The shikigami let go of me, listening, but not scared. Just curious, and not about to go anywhere.

Maybe I could possess this shikigami. A possession within a possession? What would that do to Masako? But I saw no other option.

"*I'll possess you,*" I said. "You won't like it. You better go now."

The Empress screamed in anguish again. Masako moaned, then collapsed to the floor, overcome by the two spirits arguing inside her. I took a deep mental breath, and leaped toward the shikigami's presence, willing myself to dive into its soul.

The force of my leap pushed me into the monkey-spirit, and we both fell out. Yep, right out of Masako with me in the monkey's body. The priest shouted at us, and the other medium screamed.

"Help the Empress!" I demanded. "Or I'll make you regret it. I'm the boss now!"

The monkey bounded back to the Empress's side. Sei flinched but didn't leave. Brave woman.

The monkey reached out and put its arms on the Empress's round belly. Sei screamed and batted at the monkey's paws, her hands wrapped in her sleeves for protection.

"Put your paws together and bow to show her you won't hurt the Empress!"

The shikigami did as I ordered, and Sei, her eyes wide with fear and wonder, sat back, but remained tense and ready to intervene if needed. The Empress, her eyes open but glazed, didn't react to the monkey's presence. The guards rushed in with swords up, but Sei lifted a hand to halt them from proceeding. The nun came in with them, unbound and apparently unhurt, and rushed over to the dais, ready to do battle with the monkey again. *What a warrior!*

Sei murmured a few words into her ear, and the nun clasped the Empress's limp hand, glaring at the monkey with hatred and distrust, but not yet taking action.

"Put your paws on the Empress's belly again, but slowly, don't startle her." I didn't sense a curse, but I could feel the baby lying crosswise. No wonder Sadako was in so much pain.

"Okay, Spirit-Helper, time to spirit-help. I command you to move the baby so it's pointing in the right direction!"

The monkey bobbed its head up and down with a screech, and then an electric fizzing bubbled outward from its paws like a freshly opened can of pop. The Empress's belly began to undulate, reminding me of the alien in a movie right before it burst out from someone's stomach. The shikigami was turning the baby!

Sei watched with horror and fascination, but not trying to stop us. She must have realized the shikigami was finally doing what it was brought here to do.

When the bubbling stopped, the monkey sent me an unspoken request to get the hell out of its body.

The monkey's magic paws gave me the sensitivity to feel the baby in the correct position. "Thanks, Monkey. You're the most helpful and destructive spirit-helper I've ever met. Now go away and leave us alone."

It radiated happiness at my praise, and a microsecond later it had turned back into a piece of paper which fluttered slowly to the floor, and I had slipped back into Masako's body.

Which was a huge relief. I could have ended up disembodied.

The priest bent over to make sure Masako was breathing, and announced to the room he had successfully exorcised the demon. As usual, no credit to me.

Masako staggered to her feet, and then sank to her knees, bowing her head. "I am so sorry, Your Majesty!"

No one paid attention to her. The baby was coming. Sadako stirred out of her semi-conscious state, opened her eyes, and shrieked in pain. She pushed with a last show of defiance, and the baby slid out.

The nun caught it, cleaned it off, smiled, and handed it to Sadako. "It's a prince!" she cried.

A great shout of triumph went up from everyone, while Sadako sobbed with relief and joy. Sei covered her face with her sleeves, laughing and crying at the same time. Sadako lay back, strands of damp hair clinging to her face, her eyes set in deeply within dark shadows, but her cracked lips curved in triumph. She had done it, the one thing that could save her place in history and fulfill her destiny.

The Empress gazed at the tiny baby in her arms. "Shonagon," she murmured without looking up, "find a way to let His Majesty know he has a prince."

Chapter 26

A Big Win

Twelfth Month, Chōhō 1 (January, 1000 CE)

"Your actions endangered us all. You could have killed him." Empress Sadako's sharp words didn't match her soft tone as she held her baby close, nuzzling the dark, downy fuzz on the top of his head. "I sent Lord Seimei a letter describing your actions."

Masako drew a sharp breath as shame flooded her cheeks with warmth. She bowed yet again from her kneeling position, her hands and head touching the straw mat in front of the dais. She had apologized not only to the Empress, but to everyone in the birth room at the time, especially the priest and the midwife-nun. "Your Majesty, I am a stupid apprentice," she said, her voice muffled by the mat. "I am deeply sorry."

Empress Sadako handed her baby to the wet-nurse with a last lingering touch, and turned back to Masako with a smile. "Perhaps even Lord Seimei did not understand the extent of your powers, and you saved my life as well as the life of the Emperor's first son. You will not be punished, but you must work harder to harness your power for the good of the Emperor and his family. I have asked Lord Seimei to tutor you an additional day every solar term." She dismissed us so that she could rest.

We went back to our room where Yumi was packing Masako's robes into a chest. The Empress had forbidden anyone from discussing the strange events surrounding her baby's birth, but rumors still spread. Yumi knew something strange had happened, and that it was Masako's doing.

She huffed as she pushed down to squeeze one last robe into the chest. "Will we go to your uncle's house? Or will we be-" she swallowed. "Will we be sent to your father's post in the north?"

I could feel Masako's relief and excitement humming through her veins. "We will stay with the Empress. She will not punish me. In fact, she will allow me additional learning from Lord Seimei! Yumi, Her Majesty is so understanding and kind. I do not deserve such consideration."

Yumi sat on the chest and heaved a great sigh of relief.

I felt the same way. *"Masako, your magic show could have turned out badly, but it didn't because you and I make a great team. Maybe that is why Ji and Seimei kept telling us we need each other. You conjured the shikigami, and I possessed it to force it to do the right thing!"*

Masako laughed through her tears. *"But Mi-Na, what will I do when you leave me? Unless you want to stay with me forever?"*

"You know that wouldn't be good for either of us. What if I become the dominant spirit?"

"You have told me I am bosu-i, so surely I would be dominant."

"I said you were bossy compared to what I expected a young lady in the tenth century to be. Although we're on the cusp of the eleventh century. Holy kami, it's Y1K! Look out, world!"

She laughed, but I knew she had no clue what I meant.

And neither did I. I was rambling because my emotions were so mixed up right now. This working so well with someone I actually liked was new for me. And we did magic together. How cool was that?

No wonder I was confused.

Sei Shonagon had been acting cool to Masako ever since the prince's birth.

"Masako, I think Sei suspects we gave the information to Seimei that allowed Michinaga to schedule his daughter's event while the Empress was in labor. I'm the one responsible, and I want to make it right with her. Would you let me take control to meet with her?"

"I do not object, Mi-Na, but Shonagon might." Masako went to her writing table and riffled through her paper to find the nicest. She held up a sheet of soft pink paper. "You know Sei won't respond to anything written on low-quality paper. This will get her attention."

Her paper choice worked. Sei sent a message back with instructions for me to meet her in an empty eave-chamber at the Hour of the Monkey, which was late afternoon. We arrived a few minutes early so Masako could put herself into a trance before Sei arrived. The shutters were raised, and occasional gusts of wind blew flurries of snow past the low eaves, but Masako's robes were padded with silk floss and as warm as down.

I hadn't taken control since the time I won the bet, so the first thing I did was stand up, raise my arms way up high, and stretch over to one side and then the other. Sometimes the sensation of being trapped led to a ghost-cramp in my ghost limbs.

Sei walked in just as I brought my hands down. "Is it you, Spirit? What magic is this?"

"A kind of magic called yo-ga. It helps with circulation. I mean, with feeling refreshed."

"I would try it, but I've had enough refreshment. Why have you asked to meet with me?"

"Sei, I know you think Masako spied on the Empress for Seimei, but it wasn't her. It was me. I take full responsibility. Seimei is working with Michinaga—for some reason, he doesn't want Korechika to become Regent—and he threatened me with terrible retribution if I didn't cooperate. Please, please forgive me, and even if you can't, don't punish Masako for what I did. Seimei used magic to keep Masako from knowing about it. Masako and I saved the Empress's life, and probably the baby's too. Sei, the Empress has few attendants left, and even fewer friends. Masako is loyal to His and Her Majesty, and as you saw, she-"

I lost track of what I was going to say next. Sei's dark eyes were focused on me, her head tilted to one side. Her loose, silky hair slid across her red lips. She murmured a soft "eh" with each point I made. Being the subject of such intense listening was, to be honest, somewhat unnerving. Back home, when I'd hang out with other girls, we'd talk while scrolling on our phones the entire time. We never gave anyone our undivided attention.

"Um... where was I? Masako has raw talent. She needs practice and better judgment, but she'll be a powerful force for good someday. Calling up a shikigami as an apprentice is impressive, right?"

Sei tapped her fan against her chin for a few seconds after I finished. "It was a terrifying event. You are both fortunate it ended well. You tell me the Medium is loyal. What else can the two of you do to protect Her Majesty? Can you gather information about Lord Michinaga? Perhaps through Lord Seimei?"

Seimei wasn't going to tell us anything the Empress could use against the Regent. We'd have to find it ourselves. "We can dig up some dirt on the Regent, I'm sure of it," I said.

A Big Win

"Ha! Will you bury the Lord Regent in the garden? That would certainly help our situation. You amuse me, Spirit. You are correct. Her Majesty needs allies now more than ever. Mi-Na, I have a…" She hesitated, uncharacteristically shy. "I have a request for you." She took a sheaf of papers from the usual paper-storage location where the inner robes fold over the breast. "I have a new entry in my book, a protest against the humiliations the Lord Regent inflicts on Her Majesty. You know me well, Spirit, so you will understand that I can not sit and watch silently while he treats her like a dog. Would you read it and tell me your thoughts?"

I took the bundle of soft, white paper with shaking hands. I wanted to squeal with delight, but I restrained myself. As I glanced at the first sentence, I remembered the story from *The Pillow Book*. The Emperor gave his favorite cat a promotion to Fifth Rank; a palace dog barked at the cat, which violated rules of rank, so palace servants beat the dog and sent it away; how it came back and was beaten again, and they thought it was dead, but one day it came back, and only Sei recognized it.

The story was both funny and sad, and when I first read it, I had thought it was a commentary on rank. Now I knew better. The story was Sei's revenge.

"Yes!" In my excitement, my voice squeaked like an air balloon with a leak. "Yes, Sei, of course."

Michinaga sent for Masako the next day. Puzzled, we waited in his government office at the appointed hour. Masako practiced deep breathing to control her anger. Neither of us wanted Michinaga to know what chaos her rage had caused. He'd love it. Revel in it. *"We're not going to give him that satisfaction, are we, Masako?"*

"'It will help if I keep my eyes down, which is good manners anyway.'"

Michinaga walked in, his broad shoulders cloaked in purple-black silk, his hair pulled up in its usual top-knot tucked into the usual black hat. He waved Masako to a silk-lined straw mat. He sat cross-legged with a hand on each knee, his back straight so that he looked down at Masako, his eyelids half-lowered and his mouth pursed as if Masako were a puzzle he was close to solving, but not quite there yet. Masako sat *tatehiza*-style, one knee bent and raised, the other leg folded under her. She spread her robes out for maximum coverage over her cold feet, keeping her fan raised to cover her face, and her hair pooled on the mat beside her.

He stared at her in silence for several minutes without speaking. She kept her eyes on his belt to avoid meeting his gaze.

He cleared his throat. "Imperial Medium, I heard interesting rumors about the birth of the prince, very interesting indeed. A monkey-spirit caused havoc and chaos in the birthing room? *You* conjured up this magic?"

Masako bowed. "I beg forgiveness for putting Her Majesty and Prince Atsuyasu in danger. I am a stupid apprentice who over-reached."

He nodded in agreement. "Her Majesty was upset with you, and rightly so, but Seimei will teach you to control and manage your power." He paused while lifting his gaze to examine a sutra scroll hanging on the wall. Masako breathed a sigh of relief. He snapped his focus back to us. "In spite of having Akiko enter the palace as Royal Consort from the most auspicious direction and day, she has become ill."

"*He picked a very bad-omen kind of day, in my opinion. She didn't deserve to get sick, but it's her father's fault.*"

"Lady Masako, you and your Spirit Mi-Na have angered me on several occasions. You remain in the capital on my sufferance.

A Big Win

Lord Seimei wishes it, and your presence has served our purposes. Now you must do something for me."

"Sounds ominous," I remarked.

"Hush, Mi-Na! We must listen carefully."

He leaned forward. "I will request you, Imperial Medium, to attend my daughter's exorcism."

"Only the best medium for the Lord Regent. Your reputation is made, Masako!"

"Really, Mi-Na, stop interrupting!"

"The Empress is jealous and upset that my daughter's consort ceremony occurred during her labor. I believe her jealousy has caused her living spirit to possess Akiko, and is making her ill. The priest will call the malevolent spirit out of my daughter and into you. When he asks the spirit its name, you will say you are Her Majesty's *ikiryō*."

Masako gasped. "You ask me to be a false medium?"

He stood up in one quick motion, and grabbed her arm to pull her to stand as well. He towered over her short figure, standing so close that Masako steeled herself not to flinch. The fragrance of clove and sandalwood emanating from his incense-smoked robe didn't quite cover a musky male scent that made Masako's stomach roil, but made *me* want to move closer. And I hated myself for feeling that way about this jerk.

He spoke in a low, firm tone. "Not false. Simply making the truth visible to all. Everyone believes you are powerful after your recent display, and they will believe you. Do this and your future is assured. Refuse and your future is most... uncertain."

A cold sweat made her clasped hands slippery. *"I do not believe Her Majesty would do such a thing!"*

I had to think fast. *"Neither do I. Maybe I'll recognize whatever illness Akiko has, and can give advice that will help her get well. I'm sure he'd rather she got better than blame the Empress for her illness."*

Masako didn't have a better plan, so she agreed. "I will

attend Lady Akiko's exorcism," she said, and in a subtle act of defiance, stopped her bow a fraction short of what his rank required.

Strands of her long hair slipped out of her white hair tie as she paused mid-bow, waiting for dismissal. She suppressed a shudder as Michinaga reached out to push her hair away from her face.

"Well, then," he murmured. "I will send for you tomorrow." He caressed a length of her hair with his long fingers, then twisted her hair around his hand and jerked down, forcing Masako to bow deeper, the sharp pain bringing tears to her eyes as she gasped, while I gasped right along with her. "Make her well," he said.

Masako paced back and forth in Akiko's outer room while I tried to hide my lack of confidence. What if Akiko had an illness I didn't recognize?

"Masako, instead of wearing a groove into the floor, why don't we take a look at all these beautiful things?" I didn't know why it was taking so long to get an escort to the sick room, but it would be a terrible waste not to use our time to snoop around.

She stopped to gaze at a bronze statue of a monk with an anxious expression. Masako and I occupied ourselves by imagining what kind of news he'd just received.

"He got laid off. The monastery's downsizing," I speculated.

"He just learned he's been invaded by a spirit from the future," she said, all innocent.

"Is snark contagious? 'Cuz I'm clearly passing it on to you."

Masako moved over to a black lacquered table and ran her hand over its inlaid mother-of-pearl flower. She picked up a writing brush lying there, touching its soft end, admiring the heft of its perfectly balanced red cherry handle. She marveled at the gold filigree running along wood frames of portable green and yellow silk curtains. No expense had been spared to make this a place one wanted to linger.

"This is bad," I said while Masako leafed through a book of poetry. "Very bad for Her Majesty. Korechika won't be able to obtain this level of art for her rooms. He doesn't have enough clout. I bet Michinaga designed this to appeal to His Majesty so he will spend more time here than with Sadako."

"No more betting. I didn't like losing last time," she said. "Look at this! Lord Yukinari's calligraphy!"

"We share one pair of eyes between us, remember? I have no choice but to look at it." I admired how Yukinari's penmanship flowed down the page like water down a wall. An ink illustration of a nobleman sitting under a pine tree illustrated the poem on the opposite page.

"I believe these illustrations were painted by His Majesty's favorite artist, Hirotaka of the Kose Clan. His Majesty will truly enjoy this." She set it down with exaggerated restraint, her hands shaking with her desire to throw it against the wall.

That bastard Michinaga. How dare he make this room so beautiful and interesting? The Emperor had a great love for art and culture. The Regent obviously knew this, and was leveraging that knowledge to keep the Emperor here rather than spending time and energy on Empress Sadako.

Next we examined a set of two light brown wooden screens, each with six painted panels. Masako explained how the paintings illustrated the four seasons. "*Winter is represented by this evergreen, and spring by the plum tree in blossom,*" she explained. "*This ship at sea is summer, and the rising moon is autumn.*"

We'd heard from Sei that Michinaga had personally requested famous poets to write a poem about each of these paintings, and in an unorthodox approach, asked high-ranking nobles to contribute a poem as well. Some courtiers were flattered and some were too intimidated to refuse, but by participating in this event, they were accessories after the fact, and had no right to complain about this violation of protocol. The sumptuous nature of the gifts—like the screens and the attending poems—were more appropriate for an imperial princess than a nobleman's daughter, but it meant it was all anyone talked about for days, and so the birth of the Emperor's first son had been ignored. Which was undoubtedly Michinaga's goal.

But why? He already held all the cards. Why break Sadako's heart? Giving birth to the Emperor's son was her primary purpose in life, and she deserved the attention and celebration that normally attended a royal birth.

We were finally escorted to Akiko's room. The usual medical staff—a priest, two mediums, several ladies-in-waiting—looked up hopefully as we walked in, and the priest waved his censer to get Masako's attention. "Imperial Medium, we have been waiting for you to begin. The Lord Regent said your presence is required for this exorcism."

Masako bowed to the priest and explained that we needed to examine the Junior Consort. Akiko was lying on her side on a dais, her eyes closed, her small body almost lost within blue silk robes.

"Can you put your hand on her forehead for me?" I asked Masako. "*I want to know if she's hot.*"

Masako hesitated with her hand halfway out. "Lady Akiko, may I touch your forehead? It is part of my unique ritual."

Akiko opened her eyes. "Imperial Medium? My head hurts, and I'm very tired. Am I possessed? Yes, you may touch my forehead." Her voice was high, as an eleven-year old girl's voice would be, but remarkably calm.

Masako gently placed her hand on Akiko's forehead. No fever. Akiko had gone through a lot lately, probably under a lot of stress with the rituals and ceremonies of becoming an official consort, and having to behave perfectly for the past week.

"Masako, ask her if she has been drinking sufficient amounts of water."

Masako conveyed my question, and Akiko opened her eyes. "Your hand is so cool and soft, it makes me feel better already. Water? Some. I've been very busy – the ceremony, the Emperor." Her eyes brightened. "Oh, His Majesty is so clever and kind. He played his flute for me, and told me a story from the *Kojiki*. I asked him many questions, and he knew *all* the answers." She concentrated, her barely visible shaved eyebrows pulling together, her small pink mouth making a little "o" shape. "I drank sake, rather a lot. Does that count?"

"Uh, no, it does not. Tell her to drink more water, and to rest. But tell her to stay away from sake for a while."

"She's the Emperor's junior consort and Michinaga's daughter. She outranks me." But Masako did her best, couching my advice in more polite terms. Akiko listened carefully while playing with Masako's white robe sleeve.

"I will do as you say, Imperial Medium. Why do you wear white? Aren't you going to conduct an exorcism? Am I not possessed after all? I don't feel possessed, just tired. And thirsty. Yayoi, get me a cup of water! Imperial Medium, I will tell my father you made me feel much better. He will give you a robe for your service. Priest, you may leave now. I'm sure Father will give you a robe too, for waiting." She took a sip of water, lay back down, and closed her eyes.

The priest had watched the interaction with great interest, and as Masako walked away from the dais, he walked to the door with her. "Imperial Medium, how did you banish the spirit without the exorcism? This putting of hands on the patient's forehead—is it a new method to banish spirits?"

"He's looking for some on-the-job training."

His eyes lit up with possibilities. "Did you silently chant a sutra? Or was it a new practice of *onmyōdo*? Or perhaps you have a special power. Yes, yes, that must be it. Other mediums do not have such ability. Or do they?"

Between the priest's flow of questions and my silent commentary, Masako couldn't get a word in, so she just bowed. He laughed and bowed back, the portion of his shaved head visible under his hat gleaming as a random ray of weak sunlight found its way in through the blinds.

I mentally crossed my fingers for luck that the Regent would view this as a big win.

Chapter 27

Three Worms Night

Twelfth Month, Chōhō 1 (January, 1000 CE)

Korechika announced a poetry contest, to be held on Three Worms Night, to celebrate Prince Atsuyasu's birth. His mood had improved with the arrival of this blessing from the kami to his sister.

Masako explained what Three Worms Night meant. Every sixty days, apparently, three worm spirits that live in our bodies, called the Sanshi, go to heaven to report on us while we sleep. Any bad deeds that got reported meant days taken away from life. Most folks here seemed to think they had a number of bad deeds, because the goal was to stay awake all night so the worms couldn't leave to make their report, which is why the competition was an all-nighter.

Dainagon informed Masako she would not be invited to participate. "You have no social standing here, Medium," she said as we all sat in our common room sewing robes for the contest, "and I don't want your provincial upbringing to ruin the *miyabi* we will bring to this event." She allowed her eyes to rest on Masako's plain white robe, and then turned back to sewing the red garment in her hands with a little laugh and a quick shake of her head.

Miyabi was a special kind of elegance and refinement that could only be achieved by people who didn't need to work full-time. *"Burn!"* I teased Masako.

"What? Is something on fire?" Masako looked around the room in alarm, and her strange behavior caused Dainagon and Chunagon to exchange smirks.

Sei had overheard Dainagon's comment. "First of all, Lady Dainagon, she is the Imperial Medium, and Her Majesty will expect her to attend. And second, how dare you speak for the Empress!"

Dainagon bowed from her seated position and apologized elaborately, and Masako gave a slight bow back, heroically restraining her own smug smile.

"Sei defended you, Masako! And this after our success with Akiko!" Our "cure" for the young consort had been a triumph, another example of the power Masako and I had when we worked together. Perhaps the Regent was disappointed that he couldn't blame Empress Sadako, but as I'd suspected, Akiko's health was his highest priority, and Masako's reputation as a healer had grown. Maybe that made Dainagon even more jealous that "Lady Ox" was getting all the attention.

Later that afternoon we attended Her Majesty behind our usual screen. Masako mended one of her white robes while the Empress worked on sewing her own red robe for the poetry competition. Even an Empress had to do some sewing in this world.

Korechika entered with quick steps, brushing aside the serving woman who wanted to announce him. He pulled a yellow scroll out of his violet sleeve. "Do you have your team names? Here's my list," he said, holding out the paper.

"Eldest Brother, you are so excited about this competition

you forgot to bow!" the Empress said sternly, but then laughed, spoiling the effect.

He laughed like a little boy who knew he got away with something. "It will be so elegant and erudite. You know how His Majesty enjoys poetry and music, and we shall have both! He will favor us even more. Please don't tell me you have any of his other consorts on your team. That would ruin my plan."

Sadako stopped smiling. "Brother, I truly thought you had just one goal: to entertain His Majesty. Now you tell me this is one of your strategies."

He bowed his head and put his palms together in supplication. "Your Majesty, forgive me. I only seek to protect my little sister. It will be great fun, I promise. Now, let me see your roster!"

It was to be a 'boys vs. girls' competition, with the Empress and her women on the Right Team, and Korechika and his selection of high-ranking courtiers on the Left Team. The Emperor was an observer, and the judge was Lord Sanesuke, a high-ranking noble with a reputation for scrupulous honesty. Sadako handed him her scroll, which he unrolled and scanned before handing it back.

"Your Majesty, you've included the Imperial Medium on your team. Isn't she rather coarse for such an event? I understand if you want her to observe, but on your team? Really?"

She sighed with that special kind of exasperation siblings reserve for each other. "She's good enough to sit in *my* room every day, and yet she's not exalted enough for *your* competition? I won't allow you to disqualify her. She's stuck here with me, day after day, sitting over there," pointing to the screen, "getting cold and bored. So I want to do this for her."

Tears formed in Masako's eyes. *"Mi-Na, she is so kind."*

It occurred to me how far we'd come, from being viewed with suspicion and fear in our first days at court to open displays of respect and affection by Sei, the Empress, and even Seimei. Even Michinaga's attempt at exploiting Masako's growing reputation had resulted in a success.

"All the women at court have noticed Her Majesty's fondness for you, Masako. It hasn't helped your position with them, but we don't care what they think. They don't matter. Only the Empress matters." I'd become just as touched by Sadako's thoughtfulness as Masako, and it was agony to think that I'd betrayed her. I needed to make up for that, somehow.

But right now I was excited to witness my first true poetry competition. *"How do they decide the winner? What are the rules? What happens if someone takes a nap? Would the worms leave on such short notice?"*

"I do not know. Please stop asking so many questions." Body-sharing was difficult for her, too, sometimes, so I shut up.

The event took place in a large hall outside the Empress's quarters. The Empress's team sat on the right side behind silk curtains rolled up just enough to show off their red and white layered robes, but not enough to show their faces. The men, seated on the left side of the hall and visible to everyone, wore green and white layers over white pantaloons. The Emperor sat on a stool against the wall between the two groups, impressive in his stiff brocade cloak of embroidered bronze. Courtier-musicians were placed at the other end to provide court music with koto, biwa, and flutes. Male observers sat on the left veranda, and female observers sat on our veranda wearing many layers of robes and trains to keep out the chilly night breeze.

The poems were written in advance for this event by famous poets. A reader for each team would read a poem, and the judge would decide the winner.

Which was way more fun than it sounded. "Each round, all members of the losing team will drink a cup of sake," Korechika announced.

The women gasped with excitement, and the Empress laughed. "Then we have to ensure we win every round, else we shall become intoxicated, and that will never do!"

We watched through slats in the blinds as the *suhama* were carried in by four girl 'tweens for our team, and by four young men for the Left. We had spent hours making the artificial landscape that represented our poems, and I had to admit ours was a winner, with twigs made to look like trees, tiny brown paper leaves scattered on a polished metal pond, and little folded paper ducks.

The Empress requested Sei to be our reader, which was a bit shocking. Women didn't usually read poetry out loud to men.

Fittingly, Lord Yukinari read for the Left.

We lost the first round, so a serving woman brought cups of sake. "Drink it all," Korechika called out. "It must be completely drunk to the bottom of the cup!"

The sake was lighter in flavor and strength than I remembered from my Tsukuba days, but it went right to Masako's head. "*I hope we don't lose any more,*" she said.

Both teams lost about the same number of rounds, so the volume shifted from normal to loud as more sake was consumed. Masako moved restlessly, at one point knocking over her sake cup, empty at the time, fortunately. "Go, Right Team!" she shouted, shocking me with the unexpected disappearance of her normal reserve. The other women took up her chant. "Go, Right! Go Right!"

The men couldn't let that go without responding, so they started chanting "Left is best! Left is best!"

We won the next-to-last round and the women cheered. "Fill their cups! Fill their cups!"

"Yes, please! Fill it up!" Lord Yukinari shouted, holding his high for a courtier to fill it. The Left team raised their cups together and with a great "Kampai!" tipped the clear drink into their waiting mouths. It was like a frat party, only with poetry instead of bouncing plastic balls.

Sei and Yukinari read their final poems. Sei's voice shook with excitement and nervousness behind her screen. Yukinari recited with exaggerated care, gesturing extravagantly, his green sleeves like semaphores signaling self-satisfaction. If showmanship was a factor in judging, the Left Team should win.

But Sanesuke had trouble deciding the final winner, looking indecisively right and left. "Both poems are so moving," he said, struggling to conceal his laughter. "My sleeve is wet with tears!" and with a great pretend-sob he lifted his orange sleeve over his eyes. The Emperor laughed so much that real tears streamed down his cheeks.

Sadako looked at her women with excitement. "Chant the poem all together! Sei, you too! Over and over. We'll win for our enthusiasm!"

She lifted her voice. "The wild ducks remain-"

The other women joined in with "on the frozen pond so still!" but were laughing too hard to finish, so they had to start again, and then together they all shouted the last line as loudly as they could: "YET NO FROZEN HEART HAVE I!"

The men didn't want to be outdone, so they shouted their poem in unison too. "Love torments me EVEN NOW!"

Sanesuke put his hands over his ears and looked at the Emperor for help. Ichijō tried to stop laughing but couldn't, so he slid his eyes to our side, then back at Sanesuke.

Sanesuke tipped his head in acknowledgement. "The winner of the final poem is-" He paused dramatically. "The Right Team!"

The women cheered and laughed. Servants and chamberlains brought little tables loaded with refreshments such as soft mounds of rice, grilled sea bream, sweet potatoes, and nuts. Although a little dizzy from the sake, Masako ate with gusto. I'd

Three Worms Night

enjoyed tasting the rice wine, but I wasn't a fan of how it made us feel. The food was good, but it would have helped to lay a base with it earlier.

The evening continued with music, dance demonstrations, and singing.

An odd incident toward the end of the night changed the mood, though. It was Dainagon's doing. The Empress had left with the Emperor. Yukinari casually sauntered out of the room as if it was just a coincidence that Sei had slipped away seconds before.

Dainagon sat in a small circle of women behind the screen, not caring enough about the dancing to watch. She leaned forward with a look of anticipation on her long face, her painted pink lips creating an eerie contrast with her blackened teeth. "Ladies, did you hear the latest rumor about the Regent?"

Chunagon smoothed her wispy side bangs. "Perhaps. But you tell us and then I'll tell you if I knew it."

"I just heard this yesterday from Lord- well, perhaps I should not say."

The women begged her to share both the rumor and the monger.

"Well, I won't say from whom I received this information, but I will tell you it's about the prince."

A rainbow of colorful fans fluttered as the women gasped a chorus of "The imperial baby? Eh? Tell us! Do tell!"

Dainagon spoke from behind her fan and whispered so softly the other women all leaned forward to hear. "I heard that the Lord Regent will never allow the prince to be named Crown Prince."

An awkward silence fell. Even Chunagon looked away as if unwilling to give credence to the rumor. Dainagon raised her real eyebrows, sending the painted ones even higher on her forehead. "We must remain loyal to Her Majesty no matter what may happen, but I have heard that-" she looked around as if to confirm no one was listening, "Sei Shonagon has been working hard to get in favor with the Lord Regent."

Kohyōe gave a violent start, causing her hair to fall out of her loose tie and into her eyes. She used her fan to brush it away, but it fell right back. "Dainagon, really?"

I was appalled. *"Are these women trying to ruin Sei's reputation so the Empress doesn't trust her?"*

"Why would they spread such rumors if they were not true?"

"Dainagon might be preparing to leave Sadako's court, and using Sei as a red herring-"

"But such fish are not red, Mi-Na-"

"Sorry, I was just about to rephrase that. Dainagon might be accusing Sei of the very thing Dainagon is doing, so people don't notice what she's up to. Politicians have been doing that quite a lot in my country lately, so I know it when I see it."

"Oh, no, Mi-Na. Perhaps Dainagon is envious of Shonagon's intimacy with Her Majesty."

That could be true. But I doubted it.

Chapter 28

Snow Melt

Twelfth Month, Chōhō 1 to First Month, Chōhō 2 (February, 1000 CE)

The weather turned cold, and even ten or twelve layers of robes couldn't fend off the chill. Masako's bedside cup of water froze overnight while we slept under five robes and wearing four layers. Everyone gathered around braziers trying to keep warm. Except Masako. The other women formed a phalanx around the brazier so she couldn't get close enough. They didn't blame her for the Empress's difficulties, but they were envious of the amount of time she had with her. And it didn't help that Masako sat by herself for long periods of time, and would frown, smile, roll her eyes, tilt her head, and occasionally wave her hands or laugh out loud as she conversed with me. Kohyōe would shiver and run away when she saw that, and Dainagon told everyone to avoid the creepy medium.

Ironically, such behavior would be perfectly acceptable in 2019. Everyone would assume she was talking on her phone.

Sei caught a cold, making her miserable and unhappy for several days. I advised her, through Masako, to stay in her apartment for a few days to prevent passing her cold to anyone else. "Not to mention inflicting her bad mood on us."

Sei lashed out at Masako. "You've seen spirits, but you've not banished a single one! What use are you?"

Masako defended herself. "I am Her Majesty's Imperial Medium, and what's more, Her Majesty has not become ill since I've been here."

The Empress intervened, gently telling Sei she had better follow Masako's advice. Sei glared at Masako as she fled to her room.

Later that afternoon, Sadako asked Masako to play a poetry game with her. "I will say the first line of a poem from the *Kokin Wakashu* collection, and you must complete it accurately to receive one point. For every poem you are not able to complete, I receive one point. And you mustn't allow Mi-Na to help you. That would be cheating!" she said with a soft laugh.

"*As if,*" I said, because I knew very little poetry, while Masako had memorized hundreds of poems before she hosted me.

She gave up very few points to the Empress, and as a prize, the Empress gave her a white silk robe embroidered with white thread.

Masako ran her hands over the cloth, admiring its softness. "It's beautiful! Thank you, Your Majesty."

Empress Sadako gave her a radiant smile. "I wanted you to have something a little nicer than that hemp robe. It will keep you warmer now winter is fully upon us."

Thick, heavy snow started to fall that night, and kept falling all day and into the following night. Blinds were rolled down to keep out snow and wind and keep in the brazier's warmth. The

Empress plucked on her biwa listlessly. When the nurses brought Princess Nagako and sweet little Prince Atsuyasu over to say good night, the Empress handed the biwa to Masako with a murmured command to keep playing. The princess was three years old now, so lively and happy she brightened any dark room she was in, and correspondingly, the room—and the mood—grew even darker after we said our goodnights and the nurse took her off to bed.

Lord Korenaka had resigned from his post as Master of the Empress's Household. He tried to get Masako to leave, implying once again that the Empress's household was a sinking ship, and passing along the same rumor that Dainagon had floated that Atsuyasu would never be Crown Prince. He pointed out that Michinaga gave the Hitachi Vice-Governor post to one of his loyal noblemen, and assigned Masako's father as vice-governor of a province in the distant north. "He punishes disloyalty," Korenaka said. "And serving Empress Sadako is dis-" He stopped and glanced around. "You understand?"

Masako hesitated, but her loyalty to the Empress was stronger than her fear for her father's safety. She made it clear to Lord Korenaka that Seimei would not be happy if she left the Empress's court, so he relented. No one wanted to antagonize the Royal Astrologer.

The Empress had not yet moved back in with the Emperor even though she had undergone all the appropriate purification rituals after the prince's birth. Whispers floated through court that she would renounce the world and become a nun. Other whispers spread that the child was not the Emperor's.

If I knew who spread that fake news I'd have punched their lights out. After asking Masako for permission to use her fist, of course.

Sei tried to cheer the Empress by reading entries from her book. "I am still upset with Lord Korenaka for abandoning the Empress, but I can't make fun of him without serious consequences, so I made fun of his brother instead."

She read us her description of an incident that occurred the day the Empress moved into Narimasa's residence. Sei had teased Narimasa about his gate not being big enough to allow our carriage through. As usual, she had made her barbs clever and witty. Some men don't like it when women show how much smarter they are, but Narimasa was one of those who thought it was hot. He went to Sei's room late that night asking her for "suggestions about improving the gate." She had laughed him out of there, and now everyone would read about what an idiot he was.

We stayed up all night listening to Sei read, and now daylight, made brighter by thick snow outside, lit up the dark room. We heard maids sweeping snow off the veranda.

Sei went over to the window and rolled up the blinds. "Look, little snow mountains!" she exclaimed. "We should push these together and make a real mountain!"

Masako and the Empress rushed over to the window. The Empress's smile, so rare these days, matched the sunlit snow for its brilliance as she called out to the maids. "Gather all of these little snow piles and put them together. And tell the serving men to help too! All the snow, all of it!"

The maids, infected by their Empress's excitement, chattered to each other happily as they used brooms to sweep the powdery snow towards one location.

The Empress clapped her hands together. "We need more snow! Tell the other servants to come quickly. All those who help build the mountain will receive an extra three days pay!" The servants gasped in surprise, and several women ran off to tell the others about this unexpected bonus. The Empress laughed somewhat wildly and called out again. "And tell those who don't come they won't get paid at all!"

"What about those poor folks who live too far away to get the message in time? No pay for the day?"

"She's the Empress, and look, Mi-Na, she's so excited. I haven't seen her look this happy since our first months here."

Twenty or so servants were eventually recruited. They laughed and threw snow at each other, their cheeks and noses reddening in the cold. The bustling of activity – the sweeping, the moving of snow, the men calling out to each other as they lifted and pushed – drew the attention of other nobles, who came over to see what the commotion was all about and stayed to watch the fun.

The mountain was deemed complete when the top reached the height of the roof. The Empress admired the result from her vantage point at the window. "How long do you think it will be there?"

"Five days, Your Majesty, at the most," Chunagon said.

Dainagon guessed three days, and Kohyōe guessed ten. Masako said she thought perhaps fifteen days. I remembered what Sei had written about this competition in her book, so I kept quiet.

Sei examined the mountain closely, walking to another window to get a more rounded view, and then came back with her estimate. "At least until the fifteenth day of next month."

The Empress shook her head, smiling at Sei's outlandish estimate. "Absolutely not. It will be gone by the New Year."

Over the next few weeks the snow mountain provided a wonderful diversion. We ran to the window every day and with every change in the weather. It rained, and the mountain remained. The temperature rose, and the mountain shrank but stayed. New Year's Day arrived, and while the mountain was small and dirty, it was still there. Everyone but Sei had now lost their bets.

New snow fell just after the New Year, which got Sei all excited, but the Empress ordered serving men to sweep the new snow off, telling Sei it wasn't fair. It gave the Empress great amusement to watch Sei taking the competition so seriously.

Masako was relieved at the improvement in the Empress's mood. As Imperial Medium, she was charged with observing the Empress daily, and the Empress's spirits had sunk so low, malevolent spirits might easily have taken hold.

The Emperor had written many letters asking Sadako to return (*"but don't tell my mom,"* I said sarcastically.) Between that and the morale boost of the snow mountain game, she asked Masako if she truly thought her fox dream meant she should return to the Emperor.

"Yes, the black fox is auspicious, and this is the time for new beginnings. Also, the snow mountain is still there, which is a good omen."

Sadako gave Masako a bolt of silk as her thanks for her protection and advice. "The mountain gives me hope, how it goes on and on, even into a new year."

As we got ready to depart for Ichijō Mansion, Sei gave orders to a gardener. "Make sure no children climb on it," she said. "I will make sure you are rewarded if it remains untouched."

She sent a servant to check on the mountain every day. It grew smaller and smaller, and eventually, on the fourteenth, the servant reported it was no bigger than a cushion. Sei clapped her hands at the news. "It's still there, and tonight will be quite cold, which means I win! Medium, that's a good omen for me, *ka*?"

She sent a servant to the residence with an empty box to gather the remaining snow on the morning of the fifteenth so she could present it to the Empress.

The servant returned with bad news. "The snow hill is gone,

completely gone! The gardener was very upset. He said to tell you he doesn't know what happened to it."

Sei glared at the poor woman as if it were her fault, resulting in a flood of tears, but Sei had no sympathy. "Now I must tell Her Majesty it's gone. Unless you wish to do that?" Without waiting for an answer, she spun around to head to the Empress's quarters, leaving the servant kneeling and weeping.

"*Follow her!*" I urged Masako. "*This is going to be fun to watch.*"

Sei approached the Empress. "Your Majesty, the snow mountain is gone. It was there last night, and so I wrote a poem that I planned to present to you with the box of remaining snow. But how did the snow disappear? It was a clear, cold night, but now it's gone."

The Empress smiled. "I have to be honest. I couldn't stand that you should win, so I had someone carry the snow away last night. You really did win, so read me your poem."

The snow mountain competition put everyone in a good mood. Except me. I'd been thrilled to be there live and in person—or at least, in spirit—for Sei's famous snow mountain story, so why was I feeling sad and frustrated? Lack of autonomy and control, maybe, and fear of becoming a subordinate spirit to Masako's dominant one.

She acted more like me lately. Her words were a little too direct, her stance a little less humble than was proper. And I caught her starting a sentence with "Hey," or "Look," several times (not sure how that translated, but that's how it sounded to me) which made her even more of a pariah among the other women at court. Permanent binding would be bad for both of us, even if we didn't go crazy. She wouldn't fit in her own world, and I'd never see my parents again.

"Masako, it's time for Seimei to live up to his commitment. I'm starting to forget my own language. You're starting to talk like me and I'm starting to talk like you. Even if I weren't afraid of us binding permanently, it can't be good for your career to be anything like me."

She'd noticed that too, so at the next report to Seimei, Masako asked him when he would send me home.

"There is still too much at stake, Lady Masako. Tell the Spirit I will send her back in due time, and I will ensure she returns at the moment her spirit left, so she won't miss a single event in her terrible world."

Masako bowed her head in quiet acquiescence, but I was consumed with rage. "I need to go home now!" I shouted. Out loud. With Masako's voice. While she was completely awake and fully conscious.

Seimei jerked his head up, astonished at Masako's uncharacteristic outburst, but it only took a second for him to see it was my fault. "Mi-Na, even a child has better self-control!"

"I didn't know that would happen. Sorry, Masako."

Masako shook her head back and forth as if trying to shake me out.*"Mi-Na, believe me, I want you to go home too, but if you act like a child, Seimei won't help you. Now I have a headache."*

In spite of my uncontrollable anger at Seimei jerking me around, I worried about leaving Masako. Would Seimei exploit her powers to help Michinaga? Would he force her to marry Akichika against her will? Would Michinaga punish her for her loyalty to Sadako? Without my guidance, would my innocent friend fall prey to manipulative scheming?

On the other hand, my emotions were affecting her more and more. My anger caused her face to flush, my anxiety caused her heart to race, and now it appeared I had gained a level of control over her speech even when she was awake. The integration of our spirits had gone even further than I thought. All the more reason for Seimei to send me home now.

Unless that was his plan. Bind our spirits, and thus our powers, together, for his exclusive use in perpetuity.

I stayed quiet while Masako finished her lesson. She was doing well without much help from me. But if I didn't have any relevance, I might slowly disappear like the Cheshire cat, bit by bit until nothing was left of my spirit except my thin-lipped smile. I needed to do *something* to assert myself, something to keep our spirits separated until I could get home.

I just didn't know what.

Chapter 29

An Imperial Request

First Month, Chōhō 2 (February, 1000 CE)

Sei rushed into our apartment, her face flushed and tendrils of hair flying. "A note for the Medium from His Majesty!" Her eyes glowed with excitement.

"What could he possibly want from me?"

"Read it! Perhaps the note will tell you."

Masako held the note reverently, caressing the soft green paper before unfolding each flap with care.

Sei bounced on her toes as she stood by Masako's side, trying to read the note without seeming to. "Well, Medium, what does His Majesty say?"

"His Majesty requests me to attend him today. He does not give a reason. Is he known to invite ladies-in-waiting to his quarters as Michinaga does?"

"I wouldn't say it's never happened, but he has many beautiful and charming consorts, so why would he ask for *you*? He prefers to spend time with the Empress, anyway. I don't think he wants you for that. What will you wear? Would you like the services of my attendant to prepare your hair and face? You need a *lot* of work. Your tooth-blackening is rubbing off. It looks horrible."

Sei's teeth, of course, looked perfect. *Okay, that's weird. I'm starting to like this black-teeth look.*

"I will ask Yumi to help me dress and apply tooth-black. I have a fresh set of white robes. If he needs my services as Imperial Medium, I should wear white."

Sei looked disappointed, but nodded and left.

"*Could you say no to him if he wanted you as a lover?*"

"I am neither beautiful nor charming, nor do I have skills in poetry or calligraphy, so I don't think it will come to that."

"*I don't agree with your humble view of yourself, but I hope you're right.*"

One of the Emperor's palace women came for us in the late afternoon. We followed her across the garden to the Emperor's palace, and were shown into a large room to wait. We had a lot to look at: yellow silk curtained screens and painted wood screens; hanging scrolls with beautiful calligraphy, and several bound manuscripts. After we waited fifteen minutes or so, we heard soft footsteps. Masako got behind one of the standing screens just before the Emperor stepped into the room.

"Lady Medium, you may come from behind the screen," he said in a pleasant tenor voice.

Masako gasped at this unexpected and rule-breaking request. She shuffled around the screen on her knees and bowed her head to the floor.

"Please sit up. I would like you to be comfortable here," he said as though eager to make a friend. He wore a russet-bronze brocade overcoat with under-robe layers of brown and yellow, and of course the usual white face paint, under which I could see a little acne. He tipped his head toward the table, and Masako carefully poured sake from a wooden ladle into a brown glazed cup, and set it in front of the Emperor with a bow.

He sat cross-legged on the other side of the table. "Imperial Medium, you attend the Empress constantly. Have you found any *mono-no-ke* bothering her?"

"No, Your Majesty. I watch over her but have seen nothing. She is truly blessed by the kami."

"She trusts you. Seimei trusts you. Should I trust you?"

"Your Majesty, I exist to protect and serve the imperial family."

He put his hands on his knees, and started to speak. "I-" He stopped and cleared his throat. "I want to know what the kami want from me. Do you communicate with them directly?"

"Not directly, Your Majesty. The kami provided the Spirit Mi-Na with information which she shares with me."

He stared into his cup of sake. "I dreamed last night I was flying like a bird over all the land. I flew over the Hiei mountains and the bamboo forest of Arashiyama. I could turn, dive, touch down on a tree branch and lift off again. I was in my true element. Then a net dropped onto me from the sky. I struggled to free myself, but the more I struggled, the tighter the net drew around me." He shuddered. "The joy and the horror of the dream are with me still. Do you have the power to interpret this?"

Masako's heart beat faster in near-panic. *"Mi-Na, I don't know what to tell him!"*

"Calm down. I got this. He feels trapped. But tell him you need a day to consult the oracle. Otherwise everyone will expect same-day interpretations."

She agreed. "Your Majesty, might I have one day to ensure I have an adequate answer for you?"

"Seimei usually needs two or three days to interpret my

An Imperial Request

dreams. Your oracle must be quite powerful to respond within a day." He sat there for a minute, deep in thought, then lifted a fist high, bringing it down as though to bang the table, but slowing at the last second for a gentle rap.

"I have another request, and I trust you to keep what I am about to say completely confidential, even from Lord Seimei," he said, staring at his clenched fist resting on the table. "Her Majesty is the only person in my life who doesn't try to tell me what to do. And now she has given me a son, a boy who should be named Crown Prince. However, the Lord Regent tells me the kami will be displeased if I do. I need a second opinion." He hesitated. "I will not ask Lord Seimei to divine the kami's wishes in this matter, as he reports to the Lord Regent, who has made *his* wishes clear. Since you are in training to become a miko, I want you to ask the kami for their advice on what I should do."

Masako worked hard to breathe normally and appear calm. *"I should not be put in this position! I want to say yes, of course he should be named Crown Prince, but if I do, Lord Michinaga might banish me! But if I tell him no, Her Majesty's position will be greatly damaged."*

"Isn't that up to the kami? And if they don't answer, well, he can't blame you for that, can he?"

"Mi-Na, you are right. I am embarrassed you had to remind me. It is indeed the kami's will, whether or not I like their decision."

"Your Majesty," she said with a seated bow. "I am deeply honored and humbled by your faith and trust. I am but an apprentice with very little experience."

He didn't look too upset. "I know this, but Lord Seimei has spoken highly of your abilities. How much time will you need?"

"I must pray and meditate in order to conduct a divination for a question of this magnitude."

"*Ge ni, ge ni*. Indeed. Well, it has been a long time since Her Majesty visited the Imperial Shrine at Kamo. It will do her good to make a pilgrimage. I will suggest it, and she will have you accompany her." He swallowed what was left in his cup and stood up. Meeting over.

Masako shuffled backward to make room for her extended bow to the floor, and the Emperor left the room. *"Seimei will find out what we're doing,"* she said. *"But this comes from the Emperor, so he wouldn't try to stop us... I think."*

"Seimei knows you are a novice at divination, so he won't take you seriously enough to do anything about it."

At least, I hoped so.

Chapter 30

Pilgrimage To Kamo

Second Month, Chōhō 2 (March, 1000 CE)

Masako picked at her breakfast of rice gruel with little interest.

"Eat up or you won't have the energy to pray for an answer to the Emperor's question."

She ate a little bit more to shut me up, then leaned her head on her left hand, pushing food around with her right.

"What's wrong, Masako? Aren't you looking forward to this trip? I can't wait for us to meet the Kamo Shrine High Priestess. And this is a chance for you to do some networking—I mean, establish relationships—for a possible future job. It's close to the capital and you can pray to the kami all you want."

She chased a drop of gruel around the bowl. "This position as imperial medium is more exalted than anything I ever prayed for. But now I feel like rice when mochi is being made — pound and turn, pound and turn. The Emperor wants me to tell him what the kami want, when he should be asking Lord Seimei. The Empress wants me to tell her if her son will become Emperor someday, but you won't tell me."

By now I was tuned in to Masako's emotions, even when she didn't share her thoughts. I knew when a situation made her uneasy, or when fear caused her adrenaline to rise, or when embarrassment caused her cheeks to grow warm, but these doubts took me by surprise. It was time to trust her enough to admit that I didn't know. I suspected the risk of binding increased the more I trusted her, but I hated to see her this way. "Masako, I have to be honest. I don't know whether Prince Atsuyasu will become emperor. I didn't study hard enough, I guess. I don't want you to think I was holding information back from you on purpose."

She sighed. "I suspected as much," she said. "You did tell me that you have little knowledge."

"I have a lot of knowledge, just not about the details of this particular era in this particular country. Admittedly that's the knowledge that would be most useful to me right now, but I had no way to know that when I selected my courses." It was silly to be defensive about that, but I couldn't help myself. "My focus was more literature and language than a deep dive into history."

"Mi-Na, I am not blaming you." She pushed her tray away and stood up.

"Masako, the kami chose you as my host, even if we don't know why or what they want from us. You're not responsible for what will or won't happen to the Empress and her brothers. It's their fate. From my perspective, everything that's going to happen has already happened."

"So what I say to the Emperor doesn't matter? If so, why will you not tell me what happens to the Empress? Does Korechika become regent someday?"

"Please believe me when I say I struggle every day with how much to share." I didn't know why I was so reluctant to tell her the little I knew. Surely the kami wouldn't allow me to change history. "Very well, Masako. Korechika does not become regent. Michinaga will remain regent for decades. My knowledge about what happens to Sadako is, sadly, very limited."

Masako swayed slightly, dizzy from my revelation. *"Mi-Na, I am sorry to have asked. That knowledge is a heavy burden for me to carry."*

Yumi walked over, concern knitting her forehead. She confirmed that Masako was not sick, and told her she needed to get ready to leave for Kamo.

The Empress had requested Seimei to divine an auspicious day for the pilgrimage to Kamo. Apparently certain deities would take trips from time to time, and nobody wanted to run into them for fear of disrupting their business, which would bring bad luck, so diviners were kept busy determining which directions should be avoided on any given day. This created havoc with government business since every communication was either in person or by messenger. It did provide a convenient excuse for delays, however. *Uh, yeah, I couldn't get the tax report to you yesterday because that direction was forbidden.*

Seimei determined the trip should take place at the next full moon. The Imperial Shrine at Kamo was less than five miles north of the palace, so it wasn't a long trip, but even a short journey required extensive preparation due to Sadako's imperial status. Many decisions had to be made: what gifts for the shrine and the High Priestess; which of Sadako's attendants would go; what manner of conveyance to take.

These imperial visits to the Kamo Shrine appeared to be less pilgrimage and more book club gathering. Sei had described it to us in glowing terms. "A time to discuss poetry, the latest book, and to learn from the High Priestess herself, Imperial Princess Nobuko. She is wise, beautiful, and deeply faithful to Buddha. Sadly, Buddha's name must not be mentioned within the Imperial Shrine, which is of course dedicated to the kami. It is a conflict for her, but she is devoted to her duties as High Priestess."

Masako rode by herself in a small ox-carriage with two huge

wheels similar to our ride from Hitachi, but windows on all four sides were covered with fluttering red silk allowing light and air into the interior. Its structure of bamboo and yellow woven palm fronds was both attractive and lightweight, no doubt designed for improved fuel economy. Ox fuel, that is. How many servings of millet did it take one ox to pull a cart uphill for five miles?

Recent rain caused our ox and our ox-drivers to slip in sticky mud, but it also encouraged green shoots to pop up in the fields. The air, cold and fresh with the humidity of early spring, rolled straight down the mountains and into our carriage, and Masako took many deep breaths to cleanse her lungs of palace incense. When our group passed the outskirts of the capital, the Empress's women started calling back and forth to each other with a liveliness I'd never heard from them before, as though their reserve and strict manners were left behind too. Bright flashes of red, green, and gold sleeves against the light brown panels of each carriage resembled early spring flowers, and mirrored brightening spirits.

The guards called out for everyone to halt just as we approached the Kamo River, so Masako pushed aside the window curtain. A driver saw her and bowed quickly, eyes on the ground. "A dead body lies on the riverbank ahead. We will follow the guards on a detour."

Masako drew back inside. "*Commoners. So old-fashioned, and now we are inconvenienced,*" she said with an irritation that surprised me. "*We cannot proceed to the shrine if any member of our party becomes polluted. If we pass near a dead body, we have to undergo purification all over again. More fasting, a cleansing ceremony – a delay of several days. I wish commoners would cremate the dead.*"

Kenji had told me riverbanks are borders to the spirit world, so maybe these people left the dead there to shorten the journey from this life to that one. Thoughtful, but not very hygienic.

"Maybe they can't afford cremation. And how do cremated spirits get to the spirit world?"

"It doesn't matter what happens to the body after death, or where the body lies, but commoners don't know any better, I suppose. The most important thing to do is to pray to the spirit to move on. That's why I brought my little shrine from Hitachi. It has been years since my mother and sister died, and I am certain their spirits have left this world by now, but that is why I pray every morning."

The detour took a little extra time, but we got back on track and soon crossed the Kamo River to enter the shrine grounds. Once our party passed under the orange *torii* gate, the Empress invited her women to walk the rest of the way.

Masako descended from her carriage with alacrity. She walked alone on a packed dirt path through a redwood tunnel. She inhaled deeply with her eyes closed, allowing the cedar-like fragrance of the *sugi* trees to nourish her soul, and let her breath out through her mouth, as though exhaling away her sadness.

"Mi-Na, I'm home," she said.

"Have you ever been here before?"

"Never in body, but my spirit must have dwelled here in my dreams, or in a previous existence. It's so familiar, so comforting. It's as though I'm meant to be here."

After a brief stop to pray at the lower shrine, she walked to the High Priestess's residence. A tall, orange gate was covered by a roof that looked like a horizontal sail with its four corners slightly lifted. A wall extended from either side of the gate, enclosing a courtyard.

A young shrine maiden, dressed in a knee-length white robe, red hakama, and bare feet, led us through a gravel and dirt courtyard and into a large, dark hall, smoky from oil lamps. Several tall wooden screens had been set up to partition the room into private spaces. The attendant gestured to the space where we would sleep, and then led us to meet the High Priestess, who was greeting the Empress as we approached.

Princess Nobuko, the Kamo Shrine High Priestess, was taller than any other woman I had seen here, with straight posture, a dignified bearing, and an intelligent countenance. White ribbons were braided into her side bangs, and a plain wooden comb was set above her forehead. At her neckline I could see two robes of indigo and two of green layered at the neck, and a roomy pink flower-patterned robe over it all. Her eyes were long, her cheekbones sharp and high. She had to be in her mid-thirties—she'd been High Priestess since she was twelve years old and had been in this job for at least twenty years—but she looked younger than anyone else that age I'd seen in this era. Which, to be frank, was a very small group. Epidemics and high maternal death rates skewed the average age so that nearly everyone at court was younger than thirty. Michinaga and Sei were the exceptions, not the rule. They were both thirty-three years old, and so were nearly a decade older than most of the other players in these political games. No wonder Sei had become the Empress's advisor and Michinaga ran circles around Korechika.

The palace women had relaxed, the tightness in their expressions replaced by laughter. The melancholy that pervaded Sadako's court was dispelled here, as though a magic bubble allowed the women in and kept the negative energy out.

After some catching up on court gossip, the High Priestess and Empress Sadako walked away from us, going behind a tall screen for privacy.

"*Let's follow them. I want to hear what they talk about,*" I urged Masako.

"*Eavesdrop on the Kamo Priestess and the Empress? Sacrilege!*" Masako's reluctance stemmed as much from her growing devotion to Sadako as from her religious fervor.

"*At some point Seimei will become impatient with my lack of infor-*

mation. Besides, I'm curious to know if Sadako's asking for help from the Priestess."

Masako reluctantly agreed. Fortunately there was a small shrine in the wall, so Masako could sit on her knees before it as if praying.

Sadako's normally soft voice grew louder as she pleaded with the High Priestess. "I fulfilled the most sacred duty to His Majesty—and to my father—when I bore His Majesty a son. But now the Lord Regent's daughter is consort, and rumors fly that Michinaga will never allow my son to be named Crown Prince. No one will take my side against the Regent. Could you not speak on my behalf?" Her voice choked on the last few words, and we heard quiet weeping for a minute before the Priestess spoke.

"Dear, sweet cousin, you are young and have time on your side. The Emperor loves you. Be patient, pray for guidance, and do not allow yourself to be swept up in the scheming of others. The Regent's daughter may never bear a son, and you did. Return to His Majesty's residence. You have been away too long." Her tone was calm and reassuring.

I was eighty-percent sure Michinaga's daughter Akiko would bear the Emperor at least one son, maybe more, but I didn't want to depress everyone with that information. *"So that's how Princess Nobuko kept this job for so long. Usually a High Priestess is designated every time there's a new emperor. Now I see it's because she doesn't take sides."*

Masako blinked away a few tears. *"Mi-Na, how can you be so scholarly about this? No one will help Her Majesty, and you speculate on why Princess Nobuko remains the Kamo Priestess?"*

Startled, I paused to think for a second. *"I guess I'm trying to be objective so it doesn't hurt as much to see Her Majesty's pain, knowing we can't do anything about it."*

Sadako's weeping gradually stopped. "I- I will not return to the palace unless His Majesty requests it. Will you pray to the kami for me?" she asked plaintively. "As High Priestess, your prayers have more influence than mine."

"Yes, dear one. Now we should return to our gathering."

"They're coming out!" I warned Masako.

"No time to move." She said a quick prayer because she couldn't lie about anything sacred, and apparently even pretending to pray was in that category.

The two women came from behind the screen.

"Ah, Miko!" Sadako cried with forced gaiety. "High Priestess, you should interview my Imperial Medium. She is Seimei's pupil."

"I look forward to it. Perhaps tomorrow? Now it is time to begin our discussion of the book by Michitsuna's mother."

I loved that they weren't suspicious of Masako kneeling there, but sad for the same reason. Sweet, innocent Sadako.

The following morning we woke at sunrise, feeling a bit groggy from our late evening. Masako had held back from full participation in the discussion the previous night. Not having been raised at court, she didn't want to say the wrong thing, but she had listened closely and with great enjoyment. It had been a fascinating discussion. Lively, opinionated, and we had to pay close attention to understand all the double-meanings and puns. Rank didn't seem to matter as much here, and the conversation was completely lacking in the usual witty put-downs court women used to pull rank or show off their education.

"The High Priestess has created an environment where women can be free to be themselves, don't you think?"

Masako sent a wave of happiness my way. *"Mi-Na, this is*

Pilgrimage To Kamo

where I belong! When I talk to the Priestess today, I will ask her if she will take me as an attendant, or as miko, or medium, or... or... floor sweeper! I'll take any job to be here!"

I kept my sudden pang of loneliness to myself. That had always been our plan. Masako would go to a shrine and I'd go home, and I was desperate to do just that. But we'd been sharing one body for what, seven months now? And I couldn't help but feel a little jealous.

The High Priestess had sent a note asking Masako to meet her at the Upper Shrine, which was a bit of a walk. At the palace, Masako and I both had longed for outdoor time and exercise. We'd had lots of time to *look* at nature, write poems about it, paint pictures of it, but *walk* in it? Nope. So the stroll in the glorious spring afternoon—the warm breeze wafting perfume from plum blossoms, the whistles and chirps of parenting birds, the feel of sun-warmed packed dirt beneath our feet—lifted my spirits. Masako hummed a melody I recognized from her biwa practice. I'd never heard her hum before.

We entered the large shrine after the usual ritual ablutions. The High Priestess, wearing a yellow silk jacket over robes of orange and red, was reviewing a scroll with a shrine attendant. She murmured something to the young woman, who bowed and left. Rather than invite Masako to sit, she gestured with her sunrise-colored sleeves to a nearby alcove.

"Imperial Medium, I wish to know more about you and your powers," she said as we walked into the cozy space with her. A wooden statue of a woman stood in a wall insert, her sleeves pointed at the ends, her expression serene. A Shinto goddess?

"Please tell me your story," she continued. "How did you come to be possessed, and how did you persuade Seimei to take you as a pupil? He is not known for taking on women as students."

Masako described her journey, starting with the epidemics that killed her mother and sister, to the meditation during which I'd possessed her, to her assignment as Imperial Medium. She left out the part about me spying.

The High Priestess listened without interrupting, speaking only after Masako had fallen silent. "I understand your lack of interest in marriage and children. I feel the same. As High Priestess, I live a life of mind and spirit, unencumbered by husbands or lovers. But the training to be a miko takes a very long time. Have you begun to learn the dance of purification?"

"I have been studying the Kagura Dance. A local priest is my teacher. Might I learn it here? Does the Kamo Shrine need a shrine medium or miko?" she asked hopefully.

Nobuko sighed. "We use local girls for our mediums, and you are Imperial Medium now." She placed a hand on Masako's shoulder. "When the time is right, I will discuss it with Seimei. Until then, serve our sweet Empress loyally and faithfully, and do your utmost to keep malevolent forces away from her."

She was about to dismiss us, so I jumped in. *"Masako, ask her about the Emperor's request!"*

Masako blinked in surprise, so absorbed in dreams of a future at the shrine she'd forgotten why we were here. "Please, one more question, if you have a moment for this humble medium," she whispered.

The priestess looked amused and gave a slight bow in assent.

"His Majesty honored me with a request to learn what the kami want him to do about his son. My oracle Mi-Na will not advise me. Do you have any wisdom about this dilemma?"

The High Priestess sighed. "Imperial Medium, if your oracle won't give you an answer, you shouldn't expect one from me. The Lord Regent's role is to advise the Emperor. If His Majesty doubts the Regent's advice, he must pray to the kami himself."

"See, Masako? She can't take sides because she really likes this job.

If she advises against Michinaga's interests, Michinaga would pressure Seimei to 'divine' a new priestess, and Michinaga would marry her off to some clan that supports him."

"I am not stupid, Mi-Na. I understood what she said." Masako directed her disappointment at me, as she couldn't fault the High Priestess. "This meeting is over."

"Wait! Don't go yet." If this was Masako's dream of a future home, I wanted to do what I could to make sure the High Priestess would stay alive for her. "Tell the priestess that when an epidemic rages in the capital, she must close the shrine to pilgrims and not allow any of her staff to leave Kamo."

The Priestess looked puzzled and a bit worried, but she agreed to follow my advice, and then showed Masako where she could go to meditate and pray for an answer to the Emperor's question.

Masako spent the next several hours meditating, but the kami didn't answer, which upset her. Not just because she would disappoint the Emperor, but maybe it meant she wasn't a miko.

"Be patient, Masako. You heard the priestess say it takes years of training. I know you will make a great miko someday. It's meant to be, because I'm here, right? You had to have done something to draw me here. You'll be the next Seimei, or who was that Empress he mentioned? Himiko? You could be the next Himiko!"

She cheered up but told me I was an idiot. "There is only one Himiko, and one Seimei, and I have no wish to be that powerful. Truly, I just want to save the realm from epidemics and disasters. If I could do that even once, I would exceed my dreams. I will dedicate myself to the training and purification needed to achieve that. And Mi-Na?"

"Yes?"

"Thank you for possessing me. For helping me, for pushing me to take the journey to the capital, for keeping me from dying of boredom and loneliness in Hitachi. Thank you."

At last, some appreciation. Not that I deserved it; she was the brave one, the adventurer, the one the kami blessed—or cursed —with hosting me. *"Masako, you've always had it in you. I'm just the catalyst."*

I was desperate to get home, but I was beginning to think it might tear me apart to leave. Like Lord Tomohiro's poem, I could not stay, but how could I let her go?

Chapter 31

Two Empresses

Second Month to Third Month, Chōhō 2 (March to April, 1000)

Upon our return from Kamo, the Empress received two messages. One contained news that Junior Consort Akiko was leaving Ichijō Mansion to visit her father's home for an indeterminate amount of time. The other message came from the Emperor requesting the Empress to come back.

Sei speculated that the Kamo Priestess had something to do with this, but she said that privately to Masako. The Empress was both pleased and annoyed by His Majesty's request. Pleased, because it meant he still wanted to see her. Annoyed, because he'd waited until Akiko had left his residence first. "We will move to Ichijō Mansion on the Eleventh Day of Second Month," she said firmly. "And no other day. Unless it turns out to be inauspicious for travel."

Sei told us this date was important to Her Majesty because it was the one-year anniversary of Akiko's formal introduction at court. She wasn't jealous of Akiko. Well, she was, but more than that, she needed to make a statement. The Empress had lost her support at court a few years ago when her powerful parents died and her brothers were exiled. If she couldn't count on the Emperor's love and respect for her, she had nothing, and would eventually become nothing.

Once at Ichijō Mansion, His and Her Majesties had a joyful reunion, the sounds of which we could hear from our sleeping mats outside the Empress's room. I found it embarrassing that we could hear absolutely everything going on, but Sei and Masako whispered to each other in excited tones about how wonderful it was that His Majesty visited Her Majesty so soon after our arrival, and what that meant for the Empress's future.

Princess Nagiko and Prince Atsuyasu came with their mother to the palace. We spent hours playing with the lively and intelligent little girl, and trying to get the sweet baby boy to laugh. When he did, we all cooed and praised him as the most precocious baby ever.

On the First Day of Third Month, which I estimated to be about twenty days after we moved in, the nurses came to take the children away from our morning play session. Sei smoothed the little princess's hair before she was whisked away. "Young children are so pretty and sweet. It's when they get older they become tiresome," she said with a laugh.

The Empress sighed and lay back down on her dais. Sei started to leave, but just as she scooted on her knees to the door, it slid open. Lord Narimasa was on his knees on the other side.

"*Masako, what's he doing here? Didn't we see enough of him at his residence?*"

"*He is Her Majesty's Steward, Mi-Na. You know that.*"

"Your Majesty, please excuse this interruption," he said with a bow. "There is news from His Majesty. I-" Narimasa looked around as if hoping someone would interrupt him. "The news- I mean, there is an imperial decree. I don't fully understand it. It would seem to be impossible. But-" He gave up and held out a sheet of paper towards Sei. "Please read it to Her Majesty." He bowed and left, his haste to escape made clear by the rapid shuffling of his feet along the gallery floor.

Sei closed the door behind him and read silently for a minute. Then she dropped the paper like it was a hot coal from the brazier. "No! It can't be," she cried out. "It is not right!"

"What? What is it? Masako, ask her what's going on?"

"Your Majesty- this message indicates that an imperial decree has been issued. Lady Akiko is to be named Empress! And you are also to be Empress!"

Sadako sat up. "That cannot be! There can only be one Empress-Consort. His Majesty would never agree to such a thing. Is this a prank? But who would play such a cruel one? Let me see!" She held out her hand, and Sei placed the message in it with her own shaking hands.

Sadako smoothed it out on the dais, her eyes moving rapidly up and down as she read it. "It has the imperial seal. It says that Akiko is to be elevated to Junior Empress." The Empress continued, her voice cracking with disbelief. "I am to become Senior Empress. If only my father were alive! He would never have permitted this. Korechika! Where is Korechika? Someone bring him to me!" She was breathing rapidly, her unpainted face flushing while her lips lost their color. Masako went to her, hoping to provide some solace, but Sadako waved her away.

Sei opened the door and called out for a serving woman to send for Korechika and to bring cups of water. "But he is not here, Your Majesty, so it could take some time for him to arrive."

Other ladies-in-waiting came in as the news spread, crowding the room, crying and wailing.

"They are not helping right now," I said in frustration. "Can't we make them leave? The Empress is having a hard enough time with this news."

"A second Empress-Consort is unheard of. This has elevated the

Regent's daughter above all other consorts except for Empress Sadako. And it means the Regent is now father of an Empress."

"And that's always been one of his goals in life," I said. "I hope he's happy," I added bitterly.

Korechika arrived a couple of hours later, his consternation written in his clenched teeth and fists. "Did His Majesty give you no warning of this? How dare Lord Michinaga flout the law this way! He can't just declare a Second Empress! It can't be legal—we'll fight this! Takaie has gone to the Council of State to learn how this happened. Did he threaten His Majesty to get him to sign this? Do you know, Sister? Do you know why His Majesty would agree to this?"

Sadako had cried for an hour, and had then pulled herself together to face her brother, dressing in more formal clothes and painting her face to cover the dark shadows under her eyes. "His Majesty said nothing to me about this. She was just another consort. Lord Michinaga is putting pressure on him, and His Majesty's mother as well. It is too difficult to withstand both of them."

"His Majesty's mother works against me. And Sister, you have not made your case firmly enough with His Majesty. Have you brought up the subject of naming your son Crown Prince? No? You have wasted your opportunity to influence His Majesty when you had the chance, and now *he* is influenced by those who would have you demoted."

The Empress stood straight, her eyes clear and steady as she looked at him. "I have done my duty and am blameless. The Emperor has the right to do as he sees fit. We will wait to hear from Takaie about the legality of this action. Until then, speak no more unless it is to say something pleasant."

Takaie reported back that Lord Yukinari had come up with the justification to make Akiko an Empress. He reasoned that, although there were three living current or former empresses (the previous emperor's mother; the current emperor's mother; and Empress Sadako) who could perform the sacred rituals needed to keep the kami happy, they had a conflict of interest because they all followed precepts of the Lord Buddha. Therefore another Empress was needed to do certain kami-oriented ceremonies. A divination conducted by Lord Seimei concluded that the kami approved of this reasoning.

"So," I said to Masako, "*they colluded. Michinaga, Yukinari, and Seimei must have worked together to come up with this. Yukinari had to know that Sei's fortunes would decline because of this, yet he did it anyway, probably to curry favor with Michinaga.*"

"*Mi-Na, the Kamo High Priestess is also devoted to Buddha. As long as she does not recite a sutra or mention Buddha in the Shrine, she may make offerings to the kami.*"

"*Seems like a double-standard, doesn't it? I mean, if it really was a problem, they could just ask Her Majesty not to recite sutras in the palace or wherever she makes her offerings.*"

But there was nothing to be done. Even Korechika had to admit the reasoning was solid, and the Council of State had approved it.

Sadako was devastated. She pleaded her case with His Majesty, and tried using her charms to sway him, but to no avail. He told her he couldn't do anything about it, and besides, *she* was the one who cut her hair in protest when her brothers were exiled. *She* was the one who'd threatened to become a nun. Wasn't it enough that she had given birth to a prince?

It wasn't enough, and Sadako knew it, so on the twenty-seventh day of Third Month, we returned to Lord Narimasa's residence.

Chapter 32
Going Viral

Fourth Month, Chōhō 2 (May, 1000)

Due to gossip and slander questioning Sei's loyalty to Empress Sadako, spread mostly by Dainagon but possibly encouraged by Michinaga, Sei spent most of her time in her room. Feeling betrayed by Yukinari, and hurt by the rumors, Sei raged in her own quiet way, writing in her book and muttering to herself.

I persuaded Masako to let me take control so I could speak with Sei. She sent a note asking Sei to meet her in the garden at mid-day. It was a beautiful spring day, neither cold nor hot. The air was fragrant with cherry blossoms, and in the distance we could hear the haunting melody of a koto.

Masako decided to practice her deep trance state to allow me to take over. It had been several months since Seimei took over her miko lessons. Akichika was learning to be a shrine priest, so we didn't see him anymore. Masako had had a little talk with him to tell him she had no interest in marriage, so he should look elsewhere for a mate. He'd been a little fearful around her ever since she called up the curse-shikigami at their Kagura Dance, so that was just fine with him. They parted on excellent terms, and exchanged letters occasionally. Which meant Masako's divination about his importance in our lives was wrong. I told her we all made mistakes when learning new things.

But she was getting really good at self-entrancement. I took control after only a few minutes. I immediately took a long incense-free, blossom-fragrant inhale, and turned my face up to the sun. An unseen bird whistled a long note followed by three very fast notes. The last time I heard that bird song, I was hiking on Mount Tsukuba with Kenji.

I suppressed the memory. It hurt too much to remember my other life. My real life.

Sei appeared in the garden wearing a cheerful color combination of ochre over yellow robes, quite at odds with the grim expression on her face. "Medium! What do you want from me?"

"Well, good afternoon to you, too, Shonagon. It's Mina. I asked Masako to invite you here so I can speak with you directly."

Sei lifted her perfectly painted eyebrows in surprise, then bowed deeply with mock deference. "O Spirit, I am too humble to deserve such honor."

"Stop that, I'm serious. Lately you've been... well... odd. I haven't seen you attend Her Majesty in several days. She doesn't believe those ox-excrement rumors spread by Dainagon and her girl-gang, so why are you avoiding her? Are you considering leaving Her Majesty's court?"

She stiffened and looked around as if to make sure no one could hear. "Why do you say that?"

"You're acting like you aren't sure you belong here. The Empress has so few left on her side. And she's upset because the Junior Empress just moved back into Ichijō Mansion. Her Majesty needs your support. If you leave, Michinaga wins."

Sei's eyes rested on mine in an unusually direct gaze. "Spirit, please tell me one thing. You prophesied that the Empress would have a son, and she did. Does this mean her brother will become Regent someday?"

"Sei, I- uh, well..." *Screw it. She deserves to know.* "No, Sei, Lord Korechika will never become Regent."

"Ah!" Sei put her sleeve over her mouth and bent over as though I'd punched her in the stomach.

"But Sei, don't worry about that. Your writing is your future. The level of detail in your book will bring Empress Sadako's court to life for generations to come. If you stay with Her Majesty, and continue writing your book, you will be famous beyond imagination. If you leave, there will be no record of how wonderful, cultured, lively, and educated Sadako's court was, and there *will* be a record—several of them, in fact—that glorify Michinaga."

Sei's eyes glazed over as she envisioned the future I'd outlined. "You have given me much to think about, Spirit. It would be foolish to ignore such powerful words."

"Keep reading your book to the Empress. It helps her to feel better, I think."

"I have written nothing wise or weighty. It's just lists and little observations of life at court. Do you really think the Empress enjoys them?"

"Yes, your book makes her laugh. Please read to her?"

Sei agreed and turned to leave, but stopped as that bird sang its high, fast song again. "*Uguisu!*" she called out, caught up in the moment, delighting in its song, for a moment forgetting the gloom of our conversation.

How weird was that? I didn't know that bird song in the 21st century, but I knew from my study of *The Pillow Book* that the word *uguisu* meant Japanese bush warbler, so now, hearing Sei in the eleventh century, I connected bird name with bird song.

If Sei left Sadako's court now, her book would be forgotten in history. Literature keeps memories alive. Without *The Pillow Book*, no one would remember Sadako except as a minor character in Michinaga's regency. I was merely keeping history on its course.

"More of the Pillow Book, Masako! I'm so excited!" Sometimes my emotions would be strong enough to make Masako's heart race, and she'd have a little trouble catching her breath.

"Mi-Na, calm down, please. She's just reading her little musings."

"I'll try. Maybe if you take a couple of deep breaths it'll help." My goal was to be as thoughtful of Masako as she was of me. But still – Sei Shonagon! Reading out loud from the very book I'd studied in college!

Sei bowed to the Empress. "My worthless scribbling was intended only for my own entertainment, Your Majesty, so please forgive my impudence in reading these pages to you."

Sadako gave a slightly impatient nod.

Sei began to read, her voice almost inaudible at first, then growing stronger as she went on to describe why a priest giving a sermon ought to be handsome. If he wasn't good-looking, you might not look at him, and therefore you'd look at other people, and not listen to what he's saying, which was sinful.

As Sei read, the Empress laughed under her breath, murmuring *"so, so, so"* in agreement, while Masako frowned at Sei's impertinence.

The Empress didn't want Sei to stop. "It's delightful! And so true! Read another one!"

"It's not worthy of your praise, Your Majesty." She leafed through her stash and selected another page. She described the right way for a lover to leave in the early morning hours. He should act reluctant, and need to be pushed out. And the wrong way to leave, noisily with a fuss and a mess.

The Empress was laughing out loud, while Masako was perplexed, but then, she had so little experience with men. *"It is very strange. Not at all like other diaries. I don't know yet if I like it."*

"In my world we call what Sei just read 'vague-tweeting.' The Empress probably knows who Sei's referring to, and so will all the other women here. An inside joke."

The Empress urged Sei to keep reading, so she read a long section describing a time when Michinaga bowed to his brother Michitaka, the Empress's father, who was Regent for several years.

She asked Sei to read that section twice. "Shonagon, you remember it so clearly, and it brings my father back to me, a warm, bright memory in this gloomy season."

Pleased, Sei complied, and when she finished, she promised to make a copy for the Empress.

I had a sudden thought. *"Masako, if Sei's book were to be copied and disseminated, it would be a kind of revenge for the Empress. An unpleasant reminder of how Michinaga was subordinate to the Empress's father. Let's ask Sei to 'accidentally' leak her book so it goes viral in the capital. What I mean is, everyone will love it and so they'll copy it and share it with others."*

"But will it not antagonize the Regent further?"

"Sei's writing will ensure Sadako isn't forgotten in history. The glory of this court – the culture, the beauty, the literature – should be remembered, don't you think?"

"I don't know, Mi-Na. It is quite risque."

"At least suggest it to her. Please?"

Masako didn't love my idea, but since I had asked so nicely, she requested Sei to walk in the garden with her after it was too dark to read anymore. "The rain has ended, and moonlight sparkles on the teary-eyed cherry blossoms."

Going Viral

Sei couldn't resist an invitation like that, and in the privacy of the fragrant and humid garden, Masako popped the question, making sure to clarify it was my idea, not hers.

To Masako's surprise, Sei approved. "Mi-Na understands my heart. Her Majesty's situation is tearing me apart. She has so few supporters left. I will stay with her as long as she needs me. If the Spirit believes my book will do some good, I must agree to it. When the Empress is finished with my current pages, I will add a bit more, and then leave it lying where others might see it."

And it worked. A few days later a provincial governor stopped by Sei's apartment to pass along his greetings. Sei had left her book lying on a table, and he took the bait, hiding it in his sleeves and smuggling it out of Nijo. Within weeks copies had been made and disseminated throughout court. Going viral.

Chapter 33

Find The Middle Path

Fourth Month, Chōhō 2 (May, 1000 CE)

Sei had rushed in with tears on her cheeks. "I knew this would happen, but I didn't think it would hurt so much."

Masako and the Empress looked up in surprise.

Sei bowed, never one to forget her manners, no matter how upset. "Dainagon said my book showed how vain and shallow I am, and that I made your court appear frivolous and licentious. Please, Your Majesty, accept my deepest apologies. That was certainly not my intention."

The Empress's young face glowed with delight. "They are jealous of your fame. This book reminds everyone of how wonderful my father's regency was. There has never been such a book. If you need additional paper, I will provide it."

Sei bowed. "You honor me, Your Majesty. However-"

"Yes, Shonagon?"

"Is it true? Does my book make me look shallow and conceited?"

"Sadly, it does, and will for centuries," I commented to Masako.

"I used to believe she was shallow and conceited," she said. *"But*

she shows such devotion to Her Majesty, I could never think such a thing now."

The Empress laughed. "Oh, Shonagon, asking that question makes you seem vain! Don't worry about how it makes you look. Even His Majesty laughed out loud when I read your book to him. You see how much better I'm eating now? You have cheered me tremendously."

The door slid open, and a serving woman kneeling on the other side announced that Lord Yukinari was waiting to speak with Lady Shonagon.

Sei's face brightened as she looked at the Empress for permission to leave. Sadako laughed and waved her hand. "Go see your lover. I'm sure he will have wonderful praise for your book. And Miko, you may leave too. I am strangely tired, and will take a nap."

Masako tucked the Empress's robes comfortably around her before heading to our favorite spot in the Empress's garden. It was tranquil and private, and we could spend time there without interruption. The day was hot and humid, but somehow a little breeze found its way in over the garden wall on one side and through the windows on the other.

Masako set a mat down near our favorite tree, a small weeping cherry near a little stone bridge, to practice for her next divination lesson with Seimei. She was interrupted by the sound of Yukinari's voice coming from a window in front of us. The blinds were rolled up so we could see them sitting on mats together. Apparently a woman didn't have to sit behind a screen when it was her lover, even in broad daylight.

Yukinari was writing on a sheet of paper. After gently blowing on it to dry the ink, he handed it to Sei with both hands. She held it up with exclamations of delight, and while Sei was admiring his work, he reached out to caress her long hair.

She gasped with a laugh and swatted him with an embroidered gold sleeve.

"*Aga kimi*, allow your gossamer hair to fall towards me," he said.

"Lord Yukinari, you would be greatly disappointed to feel how this gossamer has turned to hemp. The hoar frost of age has coarsened it."

"You will never age, Lady Shonagon. You grow more clever with time. And now you are famous! I hope I'm the lover you write about who leaves the way a lover should, and not the callous, clumsy one. Who was that, by the way?"

Ha! He wanted to make sure Sei wasn't making fun of him in her book.

Masako didn't think it was polite to listen to the two lovers flirting, and she needed to practice divination, so she turned back to her divination sticks.

"Mi-Na, think of a question that is really important to you."

"Oh, that's easy. When will I get home? Can you believe I've been here eight months already?"

"Yes, I believe it. It feels like a long, long time to be possessed, even by a nice and helpful spirit like you."

"Masako, you're on your way to achieving your dream. When will Seimei fulfill his promise to me?"

"Mi-Na, isn't this world better than yours? Living in the capital, honored by the Empress, surrounded by luxuries peasants could never dream of. Can your world offer the same?"

Well, I had finally stopped missing my phone, but I still missed my parents, my classes, and even the girls I used to hang with. They weren't close friends, but we shared interesting videos and funny memes. I even missed arguing with my classmates in my futile attempts to persuade them that the *waka* poetry format was superior to haiku. And I hadn't had a boyfriend since I ghosted Mick. Although was it ghosting if only a day had passed in my world?

"Masako, I love my world, even with all its faults, and I want to help make it a better place. And I want to be a better person. I've learned much from you that will help me do that."

"You have learned from me, Spirit? I am honored and humbled." Masako blinked her eyes a few times to clear away tears. "Mi-Na, I fear our spirits are becoming entangled. Will I go to your world if Seimei sends you back? Will he be able to separate us?"

I pictured Masako in my world, and mentally shook my head. As difficult as this was for me, it would be a far worse culture shock for her. "I'm sure the Great Diviner will have no trouble with that. We're still two distinct personalities. I'll miss you too, Masako. You're the best friend I've ever had. I'm sorry for the times I've been selfish and controlling. I'm so grateful for your patience in teaching me about your world."

Masako sighed again, hanging her head for a minute before cupping the divination sticks in her hands. "When will Mi-Na get home?" she murmured and threw the sticks on the ground. She examined them, memorized their positions, and threw them again. And again. And again. It was a multi-step process.

"The answer to your question is the hexagram Chi-eh, which means 'acknowledge limitations, find the middle path.'" She mulled that over. "Mi-Na, you must be like bamboo, both strong and flexible. Understand and accept your limitations."

"What, am I supposed to just wait around for the kami to send me back home?"

"Wait... one more interpretation. I think it's telling you to picture the goal you want to achieve, and relax because it will eventually come to pass."

"That's better. I can do that." I pictured that hot July day, the secret power spot on Mount Tsukuba, and Kenji waiting patiently for me. If picturing Kenji helped me get back home, I could do that. Frequently.

"Now it's my turn," Masako said. "Will the Empress's son be Emperor someday?" She closed her eyes as she gently shook the sticks in her cupped palms and focused on her question. She threw the sticks onto the mat, memorized their positions, and did this six times.

"Chi-en. The male principle." Her skin tingled with elation. "The Empress will be the mother of an Emperor! She's safe!"

"Is she, though? Isn't there more interpretation to be done, here? After all, you had changing lines."

Her joy ended. "But it's so clear. Chi-en is the creative, the male. But you're right, I need to add the changing lines. It shows that we need to get help from others, not our friends, and wait for the circle to turn. Who would that be?"

No one was going to put their own careers and reputations in jeopardy by risking Michinaga's wrath to help the Empress. Masako's magic sticks weren't very helpful. But that was for the best. A clear answer might send her into a depression.

"Sei Shonagon is willing to help the Empress. And possibly the Kamo High Priestess. Empress Sadako will need them. And she'll need us."

For the first time since I crossed through the spirit world and into this one, my agenda was not about me. We needed to do what we could to help sweet Sadako.

Chapter 34

A New Mission

Fourth Month to Fifth Month, Chōhō 2 (May to June, 1000 CE)

The end of Fourth Month brought with it soft breezes, yellow flowers, and a measles outbreak. *Aka-mogasa*, "red pox" as it was called here, was making a second wave, having devastated the capital just two years ago. A red rash covered faces and arms, fevers burned skin, and people cried out for water or screamed with nightmares. Masako said that she'd had it, and she'd survived, and her father survived, while her mother had not.

Everyone prayed frantically for this epidemic to end quickly. Exorcisms were held daily. All religious and medical personnel were called into service. Seimei, Masako, the High Priestess of the Kamo Shrine, other *onmyōji*, shrine priests, and temple priests – all conducted their job-specific rites to try to find out which divinity or *onryō* had caused this disaster.

The Empress's court had so far been unaffected, but I knew it was just a matter of time. I begged Masako to listen to me. Her confidence in her own skills had grown under Seimei's tutelage, and correspondingly, her faith in mine had diminished.

"I know what this is!" I insisted. "Let me help!"

Masako was on her way to the Bureau of Divination. Seimei was spending most of his time there rather than his office at the Bureau of Computation. "Mi-Na, what can you do? Can you help identify the kami or spirit which has brought this curse upon us?"

"Let me talk to Seimei when you get there. I need to tell him what he can do to protect the Emperor and the rest of us. Well, you've had it, so you won't get it again. But do we even know who survived it last time? If they didn't have it before, it could kill them this time."

She agreed, which I took as a sign that her trust in my knowledge from the future outweighed her trust in Seimei.

As we walked through the Bureau, the familiar smell of burning turtle shells and the sound of clacking divination sticks followed us. Several *onmyōji*-in-training were rolling dice, calling out prophecies like, "if the kami are angry, let it be a six!" And if the roll produced a six, that meant the kami were angry, so the next roll became "if that kami is Inari, let it be a five!" and so on.

Seimei was busy frowning at a star map hanging on the wall when we entered his office. After a few minutes, he put his forefinger on the map to keep his place, and glanced at Masako. "Any success?"

Masako gave an apologetic bow. "I am so sorry, Lord Seimei. I have received no answers from the kami. But the Spirit Mi-Na insists she must talk to you directly. She has some experience with this pox in her world."

Masako sat down, placed her hands together in her lap, and closed her eyes, so good at putting herself in a trance that it only took a minute for me to take control.

Seimei stared at me with his intense dark gaze. "Well, Spirit

A New Mission

Mi-Na. It's been a few solar terms since our last conversation. What sage advice do you have to offer?"

"Lord Seimei, I haven't experienced this epidemic personally, but I know it's highly... highly..." *what was that word?* "contagious. It's not quite as deadly in my world as it is here, maybe because we have vac... vaccines, and centuries of built-up immunity you don't have yet. And better health care. But the most important thing to do is to... uh... um, quarantine."

Was I really forgetting my own language? And would strange words like "quarantine" and "contagious" translate through Masako's brain and across to Seimei? When I spoke those words, there was a slight delay, like speaking with a human translator in the room.

Seimei drummed his fingertips on the map. "Stop your incantations and use plain language."

So those words didn't translate. I paused to think. This was crucially important to convey. "Okay. Let's say this disease is an angry spirit who jumps from person to person. Each time it touches a person, it leaves angry red marks that cause the illness. But the spirit can't travel to other people if they aren't in the same room. They must be breathing the same air or touching the same surfaces." I wasn't entirely sure how measles was passed from person to person, but that should cover the most likely possibilities. "So. The Emperor and Empress and imperial staff must keep others away. No one must enter or leave the palace who is not already there unless they survived the last red pox epidemic. And anyone who currently has the red pox – they need to stay in their residence, and anyone living with them must stay there too, until at least two weeks have passed with no one having the pox."

He stroked his beard while thinking over my advice. "This actually makes sense, Spirit. But I never heard of a single spirit jumping to so many people. Does it become several spirits who then jump to more people? And then they all become more spirits!" His eyes gleamed with discovery. "But-" He frowned. "Ritual ceremonies must be attended, or the great divinities may send us further curses. I know a powerful protection spell."

I didn't want to ignore the potential benefits of Seimei's spells and appeasement rituals. He did save the Emperor from dying of smallpox, apparently. But working together, with my science and his religion, would be even more powerful. "If you do your thing, and you also make sure everyone takes my advice, we can protect the imperial family. And the Regent's family too."

Seimei woke Masako from her trance. He instructed her to practice divination with the other apprentices, and told her he would send a message to the imperial family that his protection spell required them to remain in their residences until the worst of the epidemic had passed. She bowed and headed over to the divination practice room.

As we walked along the veranda, we heard Michinaga's booming baritone coming from one of the other offices in this building. "Sei Shonagon made Lord Narimasa look like an utter fool. I will burn all copies of her ridiculous book, and prevent the author from disseminating any more. And if she does, she might find herself charged with treason. If she ever thought she would come to my daughter's court someday, she was mistaken. I have found a new writer to bring to court, a much better poet. Not as witty, but Shonagon has used her wit against the wrong people."

We heard a door slide open, and Michinaga stepped onto the veranda right in front of us. Masako bowed deeply, remembering the pain of having her hair pulled.

Michinaga stopped to examine her. Not many women worked at the Bureau, so it didn't take him long to remember who she was. "Ah, the Imperial Medium herself. Still possessed after all this time. I heard your skills have greatly improved. The High Priestess of Kamo spoke highly of you."

Masako remained bowed. "I am not worthy of her kind words, Lord Regent."

He stared at her for a full minute, and Masako's skin grew warm under his scrutiny. "Medium, you will be interested to hear that your father has been doing a fine job in Mutsu Province. He put down a minor rebellion by the locals. I do believe his Taira clan affiliation makes him work all the harder to prevent rebellion against the central government and the Emperor."

Masako bowed in gratitude for the information, although her skin was now chilled with fear. "Thank you, Lord Regent."

He left and Masako and I started talking at the same time.

"My father's in danger!"

"Sei's book will be destroyed!"

Masako's fear for her father outweighed my fear for a work of literature, at least for now. *"I'm so sorry, Masako. But he's doing well, the Regent said."*

"He wanted to remind me he has the power to put my father in harm's way. That's why he made my father Vice-Governor. The actual governor gets to stay in the capital. My father had to travel to the end of the country. And it's a reminder that the Regent holds all the power."

And he would destroy Sei's book. Michinaga wanted no trace of Sei's writing to survive. She made fun of him and his friends, and highlighted the sophistication and literacy of Sadako's court, which made him look like the bad guy for destroying it.

What would my life have been like without *The Pillow Book*? I enjoyed the *Tale of Genji*, but that wasn't what made my heart beat faster. If it weren't for *The Pillow Book*, I wouldn't have changed my major to Asian Studies or gone to Japan, which meant I wouldn't have possessed Masako. I'd have remained an anxious, insecure mess of a young woman in the wrong major. Masako would be a Buddhist nun or keeping house for her father in the cold, dangerous north.

Finally I knew why I was here.

Masako and I would save *The Pillow Book*.

Chapter 35

Three Omens

Fifth Month, Chōhō 2 (June, 1000 CE)

The fifth day of the fifth month was the Sweet Flag Festival, held to ward off illness. Various fragrant grasses and herbs such as sweet flag and wormwood were spread on the roof for that purpose, and Sei, Masako, and other ladies-in-waiting hung herbal balls throughout the residence. The summer rains hadn't begun yet, and pleasant breezes wafted floral notes throughout our rooms, clashing a bit with incense fragrances, but overall, a lovely start to the month.

I hadn't told Masako yet about my goal to save Sei's book. I wanted to think about how I'd do that first, so she wouldn't brush me off as some ignorant foreign spirit who had no clue how things were done here. *I mean, she'd be right, but still.*

The Emperor fell ill in spite of the sweet flag festival, and he requested Masako to assist with the exorcism. The Empress, pleased with this show of trust in her Medium, gave Masako the use of an ox-carriage to get her from Narimasa's residence to Ichijō Mansion. I was concerned he might have measles, but Sei told us she'd heard from one of his gentlewomen that he had no rash and no fever. Masako had already had it, so we weren't in any danger anyway.

Masako peeked through the ox-carriage curtain as the drivers got ready to move the ox.

"Mi-Na, that bodyguard is the wrestler who helped us get here from the mountain!"

"Call out to him and say hello! If it's not too improper, of course."

"It's certainly not proper, but I will, anyway." She called out a tentative greeting through the window.

"Spirit Lady? From the mountain?" Taro's broad face accommodated a wide, nearly toothless smile as rain dripped from the brim of his hat.

Masako laughed at the nickname. "I saw you win the New Year wrestling championship last year. I told the Empress you guarded us on our journey through the mountains."

He bowed again while the drivers looked at him with more respect. "Thank you for mentioning this humble wrestler to Her Majesty. My win was seen as a mark of favor from the kami, so I received the honor of assignment as imperial consort bodyguard."

"I wish you didn't have to escort us in the rain," Masako said. "But the Emperor needs us."

"It is our honor, and this rain doesn't bother us. It's warm, and will give the rice plants a good start in life. And now we must get you to His Majesty!"

All four drivers jumped into action, crying out to the ox, who began moving slowly through muddy streets, with Taro striding along next to the carriage.

Once at the palace gate, Masako exited her carriage, thanking the drivers for the smooth and speedy trip. I allowed myself some credit for her new and improved attitude toward commoners, although it might have negative ramifications for her. She had to live here forever. I'd get home soon, fingers crossed.

A second carriage came to a stop behind us, and the passenger inside dismounted.

"That's Seimei!" Masako exclaimed. "He must be here to help the Emperor too."

We were shown to the Emperor's sick-room. He was covered with green sleeping robes and laying on a raised platform with curtains around him, similar to the Empress's sleeping space. I'd learned this style of bed was called a *michōdai*. The room was crowded with monks and priests, and the air was thick with incense and sweat.

"No wonder the Emperor's having trouble breathing," I said. "Too many people, too little air. Can we roll up the blinds?"

"It's raining and windy."

"All right, then, just let me get a good look at him."

Masako moved a little closer to the platform, and the Emperor turned his head. "Ah, Imperial Medium. My head hurts and my eyes burn, and I keep coughing. Have I displeased the kami?" His voice had the nasal sound of a stuffy nose.

Seimei, who had arrived in the room seconds after us, also moved closer. The Emperor glanced his way, then closed his eyes as if it hurt to look at him.

"It looks to me like a bad cold," I told Masako. "*Tell him he needs to drink a lot of water, rest in bed for a day or two, and get some fresh air. It's probably all the incense that's giving him a headache. I find it hard to believe the kami would be upset with him. He's so diligent about his ceremonial duties.*"

The bizarre had become normal. Life here had convinced me that it was equally likely for illness to be caused by a virus or by supernatural intervention.

Masako started to speak, but Seimei jumped in first. "Your Majesty, I have conducted a divination to determine the cause of your illness as well as the reason for the palace fire."

"*Divination to determine the cause of the fire?*" I murmured. "*I can't wait to hear the results.*"

"*I, too, am feeling a bit... what is that word you taught me? Skeptical.*"

Masako had been in awe of her tutor's magical skills when we arrived at the capital, so I was proud of her for seeing that his other skills included opportunism and manipulation. Although that maybe wasn't the best thing for her career. But still, it showed growth. She'd matured too, over the past year.

Seimei bowed even though the Emperor still had his eyes closed. "Your Majesty. There has been a disturbance in the spirit world. The kami have sent three omens to warn us. The first omen—the red pox epidemic, which killed many nobles three years ago, and has returned to kill yet more. Then-" Seimei's voice got lower, more dramatic "- the fire that destroyed the imperial palace last year. Third, your illness. These are all signs we have strayed from the kami-blessed path." He paused to allow his words to sink in. The Emperor was frowning but his eyes were still shut, so Seimei continued. "Your Majesty, the kami wish us to hew to the path I identified as the righteous one."

The Emperor sighed and put a sleeve over his eyes as if to block out the Royal Astrologer.

Seimei must be accustomed to the Emperor ignoring him, as he continued unfazed. "I will select an auspicious day to hold an *onmyōdo* festival for your health and for the health of the populace. I have also been conducting fire prevention rituals, and will teach the Imperial Medium these rituals as well. They are more effective if conducted regularly." He bowed again.

Masako clasped her hands in her sleeves with excitement. "*A new ritual to learn – and such an important one!*"

So much for her skepticism. And what did Seimei mean by the "righteous path?" It probably wasn't good for Sadako, and whatever he wanted the emperor to do would further his own plan. I still couldn't quite believe his prophecy for Japan's future included destroying the great love affair between the Emperor and the Empress.

The Emperor snapped his eyes open. "Do what you must. Now leave." Seimei bowed again and started to back out, gesturing to Masako to leave with him.

The Emperor sat up. "The Imperial Medium stays. She must assist the priest."

Seimei squinted as if doubting the wisdom of that request, but bowed and departed without another word.

Masako stood frozen in shock. The Emperor had asked Seimei to leave, but wanted her, the lowly pupil, to stay?

He lay back down. "Tell me, Imperial Medium, what does Mi-Na have to say about my illness? And I want to hear if Mi-Na has anything to say about the palace fire. Are these omens? And if so, does the Spirit agree with Seimei?"

She knelt by his dais. "Your Majesty, the Spirit tells me you must drink water in great quantities. And breathe air from the outside. Mi-Na does not believe the fire was an omen. However, it did occur on the same day that Mi-Na arrived in this world. But it was most likely a clumsy servant knocking over a lamp."

He smiled. "My thoughts, exactly. Maybe I am an oracle too! I wish everyone would stop telling me what to think all the time. But Medium..." he paused to cough and call for water before continuing. "How did Seimei know?"

"Know, Your Majesty? Know what?"

"You don't know? You spend so much time with Her Majesty! She is pregnant again."

No, we hadn't known. Sadako wore between five and twelve layers of robes. Although come to think of it, she hadn't gone into abstinence for her monthly pollution since her stay at Ichijō Mansion three months ago. That would explain why Seimei said the omens were unlucky. If Sadako had another boy, it would become absurd that neither boy was designated Crown Prince. But according to Seimei, Michinaga's regency was the one blessed by the kami, and therefore Michinaga must remain Regent even if Korechika's nephew was the next Crown Prince. That must be the righteous path from which the Emperor must not stray.

Seimei performed his *onmyōdo* festival, and the Emperor recovered from his cold, so clearly causation, not just correlation, right? Everyone thought so, anyway. The measles outbreak slowed, too. Thanks to my advice, those at court survived, but did I get any credit? No, Seimei took it all for himself.

Which was fine. Really.

Chapter 36

Dominant Spirit

Sixth Month, Chōhō 2 (July, 1000 CE)

The summer monsoons had dragged on. And on. And on. Hot, humid, and dark. I thought it would never end. My initial energy and enthusiasm for supporting Empress Sadako and saving Sei's book dissipated over time as Masako focused on her training. She spent her time memorizing incantations and hexagrams, and snapped at me for interrupting her. I couldn't help but get upset by that, although I knew having me in her head made it hard to concentrate. I tried not to talk to her while she was studying, which was most of the time.

Which meant I had nothing to do. I learned everything she did, and amused myself with picturing the shaman business I could set up as a part-time job when I got back to Michigan. And I decided to tell her more about my life, about the awful years when everything fell apart.

About Aya. "Masako, I was a terrible person. *I was so angry when my friend Aya told me her family had to go back to Japan that-*" I hesitated. I'd never told anyone this. My guilt and anger had consumed me for years. But somehow I knew

Masako wouldn't judge me. "I was furious. I- well, I hit her. I spun around to get momentum and whacked her with my hand while screaming at her. Of course, she ran back home, and we never spoke again. I was angry with her for years! And no doubt she was just as angry at me. But one day in high school—um, around fifteen years old or so—I suddenly felt horribly guilty and ashamed of my behavior. I wasn't in therapy or anything—we couldn't afford it—but all on my own, I realized Aya's news had been the last straw for me. Dad had lost his job the year before and we were about to lose our house. My parents had started arguing all the time. Plus, I was twelve and had raging hormones. Um, I mean I was close to my coming-of-age ceremony, and it's hard to control your temper when you're going through that, you know? I missed her so much. Years later I did lots of internet searches for her. The internet is a kind of divination, where you can ask questions and find answers. But there were too many Aya Sato's. But anyway, Aya was the only best friend I ever had before y-"

"You hit your friend?" Masako's tone was casual and a little curious, but not horrified or judgemental. "I do not understand the rest of what you said, but for now, please stop talking. I must learn this, and it is a very difficult ritual."

But I'd shared my turbulent past! I'd allowed myself to show vulnerability, and she was ready to move on like it was nothing. "But Masako, it's lonely in here. Talk to me."

"Mi-Na, be patient! You act like a child, demanding attention when you know how hard I am working. I must interpret this omen before the new moon tonight."

"A child, am I? Demanding, am I?" And did she say new moon? That meant tomorrow was the beginning of Sixth Month. The month I'd arrived here. Which meant I'd lost an entire year. The ultimate gap year, and not in a good way.

I knew it'd been a mistake to bond with her. She didn't care about me any more now than she did when she tried to have me exorcised. I'd been right all along. *Don't invest in people or places. You'll only lose them.*

My frustration caused Masako's face to flush. Her muscles twitched randomly, and her left arm jerked of its own accord, sweeping her hexagram sticks off the table and clattering onto the floor. That sort of clumsiness was very unlike her.

"Masako?"

Silence.

"I'm sorry! I wasn't being rational. Maybe this is what the Shrine Miko warned us about. Don't blame me for that!"

Still nothing. "Come on, Masako!" I pleaded. "Don't isolate me. You know how I hate that."

Masako's arms moved up and she pressed her palms together as if praying. Or pleading? Was that me? Was I in control without realizing it?

I tested that hypothesis by standing up. This was bad. Very, very bad. Somehow I'd taken control without trying to, and now Masako couldn't even communicate with me.

It was time to pay Seimei a visit. Fortunately Masako had been studying in the Bureau of Divination, and so it wasn't far to the Bureau of Computation.

Not far to go, but far enough to lose my way. The sun had gone below the buildings, and it was dark in the walkways. I looked back and forth, trying to find a recognizable landmark. A staggering shuffle alerted me to a young man weaving his way toward me, so I put my fan up.

He came closer. And closer. So close I could smell the sake on his breath and see a familiar protuberance on his forehead. The same sneer twisted his mouth. Kanechika was still alive? With a tumor like that?

"Imperial Medium. Snake curse. Banish-" He took a breath. "Banish it. Or else."

He grabbed my sleeve. I pulled my arm away, but he grabbed it again, and then grabbed the back of my neck. My fan fell to the ground.

"Your face. I see it. So you like me. You... you want to be a shrine maiden? Very, very bad idea. No men. Come. Here."

I pulled back to get away from his sweaty, stinking body, but in spite of his inebriation, he was strong.

"Let go of me!" Someone would hear me, right? "Help!"

He pushed me against the wall, and my head hit the veranda with a painful smack. Using his body weight to keep me pinned, he fumbled with Masako's white jacket. "Come on, Medium. Banish this curse and I'll give you some of me as a rewar-"

"Get away from me! Help!" Masako's body was sturdy but small, and Kanechika, although still in his teens, had the height advantage.

"Masako, wake up! We're both in danger!"

No response. What had I done to her? *"Masako! This would be a good time for a shikigami!"* I twisted and pushed against the drunken adolescent in front of me. *"Masako! Come back, please!"* I didn't even sense her presence. This was her body under attack, so no matter how angry she would be at me, she wouldn't stay away on purpose. Something was wrong.

Kanechika slipped, and his weight shifted away from me. I threw myself against him, which he wasn't expecting, and so that weight shift combined with his lack of coordination caused him to fall to his hands and knees.

I started running but immediately stumbled and fell to the ground, my feet caught in my long robes. I heard him coming after me and cursing. How could he even do that? Drunk and with a brain tumor?

I jumped to my feet, grabbing handfuls of robes and hakama

to hitch them up. I was out of breath. The past year had been sedentary, and Masako wasn't as fit as she'd been in Hitachi. I turned a corner and saw stairs. Without stopping to think about the pros and cons of going into a building with a guy like Kanechika hot on my heels, I ran up the stairs and into a small empty room.

I caught my breath as quietly as I could.

Kanechika came around the corner. "Medium, I could be regey- reggie- regent one day! Come here!"

"Masako! Wake! Up!" This couldn't be happening. I couldn't have subsumed Masako. It was her body, her life, her culture, her era. How could I possibly have been the one to dominate?

I heard Kanechika on the steps. How had he known I was up here? I looked around. The room was empty—nothing to use as a weapon. Each of the four sides of the room had closed sliding doors. I ran to the farthest wall and pushed to slide the door open. It didn't budge. I spun around to run to the left side, nearly tripping again on my robes. That door was locked, so I frantically ran to the right wall. Those doors were also locked. Doors on all four sides, and the only side open was the one I'd come in.

I heard Kanechika's uneven footsteps on the wooden veranda floor. I moved toward the door, mentally preparing myself to jump over the railing.

The snake obake! I hadn't studied for forty years like Ji had, but maybe I could get Kanechika's curse to work for my benefit. I moved to the back wall just as he stumbled in. While he peered around the dark room, I focused on the shimmer just over his head. It changed to a fog-like mist, curling and moving, and then formed into a snake-shape, looking at me just like it had before.

Should I speak out loud? Or would the snake respond to my directed thoughts? Oh, why hadn't Ji taught me how to speak to *obake*? Kanechika still hadn't noticed me, which meant I'd better try the silent method first.

Looking at the serpentine mist, I focused like I'd never focused before. *"O-snake-spirit, you have cursed this horrible man, no doubt for good reason. Please help me. Please stop him from finding me."*

The *obake* rose higher above Kanechika's head. A ghost-like slithering tongue flicked out. I held my breath, not wanting to break concentration for even a second. Then the snake swiftly jabbed Kanechika's tumor.

"Ahhhhh!" He put his hands over his ears as if in terrible pain, and then collapsed onto the ground, shaking his head back and forth and moaning. The snake-mist dissipated, and I stepped over the crying man and headed toward the stairs, turning back for a quick bow to thank the *obake*.

I ran from alley to alley, dodging small animal carcasses and various kinds of excrement as I went, not caring about the smell, only caring about getting to Seimei. This time I remembered to take advantage of Masako's muscle memory, deliberately *not* thinking about where I was going, and arrived at the Bureau of Computation without further trouble.

Seimei glared at me with arms folded. "Mi-Na, why have you stolen your host's body? I am disappointed in you, although somewhat impressed."

"How did-? Never mind. Lord Seimei, I think I might have become the-" My voice cracked. "The dominant spirit. I hope it's only temporary but- anyway, I became very angry at Masako, and yelled at her, and then, all of a sudden, I was in control and I haven't heard from her since. It's like she's not even there. This is *your* fault. I've been here for a year. I did what you wanted me to do. I spied for you. I gave you reports and updates. Why haven't you sent me home? What are you avoiding? Do you even have the power to send me home? Tell me now or I'll- I'll-" What could possibly be a threat to this high-ranking sorcerer? "I'll jump into a lake and drown."

He lowered the arm he'd raised to hit me for my insolence. "And hurt the innocent Masako? She has done nothing to deserve this. You, on the other hand..."

"What? What have I done? *She* pulled me into this world. I didn't ask to come here. Aren't you worried that I might become the dominant spirit permanently? Do you want to deal with *me* all the time? I've learned everything Masako has learned from you. I could be a miko, a powerful one. Is that what you want?"

"Mi-Na, you are like a child with your whining and your questions."

What was it with people here calling me a child? I'd lived on my own in a foreign country for three months, and then came to this place where I'd had to work on surviving in this strange world for a *year*. I was so friggin' mature my head hurt just thinking about it.

He gazed into my eyes searchingly. "Ahhh... yes. You have indeed become dominant, but it is not permanent. I promised I would send you home, and I will. But be patient just a little while longer. It will not be long now."

He was conciliatory, which was very unlike him, but my frustration receded, and I exhaled a long sigh of relief.

"But Lord Seimei, what are you waiting for? You gave my reports to Michinaga, and he used them to humiliate Her Majesty. Isn't that enough? Haven't *I* done enough? And why do you condone his behavior? Her Majesty is so kind and sweet, and loves His Majesty with all her heart. Michinaga doesn't want what's good for the country. He only wants to enrich his family and become grandfather and great-grandfather to future Emperors. And his actions so far have been shameful. Why would the kami bless that? Why shouldn't Korechika become regent? Or even His Majesty – he's almost eighteen. Does he even need a regent?"

He listened to me with one hand smoothing the point on his silver beard. When I finished, he paused as if trying to find the right words. "Well. Yes, a regent is necessary. Emperors are descended from the Great Kami Amaterasu, the Sun Goddess, and their duty is to protect the realm by serving the kami. A regent's duties are secular and political, but I won't go into that now." He paused, looking at the astrological chart on the wall behind me, and then sighed and nodded his head as if his internal debate had been resolved. "Mi-Na, I have a natural talent for seeing the future, a way of looking at each possible path and each possible outcome. This is unrelated to my magic skills, but it is the primary reason I became a diviner." He picked up a cracked turtle shell from his desk, and examined it closely. "When I was young, I realized that if my fa- if Taira no Masakado had succeeded in his attempt to become Emperor, it would have changed *everything*."

He almost said "my father," which meant Seimei really was the son of Masakado, which meant I was right. How did he survive at court with that family history? He must have hidden it well.

He noticed my distraction, and rapped the shell on the desk. "Mi-Na, pay attention! If any clan leader can name himself Emperor, what's to stop a future Fujiwara from doing it? Or any strong leader?"

I'd never thought of that before. What were the factors that made Japan the only country with an unbroken line of succession for almost two thousand years? And what did this have to do with Michinaga?

He put the shell down and stared at me. "And no war will be

as bitter as one fought to determine the true Emperor. Even as a young man, I saw clearly that should Masakado or-" He cleared his throat. "Or his son succeed in overthrowing the current line of succession, this empire would be torn apart from within, and become too weak to defend against outsiders, and so China or Koryo would conquer us."

I put a hand against the wall for balance, dizzy from the enormity of his prediction.

He had more to say. "Lord Michinaga has no interest in the trappings of royalty. He wants power and riches, as you say, but he is content to marry his daughters to crown princes and to know his descendants will be emperors. He has no interest in becoming emperor, and that sets a precedent that others will follow. Yes, there will be wars, and I know Fujiwara power will eventually fade away, but the line of emperors will remain unbroken, and this country will remain strong enough to defend ourselves against outsiders. I read in the stars many years ago that Lord Michinaga's regency will protect the realm from a terrible future, and while I sympathize with your point of view, I am compelled to complete my plan as the kami have indicated I should."

Chaos and conquering if Michinaga weren't regent? How could one person have so much effect on history? "But Lord Seimei, Korechika doesn't want to be emperor either. He would never push His Majesty out and put himself in his place. They're like brothers."

"He would not, but he is weak and rash and would be replaced by someone stronger, who would then be replaced by someone stronger yet. And that person will proclaim himself Emperor, and terrible wars would tear this island apart, leaving it vulnerable to conquerors. This is as certain as the sun rising at the Hour of the Rabbit."

Japan conquered by Korea or China? I wanted Korechika to be regent in order to save Sadako from Michinaga's endless humiliations, but if he was, the Japan I knew might not exist.

I sank to my knees, holding my hands over my burning eyes, my head aching. "I don't care what happens to Korechika, but isn't there anything we can do to help the Empress?"

He knelt and pulled my hands down, locking his eyes on mine. "Just watch over Her Majesty. The worst has not yet come for her. Be there to brighten her darkness. You cannot save her without jeopardizing the future you know and love."

His dark eyes gleamed with sympathy, and tears formed in my own eyes. I bowed my head to hide them.

"Lord Seimei, the book that Sei Shonagon is writing. It cheers Her Majesty so much to read it, and to know that others are reading it too. Michinaga has threatened to destroy it because it makes fun of him and describes how wonderful Sadako's court is. I want to make sure the book is preserved. How can I prevent the Regent from destroying it?"

"As a spirit from another world, you have power over the Lord Regent you have not yet realized. Use that power to save Shonagon's book. Now, Mi-Na, I will bring Masako back to dominance."

I needed to trust him. What choice did I have? I lifted my head to allow his hypnotic gaze to entrance me.

And suddenly I was no longer in control. Masako was holding her head—although I felt like it was my head, too—and sank to the floor, dizzy.

"Masako, I was angry with you for ignoring me. Seimei was able to bring you back, thank the kami."

"Mi-Na, I heard what you said, and felt what you did, so I was still present in my body, but I had no power, and no ability to communicate with you. Kanechika frightened us both, but Mi-Na, you spoke to the obake!"

"It was nothing," I said modestly. "But I think the binding, or fusing as I call it, has begun for real. We don't have much longer. But Seimei said to be patient, he'll send me home before it happens. And we have a lot to think about. He said we can't save Sadako, but we can save her reputation."

Chapter 37

Historic Meeting

Eleventh Month, Chōhō 2 (December, 1000 CE)

We were comfortably ensconced in the Empress's quarters with several braziers providing warmth, and oil lamps providing light, while the closed shutters kept the cold wind out. Masako and Sei were playing their version of peek-a-boo with Princess Nagako, who laughed in the unrestrained way of young children everywhere. Sadako held Prince Atsuyasu, who stared at her with the worship and devotion she deserved.

Every time I looked at the Empress, my heart broke a little more, and my resolve to protect *The Pillow Book* grew stronger. I couldn't do anything to save her, but I could at least save her story. She'd never fully recovered from Atsuyasu's birth, and she wasn't eating enough, so she was weak and tired all the time. She'd moved back to the Emperor's First Avenue residence in Eighth Month. Her fear for her position made her plaintive and teary as she tried to convince His Majesty to make their son Crown Prince. He seemed to want that too, but he kept putting her off. I'm sure he was very polite. I'd never seen him raise his voice to anyone, not even a servant, but he was stubborn, so the

Historic Meeting 323

Empress gave up and moved back to Narimasa's place for the duration of her pregnancy.

By Tenth Month the new imperial palace was completed, and the Emperor moved in. Junior Empress Akiko moved in as well. Empress Sadako was too far along to risk giving birth at the palace, so she remained in Narimasa's cramped quarters.

His Majesty did visit the baby, though, and he was delighted by Princess Nagako, giving her many little gifts and getting on the floor to play with her just like any other parent. It was a rare bright spot in this gloomy winter to see how much he loved both children. He was excited to be a father again, and he quoted the proverb, "if one must have a child, let it be a girl."

I'd heard that a few times now, and it always took me by surprise. So many cultures prioritized boys. *"The proverb must refer to a Fujiwara baby, not to an Emperor's child. Girl princesses are problematic because they rank too high to marry most nobles, so they become shrine priestesses or nuns, or just live at court without much purpose in life."*

Masako had become very fond of Princess Nagako. *"'Mi-Na, let's do what we can to ensure a purposeful life for her."*

"I'll do my best." I didn't remember anything about Princess Nagako. Did that mean she died young? Or had I forgotten everything I'd learned in school? I'd begun to have trouble remembering things about home. I tried visualizing my mother, and drew a blank. That scared me more than Kanechika's attack had.

I pushed Masako again to ask Seimei to send me home, but he put her off the same way he did me, with vague answers. There was nothing else we could do. It could be a long time before Masako had the skill and power to send me back, and she might screw it up and send me somewhere else entirely. I believed in her, but this wasn't one of those movies where someone becomes an expert in something in three days. It took years to become a miko.

Sei plotted with the Kamo High Priestess to get the Empress out of the capital for a change of atmosphere, hoping to cheer her up. They arranged that we would all visit the Priestess's residence at Murasakino.

When we arrived, the Priestess greeted us with warmth and sympathy. She directed Masako and Sei to a small group of women gathered behind a screen, telling them that she wanted to chat with the Empress alone. We walked over to the screen and bowed to the women standing there. Masako recognized three of the four women: Lord Korenaka's wife Lady Shigeko; Akiko's mother (and Michinaga's wife) Lady Michiko; and Empress Sadako's sister, Lady Motoko, consort to Prince Okisada. A fourth woman stood there with an air of uncertainty, like she wasn't quite sure why she was in such exalted company.

Lady Michiko came forward to greet us. "Shonagon, your book excerpts are so... *okashi*, as you might say. Amusing. Lord Michinaga thought you would enjoy meeting another writer of great merit. You have much in common. She also can read and write Chinese, although *she* is too humble to talk about it." She gestured toward the fourth woman. "Meet Lord Nobutaka's wife, the author of the stories about the shining Genji." She smiled. "A wonderful tale. I dare say it will be copied much more widely than your book."

Masako watched as Sei forced a smile and bowed. Murasaki —although she wouldn't be called Murasaki for a few years yet —bowed back, looking at Sei with intelligent, melancholy eyes, her mouth tipped down but not quite a frown, looking like an academic who spent all her time thinking serious thoughts about serious stuff.

I was thrilled. *"Masako, keep your eyes on these two. This is* historic! Nobody in my world thinks these two met in person this early, and I get to see it! Nobody will believe me. But I'll know it happened."

Masako, amused at my enthusiasm, indulged me.

Sei started chattering right away. "So you read Chinese? Do you prefer Bai Juyi or Li Po's poetry? Your father is also a provincial governor? I heard you spent some time in Echizen. It must have been awful. I never understood why anyone would choose to live in those uncivilized places. If they had any choice in the matter, of course. My mother was a lady-in-waiting to the previous Empress. Who was your mother?"

"*She's talking too much,*" I said to Masako. "*We need to stop this train wreck. I mean this ox-cart crash.*"

"*It's not my conversation to interrupt,*" Masako said, and she was right, so I had to watch the whole painful episode. Murasaki responded politely but coldly, and even from my viewpoint I could see disdain in her eyes. And now Sei was going to be judged through the centuries when the future Murasaki wrote in her book that Sei was conceited and would come to no good end. Like cyber-bullying, she couldn't defend herself because she wouldn't see the post.

Lady Shigeko interrupted Sei to ask her opinion on a robe combination, saving her from further humiliation, and Murasaki turned to Masako, her eyes brightening with interest. "A medium? Do you work for the Kamo Shrine?" she asked, staring at my host with unusual intensity.

"I am Imperial Medium for the Senior Empress. I am also a pupil of the Royal Astrologer. Someday I hope to serve at one of the imperial shrines. Everyone at the Empress's court admires your tales, how your words create pictures and bring strong feelings into our hearts. I heard you recently had a baby girl. It must be difficult to continue writing, but we all hope you do."

"Yes, my little girl is nearly a year old. Do you not care to be married and have children? As Imperial Shrine attendant, you will have to be devoted to the kami."

"Marriage holds no interest for me, nor do love affairs. I do not understand why everyone talks about it all the time. I am quite the opposite of your Genji!"

Murasaki leaned closer, her eyes glinting with humor. "I will tell you a secret, Medium. I am too. That's why I married an old friend of my father's. Two other wives to keep him busy, and he's quite old so he doesn't bother me much. Yet he is kind, and we have fascinating conversations, and he allows me as much time to write as I can fit in with my other duties, so I am content with marriage."

Masako smiled warmly. *"Mi-Na, finally I have found someone else who is not obsessed with love affairs!"*

Which I thought was weirdly ironic, considering the *Tale of Genji* was all about Genji having one affair after another.

Before the conversation could continue, the High Priestess gestured at Masako and Sei to come talk to her. Masako excused herself with sincere regret. Sei, who had been happily describing the best colors for the season to Lady Shigeko and Lady Motoko, came with us.

The High Priestess sighed. "I fear for the Empress. She is not sick, but she is not well. She will not eat, so dispirited is she by these recent events. She has been ill-served in spite of her love and devotion to His Majesty. Imperial Medium, please keep a close watch on her. She is too kind and sweet to be made to suffer so. Keep her children near. They provide some joy in these sad circumstances. Ah, here she comes."

Sadako had been standing in front of a sutra scroll, apparently praying, but had turned to walk toward us. She took one step forward, and then swayed as if dizzy.

Masako moved toward her, but before she took two steps, Sadako swayed again and crumpled to the ground, looking like a patch of sasa-grass in her heap of white and green robes. Everyone ran to her with cries of alarm.

"*Tell them to get away. Let her breathe, it's too stuffy in here!*" I cried.

Masako used her authority as a healer-medium to wave everyone away. Sadako was breathing rapidly, her eyes turned up in her head. Masako waved her fan to blow fresh air into her face, while Sei loosened the Empress's belt and her many robe layers.

I was shocked at how thin Sadako had become, and how gaunt her face was. She was seven months pregnant, so she should have been plump. This had happened on our watch. Literally. We observed her almost every day. How did I not notice she wasn't eating? Instead, I'd worried about my own situation. I couldn't blame Masako. She wasn't from an era of advanced nutritional knowledge, but I was. I should have had Masako prescribe more green and orange foods.

"*Masako, it's not too late. Please do whatever you can to get tempting and tasty food to the Empress. Sea vegetables, yams, mandarin oranges, nuts—all that.*"

She ignored me. She was praying to the kami to let Her Majesty live.

Chapter 38

A Dangerous Gamble

Twelfth Month, Chōhō 2 (January, 1001 CE)

The Empress went into labor in the last month of Chōhō 2, and while another imperial birth should have been cause for celebration, no one could summon joy when the mother herself had none. The past weeks had been filled with worry and concern. The Empress's health continued to decline. She had no interest in food, no matter the delicacies prepared for her, eating at most a few grains of rice and some persimmon slices. She refused to listen to music or poetry readings. The only entertainment that held her attention was Sei reading entries from her book. Once in a while a clever turn of phrase would make her smile, and that was motivation enough to keep Sei writing.

Empress Sadako sent letter after letter to the Emperor, and he responded with loving replies, but his time and attention was taken up with the new Empress's court. Michinaga had met every announcement about Sadako's pregnancy and health with new artifacts for Akiko's salon: ivory statues from China; pottery from Koryo; a new volume of poetry. Each item was a spider's sticky strand pulling the cultured Emperor into the web of the

Regent's plan. It was a competition Michinaga had a fierce desire to win, and his opponent knew she was going to lose.

Watching Empress Sadako's despair, I raged at my helplessness.

Masako begged me to calm down. I was giving her a headache. "It's her destiny, Mi-Na. We must help her as much as we can, but we should not attempt to change her fate. Seimei and the High Priestess agreed the one thing we can do is preserve her book. Let's focus on that."

I'd been espousing that viewpoint for months, so why did it bother me she was right?

Masako and Sei maintained a correspondence with Princess Nobuko to keep her apprised of Sadako's health, but I ranted about that too. "If she cares so much, why doesn't she intervene? She's an imperial princess and the Emperor's aunt. She could at least talk him into visiting more often."

"Mi-Na, you know why. She has remained in her post for so long because she is seen as impartial."

"And you don't want her to lose her job because you want to serve her at the Kamo Shrine," I said, unable to keep a bitter tone from leaching into my words.

"Mi-Na, you know better than anyone how much I care about Her Majesty, but the High Priestess shouldn't sacrifice her position when it won't change the outcome. Please let go of your anger, or use it to save Her Majesty's reputation."

And now the Empress's labor had begun. Masako was allowed to attend after promising not to take risky actions like calling up shikigami. Sei was there, in addition to a nun-midwife (a new one because the nun who attended the prince's birth refused, and no one blamed her) and a priest. Sadako's labor wasn't long, and her new baby girl arrived without drama at the end of the cold, wintry day.

The Empress barely looked at the tiny thing. Instead, she

closed her eyes, her arms going limp so that the wet-nurse had to quickly take the baby before she fell.

Sei and Masako looked at each other in shock. "Your Majesty," Sei pleaded, "Look at your beautiful girl! See her? She's perfect!"

Actually she was very small and thin. Sadako had carried her to full term, but her lack of interest in food had kept her baby from growing to a healthy size.

The nurse knelt on a mat to hold the baby up to Sadako's face. Maybe that new-baby smell would rouse her interest?

It didn't work. She swatted the nurse's arm away, so Sei signaled the nurse to take the baby to the wet-nurse.

Empress Sadako's lack of interest in her new daughter didn't change. Even a visit from her older children didn't disrupt her lethargy, so Sei asked Lord Narimasa to write to the Emperor. A visit from him might be the only thing that would lighten her depression.

He wrote back to say he dearly wanted to see her and to meet the new baby, but due to required ceremonies and rituals, he couldn't visit for a few days.

Sei tried to make the best of it—"His Majesty will come by very soon, by the 15th day! Won't he be thrilled with his perfect daughter? He dearly loves his children" —but Sadako didn't take it well, refusing to eat or drink and turning her head when we tried to push rice or water into her mouth, not bothering to wipe away tears falling continuously down her cheeks.

Seimei divined that the new imperial princess should be named Bishi. The Chinese character "Bi" was made up of the character for "beautiful" and the character for "woman." The character for "shi" was the character for "child." Beautiful girl-child.

As Masako read Seimei's message, I had a thought. "*Masako,* an alternate pronunciation of the characters bi and shi would be mi and ko. Miko! Seimei named her after you!"

"This is no laughing matter, Mi-Na. This name was chosen after many hours of careful divination."

"Ask Sei, she knows Chinese characters. She'll tell you I'm right!"

"Sei will see that as a vain and ignorant question, and she'll mock me for it."

I kept pushing her, because if I was right, it would lighten up this gloomy atmosphere.

Masako grew tired of my nagging. "Shonagon, you are so clever with reading and writing. Do these characters for Bishi's name have an alternate pronunciation?"

Sei nodded, pleased with the flattery. "Well, it's an odd name. The alternate pronunciation would be Yoshiko. But we have been instructed to pronounce it Bishi."

Masako couldn't help herself. *"Told you so."* She had become too much like me, and not in a good way.

"Well, in my era, it could be pronounced Miko," I replied, and I felt her face grow warm.

Over the next few hours Masako, Sei, and a priest watched over the Empress as she grew weaker and weaker. The priest chanted a sutra and kept incense burning, Sei prayed to Buddha, and Masako prayed to Sadako's family kami.

The Empress didn't seem to notice or care that we were there. Sei tried to get her to take a sip of water, but she turned her head away. Could they have forced her to drink? Maybe, but inhibitions of rank kept them from trying. I had to argue with Masako to check her pulse. Touching the Empress's wrist was a breach of protocol, but she finally agreed. Her pulse was faint and irregular.

"That's not a good sign. We have to do something, but I don't know what. It's like she doesn't want to live anymore. Tell her to live for the sake of her three children."

Masako felt the same way, but of course she wasn't going to tell the Empress to do anything, so instead she asked the nurse to bring the children in again.

Princess Nagako was four years old, or five by this era's reckoning. She was a lively, precocious child with huge eyes that observed everything. She loved Sei, and would sit by her side for hours. Sei had started teaching her to read *onnade* and write *waka* poems, and even at her young age, she picked it up quickly.

She held a large scrap of green paper, her writing huge and messy, but better than my Japanese writing on my best day. She tugged her mother's sleeve. "Mama, listen!"

Sadako didn't react, so Nagako looked at Sei for instruction.

"Go on, read it. She can hear you. She is too weak to open her eyes."

"Mama, I hope you like my poem. Lady Shonagon helped me with it."

She read in a clear, high voice.

"Cold, pointy needles
poke me when I try to reach
A pine-cone under the snow.
Mother, do I stop trying?
Or will you wake up to help?"

Masako blinked away tears, and Sei held her brilliant orange sleeve over her face to hide her own. Sadako didn't react at all.

Nagako, confused at these reactions, began to cry. Sei comforted her by saying we were moved by the poem's beauty, and even the Emperor would shed tears at a lovely poem or piece of music. Nagako tucked her paper scrap into her mother's sleeve, gave a sweet jerky little bow, and her nurse escorted the children out.

An hour later the Empress stirred. Hopeful, Masako bent over her. *"Maybe she's waking up! Maybe having the children here helped!"*

A Dangerous Gamble 333

She opened her eyes, staring blankly at the ceiling, then turning her head to Sei, who was chanting a sutra. She touched Sei's rosary, and moved her lips without sound. Masako bent still closer in an effort to hear.

"*I'm not sure what she's saying. Can you tell?*" I asked, knowing it was a silly question, since we shared the same ears.

But maybe not so silly. "*She's saying Amida Buddha,*" Masako replied. "*I don't recite sutras or Buddha's name, so it's not familiar to you.*"

Sei put her rosary in Sadako's hands, and leaned close enough to pull the Empress's hands into her own sleeves for warmth.

Now I knew what Sadako was saying, I could see her lips forming the words. "Amida Buddha, Amida Buddha," over and over. She stopped, then exhaled.

She didn't inhale. We waited for what felt like hours but was probably only seconds. Still no inhale.

"*Try CPR! Try mouth to mouth resuscitation!*" I knew Masako wouldn't understand me, and even if she did, she wouldn't breach protocol to that extent.

The priest picked up his chanting, and Masako prayed harder, but it was too late. Empress Sadako had passed on to the spirit world.

The next few days brought many condolences to Sadako's court as well as covert sympathy for the plight that led to her death. Korechika was distraught, alternating between tears of self-pity and fury. Takaie, sad but practical, took care of cremation arrangements. The Emperor, we heard, was very distressed.

Sei had no future at court. She had antagonized Michinaga with her book, so of course he wouldn't allow her to become a member of Akiko's court, and Korechika's future was also uncertain. We had heard from secret sympathizers that Michinaga had already started gathering copies of Sei's book to destroy them.

Masako agreed to let me take over so I could speak with Sei directly.

"Sei, the children need someone to protect them. Korechika still has a vested interest in Prince Atsuyasu becoming Crown Prince, but they need someone who has Michinaga's support, someone who can intercede with the Regent if needed. I know you're furious with Yukinari, and I don't blame you, but he seems like a good guy. Even-tempered, not a big drinker or gambler like Korechika, and he's pragmatic. Maybe he'll accept a trade. You delete the passages in your book that make fun of him and write nice things instead, and in return he protects the Empress's children. If you publish those passages making him look like an idiot, he won't help."

Sei waved her arms in frustration, the sleeves of her gray silk mourning robes gleaming in the dim room. "But Spirit, he is the one who came up with the justification for a Second Empress. That humiliation is what finally crushed Her Majesty. Princess Bishi is not thriving. She is tiny, much smaller than Princess Nagako at birth, and she refuses the wet-nurse's breast more often than she accepts. If she dies-" She paused to blink away tears. "It will be Yukinari's fault as well as the Regent's." A servant slid the door open in alarm. Sei waved her away. "Yukinari deserves worse than being a joke in my book, which the Regent will destroy anyway."

"I understand, but you loved Yukinari. Yes, he betrayed us and now you want revenge. But you loved him for a reason. He's direct, like you. And intelligent, also like you. And sincere. If he promises to protect the children, he'll do it."

I could see she was torn, so I kept going. "I suspect the Regent fears spirits and ghosts more than he fears the living, because he can control the living, but he can't control the dead. And he's responsible for Her Majesty's death. Let's tell him Empress Sadako's angry ghost will haunt him if he destroys your book."

I didn't know if Michinaga would respond to such a threat, but he'd been upset when Masako threatened him with my "spirit fury." And I'd become better at *not* going down the rabbit hole of worst-case scenarios. I refused to think about the terrible things that would happen to us if I was wrong.

Sei eventually agreed to my logic. She would have to leave court soon, so she was spending her time writing and gathering up her papers. She was also considering whether to get another husband. Fortunately for Sei, in spite of her advanced age of thirty-five, her hair shot through with silver, her influence declining after her Empress's death, she still had many suitors. Her sensitivity to beauty, her own beauty still evident and enhanced by her unerring sense of dress and cosmetics, allowed her the pick of middle-rank nobles and provincial governors. Did she want to leave the capital for the hinterland? Of course not, but at least she wouldn't starve.

When Masako came out of her trance, I filled her in on the details. *"I need to take over one more time to talk to Michinaga. He's not scared of you. He's not scared of me either, but he will be by the time I'm done with him."*

She agreed. *"But Mi-Na, we need to get Seimei's support for this. Otherwise the Regent will run to him for help exorcising you, or if he truly believes the Empress's angry ghost is haunting him."*

She had a good point. Seimei would never betray the Regent, but he'd been deeply disappointed when Michinaga asked Masako to be a false medium, and he was saddened by the Empress's demise. It was a risk, of course. He might tell Michinaga we were bluffing.

After a period of purification, having been next to the

Empress when she died, Masako was finally allowed to attend a tutoring session with Seimei.

Masako's hands shook, and her palms were so sweaty she dropped her divination sticks too soon.

Seimei looked at her with compassion, his hands clasped inside his white sleeves. "Is it the death of Her Majesty that has made you so clumsy today, Medium? You must learn to control your feelings, otherwise it could direct the divination in an unfortunate direction."

"Sorry, Lord Seimei. Yes. But also, we—Mi-Na and I—we have a request." She kept her head bowed.

"Speak, Medium. Do you think you are ready to become a miko? Is that it?"

"Not yet, Lord Seimei. It's about Sei Shonagon's book. Remember? The only thing we could do to help the Empress was to preserve it?" Masako's voice grew stronger and she lifted her head. "The Lord Regent has already destroyed many copies. Mi-Na plans to threaten him with Empress Sadako's angry ghost if he doesn't stop. We need you to support us."

Seimei smiled like a proud grandfather. "Excellent. You found a way that only Mi-Na could execute. Her Majesty was innocent, and the Emperor loved her. He didn't mean to neglect her, you know. He will want her court to be remembered. So yes, I will support your effort. His Majesty will want me to do that for her."

Masako's shoulders dropped in relief. She thanked him with a deep bow, and we agreed to make an appointment with Michinaga for the next day.

Masako had me take over while we were at the Bureau of Computation. *"I'll be too nervous to put myself into a trance while waiting for Lord Michinaga,"* she'd reasoned.

I walked to Michinaga's office slowly, taking in deep breaths of cool, damp air. The snow had melted, the sun was shining, and a light mist rose from the ground. I focused on the moment, on the illusion of freedom, the simple joy of moving my body under my own will. And it distracted me from thinking about the risk I was about to take. I didn't have a lot of evidence to support my theory that Michinaga was scared of ghosts.

As usual the Regent kept me waiting in an outer room, the same one I had waited in twice before. A guard slid the door open and the Lord Regent strode in with his usual arrogance, a smug smile on his face. "Lady Masako, what brings to you the Bureau of Imperial Affairs? Are you looking for a new job? I'm afraid we have no need for an imperial medium here, and my daughter is well taken care of. You were not much help the last time I asked for it, so sadly, I cannot give you a good reference."

I raised a shaking fan to cover my flushed face. I wanted to cuss at him, but I didn't have confidence my swear words would translate through Masako's brain in any meaningful way. Even after all this time, I still wasn't sure how this language thing worked. "You killed Empress Sadako, an innocent, loving mother of three children, and loyal consort to His Majesty!"

His smile fell away as he folded his arms and glared at me. "Ah, the Spirit Mi-Na. Lady Masako would never use that kind of language with me, but I could have *her* arrested for those words. Do you want to destroy her life? Her punishment would be severe."

I set my fan on the table with a slap to show I meant business. And then hid my hands in my sleeves so he wouldn't see them trembling. "I have connections in the spirit world, and I happen to know that Empress Sadako's angry ghost holds you responsible for her death." I folded my arms and glared at him in imitation of his stance.

He took a step back. "I don't believe you. She died in childbirth. Many women do. I am sorry for her children, and as members of the imperial family, they will be taken care of. If that is all you came to say, leave now, before I call my guards."

"Oh no, Lord Asshole-" *oops!* It just slipped out. "I have a *lot* more to say."

Michinaga gave a loud bark of a laugh. "Spirit, you are ignorant and pathetic. I will order Seimei to send you back to your world. You are no use to us now that the Empress is gone. I'm calling the guards-"

"*Machi-na!* Wait!" I used the rudest, most masculine language I knew, and his mouth dropped open in shock. I seized the moment before he could reply. "You know in your heart you humiliated Empress Sadako to further your own selfish goals. And she knew it too. She will haunt you and curse you. If you don't believe me, ask the Royal Astrologer you love so much."

He snapped his mouth shut, and for the first time, looked like he believed me. Apparently Seimei's name worked for regents as well as shikigami.

Now for the payoff. "Sadako's angry ghost will only be mollified by one thing. Well, by two things. Protecting her children, of course, and allowing Sei Shonagon's book to be copied and disseminated, even printed. You know, with those wooden blocks like they use in China."

Disbelief fought with fear on his face, and disbelief won. "You lie, Spirit. Why would her ghost care so much for the shallow musings of an indifferent poet? Dull lists of insects or bridges or shrines? Why do *you* care?"

"The Empress's ghost cares because Sei's book will preserve her reputation, and you know, the fact *that she even existed*? We all know you're trying to erase her to make your daughter's salon known as the most glorious ever. So unless you want to be haunted to an early death, you need to preserve Sei's book so future generations can read it. Since you still don't believe me, I could call up her angry ghost right now if you like. Or even better, I'll tell her to haunt little Akiko so the Emperor will avoid her. Is that what you want?" I had no doubt he'd never been talked to this way before.

It worked. He was clearly unsettled, pacing back and forth, muttering to himself, his lips tight with anger, his painted eyebrows drawn together in a deep frown.

At last he gave an irritated sigh. "It is a nothing book that no one will read in ten years unless it's to mock the author for her stupid little jottings. And you say the Empress's ghost will be satisfied and move onto the spirit world if I don't destroy the book? Of course I'll confirm the truth with Seimei as well as order him to return you to your world. If you are lying... poor, poor Masako. She won't deserve the terrible fate I have in mind for the two of you."

Seimei had better live up to his end of the bargain. He could really screw us over right now. "And the same rules apply to Masako. Treat her well or else I'll become an *onryō* and haunt you myself. And maybe we call on a few shikigami for help cursing you. Got it?" So fun to use this rude language to the man who'd humiliated sweet Sadako. My excitement had made me reckless.

He moved toward me, his hand raised as if to strike. At the last second he turned to the wooden screen next to me and slapped it instead, making me jump at the sound reverberating through the room. "I never want to see either of you ever again. If I do, I'll have you arrested and order Seimei to banish your spirit to *Jigoku*."

I gave a so-short-it-was-terribly-rude bow and walked out the door.

Chapter 39

Millennial Plan

Twelfth Month, Chōhō 2 (January, 1001 CE)

"*Masako, wake up, wake up! It worked!*" I practically danced on the way to the palace, my feet and heart light, feeling happier and more optimistic than I'd been in months. "*You can wake up now!*"

She took control so suddenly I wasn't prepared, and as she wasn't expecting her body to be skipping along the gravel path between buildings, she stumbled and fell sprawling in the dirt, gravel biting into her hands, hakama cloth ripping at the knee.

"*Itashi ya!*" she cried out while inside I said '*Ow!*' and then we both started laughing at the absurdity of sharing one body.

"*At least no one was watching when that happened. Although everyone expects you to be weird. It's the cost of spirit possession. I love that about this place.*"

She brushed her hakama off and stood back up. "Mi-Na, my heart is beating very fast and my hands are shaking. Were you scared? Did it work? Did the Regent agree to our demands?"

"*Yes, yes, and yes! Oh Masako, I didn't expect it to go so well. I was so rude to him. He could've arrested me on the spot. But it worked.*"

He knows Sadako's ghost would be justified in wreaking vengeance on him, so he agreed! And bonus feature, he'll order Seimei to send me home! I'm finally getting out of here!"

I expected her to echo my giddy relief, but she was quiet.

"Masako? Aren't you happy? I'm saying our plan worked! Michinaga will allow the distribution of Sei's book to go unchecked! Of course he will confirm our story with Seimei, who'll back us up."

Masako sighed with either exasperation or disappointment. Or both. "Of course I'm happy it worked. It's my body that would be arrested and exiled if it didn't work. I do wish you hadn't been so rude, it's very unlike me. But I'm sure that your behavior was much more convincing than mine would have been. You are not me, Mi-Na, and I forget that more and more as time goes by. Are you so very happy to leave me? Aren't you worried you won't have a body to return to after all this time?"

Oh. Way to bring me down. "Of course I don't want to leave you. You're a part of me now, just as I'm part of you. Seimei will have to rip us apart, and I'm sure it will leave a huge hole in our souls that might never heal. But I have no purpose here anymore. You must see that, don't you?"

"Mi-Na, there have been so many times when I wanted to have my body back to myself, to have some privacy, and especially to stop your incessant comments and questions. But you opened my eyes to possibilities I never thought to pray for. You provided me with companionship, solace, and humor. You encouraged—or I should say commanded?—me to pursue my dreams. You could have been an angry, vindictive spirit, but you weren't. You made the best of your strange, unwilling journey out of your world and into mine. You are correct. It's time for you to leave me. I'm ready. It's just that- it's just-" she stopped, trying to divine the right words. "I have to relearn what it is to live alone in my body. And I will miss you."

"I feel the same way, Masako. You put up with a lot from me. I ordered you around, took control of your body without permission, and made you a pariah among the Empress's women. And you're always so patient with my unending questions about this place. Will you do something for me? It's really important or I wouldn't ask."

Masako kept walking in spite of the tears falling onto her cheeks. I guessed it didn't matter if anyone saw. Everyone in the Empress's residence was crying at random moments these days. "Of course, Mi-Na, what is it?"

"Can you record what happened to us, and try to preserve it somewhere safe? I'm going to need evidence of what I learned here. A book of some sort? It won't be easy to find a way to keep it safe for a thousand years, but maybe the High Priestess can help."

"Good idea. I will chronicle these events and I will think of a way to save it for you. But don't blame me if you never find it. A thousand years is impossible to imagine. So many things could happen to destroy it."

Just then Sei walked by, so Masako gave her the news about our intervention with Michinaga. She listened to the story with great interest, nodding her head, laughing at Masako's description of my rude behavior, horrified at the risk we took.

"I must tell you how very impressed I am with your adventurous spirit, Lady Masako," Sei said with a wry laugh to show us the word-play was intended. "You managed to best the most powerful man in the realm. But just having the Regent's word that he won't destroy my book doesn't mean it will be copied and shared over the next twenty years. I have an idea." She gestured toward a couple of mats. "Please sit down. We need to discuss this quietly."

Intrigued, Masako sat, as did Sei. I was curious too.

"Lord Yukinari has agreed to your plan. I will alter the description of him in my book, and he will protect the children. Princess Nagako will want to preserve her mother's reputation. The Kamo High Priestess has said she will oversee the Princess's education, and will teach her to maintain my book, and ensure

Her Majesty is not forgotten. The High Priestess will keep my finished book until the princess is old enough to ensure it's maintained, copied, and shared widely."

"Tell Sei I think that's brilliant! Michinaga might try to suppress the book once he thinks Sadako's ghost has moved on, but if an imperial princess is in charge of it, he would have a much more difficult time. And by then the Emperor might be strong enough to resist as well, especially if his beloved daughter begs him for help. And it will give Princess Nagako a purpose in life."

Masako conveyed my words to Sei along with her own praise for the plan, and Sei smiled. "I am pleased my idea meets with your approval," she said. "Now, go to Seimei, confirm he supported you with the Regent, and learn what Masako's future holds for her. And Mi-Na, if Seimei should send you home before we meet again? Thank you for the hope you have given me that my little lists and stories will be read one thousand years from now, and that Empress Sadako will be remembered in your world for her goodness, her beauty and intelligence, and for her love and loyalty to His Majesty. I could not ask for more. I will move to my ex-husband's estate. I have received several offers of marriage, but all of them are to men of rank who must serve in the provinces before their next promotions, and while it's awful for me to leave court, it's even worse to live in the country. How did you bear it, Medium?"

Masako perked up and started to chatter about the wonders of the Taira estate in Hitachi, but Sei stood up and excused herself. "Medium, you were supposed to answer with a sad shake of your head. You will never convince me the countryside has anything good to offer. Pray to the kami for me, and I will recite a sutra for you and for Mi-Na's journey home."

She spun around to leave, her robe hems flying out like a gray and white pinwheel.

"Sei Shonagon, always the center of attention," I said affectionately. *"Next stop for us: Bureau of Computation."*

"Seimei is expecting me later this afternoon. We will go then. Let's eat something first. I am so very hungry!"

"Spirit possession takes a lot out of you, I've noticed."

At the appointed hour, Masako showed up at the Bureau with cold and shaking hands. It was a chilly afternoon, but also we didn't know what to expect from Seimei. Was he going to send me home or decide he needed me for something else? Was he a good person underneath it all? His treatment of Masako suggested he was. Or was he secretly evil and using us both in his scheming and manipulation?

Good and bad didn't seem quite distinct as it did before my arrival here. Take Michinaga for example. Commoners and many nobles seemed to think he was the best ruler they'd had in a long time. He was generous with those who supported him, applied the law strictly and for the most part fairly, and had a pleasant personality when he wasn't trying to scare me or humiliate Sadako. No one wanted to be on his bad side, because he could—and did—deny promotions and lucrative assignments for those who were disloyal. He was religious, and his Buddhist strictures against killing meant he rarely approved capital punishment, and he didn't eat meat. Most importantly, he never tried to become Emperor himself, setting a precedent that other regents—and someday, shoguns—would follow. That alone made him good. In Seimei's opinion, anyway. But if he found out we lied, he wouldn't hesitate to do very bad things to us. So that made him bad. In my opinion, anyway.

As Masako entered the Royal Astrologer's office, Seimei was

busy dictating the result of a recent divination to an apprentice. He sent the young man away when he saw her.

"Medium! You and Spirit Mi-Na have created quite a stir! His Excellency the Lord Regent stopped by, very upset. Yes, yes, very, very upset." He rubbed his hands together with excitement, or maybe to warm them. "He wanted to know if there was any chance Her Majesty's angry ghost would haunt him, and if I could put a stop to it." He paused to observe Masako. Her cheeks were cold and she was a little light-headed, so I guessed she was pale with fear.

He laughed with mischievous glee. "And I told him yes, it was very possible—which isn't a lie, by the way, it really is a possibility—and no, I couldn't stop it. The only way to appease such a ghost is to fulfill its wish, whether for vengeance or vindication. And since her wish is to have Shonagon's book preserved, well, that is the only way to appease her. Then he ordered me to send Mi-Na home. He believes she's a *threat!*" He laughed as if that was the funniest thing he'd heard in a long time.

Masako exhaled, blood rushing back to her cheeks, and she bowed in thanks. *"He did it, Mi-Na, he supported us against Michinaga."*

"Maybe he's not so bad after all."

"And, Medium, I have wonderful news for you. The Kamo High Priestess is most impressed with your work as Imperial Medium and with your devotion to the Empress. She has offered you a position at the Kamo Imperial Shrine as Shrine Miko." He beamed at her.

Masako pressed her sleeved hands against her mouth with a loud gasp, her eyes widening in a weird combination of disbelief and joy. "Really? Truly? Did she? She wants me? My rank isn't a problem?"

"Silly girl, you apprenticed with the most famous diviner in the realm. And even though your father is only Fifth Rank, you are a Taira, descended from an Emperor. And while your experience with men will not disqualify you from this position, you must remain celibate while serving at the shrine. The kami need to know you serve them, and only them. Understood?"

She gasped out a "yes, understood," while trying to process this information.

"And your maidservant—Yumi, is it? She may attend you at Kamo. And next, the Spirit Mi-Na. I will send her home. The Regent ordered this, and the Kamo Priestess does not want a miko who is already possessed. Mi-Na completed her purpose here. Yes, she provided important information about Her Majesty, but what I believed to be her true purpose, she fulfilled without realizing it. She opened your soul to allow great power to flow in. You do not need her now, Medium, or should I say, Miko."

Masako and I were both overjoyed at this news. She paced back and forth, unable to contain herself, while I suddenly thought of a potential problem.

"What if he's wrong? What if he can't do this correctly, and I end up somewhere else? Or what if your spirit gets sent into my body while I'm left behind in yours, what happens then?"

Masako stopped cold and glanced at Seimei.

"What's wrong, Miko? Did Mi-Na say something?"

"She's concerned our spirits have grown together like two closely planted trees that become entwined, and that extricating her will be difficult. Perhaps you will send my spirit instead, or hers somewhere other than her body."

He nodded as if he expected that question. "I won't lie. It will be the greatest challenge of my divination career. That is why I need time to read the stars. There may be spiritual pain for both of you during the separation, and I can't promise something won't go wrong. Mi-Na told me previously that it was one day before the new moon when she left. The phase of the moon is more important than the time of year. I will schedule the ritual for the day before the first day of the First Month."

"Tell Seimei if anything goes wrong, I will come back to haunt him for the rest of his elderly life."

"Oh, Mi-Na, I'm so happy you won't be around to give me orders anymore."

"What? Oh, you're joking. But still. Can't you convey this message? Please? Just in case? See, I'm asking nicely."

"I won't threaten my teacher, so no. Trust him. Trust me!"

"I don't have a choice, do I? I'm joking! I trust you. Really."

Chapter 40

Separation Anxiety

Twelfth Month, Chōhō 2 (January, 1001 CE)

The ritual took place at a small shrine in the foothills east of the capital near the resort town of Uji. Seimei had founded this shrine decades before as part of his quest for career success. "We will go to a *sugi* grove that has been cut off from the mainland over time by a Kamo river tributary, creating an island," he explained. "When I meditated there, a strange power emanated from the ground, creating a buzzing sensation throughout my body, and that was the first time I was able to call up a shikigami. Considering how impractical it would be to go back to Mount Tsukuba, this is the next best location for this magic."

It was oddly warm for January. The sun shone through the tall, fragrant *sugi* trees that ringed our little clearing as Masako prepared a place to meditate. She wanted to put down a straw mat to keep the damp from seeping into her hakama, but Seimei said no, she needed direct contact with the earth.

All three of us were nervous, although Seimei did his best to hide it. He talked too much and too fast, telling us how he came up with this meditation practice, which seemed a lot like *chinkon* to me, but maybe he invented it, who knows? And Masako wanted me to leave, but was scared of how lonely she would be when I left. And I worried about whether Seimei could pull our tangled spirits apart. Separation anxiety. Literally.

At least Seimei was confident that, if he could extricate me from Masako, he could send me to the moment I'd left my body. It wasn't an alternate universe or dimension, where I'd risk getting back months or years after I'd left. It was the future. Time wasn't passing there because it hadn't happened yet. Which made sense to me, although how did Seimei figure that out? Science, or magic? Or were they one and the same thing?

Masako closed her eyes, breathing deeply, and swung her arms in *furi-tama*. She emptied her mind of all but immediate sensation and sound. Long, deep inhale. Pause. Slow exhale. Again. In. Out. In. Out. The cold crept up her legs from the ground; a raven called from high in the trees; a shaft of sunlight warmed her right cheek. Seimei began chanting his incantation, repeating strange words over and over.

Masako's body trembled, her arms and legs first tingling, then buzzing as if the ground emitted tiny electrical shocks. Her body felt heavier and heavier as if the earth was dragging her into its center, while at the same time I felt as weightless as air, moving slightly in and out of Masako's body like a balloon tethered to a railing.

We both screamed in pain as my spirit started to rip away. I didn't want her to endure this torture, so I tried to resist. Seimei shouted louder, the strange foreign-sounding words pushing me with a force of their own: *Go, Mi-Na, go now!*

An invisible force pushed me like air blowing a dart out of a blowpipe. Another bright flash of agonizing pain. I felt like my arms and legs were tearing off. I screamed again, and let go.

Then—nothing. No feeling, no sound, no warm body, nothing. I had vision, though everything was tinted gray. I saw

Masako sitting there, tears streaming down her face, shaking as if in a seizure, her mouth open in a silent scream, and Seimei, sweating, roaring his magic words, waving his arms. They grew fainter and then transparent as I moved through the gray air. Was I moving through the spirit world? *So this is what disembodied feels like. It feels like nothing.*

The mist started to dissipate, and the air grew lighter. A gleam of sunlight. A tree. Two figures sitting. The gray world transitioned into bright color, and in the late afternoon daylight I saw myself in the same position as when I left. I drifted toward it, then hesitated. A strange inertia held me back. In the distance I heard Seimei shout one final exhausted incantation, which provided a last puff of magic to push my spirit into my body.

I opened my eyes to find Seimei staring down at me. I blinked tears away, crushed with disappointment. The ritual hadn't worked.

A warm, calloused hand tenderly brushed my tears away. I opened my eyes again, this time looking beyond the eyes to the youthful face above me.

"Kenji!" How could I have mistaken him for Seimei? A side effect of spirit-separation?

"How was the meditation? Did something happen? You're crying."

He didn't look any older. Same full mouth, same black hair framing high cheekbones. Same clothes, same island, same hot and humid July day. I looked at my own clothes. Same khaki shorts and polo shirt. I caressed my thin arms and touched my face. Same thin lips, same small nose. I pulled a strand of hair to look at my fine, dirty-blond hair. I'd loved to have kept Masako's hair. But then I'd look like a *yūrei* with long black hair on a ghostly white face.

"Mina, what's wrong? You look like you've had a shock. Should I call for help?"

I scrambled to my feet, groaned in pain, and sat back down again. My legs were completely numb. "Kenji, I thought you were Seimei!" I must have sounded like a madwoman, but I didn't care. "I've been gone for so long! How much time has passed?"

He smiled. Did that mean he *didn't* think I was crazy? "We meditated for an hour, which is a long time, I agree. Or did you mean something else?" His expression was inviting me to tell him everything. What was wrong with that? He might tell everyone at school I was crazy, but something told me he wouldn't.

"What would you say if I told you I'd been gone for a year? And... that year was from 999 to 1000? A thousand years ago, give or take." I laughed weakly so if he didn't believe me, he might at least think I was joking.

He stopped smiling. "I'd believe you."

I bent over to rub my now painfully tingling feet and to hide my disbelief. Nobody would believe me, nobody. It just didn't happen. Spirits don't leave bodies to possess other bodies, they just don't. That was all superstition and myth to explain what science hadn't discovered yet. Why would he believe me unless he was crazy too?

I couldn't get too worked up about it, though. I'd survived epidemics, bandits, sorcery, and political games against a master of political strategy, so I had no fear of what might happen next.

"It's a long story. If you don't mind, I'd like to get off this mountain. We could get sushi and I'll tell you all about it. I haven't had sushi in over a year." I laughed again. Crazy-talk.

His eyes looked into mine. *My* eyes. I put my hand over my heart to feel its rapid beating. My heart. My body. Mine, all mine.

I reached my hand out and he grasped it, pulling me up with him, not letting go when we stood. "First, Mina, I have something important to show you."

Puzzled, intrigued, and unable to keep a silly, happy smile off my face, I nodded. "More important than this secret power spot?"

He let go of my hand, leaving my empty palm lonely and missing his already. He knelt down by the little family shrine, which he shifted to one side, revealing a round metal cover in the ground. He lifted it, then reached into the hole beneath, pulling out a small metal safe which he opened with a key he took from his pocket. He withdrew a light brown wooden box from its interior.

I gasped. It looked just like Masako's comb box.

He looked up at me. "Do you recognize this?" he asked.

"Yes! Well, not really. Lots of boxes look like that."

He opened the lid, and drew out a package wrapped in layers of cloth. I was breathless with anticipation. What could be so well secured in this isolated spot?

He handed it to me, and I sat down to unwrap it. After I took off what felt like the tenth layer of material, I saw it was a journal with a leather cover, the kind you buy in bookstores. I ran my hand over the embossed butterfly on the cover, and riffled through its pages, all of them covered with hiragana script written with a fountain pen. A bit disappointing after all the suspense and mystery around it. "So, what is this?" I asked, noticing he was amused at my disappointment.

"A sacred trust," he said, taking it back from me. "I copied it from an older version just a few years ago, and that version had been copied by my grandfather decades before that, and his father had copied it, and so on. My family have been shrine priests here in Tsukuba for centuries, and this book contains instructions for every generation of my family to recopy this in order to preserve it. It's the same reasoning behind rebuilding the Ise Shrine every twenty years." He opened it to the first page and showed it to me. "See? These are the instructions from an ancestor of mine."

I couldn't read it. "What does this have to do with me? Who was your ancestor? What is your family name, anyway?"

"It has everything to do with you, Spirit Mi-Na."

I jumped to my feet. "What did you call me?" My face was tingling with anticipation.

"My family name is Abe, and my ancestor, the first in a long line of shrine priests, was Abe no Akichika. He brought this book to Tsukuba with instructions to preserve it for a woman with skin like a hungry ghost and hair like millet. She would be called Mi-Na. That's you, isn't it? Although I wouldn't describe you as a hungry ghost. Your skin is more like cream."

I couldn't absorb his compliment as my mind was too busy processing this information. Akichika? Sweet, clumsy Akichika? I swayed, feeling like I did after a ride at Cedar Point. "So what's in this book Akichika wanted me to have?"

"You'll see. We can read it together, in case your Japanese isn't good enough. It'll be good practice for you. But for now, just read the title page." He flipped to the next page and handed it back to me.

I examined it closely. I didn't want to mess this up. "*Miya*... umm... I can't read the next character. Or the next. It's followed by *no* and *ki*. I'm embarrassed to say I don't understand most of it." Normal-me would have turned red with embarrassment, but post-Masako-me didn't care.

"Well, yes, the first character is *miya*, which means shrine, but it also means palace. These two kanji together are pronounced *kyuuchuu*, which means imperial court. The next word is very difficult and unusual: *kannagi*. It means a diviner, or a medium, and *ki* means chronicle or record. So the title is Chronicle of an Imperial Court Medium. Now, look at the author's name on the next page."

I turned the page with shaking hands, looking closely at the name written in beautiful cursive. Of course Kenji was a master of calligraphy. He would have been popular at court.

I could easily read what was written there. After all, I'd seen my host practice it many times. I looked at Kenji, unable to speak. I swallowed, tried again. "Taira no Masako. And what's this other part? I can't read that."

Kenji took the book back, his eyes gleaming with excitement. "This is the culmination of centuries of family tradition. This second line shows the author's title and the date: Miko of the Imperial Shrine at Kamo, Chogen Era Year 4."

I folded my arms in an attempt to stop shaking. "And when —what year- what year was that?"

"1031. Come on, let's take this to dinner and I'll tell you more about it."

He put the box and safe back in the ground, set the shrine back in its place with a hand clap and brief prayer, and rewrapped the book.

I pressed my hands over my eyes, my mind whirling, and then wondered why long, wide, white sleeves weren't covering my face. Seeing my bare arms in a short-sleeved shirt gave me an unbearable pang of homesickness for Masako. *You did it, girl! You saved your book for me.*

Kenji gently lifted my trembling hands from my face, and still holding one hand, picked up the book in the other, and we navigated our way down the mountain. I stumbled frequently, still dizzy from the transition back to the modern world, but Kenji's hand remained strong and steady, guiding me through the dusk.

Epilogue

August, 2019 (Eighth Month, Reiwa 1)

Over the next few days I tried to adjust to modern life. Spirit separation and time travel gave me jet lag and culture shock rolled into one giant, disorienting package. Was I a year older? I felt older. More mature. Wiser. And I hurt inside, all the time, but not in any way I could medicate. Heartache. Soul-ache.

I got a B on my Japanese language test. Before my travel across worlds, a B would have sent me into a spiral of anxiety and self-loathing. Now I just laughed. A B? After living in a Japanese woman's body for more than a year? How ridiculous was that?

It turned out my phone just had a cracked screen. I ignored the many texts from Mick, so he called, but I sent him to voicemail where he belonged. No regrets there. It was all Mick's fault, and if I called him some day, I'd thank him for it. But for now, I wanted nothing to do with him. I had one thing in mind. Well, two things. Reading Masako's journal, and spending time with Kenji. And I'd decided I had to find Aya, even if she refused to speak to me after the way I'd treated her. So that made three things. At least, for now.

He was willing to help me achieve the first two, and I planned to ask him for help with the third. In between classes and in the evenings we'd sit in the university library and read the book. I could read some of Kenji's writing, but I couldn't make sense of the words, so he translated each sentence after I read it aloud, and pronounced those kanji I couldn't read. He sat very close, sometimes using a pencil to point to a word, his shoulder touching mine, his faint cinnamon scent causing my heart to beat a little too fast.

When I just couldn't take it anymore, I'd start babbling about my journey. He listened intently no matter how silly I sounded, so it was his fault if I talked too much.

"So," I said when his proximity made it too hard for me to concentrate on reading, "You're descended from Akichika? He's Seimei's grandson. Was, I should say. But Masako never married or had children, according to the introduction in her book, so he must have married someone else. He had a huge crush on her. But you wouldn't be here if he'd married Masako. Seimei wanted him to, you know. He wanted Masako's kids to be his great-grandchildren. And you look like him. Like Seimei, I mean. Did you ever hear a rumor that Seimei was the son of Taira no Masakado?"

He nodded. "I've heard that rumor, but I thought it was definitive that he was born into the Abe clan. Did he admit to it?"

"Indirectly. And that means Seimei was actually a Taira, and Masako was from the same branch, so you're related to Masako, too." And what I didn't say, because it was stupid, not to mention premature, is that if Kenji and I had kids someday, they'd be related to both Seimei *and* Masako. "I have so much information for my thesis. I can prove Sei Shonagon sacrificed her reputation to save Empress Sadako's. But... only one problem."

"What's that, Mi-*chan*?"

"This is clearly a modern book written with a modern pen. No one will believe it's not completely made up. It's too bad the original copy fell apart long ago."

Kenji smiled. "Akichika's copy was not the original."

"What? He made a copy to bring to Tsukuba?"

"Yes. You'll see when you get to the end of the book. Masako writes that the original was to be preserved near the Kamo Shrine. It might not have survived the centuries, but you never know. The Obon holiday begins next week. We could take the train to Kyoto to look for it."

Together? Take a deep breath, Mi-Na.

"Yes!"

Acknowledgments

The positivity and encouragement from women in the writing organization Women Writing for (a) Change gave me the freedom to write without fear.

Thanks to my fellow writers in The History Quill's writing coaching program for their feedback and constructive criticism, and for making me a better writer with every submission. Particular thanks to my editor from the History Quill, Kahina Necaise, for her insightful suggestions and enthusiasm for this story.

A *huge* thank you to Dr. Aileen Gatten, independent scholar and Affiliate, Center for Japanese Studies, University of Michigan, for her energy and thoroughness in reviewing the story's historical accuracy. Not only did she point out many anachronisms; she also sent me information on everything from Heian period furnishings, architecture, clothing, seating positions, food, whether or not brass bells were a thing yet (they weren't), what kind of fans existed at the time (not folded!) and most importantly, the chronology of what happened to Empress Sadako and when. Any mistakes are one hundred percent mine. Thank you again, Aileen.

To the courageous young people who shared with me the impact anxiety has had on their lives, and how they manage it: Heather Brooke, Georgia Ryan, and Nya Feinstein. Thank you *so* much. You got this!

Thank you to my early readers whose positive feedback gave me the encouragement to keep going, and who showed me that the story was really about friendship when I'd been thinking it was about Sei Shonagon: Amanda Mickelson, Becky Ryan, Erin Shanahan, Georgia Ryan, Justine Feinstein, Keiko Doisaki, Madison Beck, and Martha Trott.

Thank you to my friend, author Karen Odden, for taking time from her own busy writing schedule to read my third draft and give me key advice on my plot, and to another longtime friend and author, Laura Kriska, for guidance on publishing.

And my mother Vee. English major, writer, Latin translator, archeology volunteer, art museum registrar, faculty wife, reader of many books. Oh, and she raised nine children with grace, patience, and love. Vee, you inspire me by continuing to write even as you enter your tenth decade. Thank you for your unwavering positive support.

No words can describe the impact my daughter Anne has had on this novel. Thank you, Annie Vee, for your endless supply of creativity, your encouragement, your critiques, and for giving me the language of an American college student.

Anne and my son Riley both laughed in all the right places when I read aloud excerpts from *The Pillow Book*, so thank you, kids, for showing me that American Gen Z can relate to classical Japanese literature.

And of course to my husband, Kermit: thank you for your encouragement and support over the past three years of research and writing, for proofreading, and for getting me out for a bike ride when I needed to take a break.

Author's Note

The world's first novel is usually considered to be *The Tale of Genji*, written by Murasaki Shikibu, a lady-in-waiting at court in early 11th century Japan. She wrote it in an era when nearly all women everywhere in the world (and most men, too) could neither read nor write. I first read *Genji* when I was teaching English in Japan and devouring English translations of Japanese literature. I also read Sei Shonagon's *The Pillow Book* that year. Sei Shonagon invented a new form of literature known as *"zuihitsu"* (miscellany.) In today's terms, it's more like the world's first blog. Read it, and you'll see what I mean.

So here you have the world's first novel and the world's first 'blog' invented by Japanese women over one thousand years ago. Both Sei and Murasaki were ladies-in-waiting in the court of Emperor Ichijō, and they both could read and write Chinese as well as Japanese, rare skills for women even in their erudite sphere. And yet these two intelligent, creative, literary women didn't seem to like each other. Rivals? Frenemies? And what were the circumstances that led to these two women creating new forms of literature over one thousand years ago that are still studied today?

These questions haunted me over the years, and I resolved to research them some day, and then write a novel that would explore possible answers.

And this is what came of that.

List of Historical Characters

While Mina, Masako, Kenji, Yumi, and a few other characters in this story are entirely fictional, the following is a list of those fictionalized characters based on actual historical figures.

Names written with Chinese characters have several pronunciations. I chose to use the Japanese pronunciation (kun-yomi), rather than using the pronunciation based on the Chinese origin of the word (on-yomi.) For example, Empress Sadako is also known as Empress Teishi.

These are listed in alphabetical order by first listed name or title.

Akichika: Abe clan, Seimei's grandson; eventually became a master of astronomy.

Emperor Ichijō: Emperor of Japan from 980-1011 CE. His father was Emperor En'yu.

Empress Akiko: Fujiwara clan, consort to Emperor Ichijō as well as Michinaga's daughter.

Empress Sadako: Fujiwara clan, consort to Emperor Ichijō; daughter of former regent Michitaka.

Imperial Lady: Fujiwara clan, Akiko; Emperor Ichijō's mother; sister to Michinaga, Michitaka, and Michikane.

Imperial Prince Atsuyasu: Son of Emperor Ichijo and Empress Sadako

Imperial Princess Bishi: Daughter of Emperor Ichijo and Empress Sadako

Imperial Princess Nagako: Daughter of Emperor Ichijo and Empress Sadako

Imperial Princess Nobuko: High Priestess of the Kamo Shrine for 57 years, daughter of Emperor Murakami, cousin to Emperor Ichijō; Fujiwara clan on her mother's side.

Korechika: Fujiwara clan, son of former regent Michitaka and older brother to Empress Sadako.

Korenaka: Taira clan, a middle counselor and Master of Empress Sadako's Household.

Masakado: Taira clan, a powerful provincial warrior who tried to establish himself as Emperor sometime between 930 and 940 CE, but was overthrown and killed.

Michikane: Fujiwara clan, son of the previous Regent Kaneie, middle brother between Michitaka and Michinaga.

Michinaga: Fujiwara clan, Regent after his brother Michikane died.

Michitaka: Fujiwara clan, Regent after his father Kaneie died.

Murasaki Shikibu: Fujiwara clan, birth name unknown, lady-in-waiting to Empress Akiko, author of *Tale of Genji*.

Narimasa: Taira clan, brother to Lord Korenaka; steward to the Empress's household.

Sei Shonagon: Kiyohara clan, birth name unknown, lady-in-waiting to Empress Sadako, author of *The Pillow Book*.

Seimei: Abe clan, Head of the Bureau of Computation, famous diviner (see Historical Notes).

Shigeko: Korenaka's wife, wet-nurse to the baby Prince Yasuhito who later became Emperor Ichijō.

Takaie: Fujiwara clan, son of former regent Michitaka and younger brother to Empress Sadako.

Yukinari: Fujiwara clan, famous for his calligraphy; in 999 he was a senior controller.

Historical Notes

While a work of fiction, this novel is based on historical events and figures. Even the fantasy elements of spirit possession and divination are based on actual beliefs of Heian era aristocracy. Of course, the words and motivations for historical characters in this novel are my fiction.

It was not common in this era to address someone by their given name, but that makes for difficult reading, so I use both given names and titles for frequently recurring characters, while keeping to the convention of using only position or title for lesser characters.

When women moved around within indoor spaces, they usually remained seated, and so would slide across the floor rather than stand up to walk. I can only describe someone "sliding over to the door" so many times, so I took the liberty of having characters occasionally walk when they would have scooted in real life.

Western readers might have trouble believing that women in Heian Japan had the freedom to travel, to practice shamanism, to divorce, and to run an estate, but research shows women in this era were craftspeople, estate managers, mediums and *miko*. Noblewomen were taught to read and write, so literacy rates, at least in this elite class, were high compared to the rest of the world in this period. The book *Rethinking Japanese History* by Amino Yoshihiko provides considerable detail and evidence for the many roles women played in this time period.

Jstor.org, the online repository of academic articles, has a wealth of information about everything from divination (deer bones vs. turtle shells) to miko spirit-calling practices (kami vs. the dead) to imperial poetry competitions (yes, they could, in fact, be rowdy and a lot of fun).

Onmyōji, or diviners, used their skills in astrology, calendar-making, and yin-yang rituals to determine auspicious and inauspicious directions, whether omens were good or bad, and to dispel bad luck. The most powerful of these *onmyōji* was Abe no Seimei, who lived from 921-1005 CE, and who was considered to have the ability to command *shikigami*, which are spirit servants. His title in the year 999 CE was Head of the Bureau of Computation, although I have no doubt he spent a lot of time in the Bureau of Divination. In this story, I refer to him as Royal Astrologer, which may not have been an actual title, but was a role he performed. He was known and admired for his skill interpreting omens. He was especially famous for divining baby gender before birth. It was rumored that he was adopted into the Abe clan, but more recently it seems clear that he was, in fact, born into it. Speculation does exist that he was the son of Taira no Masakado, so I took that and ran with it as my fiction. Seimei's long life, in an era when the average life span was 28 years, was rumored to be due to his mother being a fox spirit.

Seimei's grandson Akichika was a real person, but it is my invention that he became a shrine priest at Tsukuba Shrine.

The Imperial Princess Nobuko, the Kamo Shrine High Priestess, also lived a long time, from 964-1035. I believe that isolation in a shrine and not bearing children were likely to have contributed to her long life.

There is no proof that Sei and Murasaki met as early as the year 1000, but there is no proof that they didn't. Their meeting in this story is from my own imagination, but it *could* have happened.

Similarly, while there is no evidence that Murasaki began writing *Genji* as early as 999, there is no concrete evidence she did not. However, she most likely began writing it after her husband died in 1001. Also, the first chapters she wrote probably did not include the chapter I have Sei read out loud, but, as that first line of *Genji* is well-known, I decided to use it.

This story has Sei Shonagon's book being taken from her room in 1000, but it was most likely taken a few years earlier than that. The story about the snow mountain competition was probably written earlier than the year 999, but it shows Sei's competitiveness and Empress Sadako's playfulness so clearly that I just had to include it. Her anecdote about Murasaki's husband Nobutaka actually shows him in a positive light, since he got promoted after dressing so gaudily, but some researchers believe Murasaki was annoyed by this portrayal of her husband, and so it is my speculation that Sei knew that and wrote the story for that very reason. It is completely fictional that Sei Shonagon's mother died in a palace fire. No one knows who her mother was or how and when she died. It is also my fiction that Sei got the name "Shonagon" from the Empress as their little inside joke because the older and wiser Sei was a counselor of sorts to the young Empress.

I was thrilled to discover the article "*Sei Shonagon's Makura no Soshi: A Re-Visionary History*" by Naoko Fukumori. It gave me hope that my speculation around Sei Shonagon's motivations for writing *The Pillow Book* was historically valid.

I refer to Lord Michinaga as "the Regent," throughout. Michinaga held various Japanese titles, and not all of them translate into the English word "regent" but that is the role he performed in the time period of this story, so that is the term that I used. Michinaga was recorded as being very ill in the year 998. I moved that specific incident to 999 for the sake of the story.

I based the character of Lord Yukinari on an actual historical person, and he did indeed come up with the reasoning to justify two empresses. He was famous for his calligraphy, and it is thought he and Sei Shonagon were lovers.

The young man with the snake-cursed tumor, the one I named Kanechika, is based on a son of the previous regent Michikane, Fukutari-gimi, who did have a tumor that was thought to be a curse from a snake, but he died before reaching his coming-of-age. I simply extended his life span by a few short years and gave him an adult name.

The smallpox epidemic of 994-995 is historical, as is the measles epidemic of 998, but the measles outbreak in 1000 is my invention.

I translated the famous Mount Tsukuba poem from the Japanese myself, and it is a very loose translation on purpose. There are many other translations available if you care to read a better one. All other poems in this novel are my creation.

This novel takes place in the Heian Period, which historians declare began in 794 CE when Emperor Kanmu moved the capital from Nagaoka-Kyo to Heian-Kyo (modern day Kyoto) and is considered to have ended in 1185 CE after years of conflict between Taira and the Minamoto clans, resulting in the fall of the Fujiwara clan from power, and creating a military government called the bakufu, also known as shogunate.

In modern times, a new era is declared at the enthronement of a new emperor, which is why 2019, the year Emperor Naruhito was enthroned, is the first year of the Reiwa Era. In ancient times, a new era would be declared to account for some major event such as a palace fire or an epidemic, which is why Emperor Ichijō was emperor throughout five full eras. This story takes place in the Chōhō Era.

Glossary

Japanese has five vowels, said quickly, without the long sounds we often use in English, and without moving one's lips much. These vowels are pronounced the same way in nearly every word in which they are used. Pronunciation of each vowel is approximately as follows: 'a' as in 'ah'; 'i' as in 'key'; 'u' as in 'put'; 'o' as in old; 'e' as in 'get.' Japanese words are built up from syllables rather than individual letters. As an example, ka, ki, ku, ke, ko are the five syllables starting with the 'k' sound. The name Michikane is pronounced "mee-chee-kah-neh," not "mitch-i-cane." Sei is pronounced "seh-ee", although when said quickly it sounds similar to the English word "say," and so Seimei sounds like "say-may" to an English-language listener. Taira is 'tah-ee-rah', and pronounced quickly it sounds more like "tie-rah" to an English speaker. If you remember to say each syllable rather than each letter, you will get the hang of it.

- Aga kimi: Darling (Heian Period usage)
- Aka-mogasa: Measles (literally 'red pox')
- Ari-mitama: Soul of Peace
- Aruki-miko: Female shaman who don't serve a specific shrine
- Ashi-no-ke: Beri-beri
- Ayashi ya: Strange, weird (Heian Period usage)
- Baka: Stupid
- Biwa: Lute-like instrument
- Chan: An affectionate version of the honorific 'san'
- Chinkon: A Shinto meditation practice
- Desho: Right?
- Ekiki: Pox demons
- Furi-tama: A Shinto technique to begin meditation
- Ge-ni: Indeed! (Heian Period usage)
- Geta: Wooden flip-flop type sandals
- Hakama: Wide-legged trousers worn by men and women
- Harae: Purification
- Hashi: Chopsticks
- Iie: No
- Ikiryō: Ghost of someone still living
- Itashi ya: Ouch! That hurts! (Heian Period usage)

Glossary

- Izakaya: A type of Japanese bar
- Jaa: Well...
- Jigoku: Buddhist version of hell
- Ji-me Ji-me: Humid, muggy
- Ka, kawa: Indicates a question
- Kami: Divine spirits
- Kami-sama: God
- Katakana: An angular form of Japanese writing
- Ke: Malevolent spirit or negative energy
- Konnichi wa: Hello
- Kosode: Thin inner robe
- Kuchi-yo-se: Spirit-summoning
- Michinoku paper: Paper made from mulberry tree bark
- Michōdai: A sleeping platform surrounded by curtains
- Miko: Ancient: female shaman; modern: shrine maiden
- Mitama: Soul
- Miyabi: Refinement, elegance
- Mogasa: Smallpox
- Mono-no-ke: Malevolent spirit which causes illness
- Nyōgo: Junior Consort to the Emperor
- Obake: Nature spirit (such as fox-spirit, monkey-spirit)
- Oki-naga: Long breathing technique for Shinto meditation
- Onmyōdo: Yin-yang divination, or a kind of sorcery
- Onmyōji: Yin-yang diviner; shaman
- Onryō: A ghost, a vengeful spirit
- Osorashi wa: Frightening (Heian usage)
- Sakaki: An evergreen tree sacred in Shinto belief
- Sasa-hataki: One of the ways to perform spirit-summoning
- Sensei: Teacher
- Shikigami: Spirit servants
- Shogun: Military ruler or dictator
- So, Sō: Yes
- Sugi: Cryptomeria tree
- Suhama: An artificial landscape like a diorama
- Tanuki: Racoon-dog; also a mischievous nature-spirit
- Tatehiza: Seated on folded right leg, left knee bent up
- Tengu: A supernatural creature with bird-like features
- Tonkatsu: A Japanese dish of breaded, fried pork cutlet
- Torii: The gate to a Shinto shrine
- Waka: Poem format with five lines of 5-7-5-7-7 syllable count
- Washi: Handmade paper

Glossary

- Ya, ya wa: A Heian Period expression of emotion
- Yamabushi: Mountain ascetic or hermit
- *Yōkai*: A wide category of supernatural apparitions
- Yoki Hito: "Good People" meaning the aristocracy
- Yumetoki: Dream interpreter
- Yūrei: Ghost
- Zo: A Heian Period expression of emphasis

About the Author

Kate Shanahan received her MA in Asian Studies from the University of Michigan, taught English in Sapporo, Japan, and enjoyed a long career with a Japanese company in Ohio as a human resources manager, ethics officer, and new model project leader, among other roles. *Tangled Spirits* is her debut novel.

If you enjoyed this book, please consider writing a review on your favorite book website. Reviews are helpful for both authors and readers, and even a short review can make a big difference.

Sign up to receive alerts for new blog posts and updates at kvshanahan.com. You can also find book club questions, bibliography, and information about Japanese eras, month names, and hours of the day there.

Also by Kate Shanahan

The Iron Palace
An ancient curse collides with a modern quest in this exciting sequel to Tangled Spirits.

When Mina finds desperate letters written by Masako a thousand years ago, she must decide whether to risk a return to the past or leave the ancient world—and her best friend—behind forever.

Made in the USA
Columbia, SC
03 February 2025